After a degree in English at Brasenose College, Oxford, Dan went into advertising as a copywriter and Creative Director before emerging to pursue his love of creative writing.

The Powder Monkey of Algiers is his third novel.

Dan's first novel, *Stuff,* is a posthumous collaboration with his TV playwright/screenwriter father, whose legacy to him was not only his original manuscripts, but a wealth of learning, knowledge and technique in the writing craft.

Dan's second novel, *The Nearly Man*, is a work of speculative fiction based on the Apollo 11 moon landings—a thriller and a 'sliding doors' reimagining of the mission gone wrong.

Dan has written numerous screenplays.

For Ivan and Caz

'Tis a fearsome thing, to love what death can touch
A fearful thing, to love, to hope, to dream, to be
and oh, to lose...

Dan Douglass

THE POWDER MONKEY OF ALGIERS

AUSTIN MACAULEY PUBLISHERS™

LONDON * CAMBRIDGE * NEW YORK * SHARJAH

A CIP catalogue record for this title is available from the British Library.

ISBN 9781398450165 (Paperback)
ISBN 9781398450172 (ePub e-book)

www.austinmacauley.com

First Published 2022
Austin Macauley Publishers Ltd®
1 Canada Square
Canary Wharf
London
E14 5AA

To my nearest and dearest, those I love most in this world. To those I have lost. To the battles we must win. To the peace we must keep. To those who have stood up to oppressors of any persuasion. To resilience. To the many who perished and suffered in the twentieth century's forgotten conflicts. To those whose lives have been lost to history.

To those who survived. To those who are capable of true forgiveness and those who are capable of true atonement. To those who take pleasure in small things. To those who use their power for the common good of humanity, not the supremacy of nationhood. To the powerless, the disadvantaged, the downtrodden and those who live every day with the fire of injustice burning in their hearts. To those who see past the shell of people and into the soul. To those who abjure cancel culture, the new censorship. To those who evaluate talent based on merit, not box ticking. To those agents and editors brave enough to back people for their work on the page, not their experience, origins, creed, colour, gender, celebrity, or age. To the power of the human imagination.

Table of Contents

Acronyms

FLN – the Nationalist Liberation Front of Algeria.

ALN – the armed wing of the Nationalist Liberation Front.

AOMA – the Association of Algerian Muslim Ulema, a cultural and religious movement in Algeria.

DOP – the French Army Détachement Operationnel de Protection, a division of the French Army specialising in interrogation techniques.

PCA – The Algerian Communist Party.

GRE – French Army Intelligence and Exploitation Group.

ZAA – Zone Autonome d'Alger, a Muslim area set up by the FLN, located primarily in the Casbah.

Terms

Harki – native Muslim Algerians who served as auxiliaries in the French Army.

Pieds-Noirs – French citizens who lived in French Algeria before independence, from 1830 to 1962. Those of European settler descent from France or other European countries who were born in Algeria.

Fellagha – an armed militant attached to anti-colonialist groups in Algeria.

Wilaya – a province of Algeria.

Berber – group indigenous to North Africa.

Spahi – a member of the Algerian cavalry in French service.

Tirailleur – name given by the French Army to an indigenous infantryman recruited into the ranks.

Colons – French colonials.

Evolués – Gallicized Algerian Muslims —Arabs by tradition and Frenchmen by education.

Mujahidat – women combatants in the Algerian war who joined the FLN armed guerrilla bands, the ALN.

Nailiya – the women of the Ouled Nail, a semi-nomadic tribe living in the highlands range of the Saharan Atlas whose women were renowned for their exotic dances and costumes.

La Mission Civilisatrice – a political construct for military intervention whose purpose was to colonise, modernise and Westernise the indigenous peoples of Algeria.

Zouave – French Army infantry regiments initially recruited from the Berber Zwawa group of tribes in Algeria, but during the Algerian War of Independence, formed exclusively from European recruits.

The Prytanée national militaire – military school in La Flèche, France.

Centres socieaux – a network of support centres run by the United Nations Education, Scientific and Cultural Organisation to promote progress in Algerian society.

Centre d'hébergement – a place of torture used by the French Army for further protracted interrogation.

Gégène – electroshock torture.

passages à tabac – beatings used for torture.

Barbarousse – a notorious colonial prison built by the French in Algiers in 1856.

El-Biar – a suburb of Algiers housing a prison widely known for practicing torture on Muslim captives.

Lodi – a detention camp in Algeria from where French communist Henri Alleg began writing his book 'The Question', published in 1958 and detailing torture at the hands of his French captors.

Banu Hachem – An ancient tribe in North Africa. The Banu Hachem are thought to be the original descendants and family of Mohammed.

Français de souche – a controversial expression meaning 'purely of French origin'.

Ulema – Muslim scholars recognized as having specialist knowledge of Islamic sacred law and theology.

Soummam – a conference that took place on 20 August 1956 in the Soummam Valley. Here, the FLN leadership convened in secret to create a common manifesto and a new structure.

The Sûreté – that part of the French Algerian Ministry of Interior charged with maintaining law and order.

St-Cyrlen – a graduate of Saint-Cyr, a French military academy located in Brittany, France.

Villa Tourelles – the location of a special interrogation unit under the command of Major Paul Aussaresses.

Hammam – a Muslim bathhouse.

Bidonvilles – slum dwellings on the outskirts of Algerian cities.

Gourbi – huts of mud and dung.

Historical characters

Algerian

Yacef Saadi – Algerian independence fighter and a leader of the FLN.

Ali Ammar / Ali La Pointe – Algerian revolutionary fighter and guerrilla leader of the FLN.

Ali Boumendjel – Lawyer and activist against French colonial rule, tortured and murdered by the French Army during the Algerian War of Independence in 1957.

Larbi Ben M'hidi – Revolutionary leader of the FLN.

Frantz Fanon – physician, psychiatrist and philosopher, member of the FLN.

Djamila Bouhired – Algerian militant, liaison officer and PA to Yacef Saadi.

Zohra Drif – Algerian militant, moudjahid.

Samia Lakhdari – FLN militant and bomber.

Said Bud Abbot – A notorious pimp, part of the Casbah underworld.

Rabah Bitat – Revolutionary and one of the so-called six historiques, whose involvement in Bloody All Saint's Day in 1954 was thought to mark the beginning of the Algerian War of Independence.

'Little' Omar – Yacef Saadi's nephew and liaison officer between the fighters and FLN leaders.

Krim Belkacem – leader of the FLN. Sole signatory to the Evian accords ending the 1954-1962 Algerian War. Assassinated in Germany in 1970.

Abane Ramdane – Algerian political activist known as 'the architect of the revolution'.

Benyoucef Benkhedda – acting leader of the GPRA exile government of the FLN during the Algerian War.

French

Charles de Gaulle – President of France, founder of the fifth republic.

Guy Mollet – French prime minister 1956-1957.

Major Paul Aussaresses – principal intelligence collector and executioner for the French Army, working under General Massu.

General Jacques Massu – French military commander in Algiers.

Hubert Beuve-Méry – French journalist and newspaper editor, commentator on the Algerian War of Independence.

Lieutenant Colonel Roger Trinquier – second-in-command to General Massu.

Lieutenant Colonel Albert Fossey-François – second in command of the second parachute regiment.

General Alexandre de Beauharnais – General in chief of the Army of the Rhine, 1793.

General Zoegli – Prussian Army General who captured and interrogated the French spy Terrare during the French operations in the Rhine – 1792.

André Achiary – French military intelligence officer and police commissioner. On 10th August 1956, Achiary, plotting alongside the Union Française Nord-Africaine terrorist group, planted a bomb in the Casbah, Algiers, which exploded killing 73 people.

Jacques Soustelle – Governor General of Algeria – 1955–56.

Robert Lacoste – French politician who served as Governor General of Algeria – 1956–58.

Nelly Forget – a member of the UNESCO international secretariat in Algeria.

Father Jean-Claude Barthez – a worker priest belonging to the French mission, a member of the social action association bringing people together from all sides.

André Mandouze – a French Catholic academic and journalist at the University of Algiers agitating for Algerian independence.

Raoul Salan – commander-in-chief of French forces in French Algeria – 1956.

Colonel Marcel 'Bruno' Bigeard – led the third parachute regiment through the Battle of Algiers – 1957.

Albert Camus – French Algerian philosopher, author, and journalist. Played in goal for the Racing Universitaire d'Alger junior team from 1928 to 1930.

Prologue

That final fatal shot fifty years ago reverberates with me to this day. For Margot, it's not quite as loud. Now she is waiting for me with a tolerating patience on the corner of Rue St André des Arts. We are paying our respects to Eloise in a way that would have moved her to tears. I have dedicated the exhibition of photographs to her memory and used part of my stipend to sponsor the show. I have also insisted that Margot attend. To test Margot's forbearance even further, she has forgotten to bring an umbrella. She is soaked through and cannot resist telling me that I am ten minutes late. "As is your prerogative, big brother," she teases. I stress that I have travelled all the way from Oxford, she only from the outskirts of Paris—and yes, I am the older sibling, so she should allow me some latitude.

"You know I'll let you get away with anything, Shimeun-frère. You just like to keep me on my toes, don't you…?"

If only I had the energy for that kind of pre-meditation.

Margot wants to legislate for everything, but the simple truth is, after all these years, I still get lost on the Paris Metro.

Although I rarely venture out of my rooms in college, I much prefer the London Underground map with its Heath Robinson plumbing to the plan of the Parisian subway, which resembles a circuit board—too much for my comfort.

"Are you ready for this?" asks Margot.

The difference in our ages can be telling at times.

I remember everything about the world of Alice's photographs. She remembers nothing.

For me, time may have rubbed away at these recollections with a coarse wire brush—burnished some, abraded others. Paradoxically, some of the more momentous events, the historical milestones, are scratchy and vague. But the personal detail is patinated. I recall the quotidian people and circumstances with

15

a clarity, sheen and colour that can sometimes ambush me—in reminiscences that are more like synaesthesia.

Margot is the polar opposite.

Alice's portraits speak to a time that is part of Margot's life but not part of her recall. They all happened pre-memory and she is therefore insulated from them. She sees them as events rather than experiences.

She doesn't even remember the explosion at the bus-stop. Nor does she want to be reminded of it. She takes my arm in hers and gives it a reassuring squeeze as she walks me up the street to the gallery.

A large window decal announces the exposition with a self-portrait of Alice. A double exposure taken in a shop window in Rue Michelet, Algiers. Smiling and uninhibited, she's captured herself on the fly as if the camera has gone off by accident. Above her image, the words are emblazoned in large Levato type:

Alice Reyes (1923-1957) portraits 1954-1957, Algeria. 'The Tortured Spirit'.

"Do you think she was?" asks Margot. "She doesn't look it."

I step into the open foyer of the gallery from out of the drizzle and hold open the glass door for my sister. I haven't quite heard all of her question. We both take a guide to the collection off a plinth on the inside of the entranceway.

"Do I think she was what?" I ask as a woman relieves us of our coats and a young man in crisp white shirt and spotless black apron offers us each a flute of champagne from a silver tray.

"A tortured spirit…"

"Alice would have hated to think the title of the collection applied to her. Most photographers want to be anonymised behind the camera shutter."

But Margot isn't listening.

She is scanning the gallery for people she may know and already stepping towards the first print on the wall. A tousle-haired young woman in black roll-neck sweater and plaid trousers, her hands tied, sitting beside a young soldier in the back of an Army personnel vehicle.

The subject's clothes are torn and dishevelled and there is a large gash on her forehead. It looks as if she has been roughed up and is about to face a further ordeal under martial law. Although uncertain what lies ahead for her, the fear on her face is plain to see. The soldier is reaching out to put a hand over the camera lens, but the shot is taken before he has the chance and he only succeeds in blocking most of his own face out of the photograph.

The effect is stark. A cover-up.

Margot would rather I talk about who else is here at the private view. She isn't that interested in my take on photography, but I continue with it regardless.

"That's what makes them professional photographers. And the great ones truly lose themselves behind the lens. Make themselves completely invisible. I'm sure it's how Alice got such honesty out of her subjects. 'Tortured spirit' applies to them, not her."

"Well, Alice was certainly that…"

"Certainly what?"

"Tortured. By the Army. And invisible come to think of it…so invisible she disappeared off the face of the Earth…"

That's Margot—ever the judge, with her neat summing up.

We are moving further into the gallery now. I'm relieved to see there are enough people here to make the numbers respectable.

The exaggerated proportions of the space make the viewing more intense. An elongated stretch of wall buttressed by short partitions means that several harrowing portraits stare back at once. I am so overwhelmed by the scrutiny of the long dead that I have to turn my gaze to Margot.

She is a striking woman who, into her late fifties, makes younger heads turn. And she is mischievous with it. I see Mother in the former, Father in the latter.

I decide to blank out the walls of images and focus on just one.

We are both frozen in front of a massive black and white portrait of an ALN fellagha. The first time Eloise showed it to me, I shivered. It took me straight back to the Casbah and Place Jean Paul-Sartre. Now, as an actual size print, digitally re-mastered, it makes an even more forceful impact. I can see every pit in the face, the fleck of spit at the corner of the mouth, the shadow of crevices and wrinkles in the skin.

According to Alice's notebook—explained by the tombstone caption on the wall beside the print—it was taken in El-Biar prison one hour before the man was guillotined.

The notes don't explain how Alice managed to gain access to El-Biar at that moment in time. To me, it's a miracle. Even more so the photograph itself.

The fighter has an expression of open defiance—ferociously staring down the camera lens. And yet there is also an extreme vulnerability and innocence there too. I remember the contradiction in so many faces I encountered on the streets of Algiers. Father's was the same. So too Mother.

Mine was. Still is.

"Cover up the left side of his face," I urge Margot. "I mean, block it out with your hand."

She covers her left eye with the exhibition guide.

"Now the right."

She does the mirror opposite and squints with her left eye as if she's reading from an optician's chart.

"What do you see…?"

"My God," she says, "that's extraordinary."

"No face is symmetrical…she understood that, according to Eloise… That's the reason her portraits work so well."

"I never really spoke to Eloise about the technique behind Alice's photographs. Never really had the chance to before she died…"

"Ah, well," I say, "that's the genius of Alice Reyes. That's the power of her photographs. It's all in the conversations she had with her subjects, the natural light, the shutter speed of the Leica…"

Margot is repeating the trick and swooning.

"Eloise said she was an incredible woman…"

Margot can see why now.

Isolate the left side of the fellagha's face and it is the face of a warrior. Isolate the right side and it is the face of a child. It's there in the eyes.

Yes, that's the brilliance of Alice. It's exactly what Eloise would have wished—the point of this retrospective. It's the one thing I wanted Margot to see too. I'm just glad that Margot and I have shared this together. And on this day of all days.

After the private view, we stroll up Rue Seguie towards the Seine. We hunt for eateries back from Quai de Saint Augustine, looking for a modest prix fixe lunch. We aimlessly glide from one bistro to another, not able to find one that fits the bill.

"Aren't we the pair," she says, "you an emeritus professor of philosophy, me a magistrate, and between us, we still can't find a solution for where to eat."

We give up on the quai and the tourist hordes and head further back from the river.

"Who are we kidding?" says Margot, ever the optimist. "This is the height of the season in the Latin Quarter and we're looking for a paysan lunch at a paysan price."

She laughs.

"Well, isn't that just the way of the world."

The area known for its frugal dining once loved by artists living in penury has priced itself out to all but those with the deepest pockets.

Irony is rarely lost on Margot. But it's never cruel, always at her own expense. That's one of the things I love about my baby sister. Unlike Parisians, she has that same self-effacing giggle I remember in the little girl.

We settle for a modest café in Rue Savoie. Nothing to write home about, but honest prices.

I order a glass of red. She has a mineral water. We both order the prix fixe—beef stew.

I watch absently as a waiter crosses the café, balancing an unfeasible number of plates on his forearm while he gesticulates at the bar tender to hurry up with the drinks order.

Time passes as we both let the gallery images sink in. Margot is the first to break the silence. She can see exactly what is on my mind.

"One day," she says, taking my hand in both of hers across the table, "one day, you will tell me everything…about Mother, Father, Louis."

She doesn't need to add the "…but not now." I take it as read.

"I still regret I never did the same with Claude," I say.

"Some things are better left unsaid…"

"Are they? I sometimes wonder…"

This is opening the door too wide for Margot. She edges it closed again as our stew arrives.

"Eloise would have been so proud of you for arranging this. And on the fiftieth anniversary of Algeria's independence. What a clever brother you are!"

I smile, but it's a little like going through the motions.

"The thing is much as I loved Eloise," I say, "she was never our Mother."

"I hardly knew Mother…"

"I wish…I wish…" My thoughts tail off. It is not just Mother who is on my mind. Father is there too. "It's complicated," I say. "I think you would have liked him…maybe not…it's difficult to say. Just wish you'd got to know him so you could decide for yourself…"

"Well, tell me one day. Tell me all about them," says Margot, though I'm not sure she's ready to know. I'm not sure she ever will be.

19

Not many are ready to hear about that level of cruelty. That's why she talks about it as 'unspeakable'. What she's really saying is she doesn't want me to speak of it. It's a convenient way for her to deflect an inconvenient truth.

I play along with it, of course. I protect Margot from my memories now as I protected her from the actuality then.

But for me it's still very real. I have learned to live with it. I have forgiven Father to a certain extent, but I haven't forgotten. I will never forget. I owe it to my own personal god, with whom of course I have a very honest relationship.

We finish lunch and I walk her to the Metro. She is due back in Neuilly for a dinner out with friends at a local eatery.

"I've probably ruined dinner by having lunch," she says, "but there you go. Easily led by my older brother…always have been. Always will. You hanging around here…?"

"Not sure…My Eurostar leaves at six."

"Oh, well…you've got a few hours to kill…you can hang out with the American tourists and celebrate Independence Day together…may see you in London within the month. Charles and I have tickets for the middle Saturday. You going?"

"I didn't get through the ballot…not even the judo…"

"Oh, well, send Oxford my love! Love you, Shimeun-frère…"

She kisses me on both cheeks and dances down the Metro steps and out of sight.

I saunter aimlessly back up to the Seine and pick out an unoccupied bench. I have the same unease about being here in Paris as I've always had whenever I come to visit Margot or for the occasional conference. After all these years, I still feel my face doesn't fit.

I watch a young American couple brandish a selfie-stick with uninhibited glee. They're wearing rainproof 'his n hers' 'London 2012' ponchos. For them, Paris is clearly just the entrée to the Olympics plat principal.

The boyfriend asks if there'll be fireworks later. If the French Air Force will put on an aerobatic display down the Seine and over the Eiffel Tower. He thinks it's Bastille Day. The girlfriend says he's ten days out and they'll be in Barcelona on the fourteenth anyway. She explains that not every country celebrates their independence on the same day as the US of A. And she doubts if they'll find an American Independence Day party in Paris. "We're not exactly swaggy here," she tells him in her best Justin Bieber.

20

I am angry. I want to tell them that this is also the day Algeria gained its independence from France. That it's not all about America. But I'm not convinced either of them would appreciate the thought or even know where Algeria is.

Instead, I chide myself for being unreasonable. They are young. Free. Algeria means nothing to them. They are having a good time. Let them be.

Instead, I walk away. I stroll east along the Left Bank and over the Seine at Pont Royal into the Tuileries Gardens. The rain clouds are racing away towards Père Lachaise and the twentieth arrondissement beyond as the sun finally bursts through.

I find a spare deckchair by a fountain away from the allée centrale. Rainwater has puddled in the canvas. I shake it out, dump myself down and turn my face towards the warm glow.

I sit back and close my eyes to the gurgle and splash of water on stone and I am back in the ravine at Kordiat el-Markluf with Father all those many hunting seasons ago.

Part One
Lieutenant Laurent

The Low Atlas, Algeria,
23 September 1956

We are treading with stealth through the ravine. A pair of raptors wheels high above us in the bleached sky.

Father is ten metres ahead of me, moving with hair-trigger concentration. I follow closely in his footsteps. I don't know the terrain that well. He could map it in his sleep.

It is he who first spots the fallow deer grazing and browsing in a stand of cedar some seventy yards away. A young buck, without the fully formed antlers of a male—just a juvenile spike on his head that announces his first steps towards maturity.

We crouch and watch, thick as thieves.

I can feel the static charge in the air after a torrid summer. A prickling energy. Or perhaps these vibrations are coming off Father himself as he begins to hunt this shy beast.

They are both equal to the chase.

We edge closer.

The buck emerges into sunlight, playing a game of un, deux, trois, soleil. He raises his head and we set ourselves like statues as he flicks his cupped ears in our direction.

He shivers, then freezes at the shadow of a cloud passing behind him. Recomposed, he dips his nose in the stream, slakes his thirst, then stalks towards us into a hollow, unaware of our presence.

He disappears.

The scrub gives way to arrow-grass and chufa as it dips towards the creek. He is down there somewhere.

Though we have lost sight of the deer, we are downwind of him, and Father knows he is achingly close to us now.

On the way here, Father prepared me for the hunt by urging me to feel the movement of the deer in relation to the wind—telling me its nose is one of the most powerful weapons in the animal kingdom, with a sense of smell far more acute than a dog and sixty times more sensitive than ours.

This weapon is defensive, not attacking—it doesn't make the animal a super-predator, but a super-survivor. And Father says in many ways that is a far more useful piece of equipment to carry through life.

It also presents him with an irresistible challenge.

Father's rifle is poised and cocked. And, like his quarry, he is silently sniffing at the air.

It is the only sign that he is breathing at all. We have been edging towards the stand of trees for over five minutes and I have yet to detect in him the slightest exhalation of breath. Despite all the tracking today, he has hardly even broken sweat.

I know this is unusual.

I have just started studying at the Lycée René Coty in Medea. Here, my form master, Monsieur Gazides chooses to teach life sciences by bringing the subject…well…to life! Rather than make us read from a dry biology textbook he reads instead from 'The Day of the Triffids' to help us better understand the working of plants.

Fancifully, it now occurs to me that Father must be part-human part-plant and respiring through the pores of his skin as a cactus does through the stomata in its green flesh.

In contrast to Father, my breath is going like a forge-bellow. The sound is stuffing out my head.

The reedy grass now snaps and crunches beneath the rubber soles of my school gym shoes. Father could just as well be treading on thick Sivas carpet in slippers, not through dry crackling undergrowth in his heavy old Harki boots. He is the very embodiment of insouciance.

To cap it all, he is smoking a cigarette. The butt pokes out from the corner of his mouth. I taste the fumes.

I peer up to the top of the far ridge. The sun is shirking beyond it. It casts a rising shadow on the rock wall to the east. The last of the sun's rays falls on that stand of cedar trees just up ahead, dappling the forest floor. A natural spotlight on our young buck.

We move closer. Ever closer.

There is an intoxicating serenity to the scene. Here, for the first time, we can both truly forget about the horrors of Philippeville so fresh in our memories. I know there and then, right down to the marrow of my bones, that I shall remember this very moment for the rest of my days. Right now, in this split second, I am in a state of grace, as fleeting but eternal as the sunburst between clouds.

A shadow passes over the ravine.

Slowly, deliberately, Father signals and crouches again.

I copy him.

He turns to me and places a finger to his lips. He points silently at the barrel of his rifle, then to me, then out ahead towards the trees.

I swallow hard. He nods. We stand. He takes a slow, deep step into the long grass. And that's when it happens. A heart-kicking, dizzying detonation of energy.

The buck explodes out of the undergrowth, sending up a cloud of insect husks, dust and broken vegetation.

A streak of sinew and stippled hide arrows towards the sky, arcing out and up. Hind legs pumping.

Father throws the gun towards me. I catch it as a reflex to stop it crashing into my face. The gun-strap whips and stings my cheek.

"Quick, my little wing man! Aim!"

I bring the stock of the gun up to my shoulder and raise the barrel without even thinking. Already, the buck has bounded some fifty yards away. He is lightning fast, zigzagging, springing, dancing, chopping the air.

"Fire! Vites, vites! kuna sarieaan! Just behind the forelegs. A third up the body! Shoot!" I waver.

"Shoot, damn you!" Father cries. The deer is sixty, seventy, eighty metres distant now.

"madha tntzr? Qu'attends…?"

I am struggling to track the movement of the skipping beast with the muzzle of the gun. Every time I think I have him, I am at least half a metre off.

Ninety, a hundred, a hundred and ten. This way and that. Trips and jolts. Fades and feints.

"You are losing him!" Father shouts into my ear.

The buck is at least a hundred and twenty metres out. He will soon be out of range. And I'm not up to the task. I don't want to shoot. It is tearing at my heart.

"Give me that!" Father seizes the rifle from me, raises the sight to his eye and fires off a round in one clean, flowing action.

The deer drops out of the air mid-jump.

The kill resounds throughout the ravine.

Father stands and stares, shoots me a withering look, thrusts the rifle back into my hands, cries "Imbecile!" and stalks over to the spasming, supine animal.

"It's not a clean shot. You have more bullets in your magazine…finish him off."

He stands back to fire up another cigarette and take in the tableau. I glance at him.

"Go on, my little wingman. He is in pain. The quicker you do it, the better."

The buck is trembling. A big anthracitic eye is fixed on me. I gaze back into it and see my silhouette reflected in its smooth, rounded cornea—the power, the surrender, the dousing of the flame.

Once again, I press the gunstock to my shoulder.

"Aim for the head. Make it instant!"

I am shaking. Everything is flickering around me. Light. Life. Senses.

"Simeon! What are you doing?"

I point the gun. My index finger is wrapped around the trigger.

"Go for the head, I say!"

I just cannot steady my trembling hands. I am back on the streets outside the stadium, hearing the screams. The buck is trying to find its feet like a new-born fawn, but hopelessly flailing.

"Je ne peux pas avoir de lâche pour un fils! Give me that!"

For the second time he takes the gun from me. This time he instantly shoots from the hip. I start. The buck's head is thrown back. Blood and bone spatter the grass. A final convulsion. At last, the animal is still.

As my punishment, Father hoists the still-warm animal onto my shoulders and insists I carry it uphill and out of the ravine.

After a few hundred metres, I am stumbling under its weight.

"Enough!" My pratfalls amuse him. "You are like a little drunken man!"

In Father's estimation, I have now paid my penance with his laughter. He unwraps the deer from around my shoulders, lifts it up and drapes it around himself with the lightness of a child trying on a fur stole from a dressing-up box. I wonder where his head is. Is he really able to blank out everything that has happened to us with his kill dripping blood down his neck? He passes the rifle to me once more.

We keep going up for another half a kilometre, then stop at the ridge. Father disburdens himself of the animal while he takes a long swig from his canteen in the shade of a cork oak. He passes me the flask, puts an arm around me and squeezes, giving me one more reassuring hug for good measure.

"You've done well. There's a good hundred and fifty pounds of meat there, Monsieur Hommefort!"

He turns back to the ravine spread out below him and breathes in the view along with the fumes of another cigarette, before we set off again.

To my amazement, he lugs the carcass over two kilometres—the remaining distance back to the truck—without stopping to catch his breath.

Arriving, he throws the buck's limp bulk on to the open trailer, shoving it alongside the rest of the carrion haul, laid out in rows. Blood runs along the grooves in the floor of the truck. It drips down the tailboard and onto the path. I turn away. I cannot bear it.

He spits into the dirt and, breathing heavily now, scrambles up into the back. He counts his spoils and divides them, pulling the three wild boar carcasses clear of the deer. Alongside the hogs lie several clusters of dead rabbits, all ensnared in a tangle of cheese-wire which cuts deep pink and scarlet tracks into their flesh.

"This is for my good friend Jameel in the souk, along with the bunnies," he says, slapping the side of the deer. "You'll find he likes to do his own butchery and his patrons are very particular…These…" he continues, indicating the gutted boar, "…are for the fancy bar cafés in the European quarter. They do so love their piggy cassoulets, the colons. And remember, Muslims do not eat hog-meat. It is forbidden by Islam. Offer one to Jameel and beware! It is an insult. He would rather feed you to the boar than vice versa!"

Father drives back down the track, past the hide in the forest where we have waited hours for the wild boar to cross the clearing.

Before I know it, we are bumping along the road to Sour El-Ghozlane, too distracted and weary to speak of the day's adventures and conquests.

Instead, the broken exhaust of Father's truck gives us the same old crotchety backchat in its familiar rattling tongue—and keeps it up all the way home to Medea.

The Farmhouse, Medea Wilaya, 5 January 1957

Father plays baccarat with our neighbour Waleed in the kitchen. I am listening to their game as I drift in and out of sleep.

Whilst their voices are hushed, they slap down cards in explosive bursts—with the same vigour as football fans throwing down firecrackers on match day in the streets around the Stade de 20 Août.

I can hear the flutter and shuffle of the deck as the two of them spar over slugs of Sidi Brahim—gulped back in shot glasses they then slam down on the table-top to announce a refill.

The glasses are too small for wine, but tonight that is the only liquor in the house—and these are the only glasses we possess.

I hear them face off—slug for slug, gulp for gulp, slam for slam.

Mother has long retired to bed, telling the men to keep their voices down. That there is a baby and three tired children sleeping in the house. However, the truth is she cannot abide these ghastly pissing contests that descend into bouts of mutual griping. And she will do whatever she can to dampen them.

She also vehemently objects to any alcohol in the house. And Father is only too aware of the fact.

I have known her regularly hide the bottles of calvados, cognac and Pernod that Father brings back from Algiers—peace offerings from the owners of the café-bars in the European quarter when he and Waleed make their autour-du-dos kitchen deliveries of viande chassée.

Mother is prone to empty these complimentary bottles of spirits down the drain when Father is not looking so as not to incite him. Whilst there is serious intent behind this purge, she draws me into her secretive acts with a girlish giggle. I am in on it, and under no circumstances am I to tell Father what she is up to.

But he knows—of course he does. Finding a way around Mother's prohibition has become part of a strange treasure hunt. He is quite capable of stashing bottles away himself where they can't be found and retrieving his cache when the coast is clear.

I know that he has special hiding places for his contraband in the wall cavities. He switches them regularly to throw her off the scent. Father has let me in on that little secret too and I am definitely not to tell Mother.

You see…

I am in an impossible position.

This is how the adults choose to spend their time. In endless rounds of second-guessing. He and Mother prosecuting their battle over his drinking. He and Waleed locking horns over cards. That is, when they're not out and about or reporting on their fellow countrymen or when Father is delivering his meat to Algiers.

Father likes to have me along with him on his curfew sorties with Waleed. Something else that provokes Mother's ire. It is my job to watch his back while he in turn watches the streets. Just as I keep an eye out for wild dogs and snakes on our hunting expeditions in the countryside.

The French have a different name for me. 'Powder monkey'.

Tonight, however, I can tell from the late hour that this is not entirely a social. They are not being their normal selves. Father is being excessively brisk, Waleed unusually eager.

For Father, the card game is a diversion from the real purpose of Waleed's visit so late into the evening. Waleed is keen to tell him something that Father is not so keen to hear. At first, they circle around the issue. And each other. It is a curious dance.

Their speech is muffled by the improvised curtain of damask draped over a washing line that separates our bed from the rest of our house. The register of their voices rises and falls as Father, under Mother's instruction, repeatedly urges Waleed to lower the volume so as not to wake the children. He reminds him there is a baby in the house. In truth, he is looking out less for our slumbers than the sharp end of Mother's tongue.

Strangely enough, despite their attempts to muffle their exchanges, I can hear every word as it travels along the length of our makeshift walls into our sleeping area.

But then, this is a strange house.

Father originally stumbled across this roost by chance like an exhausted bird blown off course by a storm. He says he had no way of foreseeing the 'wild events' that brought about the massacre of innocents back at Philippeville, so he decided the family would be in less danger here, closer to Algiers under the protection of the French.

Mother says that shows how desperate he is. She says seeking protection from the French is like running to the shelter of a solitary tree on high ground in the middle of an electric storm.

Father built our walls back up from the ruins of the dilapidated farmhouse using materials we stripped from abandoned buildings as we moved from the east. Our dwelling contains scavenged pieces of other lives. And those lives speak to us all the time.

They speak of guilt and deceit, of bonds dismantled and trust destroyed. The cries of the dispossessed and brutalised seep out of our walls. It makes Mother feel sick to the stomach.

Waleed informed Father the house had been abandoned by a Berber farmer the Army long suspected of being a saboteur. Waleed claims that he himself is the landowner and Father owes him back-rent, but he has no papers to prove it. And Father resents his neighbour's attempts at extortion.

He says Waleed is a barefaced liar and refuses to pay. He maintains the house is on 'bastard land'. Disowned. Unclaimed. Unloved. Neither of them ever stops to think about the Berber farmer—now languishing in a containment centre—whose home it was in the first place.

A month after we moved in, Captain LeBoeuf's paratroopers came knocking at our door in the name of the French Republic. They checked our documents and left. Father thinks the French confiscated the land from the farmer so that Pieds-Noirs could move in—and we native Harkis were the next best thing. It wasn't planned that way. It was expedient. Provided we were loyal to the French, it didn't matter that we lived here—not to the Army or Governor General Soustelle, nor to the National Assembly. Father took the authorities' apathy as a nod—it was as good as putting his signature on the deeds.

Waleed says the soldiers were on a recruiting drive—and as Father's landlord, he pointed the paratroopers in Father's direction. He says he and Captain LeBoeuf allow Father to be here. But Father says he is his own man.

To Father, possession is more important than improvement. He is no master builder. He's happy to botch and plug. Our house leaks sound just as it leaks everything else—rainwater, sewage, even grain from our store snaffled by the mice that scuttle and shuttle along the empty wall cavities—just like the bursts of chitter-chatter from the kitchen that now carry through into my dreams.

I am dreaming the same dream again. A unit of paratroopers swoops down from the ramparts above the city with eagle wings. They fall on the living and the dead in the streets around the Casbah. They rip at the human sinew and muscle fibre and then turn on one another.

There is more than enough meat for the soldiers to take their fill. Despite this, they flap and squabble around the leftovers. These eagles behave more like battlefield crows. Without grace. Unlike the French imperial eagle that gazes down mockingly on the crumbling Fourth Republic from its Napoleonic eyrie.

Father says if you go out at dead of night and listen carefully, you can hear the death rattle of empire in the sound of distant gunfire.

He says French people are losing the stomach for it because empire is like undigested meat rotting inside the gut of France and making it sick.

He fears that it won't be long before De Gaulle assumes power again from that fake socialist Guy Mollet and when he does, he will leave us to the vengeance of our countrymen. He says this would be a poor return for the loyalty he has shown the colonials. I think he tries to play down the danger for our sakes.

I can tell that behind it all, he is very scared indeed.

Father's nervy laughter drifts along the walls from the kitchen.

After some small talk, Waleed finally brings the conversation around to the business in hand—he speaks of a reputed optician in Algiers. I am listening in.

"Monsieur Courvois?" I hear Father respond. "You mean the short-sighted spy who makes spy-glasses? He clearly didn't see it coming."

"It is no laughing matter, neighbour." Waleed takes too much delight in the sound of his own voice to appreciate Father's joke.

Waleed swoons at Father's show of cards. Another drained glass of wine hits the table. Another splash of liquor. Another glug. Waleed is a live one tonight.

"Okay, now you are the banker. Now the boot is on the other foot and I will kick your Harki arse."

The next game starts with a frantic shuffle of the deck. Waleed deals and carries on talking.

"Courvois has been unmasked as a Pied-Noir impersonator. The FLN knows he is a pliant Muslim and a 'responsable' to the French. It doesn't surprise me.

He whistles the Marseillaise behind his counter, has made no secret of the fact he is an Algerian Muslim and a veteran of the French Army. LeBoeuf has the file."

"And no doubt you have seen the file on Courvois too," says Father with a degree of irony. "I'm sure LeBoeuf is only too willing to share classified state documents with a man of your calibre. You would be the first person I would think to tell if I wanted a secret kept."

Father's sarcasm is wasted on his neighbour. Waleed is too intent on telling his own version of the story to appreciate anyone else's contribution.

"During the war in Europe, Courvois—aka Ahmed Selmane—served his country as a medic. He moved to Lyon from Oran, with the specific plan of marrying a French woman and taking French citizenship. He had that intention from the moment he was conscripted."

I hear Father yawn. Waleed bulldozes on.

"Sure enough, he met Marie Courvois in Lyon, and brought her back to Oran, married the woman and took her family name for himself… On his return to Algeria as a Pied-Noir, he grabbed the same privileges of French citizenship as he would if he'd settled in Lyon. Not least all the lucrative business connections within the community.

He changed his given name from Ahmed to Alain when the Courvois couple moved to Algiers to open their practice and shop—with the help of a handsome grant from the Governor-General…

Read into that what you will."

Father goes along with it. Though he knows he has given his children French names too—to please his paymasters.

"That the authorities recruited him as a Pied-Noir spy in return for financial support," Father mumbles by rote.

"Hard dinar, my friend…blood and treasure."

Behind the damask curtain, I imagine Waleed is busily raising an eyebrow.

"The business grant was not freely gifted, of course. It required a certain surety in return. Information of a hidden nature."

To all intents and purposes, Waleed sounds like the inspector at the end of an English country murder mystery pulling all the missing threads together.

To Father it is an irritant. Father is not a man to be teased and manipulated. He would rather be raking the grain, feeding the chickens or cleaning his gun.

He doesn't have time for Waleed's detours and divertissements. The impatience is there in his voice.

"And?"

"Courvois used his gloomy consulting room off the main shop for eye tests and private consultations, but I can tell you, a lot more business went on in there than optical examinations.

He shared that space with people he hardly knew. Exchanging secrets and passing them on to Army intelligence. It was murky."

"His mistake was forgetting who he was." Father interrupts.

"No, Farouk. I believe he made a far bigger mistake than that. He forgot who he was supposed to be…"

Waleed takes great pleasure in contradicting Father—besting his supposed 'best' friend.

"I've no doubt being either side of an optometer in a gloomy chamber, eye to eye with people he hardly knew, brought with it an artificial familiarity and false confidences. Imagine being so close to a stranger in a darkened room that you can feel their breath on your face!"

"I'm trying to." Father's droll irony is tipping into belligerence. His fuse is shortening. He slaps down another card, pours himself another drink. But Waleed is on a roll.

"I think he allowed the mask to slip. It only takes a few seconds to spill something you regret. And once it's out there you can't unsay it.

A parvenu like Courvois—that pedlar of innuendo and lies—was all too eager to bandy gossip with patients in the consulting chair if it won him favours on the social circuit. I think he got careless and just fucked up."

Louis starts to stir under my right arm. He has been lying on one side for too long. His hair is wet and matted with sweat. His head searches for another cool patch on the linen pillowcase. He finds the spot and, still fast asleep, burrows into it. Margot is dead to the world, her thumb firmly in her mouth and her tiny fingers touching her button nose.

Waleed's voice is more strident now.

"Some of those patients would not have been too pleased to hear a Muslim rat on a Muslim—particularly if they happened to be associated with ALN militia…and if they found out Monsieur Courvois had been supplying the names of maquisards to Major Aussaresses' torturers. Well, he wouldn't just be digging his own grave. He would be handing the ALN the bullet to put him in it…

35

Unfortunately for Monsieur et Madame Courvois, a bullet in their heads…"

"Keep your voice down, Waleed," Father urges. "There are young children in the house and a baby who doesn't need waking."

Waleed obliges. He lowers his voice to a hush.

"A simple bullet in the head would have been far more painless than the fate that befell them last night…" I just about catch these last words and it sends a jolt through me—a shudder that causes Louis to stir again beside me.

He quickly settles.

It strikes me that when Waleed describes Monsieur Courvois, he could just as easily be drawing a picture of himself.

Mother says Waleed loves the sound of his own voice. That he is an inveterate rumour monger and a know-all with an inflated opinion of himself. A socialite manqué. He'd like nothing more than to trade stories over pastis down at the Yacht Club, ski up at Chrea in the winter and swan around at the Hussein-Dey racecourse. LeBoeuf has promised him these things, knowing that the only way Waleed would be allowed into the French club to share the company of 'Pieds-Blancs' would be to serve at their tables, not sit at them.

Instead, Waleed drives a bus from Medea into Algiers.

It's a drab routine. He takes no real pride in his work. But he's good at tinkering with engines. He has to be. The bus company has no maintenance crew, which means a bus driver has to double as an amateur electrician and engineer. Waleed can wire and calibrate. That's what makes him so useful as a bomb-maker to the agents of General Massu. Bombing people in the street and then pointing the finger at the Algerians is the French way of mixing things up. And it is a most effective deception when it comes to stirring up public opinion in France too.

Aside from the gossip, it's what livens up Waleed's grey world—planting explosives in doorways and blowing his fellow countrymen to kingdom come.

Our neighbour is back on his game.

"You know what happens to spies once the FLN gets a hold of them?" Waleed loves to play the shock card. "He and his Madame…" He makes a lurid choking sound, "…decapitated yesterday evening. Like a guillotine, only not as clean a cut…their heads decorate the shop sign."

I listen in to Father's silence. He has stopped playing. Waleed has his attention for sure.

"A curious piece of ironmongery. Captain LeBoeuf wants Ali La Pointe's murderous ALN accomplices done away with…so he sent me to set the trap during the night…and you, neighbour, are the blue touch-paper that will light it up."

"You have been into the city already?"

"I have just returned after a good night's work. The ALN fellaghas are still holed up at Courvois' shop. We have them, Farouk! They are pinned down by the snipers of the tenth para. And now they have it coming to them…"

Father is more attentive. Though he hesitates into his next question. "So what do they want from me?"

Waleed needs no second invitation. He jumps straight in.

"Before first light, you will rendezvous with Captain LeBoeuf. He will give you further instructions, along with your rounds for the day. You will then go to Courvois' shop and lure the assassins out. You will lead them into our trap…and boom!"

"Why me?"

"Who better than you, Farouk? A skilled hunter who knows his way around the Casbah and can ensnare them?"

Waleed's flattery is a dud. He tries a more incendiary approach.

"Besides, it is your turn. LeBoeuf says he has yet to be convinced by your…desire. Give him what he wants. A sign of your undying commitment to the cause."

It's worked. Father, suddenly inflamed, snaps back.

"Undying? That is rich. Why should I risk my life for that drill-square megalomaniac?

'Desire' and 'Commitment' are the hollow words of men who have never seen a baby run through with a bayonet or an old woman lying in the dust with her eyes gouged out."

But Waleed is not going to take Father's bragging rights to heart. The mission he has accomplished this last evening at LeBoeuf's behest gives him the upper hand on his neighbour—and on this occasion he will play his cards for all they're worth.

"You underestimate LeBoeuf. I am sure he has not only seen these things but been a party to them. And more. Which begs the question…have you, Farouk?

Do you have it within you to kill one ALN fellagha so that hundreds of our citizens will live? Rather than just run errands, listen in at cafés and tell tales on curfew-dodgers?"

Waleed has him.

"That is what LeBoeuf means by 'proof of desire'. And that is what is required if we are to free ourselves from this unholy mess—that is to match fire with fire. Isn't that what the good Frantz Fanon says? Mirror violence?"

"You have some brass neck quoting that shit-for-brains propagandist in my house."

Waleed pauses.

"Just because Fanon is an FLN apologist does not make him wrong. Often we learn more from our enemies than we do our friends..."

He presses home the advantage.

"You cannot blame LeBoeuf for wanting you to show him some fight. It is he who allows you to stay here, Farouk, without moving you on. You and Basira and the children. You have him to thank—as well as me, of course."

Father slams his glass down on the table.

"Do you want another card or not?"

Waleed does not rise to it. He presents his hand and Father is silenced.

"You say you have led Harkis on ratonnades in Skikda Wilaya, but really there is no way of LeBoeuf knowing, as that was not his principal theatre...

Algiers is.

For all he knows, you could have spooked at the fight and fled with your tail between your legs. You may not even have stayed around long enough to witness these barbaric things of which you speak.

I know you are proud of your service record, but LeBoeuf only has the Harki word for it. You could be tirailleur informant, spahi spy, or an acrobat in the Cirque National. To the captain, your curriculum vitae is still a blank page. He will only trust to the evidence of his own eyes to know who you really are."

There is a jauntiness in Waleed's voice now. He thinks he has won the argument if not the card game. But Father knows deep down that LeBoeuf and he have witnessed the same things out in Skikda Wilaya. And more. They have been together at the same time in the same place.

LeBoeuf is just intent on stringing Father along. Putting him through continual tests of allegiance. Dangling the rotten carrot of French citizenship in front of the Harki. And he uses his neighbour as his spy and stool pigeon to this end. They are both in limbo. For LeBoeuf, it is the most exquisite form of torture he could conceive.

"Anyway, whatever you think of the good Captain LeBoeuf, he is your way out of Algeria to France if it all goes belly-up. Your insurance policy, if you like. You and your family.

This is your chance. Grasp the opportunity by the head as you would a whip-snake—don't let it slip by because if you seize it by the tail, it will recoil and bite you."

Father is processing it.

"So…this is LeBoeuf's test."

"Of course. He is not stupid. And he will not make it easy for you. Count on it. He will present you with some tricky hoops to jump through tomorrow."

"And what favours have you gained so far for jumping through your hoops, Waleed?"

"LeBoeuf has promised me safe passage out of Algiers when the time comes. And that is good enough for me."

"And do you trust him to deliver?"

"What choice do I have? I'd rather put my life in his hands than serve myself up as a feast for that ALN mastiff, Boumedienne."

From half-wakefulness, I slip back into my dreams, where some of the eagles are dropping their live human prey from a height like Major Aussaresses' helicopter flights of death over the bay at Algiers.

The condemned jitterbug as they fall through the air from the battlements. As their bodies hit the ground they pop and spill their innards. Other eagles are falling on them and carrying off the carcasses and offal. They make upwardly spiralling circles as they climb the hot air currents to their eyries atop the castle walls, settling down to feed their young the carrion offcuts and sloppy organs—fresh Algerian meat.

The ravening eaglets reveal themselves to be the assembled citizenry of France—bankers, clerks, schoolteachers, doctors, bureaucrats, advocates, engineers. Their tiny chick bellies are distended with Algerian pickings and they are regurgitating pellets of bone, skin and hair.

Regardless, the feeder eagles keep stuffing fresh gobbets of meat down the scrawny gullets of their young. Swallow. Vomit. Swallow. Vomit.

It feels like minutes, though hours have elapsed. It is dark outside. But I know morning is here because I smell Mother's coffee.

My moment of waking has come too soon. Much too soon. I feel Father's calloused hand on my shoulder. His leathery palm is rough on my collarbone. He is shaking me out of sleep. His tobacco voice is rough like his hand. It scrapes.

"Come," he croaks, "While we still have cover of night. We have an appointment with Captain LeBoeuf."

Waleed is long gone. Mother is at the stove, a sleeping Baby Claude wrapped in a muslin shawl and nestled in the crook of her arm as she warms a pot. She is reheating a sloppy stew of spiced vegetables and chicken. Making flatbreads on the hot plate. And pouring black coffee thick as oil. It is a balancing act that she manages with remarkable composure.

I sit up and rub my eyes with my knuckles to clear some sleep. I am careful not to wake my little brother Louis and my baby sister Margot. They are snuggled into my armpits once again and are breathing softly by my side. I pull myself up slowly and their heads slip down onto the pillow without stirring.

I blink at my reflection in the mirror of the beaten old chiffonier that stands beyond the footboard of the bed. My hair is angry like a porcupine. My eyes are sunken in their orbits and dark.

Father throws me my trousers and goes to sit at the kitchen table, leaving the makeshift curtain pulled back. He spits on the stock of his rifle and rubs it with his sleeve. I see it is frayed and stained with blood. In contrast, the grain of the wooden gunstock is smooth and shiny. Its patina glows in the light of a single candle.

"What are you doing?" I ask innocently.

Father growls back.

"What am I doing! What do you think? Never mind what I'm doing. Think about what you're doing. And get up!"

But Mother won't stand for his hectoring.

"Don't be cruel to him," she snaps back at Father. "Pick on me instead! I too need an explanation."

Baby Claude starts to stir and wriggle under the shawl.

"For what? I don't need to explain myself."

She won't let it go.

"Explain to me why you care more for that gun of yours than you do for your own flesh and blood. Look at you caress that rifle! Explain to me why you slink off into the night with our son and he returns shaking and pale?"

Father swats away her question with a flick of the hand, but the question refuses to go away and still hangs in the air.

Baby Claude starts to move. Mother won't allow herself to be distracted.

She is staring at Father, pressing for an answer. She is standing her ground. There is fire in her eyes and her belly. Her silence creates in him an itchy heat. He carries on stroking the gunstock. He scratches at his neck, but the itch won't go, so he performs a familiar trick. He answers her by addressing me.

"If I look after this gun, this gun looks after me. And if it looks after me, it looks after you. Your mother, your brother and sister. Just remember that."

Mother's eyelids narrow over the pupils of her eyes. They are hooded now and that doesn't bode well. She is grinding her teeth behind tight lips. Clenching her jaw in a mouth-fist. She will not let him get away with it.

"You know, husband, the only thing that irks me more than our so-called democratic socialist government or the colons is a charlatan. And you are the worst sort. You don't even have the guts to tell me what you are up to. It is the behaviour of a traitor."

"Where our freedom is at stake, I am happy to be branded a charlatan and a gutless traitor-if it so pleases you." He doesn't mean it. It's a throwaway remark and I know he will regret it instantly.

Sure enough, the dam of my mother's anger bursts open. Father is forced to stand there and pay the price for years of her dutiful tolerance.

"Freedom! You fall for the propaganda of these so-called 'humanists' just like the rest of you myopic misfits. The French have been doing it to you without you knowing. 'La mission civilisatrice' indeed! You swallow De Gaulle's platitudes without the remotest idea that they exclude you. Parroting the rights of man, as if you belong to the exclusive club de La République. You never have and you never will!

You talk of the Rights of Man!

When did you ever have rights with these colons?

Of course, I know where you go and what you do, you idiot man."

"So why ask, woman?"

"Because you have never had the decency or courage to tell me to my face. And I have been praying you finally prove yourself to be the man I married and stand up to these bullies. For the love of Allah, Farouk, I am your wife. Men like Captain LeBoeuf will never understand you as I do. Not in a million years of trying.

They will never believe you have the same rights as them. They abuse your trust. And yet here you are crawling to LeBoeuf's side in the night, like a cur to the crack of its master's stick. He only has to throw you a dry old bone and he knows he has you on the end of his leash...

I would rather you went skulking off to the bordels to fuck one of your Nailiya whores than consort with that man. Can't you see it, Farouk? LeBoeuf will never see you as human. As his equal. Or as his brother-in-arms. You are sub-human to the French. You have no right to 'liberté', let alone 'egalité', or 'fraternité'. These are just words that these so-called 'humanists' believe only apply if you are human in their eyes. And we are not.

Muslims, Berbers, Arabs... we do not qualify. If you believe the French, you have been duped—and yet you give your children French names—Christian names—to impress your false masters!

You are a child of Islam, Farouk, not France. And your family is right here. To be with us, you only have to cross the room, not the Mediterranean. And yet you continue with this idolatry of the Fourth Republic."

Father is unrepentant. Rather, he is messianic.

"Better deluded than dead. Yes, that goes for you too, Basira. This gun will save you too. It will guarantee you the freedom from being snuffed out."

Father wets his fingers and pinches the burning wick of the candle. "There!"

The guttering flame is extinguished instantly with a curling wisp of smoke. Mother is unimpressed. The flame was failing anyway. She thinks it an infantile gesture. It's the kind of theatrical sulk my little brother puts on when he knows he has lost the argument before he's even opened his mouth—when he hurls himself to the ground like a fallen infantryman and wails his little heart out.

All this while, Baby Claude has been gearing up to scream. Now he lets go of an ear-splitting wail with all his might. I can't fathom how those tiny lungs can produce such a massive noise. Mother is jigging him in her arms, holding him close. She raises her eyes to the heavens and tears of frustration streak her cheeks. She is determined to have the last word if she can't have her way. But she no longer tries to shout above the baby's cries. She is resigned to Father going.

"Sorry, I was wrong, Farouk, my love. You are not deluded. You are demented. And you will get us all killed."

Father gobbles up the remains of his breakfast and kicks the chair out from underneath him, leaving it to Mother to right again. He drains his coffee cup, grabs the rifle from the table and lifts his binocular case off a coat-hook by the door. He motions for me to follow him out.

Mother is silently weeping now, calming a wailing Claude. As I hurry past her towards the door, she pushes a rolled-up flatbread into my hand and kisses me on the top of my head.

"Be careful, my beautiful boy. Stay close to your Father. He puts us in danger with his strange ideas, but he is all we have, and we must trust that blood is stronger than his false rhetoric."

It is pitch black and moonless outside. Father tugs his folded hunting cap from his coat pocket and puts it on with a grunt. He pulls the peak low over his brow thinking that I will not see the hurt and fury in his eyes.

There is a chill in the night air. Father pulls his coat around him. A fussing chicken flaps and curses under our feet as we head for the truck. I think about the soldier eagles in my dreams, wheeling and swooping down from the heights with long sharp talons poised to pick and pull at the elastic tendons and entrails of the human carrion.

I want to shake myself free from the remnants of the dreams still in my head. Thankfully, the faulty suspension in Father's old truck does the job for me.

Father jerks on the gear stick with a grinding clunk and we bump along down the dusty farm-track to the potholed road. The lights of Medea shimmer as we pass Waleed's place. His dogs snarl and growl at the consumptive cough of the truck's exhaust. But this time we are not stopping to pick him up. I think of Waleed asleep inside, knowing his job is done and favours won. No doubt he will sleep the sleep of the dead tonight. He will probably even sleep through the muezzin's call to prayer.

Father is silent for most of the journey and appears calm as he drives steadily towards Algiers.

Driving his truck is his only peace. Maybe he is thinking about LeBoeuf's test. Or perhaps he is making a conscious effort to erase the gruesome picture of Monsieur et Madame Courvois—aka Selmane—from his mind's eye. One more image to add to the gruesome back-catalogue.

I do not know what is out there, but I sense something monstrous is waiting for us.

A while later, the old fort emerges into view. Ruined battlements loom above us, uneven and broken—a row of goatherd's teeth along which the odd camp-fire glints like a gold filling.

"You are more than my lookout today, Simeon. You are my spotter and my little wingman. Imagine we are out hunting deer and you can't go wrong."

I nod.

Father pulls the car off the road beside a trickling culvert, partially hidden to passing traffic. He yanks up the handbrake and turns to me.

"Do you remember the animal hide outside Sour El-Ghozlane, on the way to Mansoura? Where we used to shoot boar?"

"I think so."

"Do you think so, or do you know so? It's important, Simeon."

"I know the place."

"Good. Keep it to yourself. You have to promise me. It's vital that you tell no one. Not even your mother. You hear me?"

"I hear you."

I don't have to question why Father is asking this of me. We both know it's his place of safety should anything go wrong later.

Father jumps down from the driver's cabin and sets off on foot. I scramble out after him and follow.

He runs nimbly with the speed of a jerboa. I keep my eyes on the heels of his boots in front of me, being careful to place my footprints inside his. He weaves around rock and brush on the way up and I shadow him until the incline meets the vertical face of a stone wall.

Father stops to catch his breath and check that I am still there behind him. "Stick to the wall and follow me!"

The lights of Algiers wink at me from below. The city is a way beneath us now. We are high enough to see dawn tracing a halo of gold around the peaks of the far Atlas Mountains to the southwest. We edge our way along the vertical wall, feeling the cold stone with our fingertips. The drop is dizzyingly steep. Or maybe it just seems that way. I find that in the dark, distance deceives the eye and objects seem further away than they really are.

A voice punctures the still early morning air. It booms down from the ramparts above.

"Ah, Farouk, sidewinder! You're on time for once!"

Up on the battlements, a soldier peers down at us, legs astride, hands on hips.

He appears have a red-hot ember for a mouth. A fire-breathing warrior against the night sky.

As my eyes readjust, I can make out the end of the fat cigar he holds between his lips.

I cannot for the life of me comprehend how he has picked us out in the gloom, though I'm told it is a sniper's skill. A paratrooper's night-sight becomes his sixth sense.

"I see you've brought your powder monkey with you."

"Yes, he is a good boy…" Father's voice has changed from that of master to servant.

"Catch, powder monkey!" shouts the soldier. He drops a heavy leather pouch down to me. It rattles with metal inside. I fumble it. Captain LeBoeuf laughs. "You'll need to be quicker than that with the ALN fellaghas. Or they'll cut your head off."

I am trembling. And LeBoeuf knows it is not with the cold. He has done with scaring me. Now he goes to work on Father.

"Waleed briefed you fully I take it, Farouk!"

"Yes, Captain."

"Good. Then you will know he has the bomb in position. It is under a beer crate at the southern entrance to a courtyard in the souk—the one named after that soi-disant Sartre. The detonator and charge are located behind a boarded-up alcove in the western entrance. The Muslims use it as some kind of street shrine. You'll have no trouble finding it.

"I have a party of my men watching the optician's shop in Rue Kadi Said. Those ALN fellaghas need shifting. You will get their hackles up. That's what we need. To rile them. Force them into a rash move. Blunder.

"You will be the bait, Farouk, drawing the treacherous jackals out of their lair towards their Hour of Judgement. But make sure you run ahead so you give yourself time enough to connect the charge to the detonator. Mark my words, the end of them will be the making of you. France beckons, Farouk. But only if you do the right thing the right way."

Father hesitates, then stiffens beside me. "Liberté!" he shouts back at LeBoeuf obediently.

It is the pledge of a reluctant patriot—and it causes something to rise in my gullet that I have never tasted before. I think it is shame.

"We'll see whether you get your 'Liberté' or not," says LeBoeuf.

Father and I make our way around to a gentler slope. We slip-slide and scramble down towards the city. Part scree, part sand soon gives way to the concrete and mud of the Casbah. Shadows of buildings are starting to form in the growing light. We scuttle between pools of darkness, between streetlamps, metal tapping metal in the leather pouch that I clutch to my midriff as if my life depends on it.

This is my duty to Father. This is Father's duty to captain LeBoeuf.

We pass through deserted streets that cling to the hillside. And the unease grows in my belly.

Father turns and motions to me to keep my head down. "Careful, my little wing man. LeBoeuf's snipers are around. They become more trigger-happy as the light comes up. They could easily mistake us for maquisards."

A short while later, we make it to the entrance of a narrow passageway leading off into the souk. It is barely the width of a single man's shoulders. Father peers down into it.

"Make a note of it. It's our escape chute."

We huddle down by a news kiosk on the opposite side of the pavement. The kiosk is shuttered and shields us while giving us a clear view down Rue Kadi Said to Courvois' shop.

The place is easy to find—marked as it is by a giant pair of golden pince-nez suspended above the street. Made from tubes of gilded metal, they look heavy enough to break a giant's nose.

At either end of the sign there is a pair of rusting iron spheres. They appear to have been hastily beaten out of shape by a ham-fisted blacksmith.

Father steadies his gun and swivels his hunting cap around on his head so that the peak faces backwards. He takes the binoculars and scans the fascia of Courvois' shop through the gathering light of dawn.

He looks up from the binoculars and throws me a sideways glance. His face is ashen and bloodless. He is about to utter something but thinks again and draws his eye back to the gunsight.

"You see the fellagha in the opticians' first floor window?"

He points ahead. I peer down the street towards the sign. Father hands me the binoculars. I make out the muzzle of a gun angling out above the sill through an open shutter.

"That's our target. Quick! A magazine!" he snaps, holding out his hand.

I put down the binoculars and plant my hand into LeBoeuf's magazine pouch.

Something barbed inside pricks me and I withdraw my fingers with a start. I think I have just caught them on rough stitching, so I do it again.

This time I am pierced by what feels like the point of a map-pin.

My eyes water and flood. I fish out an empty magazine and feed some bullets into its pinching, greedy mouth. Repeat. And again. My fingertips are being sliced open. They are bloodied with raw scratches and cuts. I try not to feel pain and keep pushing bullets into the magazine. It is as hungry as I am.

Father tells me to hurry as he holds out his hand for the magazine. "You goat! Faster than that! You should have it ready for me!" I fumble.

"I'm sorry, Father. The bullets are loose. Why couldn't LeBoeuf give us full magazines?"

I am dripping blood from my hands even before a shot is fired.

I think LeBoeuf has put something sharp in with the ammunition. I peer in and see a loose razor blade. I shake the bag and another naked blade rises among the stash of bullets.

The paratrooper captain has made it even more difficult for us. Is this the test of which Waleed spoke? Is it a game? Or worse still a practical joke?

Father's hand is beside me fishing the air for ammo as he trains his eyes on the target, but I am not ready yet.

"Remember. You are my side-gunner and my spotter, my little wing man. I am relying on you. Give me that!"

Impatient, he grabs the magazine from me, locks, loads and raises the barrel level with the street. His hand is shaking as he winces down the gunsight. The muzzle quivers. He wipes the sweat from his left eye. His right eyelid is crinkled shut.

I do not see the same man who only this morning slopped matbucha on a flatbread with a sure hand and rolled it up like one of those cigars LeBoeuf smokes. Neither do I see the man who coolly tracks down deer and boar at our happy hunting grounds in Koudiat El-Markluf.

He is panicked. He is grimacing. He is dripping sweat. He is cursing. And he is shaking like this is his first time.

He stinks—as if his clothes have been soaked in the dust and sweat of a thousand years. He has dribbled matbucha juice down his tunic—and he smells sweet sour—of vinegar and cat pee, cinnamon and battery acid. I notice that a small dark patch has formed around his groin. And it is spreading. Piss is running down his legs.

A fizzing sound tickles my ear. I want to laugh. A shiver goes down my body. And the wall behind me pops and spits dust. I turn to see how close the fellagha's bullet has passed. Father rests the gun and passes me his binoculars.

Sometimes I will take these binoculars from the hook by the door and head outside to gaze at the night sky.

Now I am thinking how much the wall behind me resembles the moon's surface as I gaze at it on those nights. Scarred and streaked, the whitewash is going grey in patches like the lunar seas. Powdery render drifts down from the walls to the paving stones. Another near miss.

A shot zips through the air just to my left, punching into the side of the kiosk. Then a whole volley of them.

I plug my ears with my fingertips before I realise my work is not yet done. As Father has reminded me, I am the spotter to his sniper.

This is the part I play when we go hunting for boar and rabbit in the mountains.

I press the binoculars to my eyes to guide him towards his target.

I tell him he is firing low. His shots hit the lintel above the side door. The wood splinters and the paintwork cracks…

He needs to raise his sight by two feet and slightly right…

A fissure in the plasterwork, but closer this time as he finds his range and distance…

He aims again and shoots off one…two…three…four in rapid succession. I see a small spurt of blood spatter the window frame and the muzzle in the window is quickly withdrawn.

"You've hit him!" I expect Father to acknowledge me, but he is stony-faced, in the thick of the hunt.

I look through the binoculars again watching for movement. Scanning the fascia of the shop, it is then that I see the bloodied heads impaled on the fleurs de lys filials of the hanging sign. Not iron balls. Têtes sans corps. Décapité.

My first thought is how strange it is that a head should be placed on either side of a pair of pince-nez rather than the other way around. The fellaghas have created a macabre visual pun.

And then I feel a great chill. Ice in my veins. My body freezes.

Father screams at me. "Ghawel! Keep it up! We need to rub salt in their wounds."

I should be loading a fresh magazine, but I cannot move. Duty calls, but I am beyond making sense of Father's words. He is now grabbing the pouch and reloading for himself. He winces at the cold razor edges that slice at his fingers, cursing everyone and everything—LeBoeuf, La Republique, the colon, the FLN and the Man in the Moon. He is swearing and firing indiscriminately now.

There is movement in the doorway of the shop and three fellaghas break into the street, darting for cover, firing back at us from boarded doorways, from behind lampposts and burned out cars. Between them, they send a fusillade in our direction. Father returns in kind. It's a firestorm. A frenetic hail of bullets all around. We are peppered with paint flakes and plaster-dust.

"I don't understand. Where are those French sharpshooters LeBoeuf mentioned?" I ask Father.

He hears my panic, grabs another magazine, fills it with bullets, locks, loads and keeps firing.

"LeBoeuf is leaving us to our own devices. He wants his snipers to lay off so these ALN bastards are free to chase us down. Why else do you think he left it to first light for us to make our move? So that they can see us better to hunt us. We are LeBoeuf's decoy and the trap is set. So come, little wingman. Let's go!"

Father pulls me to my feet by the collar of my jacket. I grab the binoculars from the floor on my way up. He tows me across the pavement. Together, we tumble into the darkness of the passageway. He picks me up again and we run for our lives.

The souk is dead to the world in the early morning. The stench of decay is overpowering. It smells of Father a thousand times over—of rotting vegetables and spices, vinegary sweat and shit.

I slip and slide on the pulpy skins of lemons as I fly through the narrow passageway, leaping over broken crates and stumbling into stalls long emptied of produce.

In the midst of the shuttered channel, a tanner's workshop is open early for business. The place reeks of hide-softening piss. I collide with a tiny mannequin stood sentinel outside, wrapped in an outsized pigskin coat with rabbit fur collar. Its fixed smile mocks me. I send flying a bookcase whose shelves groan with leather belts, wallets and shoes.

Father storms on ahead. He swivels and dodges through the ruined rat-runs. He knows every inch of the Casbah, having supplied the local traders with his quarry. But the passages are alien to me.

Shouts echo through the souk. From behind me comes the sound of feet hunting me down. I turn to look. Three men are crashing through the debris. The ALN slayers of Monsieur Courvois and his wife.

My breath is as loud as the faulty exhaust pipe of Father's truck. My chest rattles with phlegm. I am not so much breathing as churning the air in my lungs.

Long before the eagle-soldiers invaded my dreams, I had a recurring nightmare even more intense.

It started happily enough.

In that dream, I am out with Mother and Father strolling on a dry salt-lake. They are either side of me and each of them is holding my toddler hand. They are in love. It's a pleasing sensation. I am euphoric as they swing me high between them.

The higher they swing me, the more weightless I feel. And the more weightless I feel, the less power I have in my legs.

A creeping paralysis sets in as I put more of myself in their hands with every swing.

Having longed for them to propel me higher, I now start begging them not to let me go. Yet they can't hear me. They start teasing one another and their teasing turns to bickering about things I don't understand.

They have stopped swinging me in the air and are dragging me along by my hands like a sack of grain. I am heavy, dense. My arms are going numb now and so is my grip. I try desperately to cling on to them, but they let me drop to the floor.

They walk on, too occupied by their feuding to notice me, but I cannot follow them, no matter how hard I try.

I am now fully paralysed, weighed down. I implore them to come back for me, but they are deaf to my entreaties. I shout as I watch them walk away. I scream, but they do not hear me and cannot not see me. They have left me behind, forgotten me. I have nothing left to give as they move further and further away into the far distance towards a vanishing point and disappear into a heat haze.

That dream was beyond frightening. Beyond all terror. It was unthinkable.

But it is happening now. It is happening to me for real as I watch Father swivel and skid around corners, side-step stalls and duck under sagging awnings. He moves further ahead of me as I try to keep sight of the tailcoats that whip behind him.

I am running forwards, but feel as if I am going backwards, wading through an ocean of molasses. And the fighters are closing on me.

Father turns to wave me on as he runs, urging me to keep up. I want him to wait for me. I shout "Arrêtez, Père. Qf!', but the words are lost in my heavy breathing and tears and he doesn't stop.

The ALN men are firing off more rounds. Bullets whistle past me as we chase-race through the souk. One of them hits a roll of rug with a dull thwack.

Another bullet splinters a cedar-wooden carving of a Berber horseman in a shop entrance. I think one of them has pierced my side only to find I have caught the sharp edge of a bench with my hip.

I pass a group of elders sharing a shisha outside a café. As I rush by, I notice one old boy offer me a smoke from his pipe. I brush another table and a hookah clatters to the floor, bouncing and somersaulting in front of me. The patrons grizzle and curse, thinking me rude for ignoring their hospitality.

"Arrêtez, Père! Qf!"

Ahead of me Father bounds up onto a water butt, using it as a step to scale a wall which he traverses before hauling himself up onto a roof terrace. I watch him leap from roof terrace to roof terrace above me, ahead of me. Like a leopard. And he is gone.

Somehow my legs still carry me onwards as if they know the way. The passages are strewn with rubble that grazes my shins and broken tiles with sharp edges that cut at my ankles. I hear more gunfire whizzing through the air and cracking against walls.

I think I am done. There is no sign of Father. The air has gone from my lungs and I am gagging and stumbling. The footsteps are growing louder in my wake.

But then something happens. Something extraordinary.

I emerge from the dark passageway and am smothered in light and cool air. I squint at cobalt blue sky up above. I pause and sniff at the perfumed scent of oranges. The gurgling of water from a fountain bounces off the walls all around and momentarily drowns out the sound of footsteps, the cries of men and the crack of gunfire.

I am standing in a small open courtyard. A plaque on the wall announces: 'Place Jean-Paul Sartre'.

Aside from the route I have just come along, I see three other passages running off this courtyard back into the souk. I gather my breath as I step across the colourful mosaic tiling that surrounds the central fountain. Spouts of water issue from the mouths of three spinning dolphins into a sparkling pool that is strewn with treasure—dinar coins of varying sizes. An orange tree in one corner explodes with fruit.

The sound of footfall snaps me back into my reality. I move towards another of the passageways when I hear the familiar tobacco voice.

"Pssst…Simeon…Simeon." I turn to see Father crouched in the shadows across the courtyard from me. My heart leaps into my mouth.

He is ushering me to join him.

But it is too late.

The three fellaghas burst into the courtyard. Men with sallow faces and cratered eyes. Hungry, drawn, twitchy. They stop stock-still as they see me facing them.

We are staring at one another as if on either side of an enclosure fence at the Jardins d'Essai du Hama zoo. We are seeing in one another a rare animal in captivity for the first time at close quarters. We are both working out which of us is the observed and which the observer.

My hands are raised in surrender though I cannot recall lifting them. I am here in body but not in mind. It is pleasantly painless to find myself floating above the end of my life.

The first fellagha steps towards me and takes my chin in his hand, breaking the spell. I smell in his sour sweat traces of cologne and tobacco and fear surges inside my chest. He forces my head high so that I am impelled to look up into his face. He thinks he can read the truth in my eyes. But I am good at hiding it. I have learned that from Father.

"How old are you?"

"Old enough," I reply. It just comes out.

"Old enough?" The fellagha laughs and turns to his brothers-in-arms who share in the joke "What kind of answer is that?"

He pulls a knife from his belt, raises it to me and holds the point to my throat. "Are you old enough to die?"

My throat burns as I try not to swallow. My eyes flicker across to Father. He is trying to wave away my gaze. I cannot give away his location.

"Are you old enough to decide that matter for yourself? Or should you ask the permission of an adult, perhaps? I believe you will find one close by."

The fellagha scrutinises me. I have the notion that if I swallow, he will cut out my Adam's apple and hang it from the orange tree like a rogue fruit.

"Are you old enough to tell me why that older man you are with is trying to kill us?

Or better still, where he is right now?"

The cold steel nicks my throat. I shiver. And I can't help but look back at Father.

"How old are you?"

I will not tell him.

"You are the son of a Harki, yes?"

I don't answer.

"Are you a Muslim? You could be a Pied-Noir. Your accomplice is near?"

My mouth is sealed.

"Your father, perhaps?"

I cannot speak.

"An ally of that traitor, Courvois? A Muslim-denying colonialist collaborator? A flunky of the French?"

I am saying nothing. I fight back tears.

"You know we will take you and we will find out."

Behind my interrogator, I notice the second fellagha edging closer to me, keen to join in this free-for-all.

The third—younger, less bold—hangs back. I see him nursing a limp arm, wrapped around with a bloody tourniquet which he tugs on with his teeth to tighten as he keeps his weapon pointed directly at my chest. I determine this is the gunman in the window who took the bullet from Father's rifle.

The third fellagha is flagging. His face is shiny with sweat and he is panting hard. I feel sorry for him. But then I recall the horror of the optician's shop sign and realise this man—not many years older than myself—has spent part of the previous night hacking away at the necks of Monsieur and Madame Courvois.

"You go to school?" asks the first fellagha.

I choose not to reply.

"Your gym shoes tell me you do. Have your teachers taught you the basic physical laws of cause and effect?"

I cannot see where he is going with this.

"Cause and effect. You tell us now and you will spare yourself later. It really is that simple."

The fellagha grows impatient with my silence now.

"Listen to this man who stands behind me. And listen to him carefully!" he snaps, "He will tell you what we will do to release the cork from the neck of this bottle."

He tightens his grip on my jaw, pressing on my nerve that sends pulses of searing pain around my head. I gurgle louder than the fountain.

"He will tell you what will happen to you if you continue to play dumb". His hand squeezes ever tighter, forcing my eyes to bulge and my jaw to click and pop with the pressure.

The second fellagha steps forward.

"General Massu's men took my little brother here off the street one night."

The second fellagha turns to the third and forces my eye-line to follow. It is hard to hear what the fellaghas are saying. I can't compute. Blood is coursing through my ears at screaming pitch—a shrill and insistent hiss.

"They took him to the derelict sweet factory, tied him to a chair, put electrodes in his mouth. The electricity soldered his jaws together. His teeth locked to the point they cracked. He saw lightning flashes and fire across his eyelids. And it made him so very thirsty he could have drunk the Chelif dry. But for three hours they kept going, keeping him tied to the chair in spasms without giving him a drop to drink. And you know what they did to him then? They attached the same electrodes to his cock and balls and started over. He lived. He escaped. But he can no longer father children. And he still suffers the cries of the old muezzin who saved his skin.

You see, as the infidel set about my brother, he could see the old man through the cracks in the sweet factory floorboards—and he could hear that ancient muezzin begging the French paras to let my brother go by swearing false allegiance—"Allez la France!" They made that old man chant it over and over again. "Allez la France!" The muezzin hoped if he sang their tune for long enough, it would save my brother's life…and it did.

Can you believe that? A muezzin forced to sing "Allez la France!" when his voice is reserved for Allah.

What do you think that did to the spirit of that sacred man? It violated the most precious thing he possesses. His faith."

The first fellagha interjects.

"So… when we get our hands on the French and their friends, we give a dose of Massu's gégène right back at them."

"What perfect symmetry," concludes the first fellagha, staring me down again. "We do to you what you have done to us."

I want to tell the fellagha that their grievance is nothing to do with me. But I am mute. If I talk, I know they will kill me. If I say nothing, likewise. Instead, I plead for my life with my eyes. First, I plead with the fellagha to spare me.

Then I silently plead with Father in the shadows to save me.

As I do, I see Father's hand hovering over a switch attached to a battery. I see the wires running along the base of the walls to an upturned wooden beer crate which I can make out in the shadows of the passage beside me.

I look towards Father. My eyes plead. Please, please, don't. His eyes are glistening. I can read his face in an instant. It's the same calculating look he shoots Waleed in their card games. Stick or twist. The same look he gave that wounded young buck in in the ravine at Kordiat el-Markluf. If he leaves me with these men, it will be a slow death. If he detonates the bomb, it will at least be instant. And he'll gamble on the slimmest of chances that I may survive the blast. The fellagha registers the direction of my gaze. He slowly turns his head to follow my eyeline.

My world is starting to blur through stinging tears. I am feeling feint.

The fellagha spots Father in the shadows.

"There! Quick! Take him!" The first fellagha points to the dark passageway. The second fellagha sees Father and raises his rifle to fire. The first fellagha seizes me, grabbing me by the arms—and starts to drag me, using me as his shield.

There is a loud click from across the courtyard. The fellaghas stop and turn to face Father.

There is a white flash and a ground-rending crack followed by a roar. Blackness.

Seconds. Hours. Days.

I am hot. The inside of my mouth is caked with cloying phlegm and dust. I am choking on it, struggling to breathe. There is a crushing on my chest. I hear frantic voices, hands clawing at stone. A hole of light opens up. The ridges on the sole of a boot. The leopard-skin pattern on fatigues. A helmeted soldier peers in and shines a torchlight into my eyes. The light goes off.

Dazzling orange fruit blazes out against a gloriously deep blue sky.

The Trinitarian Hospital, Algiers, 9 January 1957

I am on my side gazing out through glass to a vertical horizon. Green-grey sea. A brooding gunboat climbs the skyline in a trajectory that is more rocket ship than ship. Or the direction of the mercury in that thermometer that is right next to my head.

Mother's voice is dancing around my skull.

"Shimeun…Shimeun, darling…mon petit…"

Her cool fingers are on my brow.

I am now trying to follow the fast hands of a street magician in the souk. He swishes a cape with a matador's flourish. I delight in his legerdemain. He is summoning all sorts of wondrous things from behind the cape; a rabbit; a steel ball; a bunch of irises; the decapitated head of Monsieur Courvois. He smirks beneath his gigolo moustache, raises an eyebrow at me with a showman's smile that creases the corners of his mouth and lends his eyes the twinkle of a boulevardier—and smoothly sweeps the cape over my head.

I am now watching a nurse in starched white cornette and apron. She is tapping at the joint of a drip to release a bubble of saline. She is demur and gentle. I am in love with her. For the first time in my life, I am in love.

I am now up with the eagle-soldiers again. This time, I recognise one of them as De Gaulle. He has a most handsome parabolic beak. And he wears his trademark kepi well over his majestic, crested eyebrows. I cannot imagine De Gaulle without his kepi. I am sure he emerged from the womb with one already attached.

The citizen eaglets have grown now. These upright middle classes are more savant, more nourished and are now able to spread their own wings. De Gaulle's wings are extended wide too so they can envelop the sons and daughters of

France in equal measure. His is a magnificent span, layered in drifts of the softest white feathers—fully extended, they cover the whole length of the battlements.

No longer hungry chicks, the eaglets now turn down the fleshy titbits offered to them by the soldier-eagles. Instead they feed off De Gaulle's paternal gaze and take heart from his protective embrace.

This defiant refusal to take the food diminishes the feeder eagles. They are thwarted further by De Gaulle himself, who swats them out of the air with one casual swipe of his muscular wing and a snort of disdain. Guy Mollet sits like a brooding mate to one side of the parapet watching these antics.

De Gaulle traps one soldier eagle in his powerful, levered talons and won't let him go. The eagle writhes and shudders and shrieks under De Gaulle's firm foothold. "I am your general. Stop this now!"

The eagle De Gaulle is now speaking through a microphone to the people of Algiers assembled below. Loudspeakers carry his words to every Quarter of the city, every town, every commune, every province across the land. And people quake. In the European quarter of Algiers, everyone stops to listen. In the markets of Corinthia, farmers and townsfolk prick up their ears. In the uplands of the Hautes Plateaux, shepherds pause to take it all in. Right down to the Sahara, he sends a frisson of fear and excitement, a collective shudder of apprehension and anticipation across a depleted nation.

"Let us be clear. Eagles do not feed on the dead. That is not what eagles do. We are not vultures, nor are we crows" (shrill feedback, static interference, white noise).

"We do not demean ourselves by stooping to their level. It does not become us. We are proud eagles. Fair and just. We uphold the Rights of Man."

"Shimeun…he is awake…Shimeun, sweet boy…" It is Mother, fretting and fussing over me. I open my eyes. "Shimeun, my boy!" I close them again.

She is gone. The room is dark. A man in the next bed is shining a pocket torch onto the page of a book. I can see it is more of a manual. The man can hear me stir and groan and reaches out a hand. Our beds are too far apart to allow any touch, so he waves at me.

"Do you want me to call the nurse for you?"

I am confused. He resembles the street magician in my dream.

"What is this place?" I ask.

The man frowns.

"For the life of me, I can't recollect the name of it. Isn't that strange!' He whispers so as not to wake others.

My eyes adjust to the gloom. I can just make out a row of beds with rails and curtains flanking both sides of the room. There are snoozing bodies, a notice board, a gurney, a twin-shelved trolley bristling with plastic water jugs, wipes and blankets.

At the end of the room nearest to me on the wall above double swing doors with porthole windows sits a giant clock. At the other end, a solitary figure with large white wings sprouting from the sides of her head is hunched over a desk in a pool of light under an enormous fresco of the Madonna and child. I gasp at the sight. God sends an angel of mercy down to help guide Mother and baby boy. And there she is in the flesh with pen poised. Perhaps she is going to put my name in her register before I am lifted heavenward.

"Ah, yes, now I remember. Trinitarian hospital," says the man in the next bed.

"Have you seen my Father?"

"Just the Holy one. They never let you forget Him here."

"My Mother…?"

"If you mean Our Lady of Sorrows with the deep-set mascara eyes…then, yes. She's been here. When is she not? She hardly ever leaves…"

I smile as I picture Mother's strong face—her large hazel eyes with a hint of tristesse, the aquiline nose and sharp cheekbones that she would use to cut men down to size. Mother always possessed poise and power in her visage.

"That is not mascara. She has dark lashes…" I hear myself say.

"Oh…I stand corrected. She carries herself like a mujahidat," says the man in the next bed. Suddenly, my tightly tucked sheets feel like restraints.

I am quick to shoot down his assertion, perhaps too quick. "My Mother is not a mujahidat."

"Well, whatever she is, you have inherited her features. You too have sad eyes but good eyebrows. And those long lashes of yours will carry you far. Maybe all the way to Hollywood one day. They come in handy for winning the attention of that pretty nurse, do they not? Strong women love strong eyebrows and lashes on their men as they do on themselves. They say the quality of the frame is every bit as important as the picture they surround."

I cannot tell whether he is gazing at the fresco of Madonna and child or the sister at her work-station underneath.

I feel my face flush.

"How long have I been here?"

"Five days. Six if you count today. But today is barely three hours old. And you are too young to start counting your days."

"Do you know what's wrong with me?"

"Whoah! Too many questions for this hour of the morning. That's what the sister is for, my fellow. This is way beyond my compass. I am not a qualified doctor. I am a trained soldier. Lieutenant Laurent." He extends a hand between the beds.

I tug on my sheets and pull them up to my face. I will not share my oxygen with this militaire de carrière, let alone a handshake.

"I'm sorry," I say, by way of an excuse. "It hurts to move."

"That's quite alright."

"Goodnight" I murmur.

"Yes. Sleep well."

The night terrors come. We are in the Hautes Plateaux in a carpet of snow.

We are nomads leading a flock down to winter pasture. We are being tracked by a snow leopard. We are vigilant. Our dogs are watchful too but cowed by the presence of the stalking beast. We travel for miles across bleak, wind-swept ridges. The leopard slinks after us, always downwind, waiting for its moment to strike. We reach an impassable bluff and start to marshal the flock down and around the steep promontory. The tight huddle of sheep is stretched out now and the big cat knows it has the advantage. It launches itself. Full pelt. Running at the stragglers. It cuts one hapless sheep off from the flock, chasing it in circles, then seizing it in its jaws. Father charges through the snow, yelling, waving his arms and throwing himself on the leopard, trying to wrestle it to the ground with his bare hands. Our two dogs follow, forgetting their fear. Along with Father, they set on the creature, but they are no match for the predator. The leopard rips the dogs' throats out with two tearing bites while Father struggles to bring the animal down off its hind legs. He has the leopard in a headlock as it writhes and snarls, its fangs buried deep in Father's shoulder, its jaws coated with his blood. His feet kick out and slip on the wet grass. They find purchase on a rock as he lies tussling with the beast. Father braces himself, turns the leopard's head with a swift violent motion, twists again, and manages to break the animal's neck. The leopard convulses and is still. Father is bleeding out into the snow.

I feel nothing for him. I stand over the limp body of the snow leopard as the light dies in its eyes. It is breathtakingly beautiful, and I weep uncontrollably.

It is then that I notice the wolf-pack massing on the bluff. The line of wolves has been standing off the leopard until now, but with the beast despatched, they too are eyeing up the sheep. Father lies squirming in the snow which blushes with his blood—and I realise it is now up to me to fend the animals off.

Still night-time. Early morning. I can see Lieutenant Laurent out of bed across the ward. He is exchanging whispers with the patient in the bay opposite. The patient is agitated, reluctant, sheepish.

I drift in and out of sleep.

I want to sit up in bed. And yet there is no strength in my limbs. I reach down to my thigh and touch a brittle cast. I start to panic and wiggle my toes. All present and correct. Then I feel a vague itch behind my ear. I go to scratch it and my fingers connect with lint and surgical tape. I touch my forehead and cranium, swathed in bandages. I am sedated and numb and sleepy.

But I do not sleep. I wait for the nurse to do her round and watch the giant clock count down the hours until daylight. Gradually, a flat, milky light permeates the room, rinsing it of night-shadows and dreams. The terrors flee.

The nurse checks in on me.

I annoy myself by being bashful.

"Good morning, young man. It is good to see you awake."

Laurent is back in bed, but sitting up, his nose buried in a copy of 'Le Monde' and pretending not to listen. The nurse draws a curtain with the swish of the street magician's cape.

"Now I'm sure you have many questions. But you are not yet strong enough. Take it from me."

She wraps a rubber cuff around my upper arm and squeezes a gauge. The cuff inflates and constricts.

"Open!"

I open my mouth but only to a narrow slit.

"Wider…" she urges.

My jaw is bruised and sore. I remember the vice of the fellagha's hand around my chin, the shooting pains in my head as his fingers tightened around my jawline.

I strain to open my mouth wide enough so that the nurse can wedge a thermometer under my tongue. She calmly slips it inside.

"Close!"

She needn't have bothered to warn me off asking questions. The thermometer stoppers speech.

She is checking my pulse, holding my wrist with a marked tenderness.

I want to cry.

I resist.

The nurse brings her face closer to mine. She gently reaches out to raise one of my eyelids with her thumb.

"Open!" She commands, as she shines a beam into my eye. I see an orange tree in sunburst. She clicks her torch off.

"You are lucky to be alive. By the time the soldiers brought you in you had lost a great deal of blood.

You have suffered damage to your internal organs. The surgeon removed a three-inch wooden splinter from your kidney and stitched you up again. It's a good job you have a spare.

If you feel bruised in your sides, that is why—that and the surgeon's scalpel. Your back muscles will take a little while to heal. The wound was deep.

Oh, and your leg—it is broken in two places. That will take longer. You have also suffered severe concussion.

But you have youth on your side. We will have you up and about in no time. Recovery should be rapid in a boy of your age."

I find this last remark withering. 'Boy of my age'? There must be…what…only five, six years between us? Seven at most. She removes the thermometer and checks it with a cursory "that's better…"

She moves to the foot of the bed, lifts a clipboard hanging by a string and scribbles on a sheet.

"By all rights, the blast should have killed you. There was enough explosive to bring down a three-storey building. You were buried under rubble for several hours. Questions can wait until later."

I have too many. Of course, I am not going to wait. There is one above all. "My father?"

"No questions, I said."

"My father?" I repeat.

She sighs at my impudence.

"The Army would like to talk with you—when you are stronger. Captain LeBoeuf of the tenth para has visited. Though we sent him away. Perhaps he can give you the answers you seek. Or your mother? She will be here soon. Anything you need?"

I shake my head. I feel tired. The nurse draws back the curtain and floats away down the ward.

"The notorious Captain LeBoeuf? My, you are honoured to be visited by such a…" from the adjacent bed, Laurent is reaching for a word, searching for inspiration in the ceiling mouldings. He can't find any.

"…fellow."

I turn my head away from Laurent. His stare bores into the back of my skull. I close my eyes tight to shut it out.

Sleep comes easily.

Mother is here now. She is pushing a pram and stops to talk to the nurse in the open ward. They both notice me and Mother wheels Baby Claude to my side.

"My darling child!"

I am embarrassed. I do not want the nurse to hear Mother treating me like her other baby boy. I try to sit up. Mother places a gentle, restraining hand on my shoulder.

"No, rest, Shimeun. The sister says she will get you up later."

Mother's face is over mine.

"Are you comfortable?"

I nod. She takes my hand in hers and squeezes it against her cheek, then kisses my knuckle. She looks older than when I last saw her. She weeps a little. I am embarrassed. I let it pass.

"Where are Louis and Margot?" It clearly pains her to utter her children's French names. She lost the battle with Father over their naming. Not so mine.

"They are being looked after." It is unlike her to be so vague. "I brought Claude in to see you, though."

I smile wanly at my tiny little brother and crook a finger in his direction. "And Father?" I am desperate to know. "Where is Father?"

Mother shakes her head. She presses my fist even more firmly into her cheek. She grips my hand as if letting go will make me vaporise in front of her eyes.

"Is he dead, Mother?" I ask.

"Worse," she replies. "He is gone."

"Where?"

"I don't know. Vanished."

"But he…" I try to collect myself.

"He what, Shimeun?"

I see Father's eyes flashing at me from the entrance to the passageway, his fingers on the switch. His eyes so full of panic and fear have been replaced by Mother's so full of regret.

She finishes my sentence for me.

"He is a hunted man. He was seen by quite a few people in the Casbah running from the ALN fellaghas."

"I was running too."

"Yes, Shimeun, but they think you were chasing your father to try and prevent it. They say you were shouting "Arrêtez, Père". They took it that you were trying to stop him setting off the bomb. Which is just as well, because many who live in the Casbah have learned how to look both ways at the same time. And will therefore no sooner look at you than betray you."

"But Captain LeBoeuf knows what we were doing. They were his orders. He knows…"

Mother looks away. I am confused.

"Have you seen Captain LeBoeuf? The nurse tells me he has been here."

"Maybe…" Her reticence is maddening.

Baby Claude is starting to clutch at the air with his tiny hands. His face is reddening. Mother plucks him from the pram, holds him up and places her nose at his bottom. She winces.

"Baby Claude has blown a gasket. Time to change him."

Mother tells me she will leave me to rest, that she will attend to Claude. They will head back to Medea on Waleed's bus, stopping off to collect my little brother and sister from Madame Hachemi en route. She will be back tomorrow.

I watch her push the pram away. Laurent does too. "She is not a very good liar, your maman."

Laurent is at it again.

"It's to her credit. But it means she leaves herself exposed. And you too."

"You don't know my mother."

"It's true. But I've known many like her. Women who look like they've just arrived from the country without a clue. These women are not paysan stock. They have bucket-loads of guile about them. They are perfectly capable of playing the urban sophisticate and merging in with the European crowd."

"Djamila Bouhired, Zohra Drif, Samia Lakhdari. Do these names mean anything to you?"

"No. Why should they?"

"Because they have killed many civilians. And because your mother is so like them in appearance and manner. Fortunately, that's where the resemblance ends. I know only too well the M.O. of these women. Hiding bombs under their jellabas. Placing the deadly devices, throwing their Muslim garb into refuse bins, ditching their boots for stilettos and hanging out in the more vogueish bars of the European quarter to escape detection. My group were charged with stopping them. But this shapeshifting threw us off the scent.

They are chameleons, these women. Your mother is capable of it, certainly. That pram is a ready-made bomb carriage, after all. I see all the qualities of a bomber in her. Except for one. She is too honest. She would be incapable of planting a bomb without giving herself away. And she'd make a lousy spy."

The man in the opposite bed is moaning. The nurse arrives. Swish!

"That prick over there shouldn't be here by all rights. These bleeding-heart Red Cross want common terrorists treated as prisoners of war and given full access to the treatment our soldiers receive. It's a fucking disgrace."

Laurent's voice is incessant. I so want him to shut up.

"That man's name is Mustafa Behari. He has murdered people, ordinary citizens just having a coffee or watching a movie. Fortunately for us, he has also blown himself up. His legs have been ripped off at the knees. Otherwise he'd be at our bedside in the night slitting our throats."

I wonder why he is sharing this with me.

"He thinks he is a prisoner of war with rights under the Geneva convention."

He makes mocking quote marks in the air with both index fingers.

"He is just a thug with a gun."

I feign disinterest, but I am all ears, and Laurent knows it.

"Mustafa escaped from Berrouaghia accommodation centre. He was one of La Pointe's group. Disappeared into the souk, hiding out in the tunnels. Worked alongside master bomber Yacef Saadi in 'L'impasse de la grenade' down in the Casbah. It's a hive of FLN assassins down there. A production line of death. Body maker. Explosive expert. Delivery Team. Bomb placer. And yet he's nothing more than a pimp, a fraudster and a hit-man."

Laurent reels off the résumé with such assurance he could be quoting verbatim from the file.

He sniggers to himself.

"He knew so much about blowing other people up he forgot to learn how to avoid doing it to himself. Kaboom! Goodbye legs, hello lieutenant Laurent."

I am listening hard to Laurent. My heart is thumping, and my mind is trying to tune in to him so intently that I think I can hear radio static in my ears.

How else can a man know so much about another patient unless he is building a dossier on him?

"Mustafa's targets are never the Army. Not the government, not even the Pieds-Noirs or the colonialists. His real target is not in Algiers at all. Or Algeria for that matter. It is the bourgeoisie of France. He blows up citizens here in the quadrillage of Algiers and it loosens the resolve of ordinary men and women in the arrondissements of Paris."

He pauses and gazes over at the sleeping body of his subject as if checking that his description matches.

"Yes, his bombing missions have been entirely political. The FLN believe that the quickest route to independence is to incite public opinion back home. I have at least figured that one out."

I am thinking that Laurent is sounding off for the hell of it, that these are the ramblings of a man with too much time on his hands, a compulsive conspiracy theorist or madman—and that I can continue to lie on my side and safely pretend to ignore him. I cannot imagine he'd waste his breath on a fifteen-year-old boy.

I am mistaken.

"Pardon. I should introduce myself properly…"

"It's okay," I say.

There is steel in his voice.

"This acquaintanceship is not a negotiation, you know. I will introduce myself properly. And you will listen. Because you need to know who I am."

I go rigid.

He reminds me of the relief teacher at school who was brought in to replace Monsieur Gazides. Desperate to make herself known.

"I am the adjutant to the Head of the GRE."

Laurent registers my blank look.

"The Intelligence Exploitation and Collections Group. We have infiltrated the FLN leadership in the Casbah. We weed out men like moaning Mustafa over there by dividing Algiers into sections and having a network of our veterans keep close tabs on them as leaders of their blocks—the block-leiters.

Following me so far?"

I nod.

"Good. Stop me and tell me if you don't. It's vital you understand.

It's a tight network in the Casbah. A hotbed of insurgency. But we rather like it that way. It plays into our hands.

You see, the more brutal our enemy insurgents become, the more they act as unwitting recruiting sergeants for the French among all those families and friends in the blocks who have lost dear ones to FLN bombs. And lost them in such a hideous way.

Of course, we cannot claim we have not been complete putains ourselves. We are hardly whiter than white. The terrorists are merely following our lead in that respect. We have carried out gross and cowardly acts in the name of the Fourth Republic. Unspeakably dark deeds. Torture is one.

The 'time-bomb test', moi connart! Extract truth by torture or innocent people will die. It is a rationale often used. But my experience of torture is that it is only good for conjuring truths out of thin air. It helps no one.

I personally do not believe in torture because it stains our record. It wins more moderates over to the FLN cause. And vice versa.

When they torture, it loses them support too. We have seen that pendulum swing every single day. Tit-for-tat. Symmetrical warfare. Mirror violence. Call it what you will. Someone needs to break the cycle of slaughter. And that is us—my boss and his operatives, of which I am one.

We have to be smarter than raw bloodlust, don't you think?"

I nod again. This man is beginning to grind me down with his incessant chat.

"We have to make sure that moderate Muslims in the Casbah are incensed by the FLN's murder and torture squads rather than get behind them. That they report on suspect behaviour in their blocks. That way we catch abnormal movements such as the one the ALN fellaghas conducted the other day—the double execution of Monsieur et Madame Courvois, may they rest in peace. We were all set to use that incident to bring more moderate Muslims behind us."

I turn to face him. He catches my unasked question as if snatching a fly out of the air.

"And yes, your Father is part of that web. A Francophile Muslim who has put aside his Harki uniform for the time being and works as an agent for Army Intelligence. Or at least, that was until Captain LeBoeuf commandeered him for the operation that blew his cover and landed you here.

LeBoeuf's method is the cleaver, mine the scalpel. There is no love lost between a butcher and a surgeon.

I prefer to do my interrogative work in places like this where the sister is sympathetic. She can help me administer pentothal to suspects like Mustafa over there so he will tell the truth.

Captain LeBoeuf, he believes in doing his more intricate work at police headquarters or at El-Biar jail where he can subject his suspects to all manner of passages à tabac and gégène.

But it is not good policy. It gets representatives of the National Assembly in Paris all worked up. There is now talk of civil disobedience back there and Le President is jumpy."

He seizes the copy of 'Le Monde' from his bedside locker and slaps it with the back of his hand. He throws the oblong of folded newspaper onto my bed.

"Here!"

I pick up the paper and blink back at him blankly.

"You can read, can't you?"

I scan a sea of type.

"That's Beuve-Méry's leader column today. He is banging the same drum. The nation that brought the Gestapo to justice and condemned the massacre at Oradeur during World War Two is the nation that is guilty of Sétif, Philippeville and now Algiers."

I blink. I am struggling to focus.

"Read! That is what they are saying in France. And beyond. You'll find torture does not cut much ice in the company of nations in New York either. Yet iron-clad, cloth-eared General Massu up there at police headquarters still plies his medieval chamber of horrors. With the help of Captain LeBoeuf. He is bankrupt, all out of ideas. Fortunately, my boss sees beyond that. So…now the question is this."

I think I already know what his next question will be. "Which course would you rather I take with you?"

To Laurent my silence speaks volumes.

"Ha! It is compelling is it not? A moral dilemma. Your teachers would approve, non?"

His face is set stern like the proudly beaked De Gaulle eagle.

"Now that I am here, I think it would be wise of you to relate everything you know about the operation the other night."

I stare at the slabs of type on the page to avoid catching his eye. But I cannot take it all in. An aching exhaustion permeates my bones.

I am convinced Laurent is trying to deprive me of sleep. Perhaps this is his chosen method of teasing out the truth. Sap the human spirit with a wall of rhetoric rather than stun it with electrodes, jump leads and waterboarding.

Or is this treatment reserved exclusively for juveniles like me—people who are only just beginning to see the world for what it truly is? A cesspit of mutual suspicion, fear and loathing.

For us, the drip-drip of stark reality is surely the most effective form of torture. Laurent is a past master at that. His speech confirms it.

"Captain LeBoeuf has been itching to talk to you so he can prevent you from speaking to anyone else. But LeBoeuf is an idiot. He would never guess I have inveigled my way in here with an erroneous case of appendicitis so I can keep a close watch on you night and day. The eyes and ears of intelligence are everywhere in this city, even here under the neutral auspices of the Red Cross and Red Crescent.

You will need our eyes and ears yourself soon, Simeon. To keep you alive.

You see, the operation you witnessed the other night has exposed your father to all sides.

Take it from me, Captain LeBoeuf has fooled him with false promises. LeBoeuf has no more time for Harkis than he has for the FLN. Your father is a necessary instrument of the French state, to be endured rather than befriended. And to the FLN, he has become more than an irritant—a gutter-snipe snitch. He has become their number one target. LeBoeuf's mission has backfired spectacularly."

"I don't know..." I start to say.

Laurent interrupts me.

"In that case, you need to know. LeBoeuf's paratroopers pulled fifteen lifeless bodies from the rubble of Place Jean-Paul Sartre...

Three fellaghas—well, no one will mourn those assassins...

But there are also twelve citizens dead. They include five children, three women—one of them heavily pregnant—and a veteran of the AOMA. A highly religious man. A great man, a scholar, a teacher in the madrasa and a thought leader within the community. The explosion crushed his rib cage, ground his organs into the dust and flattened his body like a crepe. That is all your father's handiwork.

These were good people for us. People we needed. Good Muslims who were loyal to France. We cannot afford to lose them. For the sake of a Fifth Republic. These are the exact people we have been cultivating in blocks in the quadrillage.

But your father's few minutes of madness in the Casbah has put pay to that. It will incite reprisals from those blowhard Arabs. Not to mention my boss. He is not a happy man."

Laurent leans towards me and lowers his voice further.

"If your father is still alive, he is in a tight spot.

On the one hand, he can no longer count on the support of the French Army. They will now disown him for this heinous act of alienating the very Muslims we need on side in the Casbah.

And on the other, he is wanted by the FLN for killing three of its finest, plus an additional fifteen Muslims who are innocents. This is bad news for you and your mother—as you are all in the same canoe.

Your best bet is to talk to me. I will offer you the protection of the security forces. Or at the very least throw you a paddle so you can make it to the safety of dry land!"

"I don't believe you!" I say. "Protection is what LeBoeuf has promised Father and I don't believe him either. You are as bad as each other."

For the first time since he has spoken, Laurent appears agitated.

"Oh, you will believe me! You may be as pig-headed as your father. But you are by no means stupid. You are more intelligent than him."

He leans in further to me. He is practically whispering now.

"Think about this before you play the big man with me.

Mustafa over there has given me some fascinating insights into your old man. Pentothal is even better than liquor at loosening the tongue. He tells me one Farouk Abou—your father—has met with both Ali La Pointe and Yacef Saadi of the FLN. In the Casbah. Mustafa has seen your father around Saadi's tunnels. Your old man is known in the Casbah. Playing for the other side. How else does an agent of the French gain admission to Saadi's tunnels?

What do you think LeBoeuf would do to your father if he came into possession of that precious little nugget of information?"

I cannot believe what Laurent has just told me.

"You…you are lying."

"I wish I were."

"Does anyone else know this?"

"I have no idea. I think not. Can anyone count on information freely supplied by a man with no scruples or morals like Mustafa Behari?"

"So, you don't know for sure."

"No one can know for sure. But I believe Behari for two reasons. Firstly, it is beyond belief, and if he were lying, why would he invent something so ludicrously far-fetched to masquerade as the truth."

"And secondly?"

"Mustafa Behari is dying. He has nothing to lose, nothing to gain from lying to me except knowing that somehow somewhere in his unrelentingly miserable life, he can shine the light of truth into a dark corner. I believe even within the most callous and hateful soul, there is the capacity for redemption.

Look, I know these terrorists. I know these bombers. I know them. They are not monsters. They are passionate believers. They are you and I without brakes. That's why they take everything to the limits.

Your father is the same. And if it is the case that he has been in the company of the FLN, it's a Jovian trick. One to be strangely admired."

He thinks again and corrects himself.

"Or if not exactly admired, gawped at. He is performing a high wire act without a safety net.

You see, no one quite knows who your father works for. Or why.

It's my theory that he works for no one but himself. He is a freelancer and will do whatever he can to get out of Algeria.

I for one want your father gone before he does any more damage to De Gaulle's project. By gone, I mean out of the country."

Laurent smiles at what I assume to be unintended ambiguity.

"Whilst he's still here, he is a loose cannon because he is desperate. He is marked on all sides. If he is alive, we must find him and put him out of harm's way before the likes of LeBoeuf or La Pointe do for him. I can feel a storm coming."

I recall Father's eyes flashing back at me from the darkness of the passageway. He is beseeching me not give away his position. At the same time, he is just a muscle twitch away from blowing me to smithereens.

"You know his lairs. The places he likes to go. After all, he takes you everywhere with him on his hunting expeditions. Surely you have been to his sacred spots, the places no one else can know anything about. The nooks and crevices, the isolated hides and holes in the mountains? Caves, hunters' huts, points of concealment? Tell me, Simeon. As I say, you are not exempt from danger yourself, you know."

The nurse is on her rounds. He quickly straightens back up in his bed.

"Think about it. You are not going anywhere. Neither am I. I have fake appendicitis remember. It's a useless appendage I can live without. Like Algeria. Not so France."

He sniggers like a schoolboy malingerer at the thought of deceiving the doctors and nurses. Faking his own illness.

Thankfully, the nurse comes between us. Swish! Another terminal sweep of the sterile curtain.

I breathe again. I quietly ask to be moved away from Laurent. I tell her that he is making me uncomfortable, that he keeps staring at me. That the soldiers and prisoners in the ward bring on bad memories and even worse dreams.

To my surprise, my move is sanctioned by the ward sister and my request granted.

Later that morning, my bed is wheeled along the ward away from Laurent through a whitewashed corridor to another ward for non-combatants.

I question whether Laurent has as much influence over the sister as he maintains. Has she given me a dose of pentothal too? Does it even work? In my feverish state, have I already told the Lieutenant what he wants to hear?

I wonder how much of what he says is true. And how much simply designed to prey on me so that I spill the one thing I have vowed not to reveal. The one thing that will give Father away. His place of safety.

The Trinitarian Hospital, Algiers,
12 January 1957

I am now hopping and shuffling on crutches through the cool shade of a cloister, making my way around a garden overrun with bougainvillea.

This is where I have sat with Mother when she has visited over the past week. She seems to like it more than I. But then, she doesn't have to put up with the physio and can sit and admire the bougainvillea while she nurses the regrets of her own broken life.

She has just left me to meet Waleed's bus. He is dropping her off at the house of Madame Hachemi, a washerwoman and child-carer in Medea—a lady with a family of seven raucous foster children who treats my little brother and sister as part of her own brood and lets them run riot.

It costs Mother five dinars for the childcare. With Father having disappeared, parting with each dinar is a step closer to the gutter. So, she hasn't stayed with me at the hospital for long spells. Just enough to make her presence felt.

The nurse encourages me to take it slowly. But I am inclined to treat my constitutional like a Grand Prix. It is her mission for me to complete two laps of this walkway. It is my aim to do three, as I want to be out of this hellish sanatorium as soon as I can.

The cloisters are a runway for broken men. Amputees with prostheses, the disfigured, deformed and mutilated circle at the same time every day. I pass by them as they pick their own pathway around the circuit with lines of bitter concentration etched on their faces—slowly chasing a more agile, more upright, more able version of themselves round and round the garden.

I am not quite sure which scares them more about this race against themselves. The fear of not being able to catch up with their own ghosts or the terror of being caught by them.

Conversely, I see Lieutenant Laurent sauntering along the colonnade in silk shift and pyjamas. He is out of time and out of place. A matinee idol mooching on a soundstage between scenes. He steps out in a pair of soigné monogrammed red velvet slippers, embroidered with the fleur de lys.

He is every inch the showboating street magician who appeared in my dreams, belonging more in a fin-de-siècle Paris salon than this grey exercise yard.

He shoots me a louche smile under his neat moustache and waves. He waits for me to hobble around to him.

I resist the urge to turn and pretend I haven't seen him. There is no escaping Laurent. The fact he hasn't found me so far is his choice, not mine. Part of me has been expecting him.

I prop my crutches against the wall and park myself alongside him. The nurse says she will come back for me in five minutes. I tell her I can find my own way back to my bed.

Laurent pats his belly gingerly.

"They have taken out a perfectly serviceable appendix for no good reason. Just so I can be here with you. So I can keep an eye on the stricken and squeeze the last blobs out of the toothpaste tube. That includes you, of course."

Laurent offers me a packet of cigarettes.

"I am fifteen."

"If you are old enough to fight, you are old enough to smoke."

"And to die…" I mutter, channelling the fellagha's opening gambit to me in Place Jean-Paul Sartre.

I take the pack of 'Disque Bleu', turn it around in my hand and pass it back to Laurent.

"I just saw your maman leave here. My, oh my, what a fine-looking woman she is."

This causes my lip to curl.

"Don't worry. She's not my type. I'm more a Jeanne Moreau man than Leslie Caron. But if I were your papa, I'd be staying closer to home."

He is fishing. Isn't he always?

"You gave me the slip the other day. Quite a disappearing act. Was it something I said?"

Despite my refusal, he lights up a cigarette for me. He passes me the lit stick. I suck on it like a straw. My cheeks form hollows and burning tar hits the back of my throat. I splutter.

Laurent smiles, lights another for himself and puffs away as we sit in silence, watching the slow progress of patients around the circuit.

"Look at this sclerotic carnival. They don't want to answer their pain. They want to deny it. The nurses won't let them. Like you and I, it's a battle of wills."

He flicks ash in my direction.

"Have you thought any more about giving me a full account of the bombing at Place Jean-Paul Sartre?"

I remain quiet on the subject.

"You know your passive silence is an active choice. Your choice is to give yourself up to Massu's torture squads. Or talk to me.

Once I leave this awful place, you will not have the option. And there will be no way back for you. Even though you are only fifteen, the Geneva convention will not protect you. Army combatants, yes. Scrawny collaborators, no such luck. Your one hope is to talk to me. And soon."

We sit breathing in the bougainvillea. I will hold my tongue.

"Have you given a thought over the last few days as to why I am telling you all of this? The reason why, despite every effort to conceal myself in this place, I am volunteering to disclose everything about who I am, what I do and my reason for being here? All neatly wrapped up in crepe paper and a little bow for you.

Don't you think it strange that I am risking everything for a boy of no more than fifteen years old who can barely sport fluff on his upper lip? I mean you must have wondered how lacking in intelligence this is for an intelligence officer."

He stares me down.

"You are not my only suspect here, you know. Or Mustafa Behari. They swarm all around me. They are here now in this bizarre circus. There! That man gathering dust over there…"

He nods to a young man standing in the garden, gently rocking on his heels with upturned face harvesting the sun's rays.

"His name is Eric. Eric DeMornay of the 20th infantry division—the 4th Rifles Regiment to be precise. I believe that man ran away from a firefight. A deserter. Which is why he has a bullet in his spine. His commanding officer thinks so too. But Eric denies it. I am here to prove it. I have shared a few games of chess with him and teased a few confidences out of him already."

He singles out other of his 'sclerotic promenaders'.

"Over there is a black marketeer infantryman. He got his balls shot off by an irate shopkeeper he was trying to scam one day on a patrol in the Casbah. He killed the shopkeeper. He says it was in self-defence. I need a confession from him as we cannot allow him to return to active duty. If he is a cheat and a scoundrel, he is a liability. And he should be court marshalled.

There, you see that old boy passing the fresco of the Ascension of the Mary? He is a Harki informant like your father—a veteran of Sétif. However, surprise, surprise! It turns out he has a brother-in-law who fights for the ALN and is a constant thorn in our side. He knows more about the FLN than you'd think.

He will help swell the dossier of deceit. They all will. They all have their tender spots. We just need to find them. We will win this war more through information-gathering and analysis than bloodlust.

The point being they do not know who I am. To them, I am just a swanky lounge-room lizard—a cocktail-quaffing colonial with a bad case of appendicitis.

Yet you know. You and a few of the staff. You could easily go over there to DeMornay and blow my cover right now. But you won't."

"How do you know I won't?"

"How? Because out of all these shirkers, liars, cheats, crackpots and demimondes, I only trust you. I trust you to know that I am right about your father. Your need for me is far greater than your need to tell them."

"You assume far too much," I interject.

"Do I? So go and shop me to your fellow-patients, then. Go on. Be my guest. Do it now."

I am fiddling with the lit cigarette, rolling it between my fingers.

"No. I thought not. You can't, and you won't. You will talk to me. I know it. You are too clever not to. I just can't understand why you have not done so already. The longer you take to tell me, the more at risk your papa is. The more at risk you all are."

I do not blink.

He throws his spent cigarette down and grinds it out under a velvet slipper. He breathes in the cool garden air. A deep breath right down to the base of his lungs.

I hear the drill of an automatic rifle from a long way off.

"I think complications may develop with my appendectomy. Septicaemia, perhaps? What do you think? It may keep me here in hospital for longer than I anticipated. But then again, it may not. It will take as long as it takes, I suppose. Sickness can be a capricious mistress."

He lights up another cigarette. I am impelled to ask him a question. Curiosity gets the better of my silence.

"You're telling me you are on surveillance now? You are spying on the sick and the wounded?"

"Ah!" Laurent leaps to his feet and stoops to look me straight in the eyes. "He speaks! I thought you were Lot's wife and you had turned to stone."

"And the dying?" I ask. "That man Mustafa opposite me in the ward. The one you say has ratted on Father. You said he is dying?"

"Yes. And that is why I'm here feeling sore from a pointless scar left on me by a needless operation. To squeeze the last morsel of toothpaste out of his tube. Even though it may have looked as if there was no more in there, it still yielded some fascinating insights into your father's behaviour.

Who knows what other secrets lie within this freak show? These men are far more likely to give them up when they are at heaven's gate begging for admittance. I have Saint Peter on my side. And he is far more effective than Massu and his goons at forcing confessions. For your information, Mustafa passed away two nights ago…"

"Poor man…he died alone no doubt."

"Come, come, he had me there with him holding his hand…"

"Army intelligence…I'm sure that was a great comfort to him."

"By God, that's it!"

Lieutenant Laurent snaps his fingers excitedly. He leaps up off the bench, stoops down and peers straight into my eyes.

It's as if he can see a whole world in my iris. He steps back and snaps his fingers with glee.

"That's it! Army! You won't talk to me not because you don't trust me, but because you don't trust them. Because I have worn epaulettes on my shoulder and stripes on my sleeve and a tin hat. Because despite this alter alias, I am a soldier through and through. Because you conflate that with French occupation.

I get it now! We are all the same to you aren't we. We move in lockstep. We share the same code. We fight together and fall together. We are all the same occupiers, invaders, impostors. Tous pour un!"

He brandishes an imaginary épée and holds it aloft.

"That's why in spite of everything I have told you, you refuse to see any difference between myself, Captain LeBoeuf and General Massu. We are all tarred with the same brush. At fifteen, there is no room for nuance."

I scowl at him.

"That look could bring down a buffalo at a thousand yards…

I don't blame you. At your age, you want cowboys and Indians. Goodies and baddies. You desire chiaroscuro. You are desperate to turn the grey areas to black and white. You absorb facts but not truth. You are certain life will go on forever, therefore everything else should be as certain. There is a reassuring certainty in thinking the French are all cut from the same cloth. It gives you something to kick against.

Anything else and it dampens the fire of hostility. Keeping it binary makes it so much easier to locate yourself in your world. The generals are happy with that. Because that is the way they see it too."

I am ready to take him on.

"I see no reason to trust you any more than any other soldier."

"Thank you! Thank you, Simeon. At last! We have got to the bottom of it now." He is dancing from one foot to another as if he needs a piss. "Imbécile! Pourquoi n'y ai-je pas pensé avant!" he chides himself.

"Simeon, don't you see? I do not trust the French Army either. And like you, I want them out of Algeria for good!"

I am still none the wiser.

"It is plain as the nose on your face. The very fact that I do not trust the French Army as a lieutenant in the French Army is the reason you can put your trust in me! Because we are the same. It's not me and the Army! It's you and I. Us!"

I am struggling with this. He can see it.

"This is not about the French Army. This is about the world I want to build and you want to inherit. The world we both want to live in. The France I want to live in now. The Algeria you want for the future.

He acknowledges one of his 'sclerotic promenaders' before sitting back down beside me and placing a hand on my arm. Now that he has me, he won't let me go. He is fired up. Excitable.

"I will not detain you much longer, Simeon. But I want to tell you—no, no, I must tell you—about one of my military anti-heroes. A soldier in the self-same French Army. It will make everything clear to you."

The nurse is returning along the colonnade. Laurent discreetly salutes her, then ushers her away. She turns on her heels and retreats. I am astonished.

"Do you command the nurses here as well as your Intelligence officers?" Laurent is impatient with the interruption, eager to relate his story to me.

"I don't have to. She knows when to give me time and stay away. It's a sign we have. A simple salute. A patriotic gesture. Who could possibly suspect that? Now, about Terrare…"

"The nurses are in on your surveillance?" I interject again. He humours me.

"Not altogether, no, but they respect that the business of Army Intelligence does not stop at the hospital gates. That would render the wards unsafe. And the safety of their patients is the primary concern of nursing staff and doctors everywhere on the planet. It is key to the Hippocratic oath, is it not? Saving lives at all costs. We share that same aim, if not the same methods to achieve it. The doctors and nurses ensure their patients' safety through care and surgery. I do it through intelligence and spy craft.

Now about Terrare. Are you familiar with the name?"

"Is he another of your watched subjects? Your victims? Your walking dead? Or whatever it is you call them?"

"Don't be ridiculous. He lived almost two hundred years ago. A courier in the Army under the command of General Alexandre de Beauharnais."

Laurent now stops to greet rifleman DeMornay who has had his fill of the bougainvillea blossom and is absently heading back along the colonnade to the sanctuary of his sickbed.

"Eric. We must finish that game of chess. You have me on the run. But while I control the diagonals, there is hope!"

We watch Eric pad towards the arched doorway back to the ward. He is unimpressed.

"A man with an extraordinary natural gift."

I think Laurent is talking about the rifleman.

"No, not Eric, you fool! Terrare!

Pay attention, Simeon. You are flagging. Keep up!

Terrare was an extraordinary recruit to the French Army. Because he had the most amazing superpower.

Not his marksmanship. Not his warcraft or his tactical nous. Nor his guile or his capacity for survival, or anything else you'd associate with a successful career in the military. No, this was a phenomenal one-off talent."

I am intrigued. Laurent has his eyebrows raised in expectation, prompting me to guess at Terrare's superpower. I take a wild stab…

"Don't know. He can fly…?"

"Nope."

"He can make himself invisible."

"Ne sois pas absurde, Simeon!"

"He can pull himself apart and rearrange himself in any way he chooses?" I snort.

Laurent knows I am warming to him.

"No. It's his appetite. A voracious appetite. Terrare's mouth was as wide as a sluice-gate. And his gullet even wider!"

"This soldier could cram six hard-boiled eggs and four apples inside his mouth at once. His alimentary canal was literally that. A veritable Suez!"

I puff out my cheeks and pretend to vomit. My face reddens.

Laurent hasn't noticed.

"Let's go back a bit…

When Terrare was just a babe in arms, he went straight on to solids, consuming twice his body weight in meat. So much that he impoverished his parents.

His appetite just grew larger through his childhood. Quel horreur! By the time he'd turned ten he could eat a quarter of a bullock in a single day. He was eating his family out of house and home. Quite literally!"

"Literally? Not literally…" I suspect this is Laurent's fantasy, a work of complete fiction.

"Yes, literally. His parents found tooth marks in the skirting boards of their home and gaping holes in the wall panels. The poor couple concluded the bites were too big for rats and were down to their son. So you can understand why they sent him packing once he was old enough to fend for himself."

I take the story for what it is. A fiction.

"He travelled France with thieves and harlots, before becoming the warm-up act to a travelling charlatan. To the delight of the crowd, he swallowed corks, stones, whole basketfuls of fruit, even live animals!

He took his act to Paris as a street performer just before the opening salvoes in the War of the First Coalition when his performance was weaponised.

Once Terrare was conscripted into the French Revolutionary Army, they had to put him on quadruple rations. But even that wasn't enough to satisfy the mountainous appetite of the man.

He was starving all the time. So he ate rubbish and waste out of the gutters to supplement his diet.

No matter how much he consumed, the poor hombre still felt hungry to the point of exhaustion. His condition got so bad that his commanding officer consigned him to the military hospital.

Here, the doctors put him through a series of bizarre medical experiments to test his eating capacity.

They prepared him the most stomach-churning banquet you could think of. Enough for fifteen to gorge on. Yet Terrare was the only diner. And he consumed the lot. You'll never believe what was on the menu."

"What was it?"

"It is straight out of a horror show."

"Tell me, you have to tell me now."

"Alright, don't say I didn't warn you!"

Laurent counts the courses off on his fingers.

"For amuse-bouches, snakes and lizards…for entrée, puppies…and for main course, he swallowed eels whole without chewing.

For dessert, they served up a live cat. He tore the cat's abdomen open with his teeth and drank its blood like a bordeaux."

I clap with joy.

"And the cheese course?" I ask and clap again.

I am not applauding Laurent. I am five years old again listening to Mother reading Brothers Grimm and spurring her on whilst pulling the covers up against the gruesome events leaping off the page.

"He ate the entire animal aside from its bones, before vomiting up its fur and skin."

My eyes are wide as my five-year old self. My lower jaw slowly drops open and my mouth goes dry.

Laurent pauses to extinguish his cigarette against the side of the open packet. He drops the spent stub in with the fresh ones and pulls out another two sticks. This time, he doesn't ask me but lights both together and passes me one.

He draws and picks a speck of tobacco off his lower lip.

"The remarkable thing is Terrare was as light and slim as you are, Simeon. And he showed no signs of mental illness other than being quite docile.

It was then that a physician attached to the ninth hussars had the most ingenious idea.

He thought to use Terrare's appetite in the service of warcraft. So he organised another test, this time more precise.

A document was placed inside a wooden box which the Army doctors fed to Terrare. Two days later, the box was retrieved from his stool, with the document still legible."

"By stool, you mean…"

"His shit, my boy. Poop. Crap. Fundament. Excrement. Ordure. Whatever you choose to call it, it's all the same to me. It's brown and it stinks."

I try to envisage a turd large enough to carry a document box. And then estimate the size of orifice required to expel it. But it is beyond me. I give up. I cannot conceive of birth either. Mother nearly died having Claude. It is not something I even want to think about.

"And that's where General de Beauharnais comes in.

The Army doctor proposed to de Beauharnais that if Terrare was capable of swallowing documents, he could pass through enemy lines with them concealed, not about his person, but within it!

So General de Beauharnais called on Terrare to show off his abilities to the commanders of the Army of the Rhine.

As a reward for which he was given a wheelbarrow full of thirty pounds of raw bulls' lungs and liver, which he immediately devoured in front of the assembled generals.

From that day, Terrare was employed officially as a spy…"

"For the Army of the Rhine?"

"The Rhine was their front. A little like the Zone Autonome d'Alger is to us. Though some argue this is not war. It is attritional slaughter.

As for General de Beauharnais, he may have been convinced about Terrare's physical capacity to carry messages inside his gut, but was as yet unsure about his mental state—at least not enough to entrust him with vital military documents.

So, as a first test assignment, de Beauharnais ordered his newly recruited spy to carry a message to a French colonel imprisoned by the Prussians near Neustadt.

Terrare was told that the documents were of great military importance, but in reality, De Beauharnais had merely written a casual note asking the colonel to confirm that the message had been received. And if so to return a reply of any potentially useful information about Prussian troop movements.

One night, Terrare crossed Prussian lines under cover of darkness, disguised as a German peasant.

But here's the rub, right?

The locals found it peculiar that a German peasant couldn't speak German. They brought it to the attention of the Prussian authorities, and Terrare was captured.

A strip-search revealed nothing secretive on his person, and despite being whipped by Prussian soldiers, he refused to betray his mission.

He was brought before the local Prussian commander—a man named General Zoegli. Again, Terrare refused to talk and was put behind bars.

Terrare was certainly a formidable gourmand with a gargantuan digestive tract, but he had absolutely no stomach for heroism or bravery.

After twenty-four hours of captivity he confessed. He gave the whole plan away to his captors.

Discovering the true nature of his superpower, the Prussians chained the poor benighted man to a latrine and waited…and waited…and waited. Terrare sat…and sat…and sat.

Despite some…err…false alarms…"

Laurent raises a buttock cheek off the bench and blows a raspberry. I steal another laugh as if I am in class.

There is a dramatic silence while the lieutenant takes a long draw. He puffs rings of smoke this time. I am spellbound.

"…day turned to night and night turned back into day. And then at last, with a rumble like you've never heard (that is unless you've stood at the mouth of the Simplon tunnel as the trans-Alpine Express emerges) the long-awaited bowel movement occurred.

You can imagine the relief of General Zoegli (not to mention that poor sod Terrare) when some thirty hours after being swallowed, the wooden box dropped from his wretched, ragged arse hole.

And then…

Relief became anger…

When the documents, which Terrare had said contained vital intelligence turned out to be de Beauharnais' dummy message.

Zoegli was outraged at being so humiliated.

"I have placed a round-the-clock watch on your bum-hole for this?" Laurent stops for another infernal puff on his Disque Bleu and chuckles to himself.

"And?" I urge.

"He duly ordered his company to have Terrare executed without any further ado."

Another drag. I am incredulous.

"Okay so whether this last bit really happened, and Zoegli actually fished out the box from the vile excrement with his own hands is a moot point.

My sources tell me Terrare had the presence of mind to recover and eat his own stools before they could be seized by the Prussians. So the documents were sent on yet another, ahem, tour of duty."

Either way, the starving man was dragged to the gallows and a noose put around his neck."

He pauses again. I am impatient now…

"Come on. You can't leave it there. What happened to Terrare? Did he swing for it?"

Laurent stares back at me.

"What do you think, Simeon? What do you want to happen to him? That's the question."

"I don't know. Maybe he should eat the noose, maybe the whole scaffolding, maybe even the hangman!"

Laurent finds this amusing.

"That's very good, Simeon. You are a bright boy. Brighter than Terrare or de Beauharnais, or the whole French Army for that matter. I wonder if Terrare even thought of it." he muses.

"Well, as it happens it never came to that. Zoegli must have been overwhelmed by the sheer weirdness of it all. Just as you are now. Because at the last minute, Terrare dodged the gallows and the Prussian gave him a severe beating instead before releasing him close to French lines.

Well, you can imagine for a man like Terrare who had gone through a near-death experience like that, any further military service filled him with dread.

He'd never thought of his condition as a gift, more a severe affliction. So, he returned to the military hospital, telling his doctor that he would put himself through any possible cure for his bottomless appetite.

They tried plying him with appetite suppressants. Laudanum. Wine vinegar. Tobacco pills. Dozens and dozens of soft-boiled eggs. But nothing worked.

And needless to say, all efforts to keep him on any kind of diet failed.

Whenever the hospital orderlies weren't looking, Terrare would sneak out to scavenge for offal outside butchers' shops and fight stray dogs for carrion in gutters, alleys and on rubbish heaps.

They also caught him several times trying to enter the hospital mortuary to feast on the cadavers."

The image of the eagle soldiers assails me again. Terrare! They are like Terrare!

"Of course, other doctors believed Terrare was a lunatic and wanted him transferred to an asylum. But his Army doctor insisted on keeping him there in the military hospital under his careful supervision so he could carry on experimenting.

A decision everyone came to regret…"

"Why so?" I am spellbound as Laurent puts more twists in his thread.

"One day, a fourteen-month-old child disappeared from the hospital, and Terrare was suspected of eating the boy."

"You are joking! He swallowed babies too?"

"It is documented. I am no expert, but I have it on reliable authority from the librarian at Prytanée National Militaire. He told me this story."

"So, it's true?"

"There are hospital records in the Archives Nationale. Terrare's doctor was either unable or unwilling to defend him, and the hospital staff chased him away, never to return.

They say he died of tuberculosis."

The cigarette is burning my fingers. I let out a whelp and drop it.

Laurent tuts.

"Waste of a perfectly good smoke."

He leans forward to pluck the smouldering cigarette from the ground and passes it back to me. I take it and hesitantly draw on it as he watches me. I kill the urge to cough.

There are fewer patients walking the cloisters now. Fewer whispers drift along the colonnades through the bougainvillea garden.

Laurent flicks his cigarette into a patch of dirt beyond the low wall to the garden.

"Et voila!" he concludes with a flourish.

"That's the most disgusting thing I ever heard."

"Why do I tell you this?"

I am none the wiser. But then Laurent doesn't require an answer from me. "Think of France as Terrare the man. The Fourth Republic. Ravening. Voracious. Consuming all in his path. Without any discernment or taste. And the result? He is sick to the core. Distended. Dyspeptic. Rotting.

The more he consumes the greater his appetite becomes. As he eats more, he hungers for more and the more he tries to ingest the more it attacks his liver, his kidneys, his stomach and intestines, the organs of state, et cetera et cetera, ad nauseam, ad infinitum. And the more this cycle of greed and excess continues, the more he decays from the inside.

That is to say the body of France rots. Its institutions. Its constitution. Its dominion. Its interests at home and abroad. Its standing in the world. And perhaps most of all its self-respect.

But it is not just Terrare that is the problem. It is the generals who try to harness his superpower. They find him fascinating. They think they can work with this insatiable man. Mould him to their ambitions.

But they are self-regarding, self-promoting and hasty. They don't treat his precious ability with the respect it deserves. They co-opt it, possess it as they do the lands they conquer. They are so in awe of the power they command that they overlook the vital factor of how to use it.

They miscalculate badly.

They send Terrare into Prussia dressed as a peasant but without even thinking to teach him German. What were they thinking! That is the self-preening arrogance of their imperial legacy.

They are culturally clueless, believing in the myth of their own invincibility. That their innate superiority alone will not just subjugate their enemy but have them eating out of their hands.

They know that in Terrare they have this amazing power at their command.

His appetite may make for the most unappetising prospect, but in the right hands, it can be marshalled to the glory of France.

Instead, the Army go in ham fisted and they squander it all. They are doing so now. Miscalculating. Wasting every opportunity to integrate with the people.

The centres socieaux backed by UNESCO are doing their level best to raise the educational standards of the indigenous people of Algeria so that they can be integrated into the Franco-Muslim project.

And what are Massu's philistines up to, in the name of the Governor-General?

Ignoring the powder keg of the indigenous inscolarises and inadaptes. Our leaders are content to let Algerians grow up in a country where eight out of ten live in inhuman conditions. And they see these essential support groups of social workers as FLN collaborators."

Laurent has a faraway look. A keening. He is grieving for something lost.

"The Army end up not with a submissive, tamed enemy, but with a heap-load of fomenting shit on their hands. It is negligent, reckless, an act of sheer lunacy, an own goal entirely of their own making.

As a consequence, Terrare dies an untimely death.

That is the pointless malaise that is the French colonial ambition. That is the fate that awaits the Fourth Republic. That is the tragedy of our Army.

So now you understand. The failure of empire is the failure of the vision of our leaders and our generals. For France in Prussia, so for France in Algeria.

They have created an all-consuming, unmitigated shit-show...

And people like me—we have been ordered to clean it up.

Make no mistake, I will do so. I will clean it up. It is my duty. And you, in your own little way, you will too. Because you too will become sick of all the shit we leave over time.

People like us, we will clear up the stinking corpse of the all-consuming Fourth Republic and build a new and better Republic in its place. One that genuinely unites the talents of the people in a common purpose. A fifth Republic. Mort a France! Vive La France!

We will clear it up, Simeon, trust me. And it starts with the mess your papa has left behind."

I stare at him. I skip a breath.

"So now for the love of God, Allah and De Gaulle, give me your full account of the bombing on the 5th of January at Place Jean-Paul Sartre."

I shake my head—a reflex that brings out a stifled cry of frustration in Laurent. His hands form knuckle-white fists ready to strike. It shocks me.

I put him straight before he has time to aim a blow.

"I mean I don't have to give you a full account. I get it. I know what you want from me. I'm not stupid. I trust you."

Laurent composes himself.

"Go on..."

"Father told me on the morning of the bombing that if anything went wrong, should we be separated, he would go to the mountains and I should join him there."

"Where is 'there'?"

I take a deep breath.

"The Biban Atlas. It's a disused hunter's hide about fifteen kilometres outside Sour El-Ghozlane, on the road to Mansoura. Koudiat el-Markluf. There's a two kilometre track off the main road that leads up to the place—somewhere Father went to shoot boar."

"You've been there?"

I nod. I see Father's face again out of the shadows in the entrance to the passageway by the courtyard. Pleading with me as I plead with him. Our quid pro quo. In his eyes: 'Do not give away my location, Simeon' And in mine: 'Do not blow me to bits, Father.'

Laurent takes a deep breath, pats me twice on the knee, rises to his feet and stretches.

"You've done the right thing."

He yawns the yawn of a man who has slept off a heavy meal and now needs to eat again. He stretches.

"Ooh, I could do with breakfast. Couldn't you?" He ambles off, his back to me, raising his hand to give me a parting flutter of the fingers as he goes.

"I could eat a horse. Thirty pounds of bulls' lungs and liver. Perhaps a viper or three. A nest of lizards. Maybe a litter of puppies. And a child, Simeon. Though, come to think of it, I'm not sure I could manage a whole one at once."

He casts a backward glance and, with a nerveless smile, disappears through the arched doorway. The heavy door slams behind him with a thud that echoes through the cloisters.

The bougainvillea sways.

What have I done? What on Earth have I done?

Central Algiers, Algiers Wilaya, 26 January 1957

Waleed drives the bus carefully. His Pied-Noir passengers are precious cargo. At least to the French.

There has been a spate of kidnappings and murders of Pieds-Noirs of late. Courvois was just one of many. The FLN have ramped up their activities openly on the streets of Algiers.

Saadi's men have been targeting Europeans of fighting age. Forty-nine of them shot dead last June as payback for the executions of two FLN men at the Barberousse Prison earlier in the year. It is the pledge of their leader Larbi Ben M'hidi that for every nationalist the French take out, the FLN will take a hundred of theirs.

It has escalated since. A former French Intelligence agency officer named Achiary has organised militant Pieds-Noirs into a para-military group. In August, this group targeted the FLN perpetrators of the Pieds-Noirs murders by planting a bomb at the Thebes Road in the Casbah. Seventy-three Muslims died in that explosion.

Since then, Ben M'hidi has sent the wheel of death off on another spin, resulting in the executions of Monsieur et Madame Courvois among other notable Pieds-Noirs. Retribution for Achiary's slaughter of the Muslims in the Casbah, no doubt. There will be more reprisals to come.

So Waleed is wary. He knows what the Army do to Muslims who kill French citizens. And how the FLN avengers even up the scales in return.

Being a Muslim himself, if anything happened to the Pieds-Noirs on his bus, he could easily find himself in El-Biar jail. And that would be a cruel joke given the lengths to which he has gone to avoid it.

My fitness is improving with every day, just as the nurse said it would. The doctor told Mother the bones in my leg were knitting well before releasing me from the Trinitarian hospital.

I have swapped my crutch for a walking stick. A gnarled, varnished length of carob wood with an ivory handle that Mother insisted I use rather than the one offered by the hospital.

The tree once stood in the garden of Grandfather's house in a mechta in the Guelma countryside. It had been uprooted by a bomb dropped from a French aircraft just five days after the surrender of the German high command in the world war.

The barrage from the air was part of the French Army campaign to rake Muslim rural communities suspected of the killings of French colonials. Grandfather carved the stick as a symbol of resilience. Conscripted as a Tirailleur in the Algerian Army during the first world war, he joined the French in seeing off the Hun. And yet after the war, he found himself without any of the privileges enjoyed by the French settlers in his own land. The French had promised the Banu Hachem the same rights of citizenship as the French soldiers they fought alongside. But the promises evaporated.

The day war in Europe ended he took up the cudgel against French colonial rule in Sétif. If he could see off the Germans, he could see off the French.

Mother tells me he once used the stick to beat off one of André Achiary's Pied-Noir vigilantes who picked on the wrong man. The assailant nearly had his head taken off with a single blow from Grandfather's stick.

Other Muslims who did not have the fighting instinct of my maternal Grandfather were not so lucky. They ended up in the mass graves of Kef-el-Boumba, their earthly remains disinterred and burned in Héliopolis to eliminate the evidence—a futile attempt to wash the blood off les mains sales Françaises.

Grandfather was a powerful man well into his seventies. He had been a boxer in the Algerian Army and his face had more cuts than a Berber warrior.

Despite that, she tells me he was very handsome. I am of course handsome too in her eyes. Even more so now that I have a large scar on my forehead above my right eye. And she will choose the most inappropriate times and places to tell me so. I know she is proud of me going to school and winning prizes for my studies and the rest, but I wish she wouldn't tell me so often in public.

Mother has always cosseted me as her first born. The very opposite of Father. She insisted on carrying my bag on the walk to the bus-stop from the hospital despite me trying to wrestle it off her so that she didn't make me look like a child and shame me.

She glided past a couple of French paratroopers, one of whom slapped her backside like a prize cow. She switched to my other side to shield me from them and that embarrassed me more. I just wanted the ground to eat me up or to kill them, whichever came first.

She said men can be like irritating insects. If a woman tries to swat them away, they buzz around her even more. If she just ignores them, they soon lose interest and switch their attentions.

She said it is the power of making a woman feel uncomfortable that spurs on the coqs sportifs of the French Army—the public humiliation they inflict, not so much their lustful thoughts.

She said they are sad, limp little men with les petits penis. And the only way they can have congress with a woman is either to force themselves on her or pay for it. While they are away, they will have their bit of fun doing both. That is their insigne d'honneur.

She said it is cruel, but it is the way of the world. She doesn't like it any more than I do. Less in fact. But that is that. Men are men.

She added that she would die if she ever found out that I had treated a girl like that. Or harboured any thoughts of that nature towards a woman.

She is very rational with me. But the soldiers' straying hands have reignited memories in her she cannot brush aside so readily.

She cannot simply forget Philippeville. It is raw and recent. She has seen some terrible things happen to friends there. At Philippeville, I know she had things done to her that she does not talk about.

Father knows. And I suspect others do too. Secrets do not stay secret for long in Algeria. The numbers of dead and wounded are too high. There are too many people involved, too many eyes on events, for word not to leak out.

Sometimes, I even wonder if that accounts for Father's off-hand attitude towards her. The fact that it is not just him who knows.

Mother says she will bring her boys up to respect their women. And she will see to it that little Margot does not accept men's abuse as a natural state.

But Mother's defiance is still only as good as the men around her. And the men around her have not been good.

Her composure just made me want to kill the soldiers even more. Because I know Mother too well. And I know from watching her take Father's blows, the calmer she appears the more she is hurting. She puts on a face for me, Louis and Margot. One of her many faces. They help her carry on.

It just adds to my anxiety—a mood that has grown darker over the last week. Of course, the larger part of that is Father's absence.

Following my confession to lieutenant Laurent, the remainder of my stay at the Trinitarian hospital was tense.

Throughout the week, I brooded on my stupidity in revealing Father's possible whereabouts to Laurent. It soured everything. So many dark thoughts have visited me since. So many questions swirl around in that vortex of ignorance.

What was Father thinking during those moments in the Casbah when his fingers were poised over that switch? Was he really prepared to sacrifice me, his own son? Is he dead? Is he on the run? If so, has Laurent caught up with him? Is Laurent the honourable man he says he is? Or a two-faced barracuda? Is Laurent just another double agent of General Massu masquerading as military police? Has he already handed Father over to the DOP for interrogation? Or worse still, reserved him a seat on one of Colonel Aussaresses' helicopter death flights over the Bay of Algiers? To be shoved out at nine thousand feet sans parachute?

Or maybe, hope against hope, Laurent has been as good as his word and put Father on the first boat out of Oran, never to return. Maybe Lieutenant Laurent will prove my instincts right. That he is a good soldier in a bad Army. And he realises that to open the gates of hell, it only takes a few good men to do nothing.

The only bright spark in an otherwise dismal week has been that Captain LeBoeuf has stayed away from me.

The ward sister told the Captain repeatedly he had no jurisdiction over the Red Cross or Red Crescent—and so it seems he gave up trying. I am sure Laurent had something to do with that.

Yes, maybe my instincts about Lieutenant Laurent will be rewarded after all. Maybe giving away Father's safe location will turn out to be a masterstroke—and Laurent will protect him. Stranger things have happened in Algiers than people doing what they say and saying what they do.

Throughout that time, Mother kept up her steady vigil at my bedside—and she joined me in the bougainvillea garden whenever her visits coincided with my hour of outdoor convalescence.

Here she was able to lose herself in her thoughts. She found the garden more restorative than many of the patients. It's why we sat in silence for much of the time.

There was no need to talk of Father. Of the bombing. Of his possible escape. There was nothing more to add other than speculation.

Frankly, Waleed has done enough speculating for us all. His idle theories feed the questions swimming around in my brain.

Of course, these questions have multiplied. I have not seen Lieutenant Laurent since we picked over the bloated carcass of Terrare in the cloisters and I have much to ask him. The nurse said the Lieutenant checked himself out that same day.

It didn't surprise me. He had what he wanted.

Between telling him where Father could be hiding out and me climbing aboard Waleed's bus today, I know that Lieutenant Laurent has had more than enough time to mount a search.

Despite all this, as Waleed's bus threads its way through the tightly controlled streets, all my guessing now leads me to one inescapable conclusion—that Father is as good as dead and buried.

It will be strange walking into the kitchen of the farmhouse I last set eyes on before our worlds were turned upside down. A house that is so full of Father's presence it's hard to imagine the space without him. But now I just want to get back there with Mother, Louis, Margot and Baby Claude so we can pick up our lives again.

Waleed, however, is doing his level best to prolong that moment. He is being extra cautious with his driving. His bus is crawling along the streets.

To be fair to our neighbour, it is not that easy for him to drive the bus through Algiers.

The city is largely shut with the quadrillage. The movement of traffic through the zones interdicts is restricted and gridlocked. From sections to blocks, everything is locked down with barbed wire and barricades.

In spite of which, Waleed presses on.

Though he is still able to make his inbound final destination of Central Square, he has a whole series of obstacles to negotiate on his way out of Algiers.

Multiple checkpoints, random obstructions in the road, nonsensical diversions.

I may have my doubts about our neighbour, but I am not entirely without regard for the man's resourcefulness.

After all, there is still a city to run. Buses are still required to transport workers into the centre. The shops are open. And those Pieds-Noirs who keep the colonials going every day still have to come in from the provinces to do so. People like Waleed—loyal to the Army as well as himself—are doing far more for the French by putting their hands to a steering wheel than an MAS-49 semi-automatic rifle.

Of course, he is helped by using the special dispensation to take his bus through the checkpoints. Every time he stops at a barrier, he flashes a handwritten note signed by Captain LeBoeuf, stamped with the insignia of the tenth para. And he is waved through.

Mother and I sit in the front seats of his bus on the way back to Medea. Waleed has reserved them especially for us and has kept the seats opposite free for my little brother and sister once they are on board.

We have left the restricted zone now. Waleed has increased his speed and the bus is trundling on towards the city limits at a steady thirty kilometres per hour along an uneven camber.

The passengers are swaying to the rise and fall of the rolling road.

"I take it we are going to Madame Hachemi to pick up the children first?" Mother puts the question to Waleed more by way of a demand than a request.

"Madame Hachemi it is," he replies, aping the devil-may-care shrug of a couldn't-care-less cab driver.

Mother has been treating Waleed as her personal run-around service the whole time I have been in hospital. And Waleed has been happy enough to comply. For now.

Our neighbour is a chauvinist. An ingratiating one at that. And there is a constant struggle inside him between these two equally loathsome sides of his character.

On this occasion, he doesn't seem to mind submitting to Mother's bossiness and even plays along with it. I know recently he has been going out of his way to drop her door-to-door, despite it being against bus company regulations to stray off the assigned route—and with a fully loaded vehicle.

There again, Waleed's passengers are a stoic bunch. They have been through greater inconveniences of late than spending twenty minutes longer in a bus than they need to. The Pied-Noir city workers have a steady resilience—what Albert

Camus terms 'peuple magnifique et derisoire'. They may be settler stock without intellect or spirit, but I find there is a pragmatic steeliness to the way they go about their lives.

This is a sore point for the 'nationalists'. The Algiers press reports daily that the FLN are spoiling for a General Strike. It starts in just two days' time and yet I am sure they will have no takers for strike action on this bus.

We are passing by the base of the hill leading up to the ancient ruins overlooking the city. The old fort is not as imposing in the daylight. I see the minuscule toy soldiers of the tenth para up there standing stiff under a postage stamp tricolour hoisted aloft on a cocktail stick—carrying rifles the size of dress-pins poised and primed in the January sunlight.

We are not far from the spot where Father left his truck that morning.

Waleed spouts his usual stream of nonsense. He directs most of it at Mother, though some of it is intended for me.

"I have something of Farouk's, Basira. I've been meaning to give it back to him. But under the circumstances, I'm sure he'd like you to have it."

Mother is surprised at this news. And a little concerned. She wonders what Waleed means by 'the circumstances.'

He reaches into his pocket and hands her a blue velvet envelope.

She hesitates to open it. Waleed is trying hard not to pay attention, whistling along to 'That's Amore' on his new Motorola radio—another of the rewards LeBoeuf has bestowed on his pet spy and bomb-maker—and casting furtive glances over his shoulder towards her whilst gripping the steering wheel tightly.

Waleed could have made this gesture at any time during my whole hospital stay—all those days shuttling Mother from Medea to the hospital in Algiers and back. I expect he has chosen this moment so that I am there to see it. And with Dean Martin to serenade her. Ça me fait froid dans le dos.

"Farouk obtained it from a jeweller in Rue Claude-Debussy. He wanted it to be a secret by keeping it out of the house…"

"Did he now…"

"I believe your wedding anniversary is coming up this month. Est-ce vrai?"

"Yes, it's true. But why would he give my anniversary gift to you for safe-keeping?" asks Mother archly.

"He says you search the house for 'things' of his quite a lot. I have no idea what he means. It's not my business to know. He just wanted me to take care of it for him, that's all. I am merely carrying out his wish."

Well, aren't you going to open it?" he urges as if this is his little token to give.

Waleed slows the bus. Other passengers are leaning in to see what a mystery gift from an absentee husband looks like. A few of them clap, misconstruing this as a declaration of love or, worse still, from those seated further back on the bus, a marriage proposal from Waleed himself.

I slide down in my seat, silently fuming at the misunderstanding. It is causing me embarrassment and shame. And I am feeling my face redden again.

Thankfully, Mother does not want such a private moment to be made so public. She slips the velvet envelope smartly into her coat pocket and pats it down emphatically.

"If it is meant for our wedding anniversary, then I will open it when he is here to give it to me himself."

Despite this, Waleed still wants her to open the gift. His eyes are all over her.

"What if he never comes back?"

I could kill Waleed. Right now. I would tie him up with those paras who humiliated Mother and gouge out his eyeball with a pocket-knife like an apple core. Mother does not so much as bat an eyelid.

"Then it will stay in my pocket. You can go faster if you like, Waleed." Then to him and the other passengers. "There is nothing to see here."

But Waleed does not pick up the pace. If anything, he is going slower than ever.

We are passing the precise spot at which Father pulled his truck off the road on the morning of the Courvois killings. Waleed is craning his neck to see down into the culvert. I am too.

Now there is no truck, though there are freshly embossed tyre marks.

The marks lead back up onto the road where they have scored the asphalt. The marks of a heavy skidding vehicle.

I catch sight of Waleed in the rear-view mirror. How does he know this is the precise spot Father left his truck that morning? He nibbles at his lower lip as he starts to put his foot down.

I sit back in my seat, still wondering.

After a while Waleed resumes his normal yammering—transmit, not receive. He jabbers away at Mother in the front seat, allowing hardly a breath between his sentences.

"Are you still finding grit in your drinking water, Basira? Farouk should have fixed the well by now. There are too many leaks for my liking. I told him that is why you have a bad well flow. The casing is cracked. You need a new liner. It's bad for the children, dirt in the water. He should know that. We are living in the modern world. Farouk must take responsibility."

Mother is oblivious to it. Her eyes glaze over. Waleed's drone becomes just another ambient sound to contend with the throb of the bus engine.

A while later, we arrive at Madame Hachemi's house in the bidonville on the outskirts of Medea. It is a modest single storey building with a large shuttered entrance.

Very little light penetrates. But today all the children are outdoors in the ramshackle yard, squinting into the sunlight and revelling in dirt.

It is chaos.

Limbless toys are scattered about. Toddlers mill around a busted playhouse and chase each other under a line pegged with washing. They play tag, screaming loudly when they are discovered behind the curtain of sheets and even more piercingly when they are caught.

I see Margot try to pedal a rusting old tricycle with the front wheel so bent out of shape that she is practically pushing it back on itself. She is going nowhere but refusing to give up.

Louis and another boy are on their hands and knees playing detectives. They have detained a gecko for questioning and are prodding it with a twig to make it talk.

Madame Hachemi is watching them from a listing folding chair by the front door. The bottom of the chair is split and sagging with her bulk and her years. It is not so much that she has settled into the chair as the chair has set around her.

She greets me as I wave to my little brother. He jumps up and charges towards me whooping.

"Shimeun! Shimeun! We captured a lizard. We have named him Marcel."

"That's nice," I say "That's a nice name for a lizard."

My mind's eye has Terrare popping Marcel into his mouth without a second thought—as mere mortals with lesser appetites and capacity would do with an olive.

Hampered by gout, Madame Hachemi has rocked herself off her chair and is now shuffling down the path towards me in her housecoat and slippers. As she nears, she fires off an icy stare towards Louis' playmate.

"Kassim, you let that poor gecko go now! What has it ever done to you?" She smiles cordially at me.

"Have you heard from your father, Simeon?"

"No"

"He is alive though."

"I don't know."

Her smile turns sour.

"Mm…Take it from me…that Farouk is a wily old dog. Saving himself is his one goal in life. He should hang his head in shame for what he did in the Casbah. Or better still just hang. As I keep trying to tell your mother. She is in pieces…"

It is no surprise that Mother has remained on the bus. She always dreads having to pick up the children from Madame Hachemi. The dropping-off is fine as she can make a quick getaway, but the thought of shepherding a five-year old and a two-year old away from so many willing playmates, whilst escaping the clutches of a busybody childminder, gives her the terrors.

Louis is at my side, trying to relieve me of my walking stick.

"Louis, go fetch your sister. Maman is waiting. You don't want the bus to leave without you now…"

Louis does what he is told. I smile politely at Madame Hachemi. I do not know what to say.

"If he were half the man Basira deserves, he would come home and face the music. Family is the most important thing anyone has in this life. More important than life itself."

Louis is taking too long to bargain with Margot. Margot is pulling a face and staunchly resisting.

Madame Hachemi is determined to have her say.

"He should at least let you know he is alive. Just get word to you all. Poor Basira, look at her. She is a ghost."

"Louis, get your sister. Now!"

"You and Farouk, you have always been thick as thieves."

I have had enough.

"Thank you for looking after them, Madame Hachemi. Mother is most grateful to you."

I stride over to Louis and Margot, grab them both by the hands and yank them towards the bus. Louis tussles with me and kicks me in the shins. Margot begins to sob and then offers up her dead weight in a gesture of supreme sacrifice.

By now Mother has left her seat in the bus and is hurrying towards us. The two remaining passengers sit on board and watch the rest of the show unfold from the safety of their elevated vantage point.

"Louis. Don't do that. Shimeun has a bad leg. He's had an operation and has been very sick. He's got a stick to help him walk. Are you blind as well as stupid?"

She prises his fingers off me and drags his resisting body up into the bus herself. I lift Margot and follow Mother, carrying my baby sister in my arms along with my stick. I am surprised just how much this takes out of me.

By the time I have calmed Margot, and Louis has given way to Mother's firm hand, I am breathless and weak.

I apologise to the remaining passengers for the children's behaviour and slump down next to Louis with Margot nodding off on my lap.

Madame Hachemi watches us go with narrowing eyelids as her foster-brood—children of the missing, the wounded and the dead—play around her.

Waleed is laughing at it all as he pulls away, grinding up through the gears.

"What a to-do, you children! You belong on the front line, not in a play-group!"

I want him to shut up. He is not their father. He has no right to tell them what's what. I am Father's son and I have been on the front line. And having seen it, there is no way I will allow my brothers and sister to go there.

"Mother, do you trust everybody around our family?" I say under my breath so that Waleed cannot hear.

"I have no choice, Shimeun. Just as your father had no choice…"
"No choice, Basira. Eh?" Waleed chips in, pretending she is speaking to him. "No choice to do what? Speak up why don't you…"

"Why don't I? Because I am not talking to you, Waleed. Concentrate on the road!"

On the way out of Medea, Waleed applies the brakes to let the remaining passengers off. He hates having to interrupt his momentum. Once stopped, it takes him a long time to bring the reluctant engine back up to full throttle.

The last two regular passengers climb down from the bus and go their own separate ways.

Waleed is free from pricked-up ears so he can talk about them now.

"She is a secretary for the Prefecture of Police. He is a lecturer at the university."

It is a Waleed-style non-sequitur. He places more value on the act of trading information than he does on the intrinsic worth of the information itself and therefore invites no further comment from us.

Instead, his attention is drawn to a column of French troops on the other side of the road—an endless train of metal heading into Algiers. It consists of some thirty vehicles. Troop transports with men smoking as they loll over the tailgates and armoured cars clad in bomb-proof grilles.

We watch the procession pass.

It's strange to me how the Army lumbers towards conflict without any seeming urgency before erupting into a surge of ceaseless energy.

Waleed cannot resist the commentary.

"They are planning to bust the General Strike. You'll see. And then all hell will be let loose on the streets."

"All hell is out there already. What kind of an inferno do you anticipate now?" Mother chimes in.

"Oh, Basira. You can see with your own eyes. This is unprecedented. The Army are arriving from their Sahara bases…from their barracks at Oran…Mers-El-Kibir…they have big depots there under the earth, you know…stores of firepower like you'd never believe…like those atomic silos the Yankees have built in the desert…the French are not fucking about…the Tricolour flies right at the top of Murdjadjo Ridge…go stand on the harbour wall at Oran and you can see it. All Algeria knows that flag will still be there in a hundred years…any cab driver will tell you. It is all coming down on Algiers. The Frenchman has endured in this city for long enough…now we will see the teeth of the empire embedded in the jugular of Algiers."

"The French! Endured? Waleed, cessez de flairer le trou de cul de l'armée française. You no longer have to play up to your Pied-Noir passengers. They have left the bus. It is just us now. You, me and my children. There is no one left to impress. Look! One of us is asleep, another is heading that way. And Shimeun is so weary with your gushing love of France that I fear he may soon be nodding off too. As frankly will I."

Margot is indeed snoozing. Her snot, tears and dribble gather on the collar of my shirt. Louis watches the telegraph poles fly by. A repetitive graph of dipping and rising lines that has a hypnotic effect on the five-year old and sends him into a trance-like state.

I am thinking of Father.

Waleed is agitated.

"You had better start believing in the Army, Basira. They may just save your life."

We pass Waleed's house and the bus cruises on by. Waleed does not even spare his home a second glance, he is so intent on reaching our farmhouse.

He points the bus up the familiar dirt road and brings it to a standstill by our outhouse. He then turns off the engine. A sure sign that he is coming in.

"Vite, vite…éveillé éveillé, lève-toi et brille, mes petites poussins."

He opens the bus door and ushers us out.

I think Waleed has some nerve coming in like this.

Mother, however, is not too bothered by it. She acts as if she expects it. Louis and Margot are also indifferent to the presence of our neighbour. They are far more interested in chasing the chickens around the yard.

I am watching Waleed's every move.

He marches into the kitchen without invitation and heads straight to the dark corners of the house so that he can flush out any imagined assassins who may be lurking there.

I thank him for transporting us—more to hurry him out of the door.

"For what? Doing what I always do? Come on! I am a friend of your father and the whole Abu family. Nothing is too much trouble…"

Mother offers him a cup of coffee. I am vexed. I cannot understand why she is playing the good host to our neighbour. In my estimation, Waleed overstayed his welcome from the very moment he set foot inside our home.

Of course, he accepts Mother's offer and plants himself at the kitchen table. He is like the weather now flecking the farmhouse windows—about to set in for the evening.

Mother reads the consternation on my face and tries to explain.

"Shimeun, we have a visitor coming here in half an hour. That is why Waleed is staying. He needs to be here too."

It is a weasel of an explanation. It tells me nothing about Waleed's presence.

"A visitor? Here? Well, who…I mean what does Waleed have to do with it?"

"You will see." Mother seems more resigned to the prospect than excited by it. Sad, even.

Once again, I am on the outside looking in.

I feel the same way as the night I was refused entry to a nightclub in the European quarter.

I was simply foolish to believe an Arab boy like me—the son of a Harki—could crash the party of the Français de souche and évolués. I wanted so much to breeze past the doorman that night—for him to sanction my admission to the club with a wink and a nod. He made me feel dirty.

But this time it is the adult world that is refusing me entry, not the elite Muslims or purebred colonials.

I am an adult when it suits them and a child when it does not.

It is a truly horrible place to be, this no man's, no child's land.

I feel fury towards Mother for trying to protect me from events when my duty as a son is to protect her. She is either failing to see it or refusing to.

With the rush of blood to my head, I do not even stop to think that she has seen her son almost blown to kingdom come or that her every waking hour has been taken up willing my recovery.

I choose to find her obstinate and unhelpful. It helps me to hate all those who make her that way.

I go to lie on my bed and stare at the ceiling, leaving her and Waleed to it.

Despite this protest, my antennae are up. I listen in. It's what I have been trained to do in the cafés of the European quarter. Learn how to tune in to the frequencies of others without them knowing.

"He's dead isn't he…well, isn't he? You don't have a building fall down on you and just get up and run away." I hear Mother say.

"Well, Simeon did. People are starting to call him the miracle of the Place Jean-Paul Sartre. They say like father like son. Who's to say the reverse isn't true and Farouk was spared the full force of the blast just like the boy?"

"He's dead, I'm sure of it. Farouk is dead. That is the reason LeBoeuf wants to visit…to give me the news and ask that I identify the body."

"How many times, Basira? If Farouk's body had been found, then we would know by now. LeBoeuf doesn't care about hanging name tags from the toes of cadavers in the morgue. He wouldn't come all the way out here for that! He has adjutants and office boys who are perfectly capable of obtaining dental records and notifying next of kin. No, he has other plans in mind."

"Do those plans include going after my husband to murder him?"

"You are paranoid, Basira. First you tell me Farouk is dead, then you tell me he is about to die. Which is it to be? It can't be both!"

After a while, I emerge from behind the damask curtain.

"Ah, you are back," says Waleed, draining a cup of coffee.

I stand over him.

"You sent us into a death-trap the other day."

"Of course, I did."

"Why?"

"You know why…"

"Do I?"

"Don't be so naive, Simeon. You know it was the plan all along. For Farouk to lead the murderers of Courvois to the bomb. Of course, no one asked that he take you with him. I was surprised he should endanger you like that."

I hear vehicles pull up outside in the yard. Undeterred, I fix on Waleed.

"I don't mean that. Forget about the fellaghas. I mean you set a trap for Father and myself to walk into."

"What on earth are you talking about, Simeon?"

It pours out.

"You placed the bomb in the passageway right underneath the ulema's apartment. You know where they all live in the blocks, all the moderate men of Islamic faith and the Muslim innocents. You know they are all packed in there like so many boquerones."

Waleed rolls with the punches. He refuses to dignify my accusations with a response.

"You know what a thousand-pound car bomb can do to a building. It was overkill, Waleed, and you know it. There was enough explosive in that bomb to bring down a mosque."

I am shouting now. Bawling at him.

"Shimeun," Mother says softly. I don't hear her.

"You might as well have taken down a mosque for the damage you have done! You knew ordinary citizens would die. You couldn't have placed it better…"

"Thank you," says Waleed, openly taunting me. "Job done!"

Again, Mother tries to placate me.

"Shimeun, darling…"

But I am inconsolable. My voice is cracking, raking my dry throat and the words come spluttering out.

"You set us up. You sent us in there not just to avenge the ALN fellaghas but to kill ordinary peaceable Muslims, allies of the French and of us. All the better for LeBoeuf to exploit our shame and disgrace."

Mother is tearful. She is by the stove, a cup of coffee pressed to her lips to keep her peace.

Waleed does not answer me. He appeals to her instead.

"Whooah! Does this boy of yours ever stop, Basira?"

It is a slap in the face. To Mother. To me. I modulate my voice now.

"You knew didn't you…you were in on it…you and LeBoeuf, you set us up. Father is a dead man because of you."

I hear multiple footsteps crunching in the yard outside. Some shouts. A hammering on the door.

Mother goes to open it, though Waleed is up from his chair ahead of her—all the quicker to dodge my accusation.

The very next second, I see Captain LeBoeuf standing there in our kitchen.

He holds his amarante beret in his hand, bearing the badge of the tenth para—buffed and gleaming. Three cigars peep from the top of a bellow pocket in his camo jacket. His double-buckle boots seem to take up much of the kitchen floor-too large for his short legs. Like a clown's shoes.

"Ah, powder monkey!"

Mother has no idea what he means by the soubriquet.

"You are still with us! Good boy!"

It is a pretence. As if my being alive and here in our house has come as any surprise to him—the man who has been trying so desperately to interview me the past few weeks during my stay in hospital.

Waleed offers him a chair. LeBoeuf sits smartly, pulls two of the cigars from his pocket and hands one to him. He quickly remembers his manners and addresses Mother.

"Ah, apologies Madame. Do you mind?"

Mother shakes her head. He bites at the cap of a robusto, then spits the wet plug of compacted leaf out onto the kitchen floor.

Mother stares at him. I swear I can hear the jangling in her head.

She gives nothing away as she calmly picks up the chewed nib of tobacco.

She places it on a small earthenware plate which she takes from a stack of dishes by the stove. She coolly places the plate down on the table in front of LeBoeuf.

"Your ash goes in here," she commands.

Her cold defiance adds to the froideur already in the room.

It is also an oddly intimate act.

LeBoeuf takes a zippo from out of his jacket, flips the top open and fires it up. He primes the cigar, spinning it around in his fingers. It burns evenly to an orange glow. He puffs at it like a pouting trout, sliding the lighter across the kitchen table to Waleed once he is sure the tobacco has caught. Waleed goes through the same ritual. But his action is less a faithful copy, more unintended caricature.

Plumes of smoke curl up from LeBoeuf's mouth. A toasted aroma fills the room. LeBoeuf sits back on the chair, legs splayed, puffing at his cigar. Waleed does the same, only his cigar burns unevenly. The two men take a moment to savour the tobacco.

Here they are. The silverback in his pose of possession and entitlement. The beta male paying homage the alpha's dominance. The unspoken contract sealed.

"Now…this is the way we will proceed." LeBoeuf pulls back a third chair and pats the seat, inviting Mother to sit next to him. She reluctantly joins them around the table.

I continue to stand.

"Waleed, with Farouk gone, you are the responsable here. Madame, you will do what Waleed asks. And Waleed here will take his instruction directly from me. Is that clear?"

Mother does not protest. It is as if she is expecting it, as if she and Waleed have already agreed this—signed, sealed, delivered.

"How do you know Father isn't coming back?" I ask.

"How do you know he is?" he replies.

I do not answer. Maybe I am volunteering too much. But I assume from LeBoeuf's response that Laurent has not shared with him the knowledge of Father's whereabouts. And by extension it hasn't been shared with General Massu, Major Aussaresses or the rest of the death squad.

"Waleed will be the head of this house. In return, I will give you round-the-clock protection by my men. For you now have an FLN target on your back. I will underwrite your safe passage out of the country—that is for you and your children. On the proviso, of course, that you agree to my conditions."

Waleed smirks.

I look to Mother for an objection. There is none.

"Good. We are in agreement then."

He pushes back the chair and strides to the window, parting the small lace curtains that barely cover the window-frame. Another make-do-and-mend feature of our make-it-up-as-you-go-along home.

"Your children are delightful, the way they follow my men around. My men are out there now, staking out the property. I think it is ideal for our purposes."

"What purposes?" I ask. Mother shoots me an anxious look.

LeBoeuf turns to face me.

Waleed sits with his eyes fixed on the floor and a self-satisfied grin on his face I want to wipe that expression off his chops with one of LeBoeuf's razor blades. Give him a real Kabylian smile.

"Was I talking to you, powder monkey?" says LeBoeuf.

Mother swallows hard. Waleed is cringing now.

I cannot contain my words. They spill out onto the kitchen table.

"I doubt it. You have no respect for me, for our family. You sent us to our deaths in the Casbah. You and Waleed here. You sent us in there to fight with empty magazines and an ammunition pouch full of razor blades. See!" I hold up both hands, my fingers spread so he can see the calloused scarring that has formed on the tips.

LeBoeuf rests the cigar on the plate. Rising slowly from the table, he makes his way around to me and takes both my hands in his—gently inspecting my quivering fingertips like a surgeon, though his fingers are nowhere near as delicate.

"Nicely done," he says, admiring his handiwork. "You have me to thank. The tips are almost gone. An old trick of mine. Now we will find it very difficult to identify you from your fingerprints when you are laid out on the slab. No records. No identity. You will be lost to history."

Mother is on her feet. She rushes around the table and pulls LeBoeuf's hands away from mine.

"Please! Please! No trouble…" But it's directed more at me than it is LeBoeuf. LeBoeuf backs away.

"If you'd like to join us at the table, powder monkey, you are most welcome. If not, I would suggest you shut the fuck up or leave this minute. This is the table for the adults of the house…You children belong in your rooms," he adds archly.

I stand my ground. He continues with his bullying tirade.

"No? Suit yourself. But if I hear another peep out of you, I will escort you to your room personally. And by Christ you will wish I hadn't…"

Mother touches my hand and gently squeezes it. I look into her eyes. She gives me the feintest of reassuring nods.

My head is whirring hot like the crankshaft in Father's truck. Mother returns to the table, the dutiful servant. She knows that if we are useful to LeBoeuf we will stay alive.

LeBoeuf is swinging back on the chair again, dragging his big sausage fingers through his buzz-cut. I pray to my personal god that he will set that wick of hair alight with the cigar and the flame will melt his odious face like candle wax.

He resumes.

"We have the FLN on the run. And we have made major strides. We have two of their leading lights in our sights. The head of the snake Ali Boumendjel and Larbi Ben M'hidi. A founder of the FLN, no less.

This is quite a hydra! There are so many heads to lop off this beast. That duo of pimps and swindlers Ali La Pointe and Yacef Saadi are also out there trading their carnage for publicity back in France. What a pair! Unwittingly playing into De Gaulle's hands. Their atrocities here will guarantee his re-election there.

There are just too many of these FLN hucksters to keep an eye on them all at once. They are quick-of-hand like magicians. When they move their cups around, we do not quite know which one the bomb is under.

So, we divide and conquer.

Colonel Trinquier is working to find La Pointe and Saadi with his informants in the Casbah. We are working to eliminate Boumendjel, Ben M'hidi and the rest of the FLN murderers. We are doing a better job flushing them out than the Governor-General and his so-called police force.

General Massu will not tolerate their insolence and is set on their extinction. To which end, I myself examined the files of FLN suspects we dug out from the Sûreté of the Prefecture de Police. A goldmine! We hit the motherlode right there."

I am calming down from LeBoeuf's threats right now, though my heart is still drumming in my chest. LeBoeuf has mentioned Father only once—to note his absence. Waleed is right. Father is just another blip on the captain's radar. I cannot think why LeBoeuf was so keen to interview me about his whereabouts in hospital. Why is he so indifferent towards the matter now?

"As a result, we have been picking up FLN foot-soldiers ever since. It is not unusual to detain them in our centres d'hébergements.

But unfortunately, we haven't as yet traced the heads of the snake back to their nest.

This is of course an operational oversight on our part—given that Ben M'hidi is calling for the workers of Algeria to withdraw their labour in just two days' time.

His capture at this moment would almost certainly snuff out any further striker insurrection. But then again, who knows? It may do quite the opposite…

To which end there has been a great deal of talk about what we should do with Ben M'hidi when we find him.

I have to admit, for once the generals have been at a loss to know how to proceed.

Capturing a trophy such as Ben M'hidi would be like winning the big stuffed bear at the fairground shooting gallery and then having to get it home without being seen…"

He is clearly pleased with his analogy. If he could give himself a pat on the back, he would.

"General Massu, Colonel Trinquier, Fossey-François and Major Aussaresses have all been scratching their heads as to what to do with Ben M'hidi and the rest of the FLN secretariat once they have been flushed out from their holes in the Casbah.

What makes matters worse is that there is a difference of opinion on how to deal with these high-profile FLN troublemakers.

There are those such as my colleague in the GRE, Lieutenant Laurent, who would have them treated as political opponents.

Whereas we know they are terrorists, pure and simple. Worse, they are pimps, black marketers and cheats. Self-appointed confidence tricksters and gangsters elevated to the leadership of a national movement. It's nothing more than a criminal conspiracy. And Laurent is buying it.

I'm sure he would rather have Jacques Tati question the FLN leadership at El-Biar—perhaps sit down with Ben M'hidi over a café-creme and a madeleine and humour him. They believe they can charm the reptile out of his basket through polite discourse, a merry tune.

Bollocks can they…

How do you reason with a snake?

Lieutenant Laurent is pliable. That is his way. He puts too much faith in what the United Nations have to say on the matter rather than his own Army.

It is something of an impasse. Needless to say, Laurent is not on General Massu's Christmas card list. Nor Aussaresses'…"

"You mean they prefer torture to questioning…" Mother cuts in.

"A more coercive interrogative technique…Massu has no time for the ballet-shoe stealth of intelligence officers like Laurent. Rather he prefers the boot of Major Paul Aussaresses, who will stamp out any chicanery in an instant."

"You have your solution then…" I say drily.

Mother bridles. She thinks it's risky for me to speak out like this.

But LeBoeuf lets it pass. My impetuosity has earned me the right to be heard and ignored. He answers the room, not me.

"Not quite. The issue is this. If our DOP officers capture Ben M'hidi and question him at El-Biar, at police headquarters, Villa des Tourelles, or any other known centre d'hébergement for that matter, it will bring instant martyrdom and the FLN will rally around their sacrifice.

Ben M'hidi's supporters know only too well his fondness for the songs of the French Resistance. Should they hear him singing 'Le chant des partisans' behind the walls of El-Biar prison, it will only give them another flag to rally around. Besides, they also know that if we sever the head, the snake will simply grow another one to replace it. 'Un autre prendra ma place'.

So you see, the last thing we need is Islamist protestors chanting yet another Algerian martyr's song in the alleyways of the Casbah. It will simply bring to the boil a situation that is already red hot. 'Pour chaque soldat du FLN guillotiné, une centaine de Français seront abattus." That is the only negotiating position that scumbag Larbi Ben M'hidi knows.

If you ask me, we should have taken the whole FLN hydra out at their Soummam get-together while we had all the heads in one place…I would have done it personally had I not been up to my gonads in paddy fields keeping the Viet Minh at bay."

Waleed is nodding in agreement with practically everything Captain LeBoeuf has to say. Le crapaud.

"Same goes for General Massu. He has not come this far to see his opposite number in custody wrapping the French Army around his little finger. Oh, no. No, no, no—that will not do. Massu will definitely not stand for that.

That's why he wants Colonel Aussaresses in charge of questioning the FLN leadership once they have been chased down. He wants the ends neatly tied up.

And Massu requires that my unit carry out Aussaresses' orders."

Mother frowns.

"But you said this house will do for your purposes. You still haven't told me. What is your purpose?"

"General Massu and Aussaresses have decided it between them.

Once we capture Ben M'hidi, it must appear to the people of Algeria and France that the man has killed himself. And this house is where we…he…will do it."

The Farmhouse, Medea Wilaya, 27 January 1957

I gently raise the latch and steal out of the house. Two of LeBoeuf's men are leaning on rifles outside taking a cigarette break. They have been there all night.

I say a cheery "good morning!" and announce that I need to fetch a sack of feed for the chickens from the outbuilding.

Once inside, I part a couple of loose boards at the back of the grain store and slip away unnoticed.

I make my way across the fields to the main road, staying clear of the farm-track in the unlikely event that others in LeBoeuf's unit are using it at this early hour.

The soldiers are looking out for possible intruders, not escapees from the farmhouse. So hopefully my absence will not register with them until I am long gone—or at the very least, until I have gained a useful head-start on them.

Having reached the main road, I will walk and hitch rides south and east. I will avoid the Army as far as is possible.

There are enough tongue-waggers out and about to give me away and I will need to rely on more than good judgment if I want to go undetected.

Luck or divine intercession will have to play their part in my journey too. That is why, once I am set fair for Sour El-Ghozlane, I issue a little prayer to my own personal god.

I am expecting the touch of LeBoeuf's dread hand on my shoulder at any moment. Or to have an ALN assassin pop up from behind a hedge and put a bullet in my head.

Every step I take feels as if it is on borrowed time.

I travel along the edges of fields and skirt along the sides of ditches that run parallel with the road, hardly ever straying on to the roadway itself. It is just too exposed.

At the distant sounds of vehicles, I use Grandfather's carob-wood walking stick to take my weight as I squat down on my haunches so that I can make myself smaller.

If I spot an Army vehicle, I scamper further away from the road, behind a bush, a water trough, a tree, or gourbi. If a civilian car or truck appears, I stand at the verge and try to wave it down.

I have few takers on these escapades. It is heavy going. I imagined it would be easier than this.

I am over two hours walking before a farmer in a Peugeot pick-up truck stops to give me a lift as far as Berrouaghia.

The farmer's face is deep tan and furrowed like the earth he has tilled. At first, I think he looks as sullen as I feel—world-worn and heavy-lidded, the default setting of a hardscrabble life. But when he starts talking, a mischievous grin breaks through like sunshine from behind clouds.

My mood instantly lightens too.

With chaos let loose on the streets of Algiers, the farmer bemoans the absence of football and asks me what team I support.

If anything can draw me out of myself, it's this.

Within minutes I am declaring my lifelong loyalty to team colours and my undying love of club.

"MA Hussein-Dey. Born and bred. Father took me along to every game at the Stade 20 Août when we first came to Medea."

The farmer harrumphs.

"MAHD are a dirty side."

I can't deny it. In fact, I'm quite proud of their notoriety. They grind out results by winning ugly. With a hardened defence and a blunted attack, they have the professional foul down to a fine art.

Of course, our reputation as a team has suffered, but for that one reason alone, they are now feared more than admired.

I consider their survival at any cost a good thing. Although now, for MA Hussein-Dey, the football is somewhat academic.

"There are no more matches at the Stade 20 Août—many of the players have answered the call to arms of the FLN, hung up their boots and taken up their rifles."

"Yes, I know. Pity, that," says the farmer, "Martyrs to a fault. They martyred themselves on the pitch too, but alas it didn't bring them any silverware.

Now they will have even more chance to show off their bone-breaking skills on the side of the FLN."

He can tell that I am sad about not being able to see my beloved team play.

"Look on the bright side, young man…who would have thought every player in that third-rate outfit would be called up to the national squad!"

His sense of humour is as dry as the Maghreb.

"I'm an RC Alger fan," he volunteers. "I have been since I was a boy. If you need a substitute for your Hussein-Dey lads, you should switch your support to Racing. They are good value for the gate money."

I confess to him I don't know very much about RC Alger. He reels off the names and positions of every player in the current squad as if they are drinking partners. Having exhausted his knowledge of the current team sheet, he then reaches back into his memory banks for stories about club legends.

"I once saw Camus play."

"Albert Camus?" I marvel. "You have got to be joking!"

"I never joke about football. It is far too serious a matter."

I am in the presence of greatness by proxy…as here is a man who has been in the presence of Camus. How can this be?

I tell him I have been reading 'L'Homme Révolte' at school. That in my humble opinion, Camus is as great a writer as he is a thinker. That my form master, Monsieur Gazides—also a fan of RC Alger—thought, just like Camus, that the simple virtues of team spirit are far more civilising than the ambiguous morality of the state and religion.

I tell him that was before one day my form master was marched out of school by the police without charge and replaced with a relief teacher.

I never saw him again.

"Oh, I wouldn't know about all that politics or philosophical naval-gazing," the old farmer enjoins.

"All I know is I saw Camus long ago play in goal in the junior team. And I recall he was an exceptional keeper…

I think I must have been…what…twelve years old at the time, working on my Dad's farm. Sneaking off into Algiers whenever I could. Just as you are sneaking off now. Except that I suspect you are heading away from trouble, not towards it."

"I can't imagine what it's like to support a football team your whole life," I muse.

"It's an affliction!" says the old boy.

"An affliction that's been passed down by the father, and cruelly visited on the son.

I inherited love of team from my Dad just like his farm. It all started so full of possibility. Good harvest turned to bad just as goal glut turned to goal drought. Rich pickings followed a meagre time of it as winning streak followed losing streak.

And flashes of genius brought moments of madness in front of goal—silly mistakes. Particularly from our arrogant centre half, Ereban who has tried to play out of goal one too many times while the opposing team are pressing high up on the pitch. What a chump!

With RC Alger you never expect to be on top for long. But I tell you this— it's worth it when you are. It's the best feeling in the world!"

I ask him if he remembers the first time he watched Racing.

"Oh, yes," he enthuses, "how could I possibly forget? Dad took me along to the ground…it was as if he'd given me a shiny new coin. The green of the pitch. So vivid! The neatly tended grass. The pressed shirts with their stripes like those sweets my mother handed out at the end of Eid. All was freshly minted. And so was I…"

I tell him it doesn't change from generation to generation. Because I remember the same. Father taking me into the Stade. That hit of green when we emerged into the stadium bowl.

The old man is inspired by my account.

"I was football mad! I so desperately wanted to follow Camus into the AC side. No question! He was my contemporary and my role model—just a few years older than me, only seventeen and with such promise. A cat between the sticks! I loved watching the juniors at Racing play as much as the first team."

He is happy and glowing with his memories. And his happiness warms me too.

On the way back to Berrouaghia from the city, he offers me dates and arrow-mint tea from a flask. He drops me off outside the town. I thank him, wish his team well—though not against the boys from Hussein-Dey—and continue on foot.

There is a warm Saharan breeze coming from the south. I taste the mineral tang on my tongue.

A gaggle of farm workers pass in the back of trucks; a school bus; a minibus crammed with Sufis; a mullah on a motorcycle; several other vehicles. One armoured car on the opposite side of the road racing towards Algiers; another motorcycle—this one with an Army courier on board—going east. There is no order to the movement of people today. It is a country in flux.

All I know is that this is the eve of the General Strike. And throughout the region, the Army is taking up its positions to keep Algiers open and running.

French Algerians sympathetic to the strike calls are heading in. Those Pieds-Noirs just plain scared of the consequences are trying to flee the city.

Shopkeepers, teachers, municipal workers, gas and electricity workers, postal service workers, indigenous Algerians and FLN supporters are all massing for the big march and the street protests that will inevitably follow.

Warring factions are jockeying for position around Algiers as horses do before the start of a race at the Hussein-Dey track.

The urgent traffic on the road between Sour El-Ghozlane and Berroughia rekindles my recall of the tense stand-off of last night. Captain LeBoeuf's cigar still smouldering in the dish burns my retina. I try to resist the image.

At least twenty minutes have elapsed before I spot the snub nose of a Citroen H van further back down the road. It passes me, slows and stops about fifty metres ahead. I catch up and gently open the passenger-side door.

A European woman with bobbed, flaxen hair is sitting behind the wheel. She peeps out through small thick-framed round glasses. Her face is ageless —she could be anything between twenty-five and forty years old.

"Where are you heading?"

"Sour El-Ghozlane…"

"I am going to Bou Saada. It is on my way. Hop in."

I squeeze into the cabin of the van alongside heavy camera boxes and wires. I spot a projector and an audio recorder. A box of tapes.

If this is a bomb factory on wheels, it is an odd one. And she makes an even odder mujahidat.

She comes out with a question straight away. Its directness and immediacy startle me.

"I assume you go to school?"

"Yes."

"Where?"

"The Lycée René Coty in Medea."

"If you don't mind my asking, why are you not there now?"

"I have been sick." I hold up my carob-stick to emphasise the point.

"Your leg?" she infers.

I nod.

"You are not well enough to go to school, yet here you are walking to Sour El-Ghozlane on a gammy leg…"

My head has cleared since leaving Medea. I have watched the crimson dawn turning golden and the sun coming up over the Atlas. The light breeze from the south has blown some clarity into my head. Maghreb grit has scoured away the dark thoughts that have coated the inside of my skull like blackened crust on a burned pan.

I am not ready for another interrogation. I have had a bellyful of it recently. "Would you stop please. And let me out."

She is taken aback by my reaction.

"Oh, I'm so sorry, I don't mean to pry. It's none of my business really. I just thought with the General Strike you were…"

"Truanting…"

"Well, aren't you…getting to wherever you need to be before the strike starts. A girlfriend perhaps? Before everyone is locked down."

She pulls the car over and I climb out. "Thank you," I say, and start limping away.

She slowly passes me and guns the van up the road.

Some seconds later, I see the brake lights come on again. The vehicle stops. She waits for me to catch up. When I do, I find her leaning across the passenger seat to wind down the window.

"Look, I apologise. I got off on the wrong foot. It's my job getting the better of me, I suppose…I'm not your teacher or parent. I have no right to make you account for yourself…

Let's start again. I promise I won't judge. I won't even talk to you on the way if you don't want me to."

I am still standing there, not budging.

"You won't be able to get far on that leg, you know. So please do let me give you a lift. Come on, hop in. I could use some pleasant company. God knows there's little enough of it about."

I hesitate before pulling myself in to the passenger seat and closing the door behind me. She's right. My leg is sore. The joints are chafing. And the muscles aching. I lean forward to rub my Achilles free of cramp.

She smiles and yanks the gear shift. The van lurches forward.

For several minutes, I am lost to my recollection of the previous evening.

Despite feeling the freedom of the road, the encounter with LeBoeuf has tied me to Algiers. The further I travel away from the capital city, the greater the gravitational pull back towards it.

Having revealed that Ben M'hidi would die at our farmhouse, LeBoeuf swept out of the house, leaving us to process the news in shocked silence. Waleed, of course, was quick to follow his master, the simpering lapdog. Though before they left, Mother had calmly pointed out that it is a major sin for a Muslim to commit suicide.

"You should know it is forbidden in Islamic law. As it is in the Christian religion. That is the settled view of the Qur`an, Sunna, and the consensus of Muslim scholars."

That remark forced an indignant cry from LeBeouf.

"Forbidden? What do you call Jihad then? A picnic?"

He was so enraged that he spattered her face with his spittle.

"If one Algerian Muslim blows himself up in the Casbah, he takes a hundred French with him. One for each virgin who will then greet him in Paradise.

What do you call that if it's not murder by suicide?"

Mother kept her head. "No Muslim will commit suicide with the intention of deliberately escaping this life. No matter how much hurt, stress or fear they are in."

I could detect the pain in her eyes.

"Pah! That's rich," was all LeBoeuf could say.

All the while, I noticed Waleed busily inspecting his shoe leather. Keeping his nose out of it whilst silently scoffing at Mother's remarks. This didn't deter her. It just incited her more.

"If you take a Muslim's life and claim he has taken his own, I guarantee you no one will believe you—no matter whether they are native, French Algerian or Islamist. You will not even convince your own 'Christian soldiers'."

At this, LeBoeuf pushed himself away from the table and rocked back on his chair, scraping the chair-legs on the floor with a shrill screech.

His voice deepened with frustration.

"Would you like to tell that straight to General Massu's face?"

Mother was doing her level best to keep LeBoeuf from turning the house into a chamber of horrors.

She was extremely brave with LeBoeuf yesterday evening. Far braver than I dared to be with him. She has a way of getting under the skin. It has always been far more effective than Father's blunt approach.

Father has blundered into most of life's decisions, come to think of it, driven by appetites and instincts. Mother has always done the right things by us and in a way that has never put us in harm's way. This is what Laurent meant when he said she was too honest to be a good spy.

It was at this point during LeBoeuf's visit that I resolved to find out the truth about Father for myself. After the courage Mother had shown me, I wanted to do something brave for her.

Which is why I am on the road this morning. It is the only way I can know for sure whether Father is dead or alive. And I am heading for the one place I know he could have fled after the bombing. The one place Lieutenant Laurent also knows he could be.

My eye is drawn to the equipment in the van. It looks suspiciously like surveillance apparatus. I cannot resist my curiosity, so I break the silence.

"Are you in surveillance?"

She smiles.

"Military Intelligence?"

She laughs.

"The movies then?"

She nods.

"You could say that, I suppose. More education than entertainment, though."

I scrutinise the cargo in her van.

She has a Leica stills camera, a cine-camera and a UHER tape recorder. Boxes and boxes of photographic prints. Editing kit. And all the paraphernalia required to make and project moving images. A scroll down screen, a sturdy stand.

Behind us, in the cargo area squats a gun-metal grey Dejur eight-millimetre projector surrounded by stacks of wooden chairs. The Dejur is one beast of a machine.

There is just one thing out of place—and it sits between us in the cabin. A baby doll with a feeding bottle in its lap wrapped in a swaddling shawl. I try my best not to notice it, even though its painted eyes are defying me to look away.

"You have some good kit here…" I comment.

"It's an experiment…"

She is happy to leave it at that.

"What experiment?" I enquire, pressing her on it, thinking she must be producing propaganda films for the Army.

She glances across at me, keeping the road ahead in her peripheral vision. "You're exceptionally curious for someone who doesn't want to talk."

I realise that I have been cool towards her. And that I am now being intrusive myself, if not downright suspicious of her. I guess we're now even on that score.

"I'm Shimeun. Shimeun Abu."

She takes one hand off the wheel and extends it towards me.

"Nice to meet you, Shimeun…Eloise…Eloise Marchand…"

We shake.

"That's Ellie to my friends and colleagues at the centre socieaux."

"Ah, the centre socieaux…the one in Bel-Air?" My suspicions evaporate instantly.

"Actually, I have come from St Maur in Oran. You know Bel-Air?"

I can recall a class there. Mother and Father took me along with them just last year. They said I was now a grown-up in the family and insisted I watch this demonstration on a flannel-graph board. The teacher moved little cut-out figures around showing us how to build a basic shack. Father said it would be useful knowledge while we were waiting for a place to become available at the government housing development in Medea.

We are listed for new housing, you see."

I tell Eloise that we are not in a gourbi as featured in the film, or a bidonville like Madame Hachemi. Our farmhouse is granted to us more by the grace and favour of the French Army—but Father told us that any building tips we could pick up could only be a good thing. Particularly if they came courtesy of Governor General Soustelle.

Anything to help Father make our farmhouse more comfortable—to make sure the roof didn't leak and the gas supply was connected.

Mother thought it all part of a French Army ruse to cement the Pied-Noir settlements in Algeria. She mistrusted the centres socieaux almost as much as she did the évolués and colons.

I recall Father saying that the centre socieaux classes were the best way to learn how to insulate the walls of our property so we could keep the heat in during the winter months.

Father lost interest in the course at the centre socieaux and didn't stick with it long enough to find out how to plug the wall cavities—which is why the rats now use that space to build their nests. And why voices now carry around the house through these sound-conducting channels.

I tell Mademoiselle Marchand all of this. She is fascinated—it proves her point.

"That is precisely why we have moved from charts and static presentations to film.

We think perhaps people pay more attention to film and learn faster if we use the moving image. They take more in.

What is it Confucius said about learning?

'Tell me and I'll forget. Show me and I'll remember. Involve me and I'll understand'. Your father is a classic case in point…if you don't mind me saying…"

I tell her I have no illusions about Father's short attention span. I know he is a butterfly, flitting from one distraction to another. No sooner engaged in one task than starting another. And never finishing either. I tell her it drives Mother mad. The house is a permanent work in progress.

"You would call yourself a film-maker then," I suggest.

"It's part of what I do—but I am an educator and communicator first.

I write, shoot film, edit and play the output to classes by way of a learning experience. Writer, Director, Camera operator, Projectionist, Presenter. Aren't I magnificent? A one stop shop!"

She has boundless enthusiasm.

"Oh, and I produce our radio programmes out of Radio Alger too. They say there are better pictures on radio than on film…so we are quite spoilt for choice really…

In fact, I am on my way to the centre socieaux at Bou Saada right now. I am going to show a film and give a talk on how to feed a baby. To a group of new and expectant mothers."

"You are not Pied-Noir?" I ask.

"I am French, Shimeun…"

"Mother thinks the centre socieaux is a part of the fake civilising project of the French. It's a three-card trick to make Algeria subservient."

Out of nowhere, she slaps the steering wheel in frustration.

"Mother thinks? Do you not have a mind of your own, Shimeun? Does everything have to be so fucking political?" she snaps.

I recoil.

She composes herself and places a placatory hand on my arm.

"Sorry."

She gazes silently out at the road ahead. It feels like an eternity before she speaks again.

"I don't mean to take it out on you…It's just that I am tired of being misunderstood and spat at."

"…I really didn't mean to cause you…"

"It can bring me down sometimes—having people put up barriers to new ideas before they've even given them the time of day. And here I am always seeing the best in people—such a blind optimist!"

I feel ashamed. She continues.

"I can assure you I have no mission…we have no mission…other than to educate. Education frees people. And makes them stronger. That is it. Pure and simple."

"That's very noble of you…"

"It's not intended to be. I know what it's like to be on the margins…

I am originally from French Alsace. We will forever be cast as Nazi sympathisers, even though I am French, and my parents had no sympathy for the Vichy government. So, I know what it's like to be outside the tribe. To be misunderstood and caught in the crossfire of ignorance and prejudice."

She pushes her specs higher up on the bridge of her nose so that she can better focus on her argument.

"Education is a universal right. It empowers the poor and gives people hope. And hope is everything in this world."

I wonder how she manages to tread a fine line between the agitators and the enforcers when education is the battleground.

"So, you don't work for the FLN or the Army?"

"Mon Dieu! How many times…? You really are suspicious aren't you…I am not Zohra Drif, you know!

If I serve anyone it is the commonwealth of people, the union of nations. UNESCO. They keep us going, no one else. Their money pays for all of this."

"Have you heard of an Army officer named 'Laurent'? Lieutenant Laurent? He is in military intelligence."

"No. Why?"

"He mentioned you recently."

"Moi?" She feigns a shiver.

"Well, no, not you personally…your organisation. He says you have more influence over the people of Algeria than the Army or FLN could ever dream of. Is that right?"

"I should take it as a compliment, shouldn't I? But in all honesty, it's not saying a lot coming from the Army. They are doing their best to flatten us while the FLN are trying to infiltrate us.

Your Lieutenant Laurent is correct in one respect, though—all sides know we truly have the betterment of the people at heart. Which is what makes us so very vulnerable to attack."

"You know what I think?" I say.

"No. Do tell. I'd be interested to hear."

"I think Algeria needs more people like you."

"That's very sweet of you, Shimeun. Very flattering. If only Governor-General Lacoste would see it the same way."

"He is certainly not Jacques Soustelle…"

"At least Governor-General Soustelle worked with us. Lacoste is the opposite. He undoes all our hard work around the country. And uses General Massu as his wrecking ball."

"Many Algerians mistrusted Soustelle too. My Mother is one of them."

"Ah, there she is—your mother again. People like your mother have been under the impression the centre socieaux is trying to legitimise the colonisation of French culture among Islam.

It is further from the truth than they could possibly know. We cannot win…

To the FLN we are an instrument of the French occupiers, a means to reinforce pacification of the Algerian people…

To the Army of the French Republic, we are a recruiting-sergeant for the FLN, a convenient place to harbour terrorist cells.

In reality our true intentions are nothing more sinister than giving a leg up to people who have nothing so that they can rise above nothing…"

"My mother is a proud woman."

"I don't blame your mother. In fact, I'd very much like to meet her. People like her are perfectly justified in their cynicism. She believes we are hell-bent on cleansing Algeria of its indigenous culture and cementing its status as a Department of France. If I were Arab or Berber, I'd be suspicious of me too…

Where did we go so wrong, Shimeun? If your mother cannot see what we all know in our hearts to be true.

Well, it is for us to prove her wrong by continuing with our work in the most difficult places. It's not people's political viewpoint we want to change. It's their living standards.

That is what success looks like for us. It is our failure that people think we have hidden motives…"

"You are being too hard on yourself…"

"If only…

The truth is we are not doing ourselves any favours. We are indeed susceptible to agitators in our midst. Some of our workers are taking part in the strike tomorrow.

At the moment, we are about as popular as the teachers we work alongside.

We have also refused on principle to go with the Army when they chase the FLN into the Casbah. By rights we should be there to help people deal with the trauma. But it is far too risky at a personal level. Not to mention a threat to public relations.

General Massu can't bear it when we go against his wishes, but our neutrality stops us from going in…and yet the FLN take our staying out as a sign of our support for them…

We are damned if we do and damned if we don't."

I feel impelled to interrupt.

"You must go in. People in the zone interdite are dying on their feet. They are being starved of help. You can see it happening. They need you there."

"You have been into the Casbah yourself recently?"

"Of course. Father supplies…supplied…the souk with wild meat—boar and rabbits and dear-meat from the mountains.

He knows the Casbah well. We have delivered food to whole families who live in holes no bigger than the back of this van here…

Since the bombings at Place Bugeaud and Rue Michelet, police agents have done everything they can to wreck any trade in the Casbah. People are suffering there, Muslim children no older than my little brothers and sister…"

"It's tragic," says Eloise, sighing. "I know the Casbah is crying out for our help. But the FLN are making the place impenetrable. It's the same in the djebels of Kabylia and the Aurès. We cannot reach the children and families there—and if we cannot teach, we cannot function."

The words of my form master, Monsieur Gazides, come back to me. I have learned all about the United Nations General Assembly at school.

"Nation shall speak truth unto nation." Isn't that what they preach at your shiny New York headquarters? Surely you are supported by the most powerful voices in the world?"

"If only that grandiose statement were based on reality.

I hate to disappoint you, but it is not the case with the centre socieaux. Few in Algeria want to speak the truth. And even fewer want to hear it.

We are a very small cog in the whole apparatus of global power. We cannot allow ourselves to take sides or we will lose the little power we have.

General Massu believes we are 'separatist' sympathisers and nationalists.

The so-called free press, 'L'Echo d'Alger', reinforces his lies with false reporting.

They say that we treat FLN wounded in the Casbah with medicines. Quel mensonges!

They report that our medicines are aiding and abetting the fighters, not given freely and in good faith to people as an act of pure human compassion.

They report all this openly but then fail to report that we give medicine to anyone who is wounded, not just the FLN.

Militant Muslims see these acts of kindness as bribes from progressive Christians on a missionary expedition to convert Algeria. And we are targeted by extremists.

Of course, we have all sorts—women, Muslims, Catholic priests, even anti-colonial intellectuals—working alongside us. People of all stripes who happen to be passionate about the Franco-Muslim project.

You may have heard of them. They are prominent members of society. Highly regarded in their own right…Nelly Forget, Father Barthez, André Mandouze…they have no axe to grind, but they have all worked tirelessly to earn the respect of the Muslim population—because it is in Muslim communities that most of the poor reside.

But respect is a poisoned chalice…

If we find ourselves praised by the ALN we are then hated by the French. And the Army want us gone…

One thing is clear—we do not do our highly esteemed neutrality any favours when we are seen to take partisan positions. And within any organisation there are bad apples quite capable of doing so and ruining it for the rest …

I fear for my colleagues with this strike tomorrow. My girlfriend is among them—a teacher at the Ecole Normale of Bouzarea. Alice Reyes. She will not be in at school tomorrow. She will probably be out with her camera…"

"She photographs?" I ask.

"Ah, yes. Try stopping her! I have asked her to stay safe. I will be away in the villages. She will be back in Algiers. Who knows what will happen?

Tomorrow is another country…"

She sinks into private reflection. Mention of those close has brought a series of images to mind. My best friends Christophe and Yerma at school in Medea. Louis. Margot. Mother. Father.

At El-Ghozlane the road diverges. In the town, we pass the café where Father would down a strong black coffee and buy me a soda. I look over as we pass, expecting to see him at a table as he chats with me about the weather in the mountains. But the café is shuttered.

From here, I can see Mansoura rise in the distance. It is magisterial.

At the fork in the road, Eloise pulls the van over to the side. She points up the road to the left.

"I go this way."

"That's me," I say, nodding in the opposite direction.

She reaches down the side of her seat and passes me a plastic box.

"Here. Lunch. A flamiche. I made plenty. There's a hunk of bread in there too."

I am famished and grateful. There is no polite protest from me.

Again, she extends a hand. "Well, Master Shimeun, I wish you and your family all good things in your lives. Take good care of that leg. It looks sore. Oh, hang on…"

She reaches down for a bag at the back of her seat and hands me a card. It bears the name of 'Centres socieaux', her name, the title of 'Directeur' and the address of her head office, the centre socieaux in Oran.

"That's me…"

"Maybe we'll all meet at Bel-Air someday soon," I say.

"I hope so. Then your Father could finish his lesson. Not to mention your house."

"I will keep a look out for Alice for you."

"That would be nice too…"

I slip the card into the pocket of my hunting jacket, open the door and step outside. The warm breeze from the south has given way to a wind off the low Atlas that is starting to bite. I watch the van head away. And I start walking towards Mansoura clutching the lunchbox.

I have little idea of how much ground I am covering. The mountain is one giant optical illusion. A mirage. The further I walk towards it, the further away it is.

I am far from dispirited. The mountain is a beacon and consoles me. I could stare up at it all day long.

I am fortunate that a truck full of Arab farmhands stops for me. One of the team pulls me up into the open trailer alongside them. All is sunny and bright. The mood of the workers too.

The man beside me magics up a seemingly endless supply of cigarettes from under his qeššaba and hands them around to grateful nods of acceptance.

From a small pocket of his goat-hair jacket, a younger man who refuses a cigarette takes a soda bottle half filled with dhoka.

He places a midwhak pipe on the trailer ledge, stuffing the chamber full of green flakes from his bottle. He takes a few puffs before the slit of his mouth broadens into a grin like an Arab crescent. They all sail along on a cloud of euphoria.

Except that for me it all feels off register.

One of the hands—an older man, who I take to be the foreman—glowers at me from under the hood of his qeššaba. I notice him eyeing up the soles of my scratty gym shoes.

"Watch those. Not good for the fields. They will be torn to shreds…"

I thank him for his apparent concern.

"Where are you going?"

"Beyond Dirra. The turning for Koudiat el-Markluf."

"That's quite a way from nowhere…"

"I have business to finish…"

126

"Business, eh? A schoolboy like you?"

"I have field studies…" This is not an outright lie.

You are Arab?"

I nod.

"Berber?"

"On Mother's side."

"But not your father's?"

I now want to tell a lie. But I cannot…I am trapped here in this corner of the trailer…

"It's complicated…" A politician's answer.

"Ah, yes. Compliquée. If I had a dinar for every time an Arab told me that…"

"Well, it is…" I say defiantly.

He spits a gob of brown tobacco at my feet.

"Ask any one of these Arabs here…they don't think it is complicated at all…they think it is dead simple…"

"I suppose so…"

His sudden menace contrasts sharply with the mood of the group—now excited by the distribution of cigarettes.

Lighters are being handed around and fired up. The farmhands are leaning into one other to hear and make themselves heard above the thunderous sound of the truck. They are pressing their kufis to their heads, keeping them from being blown away as the wind buffets them.

Amid the general hubbub, the foreman is gesticulating at me with jabbing fingers.

"This is their land. It has been taken from them by the French and handed to the Pieds-Noirs. Shamefully, some of our Muslim brothers fancy themselves as évolués and have joined the ranks of our oppressors.

As a result, these men around you now work the land for the very people who took it from them in the first place. The Pied-Noir scum.

These men are scarred—some of their friends and loved ones have been forced into containment camps rather than starve. Between the devil and the deep blue sea.

They will be out on strike tomorrow. They cannot afford it. But they will. They know all is at stake. And they have nothing to lose.

Every day the French take their profit, their produce, their livelihoods and their dignity. What do they have left?

Ah yes, their rights!

They were promised equal rights with the Pieds-Noirs.

They fought for the French in two world wars to guarantee those rights…that was the deal.

Then they came home and were dealt nothing but broken promises—famine, disenfranchisement, daylight robbery, massacres…these men have been through it all at the hands of the French…

So, I ask you, how complicated is that? How difficult is that to understand? Compliquée, indeed! Shame on you…and shame on your father…"

I curl up beside the trailer ledge. I am making myself small again. I keep my eyes on the road receding behind us.

This man has not blinked once or taken his eyes off me the whole time I have been squatting here. I want to drift off to sleep, but I must stay awake and alert or I fear he may slide the point of a knife between my ribs.

After a while he slaps the side of the truck twice with his palm. The truck grinds to a juddering halt.

"This is your stop. Go on, get out of here. You are not fit to be in our company." I jump down, my humiliation complete.

The man raps on the side of the truck with a knuckle and it rumbles off up the road. He keeps his eyes trained on me standing by the roadside until the truck is no more. I watch him go.

I then realise, in my haste to escape, I have left the lunch box with the flamiche by the tailboard of the truck.

I sob—I try so very hard not to but cannot help myself. I give way to self-pity. I am all alone out here after all, blubbing like Baby Claude in the void.

I cross the road and trudge up the track. Through a haze of tears, I read the signpost 'Koudiat el Markluf'. I remember this sign—a farmer or hunter has used a blowtorch as a pen and scorched a length of crate-board with lettering in bold strokes.

Crows have used the sign for a latrine. The charred typography is streaked with bird-shit. Some artwork. Some art critics.

The sun is beyond the zenith and is losing its ferocity. There is a slight chill in the air as dusk pushes daylight into the western sky—everything is still except for the feint sound of thunder over the High Atlas. The light is dimming as lowering rain clouds form over the peaks.

I head up the track towards the intersection of hills that marks the start of the gorge. In the crevice between them lies a heavily wooded escarpment, a tangle of maple, tamarisk and brome that thickens as it ascends gently to the brow.

The land is just as I left it, just as I remember it.

I pass by the clearing and stop at the hunter's hide—an improvised brick building that resembles a municipal bus-shelter, draped in moss and clawed by briar. I circle back around and stand a little way off the entrance.

"Father!" I call. The sound is deadened by foliage and undergrowth.

I step inside and wait for my eyes to adjust to the dark, watching for snakes and scorpions.

A horizontal aperture reaching around the building, no deeper than a duckboard, admits a slice of light and a view of the clearing outside.

My foot crunches down on a broken tequila bottle. In one corner lies the remains of a campfire, long extinguished. Next to it is a smattering of dried old coffee grounds, teeming with termites who use it to build their mounds. Cigarette stubs are strewn about and spent matches litter the floor. I prod an empty 'Disque Bleu' pack with the end of my carob stick and use it to flick over the sports page of a twisted, partly singed spread of 'L'Equipe' that has made a handy firelighter.

Two buckets stand in one corner of the hide. One is an improvised latrine, stuffed with the remains of the newspaper.

The other bucket exudes a hellish stink that, even though familiar to me, makes me want to gag.

Thankfully, I know it is not human.

This is where Father disembowelled every boar, slopping its viscera and gore into the bucket. He then buried its heart, lungs and guts deep in the forest to keep the fennecs, wolverines and jackals away from this killing ground.

The walls are covered with graffiti, much of it coarse. Some is aimed at the politicians in France, drawn with faces that look like bum-cheeks blowing speech farts.

One shows General Massu as a pair of balls with a kepi surmounting his proudly standing cock. Another is the star and crescent from the flag of Abdelkader underscored with the words 'Vive Le FLN!'

I cannot imagine Father bothering with any of this. He would have regarded these slogans as a petty indulgence.

I have seen enough and step outside.

I shout for Father again, though I know in my heart that there is as much chance of him emerging from the treeline as a Pashtun tribesman.

It takes me half an hour to crest the hill.

It's well worth the climb. It always was for the view that lay beyond.

Each time I went up there with Father in pursuit of his quarry, I was rewarded with the sight of paradise.

I liken it to those moments I recounted to the old farmer on my way here—when Father took my hand, leading me up the steps through the drab stands of the Stade 20 Août into the stadium bowl, where the striped cut of the newly mown playing surface would pop against the grey in all its lush green glory.

The floor of the gorge gradually reveals itself to me in the same way. A sward of vivid colour that makes me gasp.

The stream through the ravine is a race of tumbling crystals in the late afternoon sunlight. The pale shadows of clouds traverse the valley sides—the fleeting ghosts of long-held memories casting their spell on the scene.

The gorge descends from the east and narrows into the ravine. Here is where Father killed the fallow deer with one swift body-shot. Here is where I discovered how thin the skein is between life and death. Here is where the dead dear weighed heavily on my shoulders, where I marvelled at the stars as Father snored with his bottle of tequila nestling under his arm in his old canvas bivouac. Here is where, on those bright, moonlit nights, I found my own personal god.

The Arab foreman was right. I am not fit to hold their company. I have always kept my own. Just as I have kept my own god like Father keeps his cards, close to my chest—closer in fact, so close that nobody else knows about it. Not even Mother. Especially not Mother.

It is the one ineffable thing I possess. If anyone else could describe it, they would take it from me. But this is the single thing that nobody else can take from me, no one else can own. The thing that no secrets and lies can destroy. This is my god. The god I have created. The god who has created me.

I sink to my knees at the impossible beauty of what I am seeing. I call out once again as if from the highest minaret in the world.

"Father!"

My voice comes back to me in rippling echoes.

"Father!"

I am desolate. The loneliest boy in the universe.

I pick myself up and skirt the valley edge looking for a place of shade to stop and rest my aching leg.

Some fifty yards off the path, I notice the cork oak where Father stopped to relieve me of the dead dear that day. Its boughs offer plenty of shade.

I notice I am not alone.

A line is hanging plumb to the cork oak looped around a thick bough at one end and weighted at the other.

It's as if the tree has dropped its line in the ravine and caught an animal carcass.

I am sure I see the dead weight jump, but then again it could be a tick in my tired eyes.

I draw closer. I hear the blood racing in my inner ear.

I can now see that the head of the animal is set at an oblique angle.

I come closer. It is a torso.

With a three quarters view of the head, even at this distance, I see that the neck is broken, and the skin split by a red gash. Around it is a purplish hue. The face is puffed and bloated in death.

"Father!" I shout and rush to put my arms around the lower legs of his stiff body, trying to raise him up and create some slack in the rope.

But these are not the boots, the uniform or the heft of Father. And it is far too late to help.

I look up into the face of the hanging man.

It is not Father's dead eyes staring blankly out at the ravine...but the eyes of Lieutenant Laurent.

Part Two
Ben M'hidi

Au Bon Marché Département Store,
The European Quarter, Algiers,
28 January 1957

'Fellow Citizens of Algiers and France! Rejetez cette grève! Go back to your shops. Go back to your schools. Go back to your hospitals, your offices, your warehouses, your depots, your building sites, your cranes, your docks. Do not betray your country. It is your duty to go to work. It is your Département.

Keep your Département open. Keep your Département running. Keep your Département alive…if you know of anyone withholding their labour, it is your civil responsibility to report them to the Prefecture of Police.'

There is a number to call. The notice is signed by the Governor-General Robert Lacoste.

I cannot process a single word on this sheet of paper. Nothing is going in. All I feel is the blind panic rising through my belly, up through my diaphragm, puncturing my heart, constricting my neck, inflaming my eyes.

And I am tired. Dog-tired. The last thirty-six hours have hollowed me out completely.

If it were not for my personal god, I would have given up the ghost by now.

I would have cut a deal with LeBoeuf that he could do whatever he wanted with me provided that he finished me off quickly.

You see, since I arrived here, I have been gripped by the idea that LeBoeuf has brought me up to this roof—via some dingey back stairwell—to throw me off it. Not just to torture me with the thought of the drop.

He has done nothing to convince me otherwise. He has even held me by the scruff of my neck at forty-five degrees out over the parapet, perpendicular to the angled flagpole and tricolour. He has kept me hanging there, insisting that I stare down into the abyss of the Rue d'Isly five floors below. A torn collar or loose footing and I would be dead meat on the pavements of Algiers.

My hands have been cuffed behind my back all this time. And we are a hundred feet up. My single overriding thought has not been to save myself. No, I have gone beyond that point.

Rather, I have it in my head that I could not bear to swallow dive to the pavement below without being able to stretch out my arms and somehow break my fall—no matter how ridiculous a notion that may seem.

This idea has scrambled time. I do not have a clue how long I have been up here waiting. Or even what day it is. I could swear I have held my breath throughout as if I am five fathoms below the waterline, not five storeys above street level.

What escaped me then and strikes me now is that death and torture are indivisible. And it is happening to me. Not to others. Not this time. But to me.

There is one thing I do know in the meantime. I have soiled myself. A cloying slush has pooled in my underpants and the area around my crotch feels sticky and warm.

The sound of the helicopter and the sight of the leaflet shower fills me with barely disguised relief. And I resist the urge to release the remaining contents of my bowels as my muscles relax for the first time today.

I now know I am here because Captain LeBoeuf wants to show me something majestic to behold, not to throw me off the edge of a five-storey building.

And there it is, moving steadily over the rooftops of the European quarter. Aussaresses' hovering bird of death in the sky.

This time, though, it is not casting the bodies of agitators to the winds, but paper.

I can breathe again. I have trusted to that god of mine and once again he has come through for me.

In the open belly of the helicopter above, I spot an airman crouched beside the door-gunner. He is casting batches of leaflets down onto the European quarter.

Each sheet of paper seesaws down into the broad avenues and boulevards below.

LeBoeuf delights in the reams of litho-pressed foolscap sawing the air and drifting into the canyons of Algiers. This time his target is not the Viet Minh in their foxholes but his fellow countrymen on their way to work.

He thrills to the sight of a combat helicopter. To LeBoeuf, Indochina is so very far away, but also very, very close.

He greets the fall of paper as a child does its first fall of snow. He turns his head to the sky, closes his eyes and feels the breath of the rotors against his skin like the chill air coming off the High Atlas.

Two paratroopers from his unit are with him. They stand at a respectful distance as their captain dreams of snow angels as he spread eagles in a bed of propaganda pamphlets.

So LeBeouf is not going to do away with me after all.

He is here to teach me a lesson. And I am here to take it.

He doesn't just want to punish me for absconding from the farmhouse yesterday and making fools out of his elite para guard.

He is determined to show me how the might of French willpower, let alone its firepower, sweeps all in its path. And how pointless it is for me to go against the grain of history.

He has choreographed this operation around the city on this first morning of the General Strike using his elite paras. I am not so vain as to think that he has laid this spectacle on especially for me. But he has certainly handed me a front-row ticket.

LeBoeuf snatches the leaflet back off me. I am numb and all I see is a jumble of words. He thinks I am taking too long to read it.

"It is not fucking Proust! You are not looking at an exam paper! It is a simple edict. In the form of an open letter to our citizens from their Governor-General."

He folds it and inserts it into his pocket.

Despite this scratchiness, LeBoeuf looks pleased with himself. He pivots on his heels and steps forward to look down onto the city. He leans casually against the metal 'C' of the sign that spans the right-angle of the rooftop and that dominates the streets below.

Another flurry of leaflets is falling from the Vertol H-21 over the European quarter. Its rotors send a downdraft that contrarily whips up the paper in a whirling vortex and then scatters it to all corners. Some leaflets land on the fallow ground of roof-tops, the tops of bus shelters and kiosks. Most carpet the streets. Many people deliberately ignore them. A few pick up the leaflets and glance at them. Some drop them, some screw them up into paper balls and discard them, others pocket them so they can take a furtive glance later. But everyone notices them.

LeBoeuf is encouraged by this.

"See that black-foot with the umbrella scurrying off to work? Our literature has made him think. The French government has no sway with the people on the streets. They know something our flaccid National Assembly does not. We are the de facto government here. The Army is the only steady hand of France in Algiers. And we will bust this strike wide open. This is General Massu's wish. This is my command."

At mention of the word 'command', LeBoeuf steps back smartly to exchange words with his Lieutenant. He summons a signals officer standing close by and speaks over a field radio. He gives an order urgently but expressed in a low tone that I cannot hear.

He paces towards me, pauses and takes in the whole giant sign, which he reads backwards and in reverse.

"Au...Bon... Marché...Paris," he declares, "This is Mecca for the colons."

Below, the Rue d'Isly is awash with leaflets. From where we stand, we can hear voices bubbling up from the pavements below. But they are still muted. It is too early for the assembling strikers to reach their critical mass.

LeBoeuf can't wait to see more people down there trampling on the carpet of paper—treading all over the French rule book. He knows it will give him licence to tread all over them in return.

The shops are not yet open. But he has a plan to thwart the strike, no doubt rubber-stamped by Jacques Massu's council of war. He, Roger Trinquier and Raoul Salan carving up the strike-breaking and spoiling tasks between them. This shower of propaganda is clearly just the start.

"Come!" he says "I want you to see this."

I try to disguise my relief as he leads me down the stairs from the roof. I am still alive, still breathing.

We enter the main store. It is eerily quiet.

This is the first time I have been inside Au Bon Marché.

I have been told unofficially it is off limits to Harkis and 'people of my persuasion'. But that is more Mother warning me not to be seduced by the luxury goods or put myself in places where I stand out and can attract the unwelcome attention of the Pieds-Noirs.

She sees the department store as part of the Frenchman's plan—'la mission civilisatrice'. She has urged me to stay away lest I find myself under the spell of the young ladies on the Lancôme counter. They are the sirens with made up faces, luring the unwary onto the rocks of European decadence.

I have told her not to worry, I am not that shallow. But the truth is her words have stuck.

Up until just this morning, when I was frogmarched off the street and through the side door of the store, I hadn't dared set foot inside this emporium of earthly delights.

Now that I have been brought down from the roof, I begin to appreciate the charms of the place.

Au Bon Marché has the appearance of a politely ransacked palace. It sparkles and gleams with store fittings and fixtures, all polished wood and glass, though most of the more expensive goods have been taken from the shop floor and put safely under lock and key in the storerooms. Much to Captain LeBoeuf's chagrin.

I blink at the vast swathes of floor space. The shiny counter tops, the strangely posed mannequins in the 'Département de vêtements pour les dames et pour les messieurs.' A kaleidoscope of legs, busts, feet and arms.

LeBoeuf moves swiftly past them all. Fashion is not his concern.

"I have discussed the situation with the general manager here. I have told him that if he fails to get his staff to work this morning within two hours of opening time, the Army will commandeer the premises in the name of the Governor-General and we will use them as bureaux of state."

We quickly descend through the floors as he talks.

"And we don't want to see precious staff time used up guarding the stock-rooms when they should be out here on the shop-floor. We need them to do what they do best. Sell. Retour au travail rapide!"

We pass display-cases, displaying nothing more than studded, padded satin stands where the luxury linen and jewellery would hang. Shelves yawn at us where stocks of Egyptian cotton shirts should be. Clothes racks are exposed, their steel spines stripped of camel-hair coats and Italian suits.

We reach the ground floor where LeBoeuf indicates a store-guide.

Alimentation, hygiène, layette, verrerie, musique, électricité, mercerie, mode, papeterie, cordonnerie, confiserie, bonneterie, parfumerie, jouets, quincaillerie, bijouterie, ménage, sport"

He savours every word.

"All you could possibly desire under one roof…Ah, this is the colonials' catechism. Their sacrament. Isn't this why Zola called it 'a cathedral of commerce'?"

I look at him blankly.

"Well, you tell me, powder monkey. You're the student among us."

He reads a promotional poster out loud as he passes.

"…*on trouve tout cela et bien d'autres choses encore dont la qualité est sélectionnée et la valeur incontestable…*"

"Who would have thought it. All this verbiage devoted to things. Things! Things to wear. Things to eat. Things to show off. These things are indispensable to those who desire a better life. So, I ask you. What black-foot would give up all of this to join the FLN in their shitty communes?"

We have reached the ground floor at a breathless pace. I look around and take in the whole store. I am transported.

Tester trays with their delicate air puff samplers in the perfumerie. Transparent cabinets stuffed full of cut-glass bottles and fancy boxes—forming a brickwork of summer colours, teal, mustard, lilac. I breathe in the heady scent of cedar wood, musk and bergamot.

A frieze along the far wall of the perfumerie adorned with lettering in cursive Gothic type announces 'Entrez dans la Reine de Saba'. There is an Egyptian-looking Queen, a beautiful woman with a shiny black bob and long eyelashes. She wears a silver basque, garter belt and seamed silk stockings, her forehead encircled with a jewel-encrusted tiara, hall-marked and signed 'Cartier'. She is reclining on an ornamental royal barge decorated with gilded curtains amid a bed of exotic pillows and silver drapes.

A diamanté armlet encircles her raised arm. The back of her hand is placed under her chin, languorously stroking her throat with a finger as she admires a muscular oarsman standing above her. He wears nothing more than the mask of Anubis and a loin cloth, his arms exotically tattooed with the hieroglyph of a roaring lion, a Barbary ape and an asp.

A preening gold peacock fans its feathers in the prow of the boat, bearing the insignia 'Van Cleef and Arpels'. The Queen luxuriates in a bower of flowers and stacked gift boxes, emblazoned with brand names. Louis Vuitton. Dior. Hermes.

I am transfixed.

LeBoeuf is unmoved. He pushes me along and I totter in front of him.

"I guarantee you, within five minutes of the French Army leaving these premises, those FLN agitators will be in here looting…I know human nature. Well, I tell you, part of me thinks 'let them!' If they give me cause to shoot them, so be it. The tenth para are born to do that very job."

He leads me towards the back of the store where an officer stands guard. The officer salutes LeBoeuf, unlocks the door and pushes it open for us. We step out into a side passage where a convoy of armoured cars awaits us, standing nose to tail.

The vehicle nearest us with its door agape is surmounted by a large loudspeaker system. Four loudspeakers directed to all points of the compass— rigged to a squawk-box and an intercom inside.

"Get in!" LeBoeuf shouts indicating the open door of the vehicle. I climb inside. He signals at the officer attached to the lead vehicle to move off, making a circling gesture in the air with his forefinger.

"Lieutenant Mauritz! Wagons roll!" he shouts, channelling his best John Wayne, as he dumps himself on the seat next to me. I feel the thick muscle of his girded shoulder press against my bones.

The interior smells rancid—of diesel, sweat and fear. I am surrounded by soldiers, by heavy pulleys and chains. It is gloomy inside, a thick wire-mesh screen between us and our driver. A giant winding motor sits in the back, a hawser spooled around it.

LeBoeuf is excited. He goes to pull out a cigar from his jacket pocket, then thinks twice about it.

It can wait. It should wait. He will keep it as his reward. Anyway, for the next few minutes his hands and mouth will be occupied with something far more satisfying.

"I want you to see this because I want your father to know that I take no prisoners!"

I shiver at the mention of Father. I note again that LeBoeuf thinks he is still alive.

We swerve right onto Rue d'Isly.

LeBoeuf takes the open letter from the Governor-General that he stuffed into his camo pocket back up on the roof of the department store. He lifts an intercom from a mounting in front of him and pushes a red button on its side. A shrill burst of ear-piercing feedback floods the interior.

He reads aloud from his cheat sheet—the open letter from the Governor-General—and I immediately hear his ripe baritone boom outside the car and further out across the city.

This is his moment, his platform. He is a natural with a delivery that demands attention.

He savours every word like a good cigar, making every phrase his own—the rounded vowels, the sibilants.

He has learned to be bellicose in speech. Somehow, he manages to find glottal stops in a language and in sentences where none exist and fires them off like bullets. Plosives pepper his invective. It is not silky. It is not usual. But it is unsettling, compelling and effective.

Algiers is now his drill-square and its citizens his raw recruits.

"Chers citoyens d'Alger et de France! Rejetez cette grève! Retournez dans vos magasins. Retournez dans vos écoles. Retournez dans vos hôpitaux, vos bureaux, vos entrepôts, vos dépôts, vos chantiers, vos grues, vos quais. Ne trahissez pas votre pays. C'est votre devoir d'aller travailler. C'est votre Département. Gardez votre Département ouvert. Gardez votre Département en marche. Gardez votre Département en vie…si vous connaissez des grévistes, il est de votre responsabilité civile de les signaler à la préfecture de police."

The convoy swings left onto a tree-lined boulevard—Rue Michelet. The cars halt outside a row of steel-shuttered shop fronts set back into the elegant facade.

LeBoeuf leaps out and ushers me to follow. I jump down and stand by his side.

"See these. All of these?" He nods towards the shop fronts. "What do you see? Come on, powder monkey! What do you see?"

"I see shops…"

"Yes, yes. And? What kind of shops? That's what I want to know…"

I hesitate, thinking he is trying to catch me out. Any excuse to put a bullet in my head.

"…une papeterie…"

142

"Come on!" he bullies.

"…une bijoutiere…un buraliste…un magasin de meubles."

"Wrong, wrong, wrong…and wrong again. Don't look at the shop-signs. Look at the signs on the shutters. What do they say?"

I squint across the front of the armoured car—at the one of the notices taped to the papetiere's steel shutter. I find it difficult to read.

"Come on. What does it say?"

I squint some more and just about make out the words.

"Fermé jusqu'à nouvel ordre."

"Ah! There you have it…Now you know what type of shops these are…These are closed shops. Shuttered. Shut. Fermé…

These shops are run by gutless cowards, citizens of France who would abandon their posts at the first whiff of cordite…these are the lily-livered of Algiers who kowtow to the FLN and cave in at the slightest provocation.

This, powder monkey, is an abomination. Look! It's the same with every shop in this row. They are in league with one another! Each one of these shopkeepers has served notice to their customers that the shop will be shut today until further notice—which means, for the duration of the General Strike, they are playing right into Ben M'hidi's hands."

He spits on the ground and calls for his Lieutenant.

"Lieutenant Mauritz, you may begin…"

Without hesitation, Lieutenant Mauritz runs along the line of armoured vehicles hammering on their sides.

"That man, Ben M'hidi. Another spineless pimp who won't even have the balls to turn up to his own General Strike…a no-show at his own party! Ha! He makes everyone else do the silly dance except himself. The fuckwit…" adds LeBoeuf, contemptuously.

Soldiers are dispersing and busily setting about their orders. LeBoeuf pushes me back under the boughs of a pollarded tree so that the drivers don't reverse over me.

"Watch, powder monkey…"

The drivers of the armoured cars do three-point turns and back them up to the shop fronts. It is a triumph of synchronised driving.

LeBoeuf's men fling open the rear doors, yank on the chains and attach hawsers to the handles of the steel shutters.

The engines choke into action as the winding mechanisms start cranking up. The chains tighten and strain. The armoured vehicles buck slightly. Then, with one synchronised, deafening crunch, all the shutters detach themselves from their fixings at once. Their metallic screech sends magpies scrambling skywards from the Boulevard as the shutters are ripped from their bearings and dragged into the street. A few shop windows crack and shatter.

Almost immediately, startled faces, still pale from sleep, appear at upstairs windows. LeBoeuf gives them a mocking wave and a cursory salute.

"See those people hanging from their windows? They may live above the shops, but they are not necessarily the owners…Although I'd hazard a guess some of them may be landlords.

If so, what are the odds they will already be calling their commercial tenants with the news that their precious stock is now exposed to looters?"

I notice that the faces have gone from the windows as quickly as they appeared, like timid sparrows peeking out from their nests at a marauding flock of starlings.

"You see, having the security shutters removed is a threat to the whole building. Everyone who lives here is now involved in the outcome. So, I guarantee you the shopkeepers will be here in a shot."

He chooses this moment to light his cigar.

In what seems like a few seconds, the residents start to emerge from doors at street level clamouring for an explanation. Some are half-dressed for the day, others still in nightgowns, dressing gowns and pyjamas.

LeBoeuf's men contain them, pushing them back against the walls with their batons.

"Calm down and go back inside!" shouts LeBoeuf, "Haven't you seen a shop opening up before?"

The residents are vexed by LeBoeuf's casual impertinence.

A man shouts 'You have no right…"

Another "What do you mean by this? The people who own these shops are fine, law-abiding people. They pay their rent, on time. They pay their taxes to France. They are trying to make a living. This is criminal damage."

"Worse," shrieks an elderly lady, "It is intimidation. You are Nazis!"

LeBoeuf is rattled by the comparison.

"Go back inside now. Or I shall forcibly remove you and have you arrested on a charge of civil disobedience. I mean it! I am not fucking about with you people."

The residents are shocked but comply. LeBoeuf may bark more than he bites but you underestimate him at your peril. In that voice is a caustic grit—an unsettling guttural menace. It is a voice well-suited to both the streets under martial law and the barrack room.

He takes a quick glance at his watch.

"Give it fifteen minutes and the shopkeepers will come scuttling back to their workplaces from the suburbs.

We must give them a little latitude. Some will no doubt be travelling in from Hussein-Dey and Bouzzareah. On the first day of the General Strike it won't be easy, but it's still early enough to avoid the delays."

Now LeBoeuf's men form a line with their backs to the shop fronts. He sits on a street bollard, arms folded, legs crossed, savouring his cigar while he awaits the shopkeepers' arrival.

It is clear to me how all strike-breaking actions on this day across the whole city pivot around him. He has the self-possession of a man destined to orchestrate proceedings—even those outside his immediate supervision. He is totally in command of the tenth para and his brief, wherever his men operate in the city today.

And then, as if from nowhere, he asks the spring-loaded question.

"So, did you find your father yesterday?"

The question bounces around my head. This is where my interrogation truly starts.

Not on the roof. Not in El-Biar or the police station. But here, on the side of a Boulevard in the European quarter for all to see.

I say nothing. LeBoeuf sighs.

"Congratulations! Yesterday morning, you managed what few have done. To give the tenth para the slip.

I have cautioned those officers on watch and they were none too happy you put them in the dog-house. If I know them, I've no doubt they had something to say to you about that. Did you find that was the case?"

I rub my shoulder without thinking. But it's the answer he's looking for.

"Come on, powder monkey. You are a rank amateur at deception. Both you and I know you went to search for your old man."

He waits for my response, though none comes.

"You didn't find him, though, did you? If you had done, you wouldn't be here. You would still be hiding out somewhere in the hinterland with him!"

He is playing with me. He leaves me in no doubt that he already knows the answers to his own questions.

"No, you're right. I didn't find him."

"So what did you find?"

I have Lieutenant Laurent's puffy death mask and lolling tongue in my head. It is so clearly defined in my mind's eye that I wonder if somehow the image of it has projected itself onto LeBoeuf's retina and he can now see it too. I think of telling him about my gruesome find, but I am still protecting Father, the murderer.

"I found nothing."

"No trace?" LeBoeuf asks. "Just nothing…"

LeBoeuf leaves it at that. But I know he will return to the theme now that he has me. I am convinced I too will become one of the 'disappeared' by the day's end.

LeBoeuf is right. Ten minutes later, a middle-aged man in a moth-eaten kepi—the owner of the tabac—is the first of the shopkeepers to make an appearance. A young couple pull up in a Peugeot, aghast. Another lady in a housecoat and apron, armed with a bucket full of cleaning agents and a mop, is patiently asking LeBoeuf's men to stand aside so that she can enter her papeterie.

The man in the kepi remonstrates with LeBoeuf.

"Are you not ashamed to wear the badge of the tenth para?" he says, jabbing a finger at LeBoeuf's beret.

I rarely hear LeBoeuf challenged. I know to my cost what happens to those who do. But the Captain approves of the man correctly identifying the regimental insignia.

The proud veteran clearly does not intend any flattery whatsoever.

"You are here to represent the French, yet by ripping the shutters off our shops, you are tearing the guard-rails off our democracy. You are not fit to wear that badge. I fought in Italy with the French Army. And look what you are doing in its name."

LeBoeuf steadies himself. He must not go at this fellow too soon. He can pick off the man without too much effort and it would be almost indecent to take down such a soft target with such apparent ease.

"Whatever I do, I do in the name of France…and I put the question straight back at you, sir. What are you doing besmirching the honour of the nation you served so heroically with this cowardly action?"

"What 'action'?"

"The action of closing your shop. And on this day of all days."

"Of all days? What do you mean? A General Strike has been called, man. Do you think anybody will have a mind to shop on this day? The streets are snagged with razor wire. No one can move. It will be pandemonium out here. I am protecting my property and my stock. I am safeguarding my livelihood as a proud citizen of France. Something you and your men clearly have scant regard for."

LeBoeuf has heard enough. He is fully primed and ready to attack.

"You are siding with the communist agitators."

This comes as a body blow to the stout veteran. He staggers under its force. He starts to show small signs of weakening.

"I am doing n-nothing of the sort."

LeBoeuf has registered the slight stammer. He will now open the man up.

"The FLN rely on people like you to keep their phoney war alive."

The veteran recoils.

"How dare you! I am no more a s-supporter of the FLN than you are."

LeBoeuf parries.

"And yet here you are, paying homage to their strike action. If you are not a collaborator then you are a dunderhead. Do you not get it? By staying closed, you are marching behind the banner of the FLN. Because it is their express wish that you stay shut. There is no question about that."

For a moment, I think the veteran is about to suffer a heart attack. LeBoeuf is relentless. Another volley comes flying in.

"The plain fact is, if you close your shop, you betray your fellow French citizens. …Have you not read this morning's notice to go to work from the Governor-General…It is all over the city. How can you possibly have missed it? You are blind if you have missed it. A blind cunt as well as a treacherous one."

I can see the veteran's eyes well up. Never before has his loyalty or patriotism been brought into question like this. He is faltering now. Finding speech harder.

"F…four times we tried…t…to break through the G-Gustav line. Four times! On the fourth occasion, we did it! We made that bridgehead at Mmm-Monte Cassino…and you ac-cuse me of treachery to France?"

Mention of the man's war record glances off the Captain. He is not going to be played by him. He won't let a veteran of the Second World War pull out the 'fought-for-my-country, nearly-died-for-my-country' card.

"You are Algerian by birth, non? You wear the very best in black French footwear—from 'Aubercy of Paris', no doubt—to conceal your true colours. You are a man who professes to love France through-and-through, but you bend to the will of these terrorists at the first whisper of wind."

"B-but I am F-French."

"Then p-p-prove it!"

The mimic LeBoeuf has his man exactly where he wants him. His words have the desired incendiary effect.

"It's outrageous. I will put in a c-compensation claim to the Governor-General…and your superiors will hear about this."

"You c…c…" LeBoeuf snarls, "c-count yourself lucky the Governor-General does not come after you for compensation…

…You are a disgrace to the tricolour…"

Far be it from LeBoeuf to fire off single rounds when he can strafe the man with his invective.

"…Anyway, you have no choice but to work in your shop, you cowardly cunt. You have no security shutters to speak of and if you leave the stock unattended, you will risk losing it to looters. Now that you are here, I insist you open for business. Or fuck you, you tirailleur, I will ram your shutters so far up your arse your eyes will be shuttered forever.

My men will be making regular patrols today. Do not try to deceive them. Or you will face certain imprisonment. Open your shop for the sake of liberté, égalité, fraternité."

The man is reeling, practically incoherent with anguish.

"And the d-d-damage? It will take me t-two days trading to make up for the loss, the c-cost to my b-business from the criminal damage you've done to my security screen."

"You don't fool me," LeBoeuf retorts, "I know you Pieds-Noirs with your bourgeois pretensions out there in Hussein-Dey. With your tidy houses and smarmy-arse kaffir-tended gardens. You've got enough dinar to cover the damage. In fact, I think I'll come around to your place soon to collect for having saved your business. Reckon you owe me commission…"

The man is inconsolable.

"For crying out loud, I can't afford it."

"Then you had better start working right now so you can…"

"Comme Dieu est mon témoin, you've not heard the last of this…"

"On the contrary, my friend. My word is final. This is the last word on it. Good day to you!"

LeBoeuf signals to his men to disband. They climb aboard the vehicles. He throws his cigar at the poor man's feet, crushes the stogey under his heel, pushes me in ahead of him, jumps in and the convoy moves off. Through the heavily scratched window and the webbing, I watch the other shopkeepers trying to console the tabac owner.

The veteran stands lost with sunken shoulders and arched back. Mission accomplished. LeBoeuf has broken him.

The Captain is in buoyant mood. Jovial even.

"We need to make a few examples of these Pieds-Noirs. Even the loyal ones are prone to waver…"

We pass along the Boulevards and Avenues where LeBoeuf repeats his mantra over the loudspeaker.

"Rejetez cette grève!"

We sweep past other shopfronts with their crumpled shutters left for scrap metal on the pavements, the shopkeepers surveying the wreckage as they fret about how they are going to survive the day.

We cross over to the Zone Autonome d'Alger in the Casbah where crowds are beginning to assemble. The convoy slows as it finds itself in the thick of the throng. A few forward souls batter on the vehicles, spitting on the armour as we pass. LeBoeuf is careful not to create an incident as he watches them from behind his mobile carapace. He is mindful of the fact that there are as many friends to the French here as there are enemies.

"Ben M'hidi is out there in those streets. Somewhere. Four hundred thousand Muslims in the ZAA. And yet it's just a few king rats who carry this plague around the whole population. Ben M'hidi and his cronies. Pimps.

Swindlers. Conmen and crooks like Bud Abbot. And their sympathisers in the wider community..."

He looks me straight in the eye.

"Maybe I should add you and your father to that list, perhaps? Maybe you have gone over to the other side too. We will know very soon. Either that or never."

I don't know what he means by this. I am just hanging on—grateful that my life has been spared up to this point. Although I know it is not a reprieve, more a stay of execution.

"This is where I say 'adieu'. I have my scouting to do here in the Casbah. Lieutenant Mauritz will accompany you to your next stop. He is a good man. A graduate of Saint-Cyr like me. We Cyriens stick together."

LeBoeuf opens the door and jumps down. He addresses me from outside the car.

"Congratulations, powder monkey. You are now part of our 'collection service'. I am sure that your old form-master, Gazides, will be delighted to know that. I wish I were around to see it for myself. I could do with some light relief, but as you can see, I have my hands full here."

And with that, LeBoeuf is gone.

We wait.

Lieutenant Mauritz climbs in beside me, gives a brief instruction to the driver and the armoured vehicle peels off from the convoy, heading for the outskirts of the city.

As we make the turning off the highway south, I know that I am not going home to Medea. To Mother, Baby Claude, Louis and Margot.

Instead, I find that we are heading towards El-Biar.

My stomach drops. My throat dries and tightens.

Some thirty minutes later, we turn into a drive past a gatehouse manned by paratroopers. I see the name proudly displayed on a plaque screwed to the stone gatepost—'Villa Tourelle'.

The driver draws up in the outer courtyard of the old colonial villa.

A man I assume to be Aussaresses' adjutant is there to salute and shake the hand of Lieutenant Mauritz. One administrator to another.

Lieutenant Mauritz disappears into the building.

So, this is it. This is my end.

I wait to be taken inside to my interrogators.

The driver stands by the door as I sit and wait to be 'processed'.

But no one comes for me.

Nothing happens.

I try to free my mind.

My thoughts take me back to yesterday—the ravine at Koudiat el Markluf, to the cork oak tree and the hanging corpse of Lieutenant Laurent.

I didn't know what to do.

What could I do?

I had no knife to cut his body down. I had nothing to dig with so that I could bury him deep enough to prevent the scavenging animals rooting him out and devouring his carcass.

My leg was a mess. I was suffering a deep neural ache from my buttocks to my toes. I could no more shimmy up the tree and untie the noose than climb the Eiffel Tower and place a tricolour on the mast.

I calculated and decided to leave Laurent there.

In time, I figured the crows would pick his bones clean of flesh. But I also thought that somehow this would be the best way to honour a free spirit like Laurent.

After all, I knew there would be few chasseurs passing through the hunting grounds at this time of year. Laurent's corpse may hang undiscovered for months, by which time the French Army would surely have caught up with Father. Then he would confess to Laurent's murder and lead his interrogators to the bones of the hapless Lieutenant.

Again, I was seized by a wave of anger and betrayal. Father had done for Lieutenant Laurent—and in such a brutal manner.

I felt sympathy for the Lieutenant who was doing his job.

Deep down I believed in Laurent.

He wanted to guarantee Father's safety in return for information. He would have helped us out of this mess, I was sure of it.

Father had wilfully destroyed the only lifeline we had—a way out of Algeria to France and a future for Mother and the family.

It seemed such a senseless act.

The good Lieutenant Laurent—he probably had a family back home too, just like ours. He was probably also trying to do the best by them.

Well, at least I had seen him off with a prayer to my personal god before leaving him to rot. It was not much, but it was something.

It had been quite some trek back to the highway from the cork tree. A real slog, but thankfully a downhill one. On my way, I decided to take one last look inside the hunter's hide. I checked the date on the discarded copy of 'L'Equipe'. 19th January 1957. That would tally with the Courvois killings and the bombing of Place Jean Paul Sartre, with Father's subsequent escape, my confession to Laurent and his tracking down of Father.

I concluded, with the exception of Lieutenant Laurent, Father would have been the last person here in this killing ground.

Once I'd reached the highway, I wanted to sit down rather than walk. Dusk was approaching and the flow of traffic had thinned.

But I feared if I sat on the ground, I'd want to close my eyes and never wake up.

I propped myself up on my carob stick, waiting stiffly and silently for any sign of traffic on the near-deserted highway, eventually managing to wave down the driver of a tanker heading northbound.

It wasn't easy—I launched myself into his path, giving him the fright of his life and forcing him to brake suddenly.

I was fortunate not to be smashed head-on by that cheese-grater of a grille on the front of his driver's cab. Had he not been so alert, it would have shredded me.

The driver ranted at me. But I didn't care. I told him I wouldn't move off the road until he agreed to take me.

It was more trouble for him to throw me onto the verge and he reluctantly offered me a lift.

He told me that he was heading back to the Oran refinery having made his deliveries in the south. I said that was good for me and I drifted off to sleep.

I dreamt feverishly.

I dreamt that Lieutenant Laurent and the Doctor were walking me around the cloisters of the Trinitarian hospital.

Laurent appeared as an elongated figure with a broken neck.

We were characters in a movie I had crept in to see with Verna at the Algiers picture-house earlier last year—one of the only places in the European Quarter we could spend a few hours unseen.

In my dream, I was playing the Kevin McCarthy part in 'Invasion of the Body Snatchers'. I was being restrained by orderlies in the sanitorium as I appealed to the doctor.

"Doctor. Will you stop these fools? I'm not crazy! Listen to me. Please listen. If you don't…If you won't…If you fail to understand, then the same incredible terror that's menacing me will strike in you!"

Laurent was voicing over my dream. His voice was strangulated, of course. More a pinched gurgle. His larynx was crushed, after all, and he was struggling to squeeze air through his vocal cords.

His injuries made him sound shrill and hoarse.

"They come from another world," he intoned as we stood together under the bougainvillea in the garden. "Spawned in the light years of space, unleashed to take over the bodies and souls of the people of our planet, bringing a new dimension in terror…"

My character, Doctor Miles J. Bennell was all starry-eyed and devilishly handsome. I was explaining to my colleague, the actual doctor at the Trinitarian hospital.

"…whatever intelligence is out there is forming flesh and blood out of thin air…it's incredibly powerful, beyond comprehension…"

That's when I caught sight of Mother. She was Dana Wynter as Becky Driscoll. Laurent turned stiffly to follow my eye-line as he voiced over my dialogue. He had picked a bougainvillea bloom and was now delicately placing it in Becky Driscoll's hair.

"A cursed dreadful malevolent thing was happening to those he loved," Laurent continued.

"This isn't an ordinary body is it?" interjected the doctor, looking askance at her, as though she was some kind of freak.

"I never saw one like it. It looks…unused," I replied, looking closely at Mother… "and now an unknown horror makes her life and love a vortex of fear."

I was sitting on the bench with her, the real doctor standing over us. Now Laurent's body was hanging from a beam by his uniform belt, framed by one of the Romanesque arches lining the cloisters. The real Kevin McCarthy was walking arm in arm towards us with Dana Wynter. They were visiting me.

The doctor was busy explaining something to me…

"Suddenly while you're asleep they'll absorb your minds, your memories…"

"I don't want any part of it." I said.

"You're forgetting something, Simeon." he went on.

"What's that?"

"You have no choice."

Laurent was spinning and kicking as he hung there. He squeaked and strained as the belt tightened around his neck.

"From city to city, an incredible hysterical panic spreads—as the unimaginable becomes real," he voiced, spitting out the words.

I was up and shouting at the patients—the sclerotic undead, mindlessly moving along the walkway on the arms of their nurses.

"Listen! Can't you see? They're not human. Listen, everybody! You're next!"

"Accept us as one of you!" Mother said from the bench, with a dead-eyed stare.

"Never!" I screamed. Then I could hear my own voiceover running in my head.

"My only thought was to get out of there. I ran and ran. My only hope was to get to the highway. Warn the others what was happening!"

I was out on the highway outside some sleepy California town, pursued by the body-snatchers. I ran and ran then felt an arm on my shoulder.

It was the arm of the crotchety tanker driver shaking me awake, telling me that it was time for me to leave his lorry…we were approaching Berrouaghia and he was heading off to Oran.

He let me out at the main junction.

It was dark outside and drizzling. I couldn't think what to do. So I did the first thing that came to mind.

Nothing.

I sat on the ground, cold and dispirited—and lay down on a mound of wet esparto. Out of my mind with hunger, I tore at a handful of the grass and started grazing on it like an ungulate. I quickly spat out the fibrous, undigestible mush and just wanted to howl.

By this time, a commercial traveller had spotted me and pulled up alongside.

He told me he had a son of my age, that he couldn't stand the thought of his own flesh and blood being out like this. That the General Strike was putting everyone in danger and it wasn't wise to ignore a curfew.

I thanked him over and over again.

"You are some father's son just like my boy," he declared. "That's good enough for me. Hop in…"

He drove me all the way to Medea, sharing some snacks from his glove box along the way.

I soon found myself back in the muddy field running alongside the dirt-track on the way to our farmhouse. My gym shoes were caked with clotted earth. The canvas uppers were coming away from the rubber soles, the material tattered and frayed. The tongue of one shoe had completely shredded and there were holes in the toes of both. On the way up through the field I had squelched in a few puddles and my feet were cold, wet and badly blistered.

It came as an odd relief when two of LeBoeuf's men lurched out of the darkness and started to berate me.

I knew I had reached journey's end and was ready to collapse. If it was at the hands of LeBoeuf's men, so be it. I would submit to a beating just to be home.

"Fucking cunt!" said one as he slapped me around the face with the back of his hand.

"Fucking bag of shit!" shouted the other, wading in with his rifle butt, ramming me on the shoulder and giving me a kick in the side once I'd hit the floor.

I took it. And I was fine with that. Just fine.

Mother heard my yells and came rushing out of the house, grabbing me and helping me up from the dirt. The soldiers were surprisingly restrained with her, in sharp contrast to the way they had dealt with me.

Maybe it was just too early in the morning to pick a fight with a woman like Mother. Maybe LeBoeuf's firm rebuke for their lax behaviour that morning had made them wary of overstepping the mark again. Either way, not wanting to venture across the threshold of the house, they let us back indoors unmolested and left us alone inside for several blissful hours.

We were en famille once again.

Mother placed my raw blistering feet in a bowl of hot, soapy water, dabbed them with disinfectant, then made a milk poultice for my bruised shoulder before feeding me some spiced beef stew.

She gently asked me where I had been. I told her I had gone to find Father. She said she suspected as much.

I asked her if she remembered Lieutenant Laurent but realised the two of them had never been introduced at the Trinitarian hospital—just in my dreams.

She had vague recollections of him as 'the nice man in the next bed' but couldn't quite place him.

"Father has killed that 'nice man'. He was an officer in French Army Intelligence. Now I know if they catch Father, they will execute him. He is definitely alive, Maman, but he is as good as dead."

At this news, Mother's face turned thunderous. She put me to bed alongside a snoozing Louis and Margot.

I heard her wake in the night to feed Baby Claude and I could tell she was fitful and not sleeping. I think she was keeping herself up to watch over me.

This morning, Mother stood around the door as the guards of the tenth para came for me.

To her screams and wild protests, the paras cuffed me, dragged me from the house and bundled me into a waiting staff car. Mother fell to her knees at the threshold, wringing her hands and wailing into the stanchion of the door frame as she watched me go.

I was driven all the way to Algiers for this morning's appointment with Captain LeBoeuf atop the fifth floor of Au Bon Marché.

But as I now sit in the armoured car outside the Villa Tourelle, even that event seems as if it happened aeons ago.

Hours lag and then race on. Time is just one interminable stretch, measured by a state of decay rather than a rate of progress.

The door of the vehicle opens and a middle-aged man is shoved inside.

He too is chained and cuffed.

He wears a suit that hangs off him; a crisp, neatly ironed, spotless shirt out of keeping with his shaggy look; a scuffed pair of leather brogues covered in dust, and bright red socks.

Under his straggly greying hair, I notice that the area around his left eye is puffy and flushing with the colours of a sunset—yellow, orange, crimson and blue.

There is a gash and a groove in his left upper jawline where his beard stops, indicating a fractured cheekbone.

He holds his head low and mutters something incoherent as Lieutenant Mauritz and another para climb in alongside us.

The vehicle moves off down the drive towards the gates.

So, this is another stop along the way. We are not far from El-Biar jail now. Perhaps we are going there after all.

I see buildings race past the car. A mishmash of corrugated shacks give way to rangy neo-classical villas, then adobe-style houses, then more shacks.

The bearded man keeps his head down, eyes on the ground. He is silent.

As we pass El-Biar jail and head out on the road south, my breath catches in my gullet. Another torture centre swerved. Or is this constant guessing at the hour and minute of my death a part of the torture itself?

I am trying to gather the strength to ask this question of the phlegmatic lieutenant Mauritz. Not because I fear his reaction, though his silence does intimidate me, but that I'm not sure I am strong enough to accept the answer.

The question is on its way up to my voice box anyway—it finds its way past my larynx to the roof of my mouth and the tip of my tongue where it stays for a little while before I blurt it out.

"Am I going to die?"

"At some time in your life, yes, I've no doubt."

"Are we going to a torture centre now?"

Mauritz gives a weary shrug as if my question is inconvenient.

"No. Medea."

My heart races.

"Am I going home?"

"No. You are going to school."

I think it remarkably strange.

"School…" I repeat, dazed.

Mauritz repeats and clips his words just in case I hadn't heard them first time around.

"Yes. School. The Lycée René Coty. You are going to school."

The bearded man slowly raises his head and peers through the darkness at me.

"Simeon? Simeon Abu!"

"No talking!" says Mauritz.

"But this is my pupil!"

He is sallow, gaunt, a ghost of a man, although the eyes are familiar. The way they radiate wrinkles around them when the lids narrow with thought. The cluster of tiny liver spots around his temple, the broken veins in his cheeks that give him an odd blush and a bashful look. I know him. My heart soars again.

"Monsieur Gazides!"

"And that means you too!" Mauritz flashes an angry look my way.

Monsieur Gazides smiles, nods and places a finger to his lips. All this can wait. It is so good to see a friendly face.

The Lycée René Coty is less than an hour's drive from here.

Monsieur Gazides and I sit in silent solidarity throughout the trip, whilst lieutenant Mauritz scans the roadside for trouble.

The armoured car pulls up outside the school gates. Mauritz flings the door open and hops out.

Children and pupils are decamping from a convoy of troop transports and Army cars in lieu of school buses. Other Harkis, shouting their half-hearted commands in Arabic and French, are trying to muster the pupils into orderly groups. But quite a few of them resist. A game of football has broken out among the pupils and the players move freely around the yard, weaving in and out of the throng. Not to be outdone, two of the Harkis have joined in the game, but the paras are putting a stop to their fun.

A teacher stands at the school entrance transfixed by the sight of the armoured car.

Pupils gather around us. I spot Christophe dawdling close by. Yerma is beside him, whispering something in his ear. I think they have spotted me sitting here in the gloomy interior of the vehicle. I feel a longing to be out there with them again, everything having returned to normal—to reverse the clocks as if January had never happened.

"You will wait," Lieutenant Mauritz orders, slamming the door behind him. It leaves the two of us and the paratrooper, who is still sharing operational notes with the driver.

I turn to Monsieur Gazides. Finally, a chance to talk to him without Mauritz present.

"I'm sorry, sir. But I hardly recognised you."

"That's perfectly understandable."

His voice is muted. It sounds as if he's talking through a wall or from a long way off.

"I hardly recognised myself today back at the Villa when I looked in the mirror…

They let me use Aussaresses' private bathroom to brush up. He has golden taps. I don't think I did a very good job of it…"

"Was that where they've been keeping you?"

"No. It's Aussaresses' HQ. A torture centre—their reception centre, too. I was brought up to Algiers from Lodi camp last night. I have been at the Barberousse military hospital."

"What was wrong with you?"

"They went too far at Lodi..."

"Who? Who went too far? With what?"

"No charge. No trial. No sentence...

They turned up that day at school. You remember?

They told me I'd been poisoning young minds with my Marxist claptrap...

Well, you know, Simeon, I may be guilty of very many things. Drinking in the staff room after hours...falling asleep marking papers...but teaching my class about the United Nations is not one of them."

It is good to hear some lightness in his voice. I recall the events of the day he was led away. His abduction by the gendarmes without explanation. The calmness with which he just accepted it. His sudden absence in the classroom and the aftershock that hit all of us at Lycée René Coty.

"I remember that history lesson. The Security Council, right? You told us all about the UN. You talked through the role of Secretary General. The functions of all the departments..."

"Of course. I thought it was a good thing to do...with the strike planned for this week and the General Assembly meeting in New York. Five thousand miles away, they're talking about our stricken country. Your country. And no, it's not on the syllabus..."

"No. Much of what matters isn't..." I muse.

"So, I thought...This is the world you live in, the world you're growing up in. This is the world you're inheriting. And if the past is a good pointer to the present and future, then there are lessons to be learned in ours. What is it they say? 'If you don't know your history, you're bound to repeat it'. So, this is what I should teach you...how the United Nations came about, its role as a peacekeeper...its successes, its failings..."

His voice drops away.

"I had no idea it would...escalate."

"How?" I ask.

"Someone reported me to the Prefecture. My details found their way to the Sûreté and then into the hands of Aussaresses and his men."

I am incensed by this news.

"Who? Who would report you?"

My indignation causes the para to glance across at me. Monsieur Gazides stops talking, only to resume once the soldier has directed his attention away from us and back to the driver.

"I don't know. A parent…a child…a colleague. What does it matter who? Madame Alaric said I was endangering the school…that I was veering off the syllabus…going off-piste…"

"Trust that snooty cow to know what a 'piste' is," I say, "She goes skiing up in Blida Province every winter…Mother thinks the Madame fancies herself as a chatelaine living in Paris."

Monsieur Gazides withholds judgment on Madame Alaric. He will not criticise her, no matter that what she has said or done has led to his detainment and torture.

Monsieur Gazides taught me that everyone has their own reality to deal with. Everyone their pressures and their reasons for behaving the way they do. And if people don't have the capacity to forgive, there is no essential humanity in the world. Monsieur Gazides is one of the most tolerant and balanced men I have ever known.

But I have lapsed. And I feel bad about it. Immediately, I feel ashamed for having slighted my headmistress.

He goes on.

"She told me I am a Marxist in league with the FLN…and my politics has no place in the classroom.

The next thing I knew, the Army were here.

They said I should join my PCA comrades in El-Biar jail. They told me I was lucky they weren't deporting me to Moscow!"

"You were in El-Biar?"

"I was."

"What happened to you?"

"Much…"

"They tortured you…"

"Yes…"

I don't know if Monsieur Gazides wants to tell me, but it feels natural to be curious and enquiring in his company—and yet the type of questions burning inside me are so very different to those I would normally ask of him in class.

I have an overwhelming impulse to ask them. Yet I have never feared his answers as much as I do now.

"Is El-Biar as bad as they say?"

"You don't want to go anywhere near El-Biar…"

"I've never heard of Lodi…"

"It's an old holiday camp about a hundred kilometres southwest of here…"

"What kind of things did they do to you there, Monsieur Gazides?"

Monsieur Gazides takes a long deep breath. His eyes search mine.

"Do you really want to know this?"

I nod and try to swallow hard.

"Only if you are willing to tell me."

The swallow tickles my parched throat and I cough. I brace myself as Monsieur Gazides casts his mind back.

"At Lodi, they stripped me naked, took me into a shower room, tied me to a chair under the shower…ran scalding hot water over me…It seared my shoulders, chest and thighs…then they put a towel over my head and held it back…

They turned the shower on again. This time the water was cool, but it's like every drop of water was a lit match on my body…

I took a deep breath at first, thinking I could hold it long enough to survive a drowning. When my breath ran out, I thought I could get by snatching short breaths…I tried, but the towel was drenched and there was no oxygen getting through to my lungs.

I thought I would drown…I tried not to…just couldn't breathe…I blacked out…do you want me to go on, Simeon?"

I nod.

"I had no name. Just a number. 7-8-1.

They called the number out one morning…

That was the morning they ordered my execution…

They dragged me from my bed to a washroom, blindfolded me, put a revolver to my head…

I heard the chambers spinning, then the click, but no bang…

They knew exactly what I was thinking. I didn't fear dying.

I feared going to my death as a number…7-8-1.

For a few moments I thought that number would be the only thing I would be remembered by…The only inscription on my headstone…

No name. No history. Just a number…"

It is unbearable.

"Why have they done this to you?"

"They wanted to know where the FLN leaders were hiding…They wanted the names of communist party members.

They tried to get them from me…The names of friends at the university…Teachers here at René Coty…Parents who I may suspect of being maquisards…

My sister is a doctor. They wanted her name too…To betray my family, not just my school…"

"Your family are okay?"

"I don't know. I think so. They haven't allowed me any visits."

"What's happened to all the other teachers?"

"I assume they are still here. Madame Alaric, Monsieur Chambord, Monsieur Erboli…the replacement teacher, what's her name?"

"Mademoiselle Richemont…"

"Yes, that's it. Look, there, I can see Monsieur Chambord manning the gates right there…"

He reaches to grab a glimpse out of the tiny scratched window in the side of the armoured car.

"I don't understand. Why just you?"

"I guess because I wouldn't take it back…"

"Take what back?"

"I told them I teach history the way I do because I believe in social justice for everyone regardless…

And if our records are written only by the victors and not the vanquished, then history is nothing more than a worthless stream of lies…

And the lies go on and on just as history goes on and on—from generation to generation…

So I wanted to teach my students the facts as I see them…

The Army took that as my confession. They concluded I must be an internationalist Marxist like Frantz Fanon. A member of the PCA, and plotting with the FLN…"

He has a faraway look about him.

That's when they burned me, drowned me, made me believe I was a dead man…

I couldn't give them any names because I had none to give.

I am a teacher. I am not rank-and-file FLN…I am not a signed-up member of the Communist Party of Algeria…I will teach my class as equals. I will not treat people as being worth any more or less than one another…no matter what happens to me…

It's why I teach…"

Monsieur Gazides peers out at the schoolyard.

"I have fond memories of this place. I loved it here…"

"You will be here again, sir."

A shadow passes across the sun.

"They tell me I will spend five years at Lodi. I don't think I will see it through another winter…"

I reach out to him forgetting that my hands are cuffed.

"Keep going, Monsieur Gazides…please…"

"And you, Simeon, what brings you to this point?"

"My father…" I say. But before I tell him, the door opens with a thud.

I jump.

Lieutenant Mauritz peers in. He orders me to hold out my hands and removes the cuffs. He does the same for Monsieur Gazides.

I rub my chafed wrists.

"Come!" he commands.

The paratrooper pushes us out of the vehicle.

I blink in the light and take a moment to adjust my eyes.

The throng is still there. The teachers have lined up their charges by year in the yard and are busy taking the morning's registration. Another of the tenth para checks the list and notes down the names of absentees.

The soldiers of the Harki unit look on, their rifles resting by their side. The morning's 'collection service' is done. They have completed the first part of their operation. Their quota of students and teachers is present and correct. A few stragglers, but they will be handled by the paratroopers.

At least the Lycée René Coty will be attended this morning.

Now they will have to make sure it stays that way for the duration of the strike. I imagine the same is happening in every school, in every factory and every workplace throughout Algeria.

Mauritz steers Monsieur Gazides and myself through the yard. The Lieutenant clears a path for us through the students, who step back in bemused compliance. Their reactions tell me that we are an oddity.

We go through the main doors and along the corridor to a classroom. Lieutenant Mauritz takes a chair, places it at the back of the room and sits.

"You!" he says, "Be seated there at the front!"

I do as I am told.

"You!" he addresses Monsieur Gazides, "When the students come in, teach."

Monsieur Gazides stands in front of the empty classroom, desolate.

"What do you mean, 'Teach!'…Teach what?"

He stares at Mauritz blankly.

"I don't know. You're the teacher," retorts Mauritz with a shrug.

"But I don't know where we are in their syllabus…I haven't prepared a lesson…"

"It's of no consequence," Mauritz interrupts. "Tell them how a combustion engine works, how many beans make five, how porcupines fuck…use your imagination…but just teach…"

Monsieur Gazides is struggling to understand. "Why?"

"Why!" Mauritz is nonplussed. "And you call yourself a teacher? Isn't it obvious?"

Monsieur Gazides begs an explanation. Lieutenant Mauritz obliges.

"Because you will be seen to be breaking the strike! You will be openly defying the FLN…"

Captain LeBoeuf tells me your school is full of rats and one of them will rat on you to your political masters in the PCA. One of their own breaking the strike…

Captain LeBoeuf's 'collection service' will break the resolve of the strikers…

Every teacher across Algiers, across Medea Wilaya and every Wilaya throughout Algeria will return to their classrooms this morning. All the pupils. Except for a few reckless sons of the FLN, the ALN and the PCA…oh, and no doubt a few Pied-Noir traitors, French communists and Muslim turncoats. We shall know who they are soon enough.

These are Captain LeBoeuf's orders today."

I can hear a cascade of footsteps heading towards us along the corridor outside.

The classroom starts to fill.

Christophe saunters in and heads for the back of the class with a cursory nod in my direction. The others give me a wide berth, no doubt smelling the excrement that is drying in my trousers. Verna resolutely sits at the desk next to me. She is pleased to see me.

"Simeon. Where have you been? You smell like shit…no, correction, you smell of shit…"

"I…" I find it almost impossible to explain why.

She touches my face tenderly.

"It's okay," she says.

I am so grateful to her I want to cry.

The class settles to the sight of a baleful Monsieur Gazides in a borrowed suit, looking hopelessly lost. He has the air of a lonely commuter left behind on a station platform having missed the only stopping train of the day.

His gaze is fixed on a point at the back of the class and some imagined rabbit hole leading off through the wall above Lieutenant Mauritz's head. By the looks of him, he is already half-way down it.

He cannot comprehend how his life has come to this and he is searching the universe for clues.

The class is quiet. They are all asking themselves why Monsieur Gazides is standing before them and what they should do next.

Monsieur Gazides remains silent, his head bowed as if in a state of grace or common prayer.

I want to shake him so that he puts his head up and rises above his humiliation.

Lieutenant Mauritz, however, is growing impatient at the lack of any teaching. He throws the stranded teacher a prompt from the back of the room.

"Monsieur Gazides?"

The class turns to glare at the uniformed officer, then back at the solitary figure standing isolated out in front.

"Good morning," says Monsieur Gazides, hesitantly.

The class says 'good morning' in unison.

"You know who I am, right?"

"Of course, we know you, Monsieur Gazides!" Friendly sniggering breaks out among the class. It fills the vacuum. Monsieur Gazides smiles along with us. He is finding his footing again.

"Right! Gazides! Yes, that is indeed the answer to the first question. You are on form today, class!"

He slowly and deliberately chalks up his name on the blackboard, adding the numbers '7-8-1' at the end.

As he writes, I can see the outline of his scapula through the loose creases of his suit jacket which falls around his scrawny frame.

I watch him stop mid-flow, press his forehead to the blackboard and take a deep breath. Not so much an inhalation, more a moan.

I am willing him to continue. We all are.

He turns back to face the class.

"I haven't prepared a lesson today. So, I'm handing it over to you. What would you like to learn?"

The class is silent. Embarrassed. Not a murmur. They have no idea how to respond.

A pencil rolls off a desk and falls to the floor. One of the class shouts 'merde!' as if she has just dropped a Lalique vase.

Lieutenant Mauritz appears to lose his composure entirely. The feet of his chair scrape the floor as he suddenly stands.

The class turns to watch.

He grabs a textbook at random from the shelf of the bookcase beside him and furiously flicks through its pages. He quickly alights on a spread which he then flashes at sallow-faced Monsieur Gazides.

"There! The Water Cycle! You will teach The Water Cycle!"

Bewildered, the class turn to face Monsieur Gazides again…

"Okay…thank you, Lieutenant…The Water Cycle…"

He erases his name from the blackboard, leaving the number in place, and starts to chalk up 'The Water Cycle', followed by the outline of a mountain.

We are transfixed.

The downhill diagonal chalk-mark turns into a jagged horizontal representing the sea.

He chalks up a series of squiggly vertical lines linking the sea with the sun, adding a cloud and some slanting sprinkles of rainwater over the peak of the mountain.

There is a perfunctory click from the back of the class.

Lieutenant Mauritz is taking a photograph of the teacher at work. I see him smartly stow a Minox in the pocket of his camo jacket.

Monsieur Gazides hasn't heard the sound. Or at least pretends not to. He is looking the other way, standing back from the blackboard to check that he has not missed any detail on his carefully rendered chalked diagram.

Satisfied, he turns to face the class.

"The Water Cycle. Attendez-vous!"

His flicks an index finger across the diagram, pointing out key stages in the journey of H_2O.

"The sun heats up water from the Mediterranean here…the water evaporates and forms tiny droplets…these droplets are held in clouds and fall on the Saharan Atlas as rain…the water is absorbed into porous layers of rock…it wells up at various fissures in the earth…"

The class exchanges baffled looks. Monsieur Gazides ploughs on regardless.

"From these water sources, gravity takes the water down from the high ground. Some of it in the south flows down to form wadis—perennial rivers which evaporate and drain into chotts. The water sinks back into the earth and these dry."

Lieutenant Mauritz is now checking on the state of his fingernails.

"The water that flows north creates tributaries that meet to form rivers like the Chelif…which runs some seven hundred kilometres into deltas and estuaries, back out to the Mediterranean Sea, where the whole process starts over again…Voila!"

He stops and stares out at the class sitting in confused silence.

Verna tentatively raises her hand.

"Yes?"

"Sir…" She is reluctant to ask what she knows in her heart she has to. "…We know all about the water cycle…We did it in Cinquième…"

Monsieur Gazides pauses. He knows.

Lieutenant Mauritz coughs—a sign to move things along. Verna's hand is still in the air.

"Yes?"

"Sorry, I don't understand. We're not twelve-year olds. Why teach it to us again when we know it already?"

"A very good question. You heard the officer at the back there. This is for his benefit…perhaps his teachers didn't cover the water cycle when he was at school…"

Lieutenant Mauritz has heard enough.

He marches to the front of the class, seizes Monsieur Gazides by the lapels of his suit jacket and propels him out through the classroom door.

I rise from my desk and go after them into the corridor followed by Verna and a few of the class. A Harki soldier bars my way and I can make no further progress.

I watch helplessly as Mauritz pushes Monsieur Gazides through the swing doors and into the yard before disappearing from view.

I feel like throwing up.

Before long, Madame Alaric is standing in front of us, ushering us back into the classroom.

"Asseyez-vous, tout le monde! That is quite enough excitement for one day!"

Lycée René Coty, Medea Wilaya, 28 January 1957

It slowly dawns on me that I am going to survive this day. No cuffs. No paras. No questions. No torture centre.

The Harki soldiers are still hanging around the school yard, of course, though LeBoeuf's paras have long gone. The Harkis will no doubt remain throughout the day to enforce the Governor-General's strike-breaking orders.

The Army of the Fourth Republic find the Harki auxiliaries useful in liaising with civilians on the ground. Many are known by the locals as they live among them.

That's the way they used Father, to help them quell civil disputes and mediate between the various sections of the community.

But for me, out on the streets of Medea and in the school yard, the truth has been plain to see in the way people make no allowances for the Harkis. They are heard but not listened to, remarked on but not regarded, seen but not sensed.

They are simply tolerated, nothing more.

To most Algerians, the Harkis are neither French nor Franco-Algerian. Neither colon nor Pied-Noir. An Army shorn of an identity, manned by spiritless, soulless, deracinated men.

To my countrymen, the Harki soldier is a traitorous mercenary. To the Frenchman he is an alien auxiliary, a servant of the French state. To Arab Muslims, he is a traitor, lacking in national pride. To Francophile Arabs he is an opportunistic soldier of fortune, lacking in scruples. To Pieds-Noirs he is a pale imitation of a colonial, lacking in conviction. And to the native French in France, he is a superfluous Arab national, lacking a passport.

He is mistrusted by more people than he would care to think.

There is no real affinity for the Harki anywhere on the planet. Such is the contempt in which Father is held.

The fact that he doesn't come in for the same sort of privileges as the Pieds-Noirs speaks volumes, as they are quite a way down the food chain themselves.

This was always Father's Achilles heel, because it played to latent insecurities that he carried throughout his life. I called it his 'Harkiness'. A characteristic all of its own. Like 'fecklessness' or 'cowardliness'.

His 'Harkiness' was the birch with which he used to beat himself. It always described a kind of no-man's land, a place detached from the real world, a place of supreme disconnection.

Mother berated him for it before we left the farmhouse on the morning of the bombings. This is what she meant by "you are deluded, Farouk…no, you are demented. And you will get us all killed."

In the end, Father became so removed from reality that he lost sight of himself. He refused to see himself as others in the community saw him. As the eternal outsider.

But I know with mounting certainty, the longer I live, the more of him is in me.

Like Father, I too occupy a no-man's land.

Like Father, I have long since lost the ability to see myself as others see me. Trusted by neither the French nor the Algerian and certainly not the Pied-Noir.

Paranoia has taken over where objectivity left off.

For example, I cannot recognise the apparition that has been here in school today. No, not Monsieur Gazides, though his presence here today has been a strangely dislocated phenomenon.

No, I mean me.

I suspect everyone, trust no one. I hope the people around me have pure motives, driven by the affinity of kinship, friendship or consanguinity—or failing that simply the motive to do no harm.

But I hope for it more than I expect it to be the case.

I suspect that my fellow students believe that I have brought the soldiers to their classrooms this morning. I wouldn't be at all surprised if my teachers think I am somehow responsible for rounding up the strike-breakers among them and forcing them into school.

But they may also be thinking nothing of the sort. They may just see me as a mess, an object of curiosity. Someone to be pitied in public and scorned behind his back. I have no idea.

My friends blench at the sight of me in my school gym shoes, which are ripped beyond repair and stained. I traipse mud through the school corridors. I have a pronounced limp and each left step is a heavy plod. Apart from anything, I stink to high heaven. Madame Alaric has recommended to the Harki soldiers that I go home—at least to wash and change, if not to sleep.

I don't think they can quite understand what has happened to me—or to Monsieur Gazides for that matter.

I have heard Madame Alaric many times in the past warn pupils who have been playing up "There will be consequences!"

It has become her catchphrase.

I have heard her regularly mimicked for it in the school yard.

But to our directrice, 'consequences' is just another word. A distant rumble of thunder heavy with static. Its lightning will never strike her.

In the case of Monsieur Gazides, the consequences are all too real and the proof is here today moving around among us.

Madame Alaric simply cannot imagine what Monsieur Gazides has endured at the hands of Aussaresses' men.

In a strange way, I feel for her detachment from events and their 'consequences'. But I am also past explaining myself to her.

I am happy to be back at school, of course. It's a kind of freedom and I am grateful for that.

But I hardly see school as the sanctuary she would like to think it is. Far from it…

I am neither safe from my teachers and classmates nor from the Harki enforcers around me, no matter how much they profess their respect for Father. There is no respite from threat—either here, at the farmhouse, in Waleed's bus, or on the streets.

I am haunted by the decapitated heads of Monsieur et Madame Courvois, the distended face of the hanging Lieutenant Laurent, the sight of Rue d'Isly from a hundred feet up as LeBoeuf holds me over the parapet. And now, and most profoundly, by the receding, shrunken figure of Monsieur Gazides as he is manhandled out of the school by Lieutenant Mauritz.

I am haunted by the 'consequences'. And I will only shake off these ghosts in death.

I believe my only two friends may understand this.

In the school yard, Verna and Christophe shield me from the gaze of other students.

They see themselves as my cordon de sécurité, keeping everyone at arm's length. Verna tells me she has elected to sit at the desk beside me at the front of the class—not just because she likes me, but so that, in her words, she can 'cover my flank'.

Father would be proud to know I finally have my own 'little wing man'.

At break-time, Verna wards off unwelcome intruders by conspicuously feeding me a rouleau de fromage from her lunchbox.

She does this as she would an injured bird. A peck at a time.

I am ravenous and want to scoff it all, but every morsel she tenders is gratefully taken. I don't care that the others may think it odd, and neither does she. I appreciate the affection she offers me every bit as much as the food.

She puts her arms around my neck and kisses me on my forehead.

"It's okay, Simeon. You are safe with me."

I sob again. My shoulders heave. Christophe puts a consoling hand on my back. He moves to embrace both myself and Verna, but his arms just won't reach that far around.

"Monsieur Gazides is a good man, Simeon. And he's his own man. You couldn't have done anything to help him. None of us could."

Madame Alaric approaches. She is prim and matter of fact—intent on putting a stop to our huddle. It is just not a sight she wants to see. She claps loudly, as if scaring the crows off her prize marrows.

"Come, come, you three. Enough!

Simeon, you'd better go and wash and get some sleep. A clean change of clothes for you, I think, young man."

Her nose wrinkles as the stink of my excrement assails her nostrils again.

She casts her eye over my disintegrating gym shoes. "Do you have anything else to put on your feet? Those ones are done."

I shake my head.

"Hang on, I have an idea," she says and disappears back inside.

"She is a proper witch," says Christophe.

"A bitch more like," adds Verna, looking daggers at the main doors that have just swung shut behind our directrice.

"She's just doing her job…" I say, trying to channel a little of Monsieur Gazides' balance.

Christophe takes his arm from around my shoulders and separates himself from the huddle.

"That's a touch sanctimonious, don't you think? Is that what your Dad said when he blew up those people?"

"What do you mean by that?" Verna snaps back at him, moving between us.

"I mean it's quite a thing to say really, 'Just doing her job'?
She ratted on Monsieur Gazides to the French soldiers."

Christophe continues, "You know my cousin's friend was killed by the bomb your dad planted…"

Again, my reflex is to leap to Father's defence.

"Father didn't plant it…" I assert, immediately realising that I have offered Christophe no words of sympathy for his loss.

"I'm sorry to hear that," I add, though it comes across as an afterthought.
"You're sorry? You were there too, weren't you?" retorts Christophe.

"He tried to stop it," Verna protests.

"Yes, that's what I've heard," says Christophe, "but there's another side to it…"

"What other side?" asks Verna, bewildered.

"That Simeon went along with it. Helping his old man finish the job. His old man ran away. The Army are looking for him. The ALN are looking for him. They both want to kill him. That's what I heard."

"Enough of your rumours, Christophe! Why don't you take a knife to Simeon too while you're about it…Look at him! Do you know what he's been through?"

"No. Do you? Do any of us really?" says Christophe pointedly.

"Listen, I love you like a brother, my friend. But you've got to start seeing things for what they are. The only person pulling your strings is you…"

At this, he stalks off to join his mates who loiter conspiratorially by the wall across the school yard.

"Salaud!" says Verna as she watches him go, placing a reassuring arm around me. I have managed to staunch the tears.

"Did you?" she asks.

"Did I what?"

"Did you help your Dad blow up those Muslims in the Casbah? Is that why you are under the protection of the French? Is that why that soldier brought you here today? I heard there are troops guarding your farmhouse too…"

I am silent on the subject.

"Tell me, Simeon. I am your best friend."

Madame Alaric returns, brandishing a new pair of loafers.

"I knew I had them," she says breathlessly, "They've been in my desk drawer all this time. These were left behind by one of our pupils last year, the son of émigrés. His parents took him back to France, but he forgot to clear his locker in the gymnasium. Must have left in a hurry. They look your size, Simeon."

I try them on. She's right. They fit.

"Take them! Keep them! They're kind of snazzy!" She claps her hands with excitement, "Now, vite, vite! See that gentleman over there..." she says, indicating a Harki driver sitting at the wheel of a troop transport, "...he has kindly agreed to drive you home."

Madame Alaric nudges me in his direction and away from Verna whilst keeping a discreet distance.

I mouth 'bye' to Verna. She looks desolate that I am leaving her so soon, that I haven't given her the answer to her question.

I'm not sure I have the answer anyway. Yes, I went along with Father on his bombing sortie. And, yes, I would have given anything to stop it. But maybe Father thought, by letting the bomb go off, he really was saving me. I banish the thought instantly.

It seems there are no easy answers to simple questions.

Christophe slides me an ugly sideways glance from the far side of the school yard.

He is right. I should pay heed to him. I am responsible for my actions. I cannot hide from them any longer as Father is doing now. I must learn to face up to them. Learn to look myself in the eye.

Within minutes we are on the road out of Medea heading south to the farmhouse.

The Harki driver is talkative...I am desperate to see my family again and his rasping voice is the last thing I want to hear.

"I heard what that boy said to you back there. Don't pay any attention to him. Farouk Abu is a legend."

"Christophe is a mate. He's alright..."

"A mate doesn't rubbish another mate's dad. That's family. That's bad form..."

174

"He didn't mean it…"

"Not much!" exclaims the Harki driver. "Look, it's none of my business, but your dear papa has a good reputation with us. He's got our backs. We won't hear of him being condemned…"

I can't square this fulsome praise of "dear papa" with Father's actions the last time I set eyes on him in Place Jean-Paul Sartre.

He certainly didn't have my back then.

How could he think he was saving me? Despite my pleading with him not to go ahead with it, "dear papa" was prepared to see me ripped apart with fifty kilos of explosives.

The realisation sends a searing pain shooting down my leg. Muscle memory. I let out a yelp and immediately want to throw up.

"Just saying…" mutters the Harki driver sulkily, thinking my grimace is an adverse reaction to his words.

"No, you misunderstand." I swallow my rising bile. "I have this horrible pain in my leg."

"Well, it's hardly surprising. You had a building fall down on you, didn't you?"

"Yes."

"The miracle of Place Jean-Paul Sartre…that's what people call it…"

"Do they?"

"Oh, sure. You are a legend like your old man. A chip off the old block. And legends are good PR for the Army."

So that's why LeBoeuf has kept me alive. I am useful to him. Quite simply, I am 'good PR'.

"Where is Farouk now?" he asks.

"I've no idea."

The pain relents. The queasiness is passing.

"They say your papa is a double agent, an FLN infiltrator. But we know him better than that. He is one of us. No question. He has always looked out for us."

"Has he…" It's not a question, more an expression of doubt.

"Oh, yes…"

A spark goes off in my head.

"Who says he is a double agent?" I ask pointedly.

"The intelligence services."

"Who in the intelligence services?"

"Apparently, there is this officer in the GRE who claims he knows of a meeting in the Casbah between Farouk and Ali La Pointe. That madman Saadi too...

But these intelligence people, you have to take what they say at face value... Half of it is misinformation. The other half lies...

They peddle their conspiracy theories to inflate themselves and keep their pay packets stuffed. Like the politicians, they have to justify their positions."

"Do you know who in the GRE?"

"No. Some shit-stirrer. That's what Captain LeBoeuf thinks anyway..."

So LeBoeuf is aware of the intelligence Laurent extracted from the dying amputee Mustafa Behari after all. He knew all about the lieutenant's tip-off that Father met with the FLN leadership in the tunnels of the Casbah.

I recall LeBoeuf's last words to me earlier as he left us to go to work in the Zone Autonome d'Alger. "You and your Father...maybe you have gone over to the other side too." And his parting shot "We will know very soon. Either that or never."

Lycée René Coty, Medea Wilaya, 30 January 1957

Mademoiselle Richemont, our relief teacher, likes to limber up mind and body at the start of every day. A loosener to help us focus more sharply on our schoolwork.

Mademoiselle is irrepressibly positive. Madame Alaric describes her as 'a fiery ball of life-affirming energy'. But then Madame Alaric is a drama queen with an incurable tendency to overstate things.

"There are two types of people in life," Madame Alaric told us when she first introduced the Mademoiselle as Monsieur Gazides' temporary teaching replacement. "Radiators and drains...

Mademoiselle Richemont is a radiator. She will lift your spirits as well as your marks. Her centre of gravity is positivity...

You will find her incredibly energising."

I felt protective of Monsieur Gazides and I know that Madame Alaric's praise for our new relief teacher would have hurt him.

I also know he hasn't been here over the past few months to speak up for himself—with the obvious exception of Monday's humiliating show-trial. If he had been here, I'm sure he wouldn't have wholeheartedly endorsed her teaching methods.

Every day that Monsieur Gazides has been away, Mademoiselle Richemont has gone through the same 'energising' routine with her class.

Even before we've had the chance to unpack our books from our school bags, she has attempted to drag our sleepy bodies out of their torpor and into the day.

She has made us stand at our desks, stretch for the ceiling and waggle our fingers to shake out the remains of our tiredness...and then touch our toes.

We are yet to be convinced that it does anything more for us than make us dizzy and irritable. Nevertheless, she has taught us to revere our God-given body and mind as our own hallowed property—and made us stick to her daily ritual as a kind of sacrament.

It is one of the few benefits of being off school. That I don't have to pander to the planned spontaneity of Mademoiselle Richemont's start-of-day warm-ups.

But that is about to come to an end too.

Although Mother is wary about letting me out of her sight, she insists I go back to school again today.

She says I have spent too much time away from learning while convalescing in hospital and I now need to nourish my mind.

She is certain it will make me feel more alive.

She also tells me I should be with my friends—that it will be good for me to spend more time among people my own age.

But then parents are good at telling you what you should do and feel as a result. And Mother transfers a lot of what she feels onto me.

On Monday, when I turned up at the farmhouse having returned from school, it was as if Mother had seen a living ghost.

When the paras took me away from the farmhouse first thing on Monday morning, I believe she never expected to lay eyes on me again.

When I reappeared that afternoon, she smothered me in kisses and clung to me like an adult clings on to their childhood comfort blanket.

I have become her totem. As if just touching me brings life and fortune to the whole family. That's partly why she never wants me out of her sight. And why it becomes suffocating that she clings to me so tightly. I have become the receptacle for all her grief and her hopes.

Her fear of losing me has become the dread of everything disappearing. Family. Home. Louis. Margot. Baby Claude. Religion. Tradition. History. Country. She pours all of this into me. And it is unbearable.

She thanked Allah throughout the whole of yesterday and watched over me as I slept. After a while, her joy at seeing me gave way to anger. Her eyes grew dark as I recounted my experiences at the hands of LeBoeuf.

I have to confess I didn't tell her everything—in particular how LeBoeuf had hung me out over the Rue d'Isly like a flagpole.

I now think the events of Monday were LeBoeuf putting on a show for me, not just to scare me but to cause Mother the utmost distress and let her know who was in charge. Control is everything to him. And I am convinced he has been using me to get at her.

I am also certain that if she had learned the full terror of what I had been through at the top of Au Bon Marché, it would have sent her into a spiral of madness.

I wasn't prepared to give LeBoeuf the satisfaction. I certainly wasn't going to pile any further stress on Mother's shoulders. So, I decided to keep that particular incident from her. On this one thing, I could 'pull the strings', to quote Christophe.

Instead, I chose to tell her about the way Monsieur Gazides had been treated.

She pointed out that LeBoeuf had used the poor man as a propaganda football and dragged me into his twisted game. She cursed him and—the very first time I have ever heard her say it—she wished him dead.

Through the rest of the day, she nursed me, tending to my sore and broken body.

She poured hot water into a tub, adding a slug of cypress oil, and left me to soak. She treated my bruises, applying milk poultices to my shoulder, encouraged by the sight of my bruising finally coming out after Monday's beating.

She gently dabbed at my sore feet with disinfectant as if anointing them, propping my leg up on a chair and making me gobble down a third helping of chorba.

By the end of the day, she was satisfied that I was strong enough to go back to school.

However, she made me promise first that I would not put up with anything that would make me feel threatened or mistreated in any way. And to come home the moment I did.

Thankfully, all direct communication with LeBoeuf has ceased for the time being, though Mother has sent word to him as commanded through his adjutant Lieutenant Mauritz, who yesterday checked in twice on us at the farmhouse.

I asked Lieutenant Mauritz directly what had become of Monsieur Gazides.

He was giving nothing away. All he said was "the man let himself down," and left it at that.

I would have punched Mauritz, but I am no physical equal to him, certainly in no fit state to take him on and it would have achieved nothing.

I did think I would hear more news out of school than from LeBoeuf's Lieutenant. And whilst I wasn't quite sure about being in class, concluded that it was probably best for me to go. It would keep everyone happy and at peace for the time being.

Lieutenant Mauritz mentioned that LeBoeuf was also keen on the idea. For the Captain, the fewer interruptions to normal life the better.

If LeBoeuf couldn't put an end to Ben M'hidi he would do the next best thing and see off Ben M'hidi's General Strike. To do that, the wheels of industry had to keep turning. And that included the Lycée René Coty.

It is an enigma to me why LeBoeuf is so interested in us. Why he would go to all the trouble of setting us a guard, sending his Lieutenant to mind me, and tying up precious strike-breaking resource to keep us safe.

Why he continues to make these concessions to Mother and myself is anyone's guess.

I know that Father is a man wanted on both sides of the conflict. But the family he has left behind is poor and the tiniest of dots in the wider scheme of this war.

LeBoeuf is almost obsessive in his watchfulness. It is not very…soldierly. I'm sure his commander, General Jacques Massu would have something to say about that.

Mauritz also relayed LeBoeuf's wish that one of his men accompany me throughout my school day.

Mother managed to convince him that it would be less obtrusive for Waleed to drop me off at the Lycée on his bus each morning. The Harki guard were quite capable of protecting me on the school premises. They had a soft spot for Father and wouldn't let any harm come to me.

Reluctantly, LeBoeuf has conceded…though, as a safeguard, he insists that a soldier of the tenth para accompanies me on the bus whenever I go to school.

For the eight days the General Strike has been called, LeBoeuf makes sure that bus drivers are kept busy taking workers into Algiers and dropping pupils off at school.

He sees them as an extension of the Army.

To him, municipal workers are essential strike-breaking auxiliaries, a useful addition to the Harki units.

For LeBoeuf, sending me to school, along with the thousands of other pupils and students throughout Algeria, is a clear signal to the terrorists that life continues unfazed.

But it also increases the stakes.

I'm sure everyone at school has become wary of my presence among them since the bombing of Place Jean-Paul Sartre—teachers included.

I'm certain they think that every minute I am there puts them in harm's way.

With the exception of Verna and, to a certain extent Christophe with whom I have a new understanding, they treat me as if I have some deadly virus.

I feel desperately lonely.

This morning, Mademoiselle Richemont is even more buoyant than usual. Her normalising behaviour reaches an almost hysterical pitch. I can't help feeling she is over-compensating for Monsieur Gazides' brief, traumatising appearance of Monday.

Having stretched, waggled our fingers and touched our toes, we now enter what she describes as her 'brain gymnasium'.

Mademoiselle is irrepressibly positive.

As the class wheezes and coughs behind her, she chalks a giant ball on the board with nine smaller balls in a line alongside it and throws a question out to the class.

"Right, who saw that giant gibbous moon last night?"

No takers.

I had seen it through the window of the farmhouse. And I was mesmerised by it.

But I'm not going to tell the Mademoiselle that.

I am still thinking about the wound she has done to Monsieur Gazides—a man who has never complained about anyone or anything.

"Wasn't it wonderful! It was actually rather beautiful. So, I thought…"

She turns to the blackboard and back to the class, clearly pleased with herself.

"…this morning's 'brain gymnasium' is based on the planets. Here they are. You'll notice I've drawn them all the same size to make them more difficult to identify. Except for the sun, which isn't strictly a planet, but a star…

Now…who among you can name them in order of their distance from the sun?"

She taps the board.

"Go on, work-books out! Write them down. You have two minutes to work it out. I shall go around the class and ask each of you for your answer."

We are not exactly inspired by this. It is an exercise we went through in our Sixième.

Most of the class have forgotten it. They didn't see the point in naming the planets then. And they can't see the point in it now. It is enough of an exercise for them to keep their feet planted on Planet Earth than go spinning off on an academic field trip into the cosmos.

Mademoiselle Richemont has other ideas.

She is an irresistible force. She will move us to answer even though she can see a fog of indifference creeping across her classroom.

"Right! Let's start."

She coaxes our answers out of us with care.

It takes some considerable time.

She writes a selection of our answers up on the board above the chalked circles of planets, leaving the area below free.

"Well, I'd hardly call that putting your back into it…So, let's see who's got it right shall we."

She stops herself, deciding it is time to add a little more spice to the exercise.

She moves to her drawer and dramatically places a forefinger to her chin to act out a quandary.

"Oh, hang on! I almost forgot! I have a very special prize for the winner— or winners—in my drawer here. Do you want to see what it is?"

She toys teasingly with the drawer handle, keeping her eyes on the class.

At this, the class perks up. They are easily won over by the promise of treasure.

"Ah!" says the irrepressibly upbeat Mademoiselle, "so now you are interested! What a shame you haven't put the same enthusiasm into the brain gymnasium as you have into the thought of a big fat reward at the end of it!"

She giggles and teases the class some more. Madame Alaric applauds her from the side-lines.

"Touché, Madame Richemont, touché. Very well put! I can't help making the same observation myself," she sighs.

"So, for those who have it right, I have these." Mademoiselle Richemont opens the drawer and produces a sheaf of tickets. She holds up a fan of them for the class.

"What are they, Mademoiselle Richemont?" asks one of the class. Mademoiselle Richemont fans her face with the tickets and swoons.

It is a very strange performance.

"Only…tickets to the Algiers observatory in Bouzareah!"

Madame Alaric feels the need to chip in, to reinforce Mademoiselle Richemont's generosity.

"Now these are extra special. The Observatory is not open to everyone. This is courtesy of Madame Richemont's connections with the scientific world."

Mademoiselle Richemont delights in Madame Alaric's approval.

"C'est vrai, Madame Alaric! These are gold-dust, much sought after entry passes. And if you are very lucky you will get to look through the giant telescope."

I can see Christophe mouth 'Wow!" to a classmate at the desk next to him. I can't quite tell if it is sarcasm. It wouldn't surprise me. Mademoiselle Richemont is now reverting back to her usual infantile voice.

"With that in mind, and these in my safekeeping…" she replaces the tickets and slams the drawer shut, "…you can now put some serious thought into it and have another go. But this time, write your answers down on a sheet of paper and make sure you put your name at the top of the page."

Everyone sets about scribbling, redoubling their efforts.

I ask Verna quietly if that's all it takes to turn people—a simple bribe.

"Don't be so snooty, Simeon. You and I both know that's the way it goes," she remarks, setting about the page with her pencil. "Why are you so damning of human nature?"

Whilst the class applies itself to Mademoiselle Richemont's 'brain gymnasium', the replacement teacher exchanges conspiratorial glances with Madame Alaric.

Mademoiselle Richemont is keen to pique the interest of her class throughout the exercise and offers up some further commentary.

"The director of the observatory was one Francois Gonnessiat. And he was the man responsible for discovering several 'planetes naines'—the minor planets. He even has an asteroid named after him."

Madame Alaric joins in.

"Ah! Imagine that, class. A piece of stardust named after you. Comment drôle!"

I decide to sit it out with arms folded whilst the class sets about the task. I am on strike and it is noted.

Pages are ripped from workbooks as Madame Richemont collects the worksheets. Madame Alaric is staring at me, unimpressed.

"Now, the answer!" declares Madame Richemont.

She chalks the name of each planet beneath each of the nine circles, underlining the initial capitals as she goes.

"Mercure. Venus. Terre. Mars. Jupiter. Saturne. Uranus. Neptune. Pluton."

"Hands up if you think you've got it!" she chimes. Several hands shoot up. Madame Alaric makes a mental note of the star pupils.

"Okay, let's see"-the Mademoiselle starts flicking through the pages, "Ah, it looks as if several of you have it right! Now, then…"

She takes out her blackboard eraser and scrubs the jumble of words above the circles.

"Of course, there is an easy way to remember the order of the planets. It's a simple but very effective memory technique. In America, for instance, they use this as an aide-memoire…"

She chalks up a sentence in English:

'My Very Educated Mother Just Served Us Nine Pizzas'

At the sight of the word 'pizzas', the mood of the class instantly lifts.

"See how the initial characters of each word are the same as for the planets? And in the correct order of distance from the sun! Only the name for 'Terre' is different in English. It is the literal translation—'Earth'."

A few of the class copy the words dutifully into their workbooks.

"So, here is the second part of this morning's 'Brain Gymnasium'. And you'll need your workbooks for this again…"

I turn to Verna. She is totally engaged, her pencil poised.

"I want you to come up with the equivalent en Français…

A sentence that works in the same way. Now, remember! Each of the initial characters in your sentence has to be the same as for the initial characters in the sequence of planets. And the sentence you compose must read as a sentence. You are to put them in their correct order of distance from the sun. Understood?"

The class mutters their assent.

"Do you have any more tickets if we get this one right, Mademoiselle?" one of them asks.

"Not to the boring observatory. To see MC Alger play!' shouts another. "How about rewarding us with nine pizzas?" suggests Christophe.

"Not quite," she replies, "but I do have as many tickets to the Algiers Observatory as there are correct answers. So, if you don't have one already, this is your chance!"

She checks the clock on the classroom wall and then her watch.

"Okay, you have two minutes to complete the exercise…Go!"

I push myself away from the desk on my chair, rocking backwards on its tilting hind legs. It prompts Madame Alaric to resume her disapproving gaze.

I find her laser death-stare disconcerting. I sit forward, open my workbook and pick up my pencil.

My mind ticks over. I can see nothing but the face of the heavily bearded Monsieur Gazides. He is looking up imploringly at me through the gloomy interior of the armoured vehicle.

He is resigned, submissive.

The two minutes pass in a flash.

"Time's up, tout le monde!" chirrups Mademoiselle Richemont.

Many in the class throw down their pencils, admitting defeat.

But nothing will beat Madame Alaric, who takes up the challenge as an example to the class, scribbling and crossing out in her own notebook.

"I have one!" she exclaims, jumping up from her chair and striding to the front of the room.

"May I?" she asks of Mademoiselle Richemont, commandeering her chalk and preparing to carve out her response on the board.

"Be my guest," Mademoiselle Richemont replies, "tu es les bienvenus, Madame Alaric!"

Madame Alaric chalks away happily while the class fall into a respectful silence.

'Mon Vacatiere Tellement Marrant. Jouer. Sourire. UN Plaisir!'

She emphatically nails the point of the exclamation mark onto the board with the chalk and reads aloud to the class with ringing clarity.

"My—very—cheery—replacement teacher…Play…Smile. A pleasure!" Mademoiselle Richemont is beside herself. The class is silent.

"That is very good, Madame Alaric. Very clever."

"Well, you make us all smile, Mademoiselle. And it is a true pleasure to have such a ray of sunshine in the class. I'm sure we'd all agree."

Mademoiselle Richemont notices Christophe's hand in the air. He is flapping it about, desperate to point something out.

"Yes, Christophe?"

"It's not strictly correct, though, is it, Mademoiselle? I mean, Madame Alaric has made one word out of the initials for Uranus and Neptune. That's not in the rules, surely."

Verna sniggers. She knows exactly what Christophe is up to.

Madame Alaric nods.

"You have a point I suppose, Christophe," she concedes. "Not that there are any hard and fast rules per se. But you're right—I have indeed used the definite article to cover two planets."

Mademoiselle Richemont interjects…

"Well, I think in this case we can bend the rules slightly, don't you?" Christophe isn't happy about it. "Why?" he says pointedly.

I have had enough of this. Something inside me snaps. I stand suddenly as if someone has pulled me up by an invisible thread. I am no longer in command of myself.

I feel the betrayal of Monsieur Gazides with every fibre of my being. "Simeon, sit down!"

Madame Alaric knows I am troubled, but she is not prepared to see me disrupt the class like this.

I stand. She flinches.

"I just want to give you my answer," I state, disarmingly.

"Wait to be asked, Simeon…it is only courteous."

"That's quite alright, Madame…" says Mademoiselle Richemont, holding the chalk up for me.

Madame Alaric demurs. The two teachers stand aside as I take the chalk and start writing.

I hear a collective gasp from the class as the words reveal themselves.

'Mon—Visionnaire—Tortué—Muert.   Judas—Suit—Un—Nouveau—Professeure.' Silence.

"Get out!" Madame Alaric's command is delivered softly—almost casually. She points at the door.

I blink at the string of words I have just written.

"Get out!" she repeats, louder this time.

"But it's correct isn't it, Madame…I mean, it's the right answer—the planets in their correct order of distance from the sun…"

I read aloud robotically for all to hear.

"My—tortured—visionary—dies. Judas—follows—a—new—teacher."

"Get out of my classroom…now!"

I go to my desk, sullenly pack my workbook and pencil into my bag and head for the door.

The corridors echo to my footsteps. I vow never to set foot inside the Lycée René Coty again.

The Farmhouse, Medea Wilaya,
1 February 1957

"Of course, you will!" exclaims Lieutenant Mauritz as he knocks his boots against the door frame to clear them of mud. "Captain LeBoeuf insists that all pupils and all teachers go to school during the General Strike. I will take you there myself this morning."

"Thanks, but I'm staying put."

Waleed, who has been seated at the table loudly sucking at his beaker of coffee, tuts disapprovingly at my insolence.

Mauritz is trying his best to avoid Mother as Baby Claude nuzzles into her breast and feeds.

She tears around the kitchen making and fetching breakfast while the feeding infant takes his fill. She is grateful for the Lieutenant's consideration. After all, there is not much privacy in this leaky bayt rifi.

She succeeds in shielding her breasts from view under her loose fitting jellaba and has wrapped Baby Claude in a shawl and a thin blanket to obscure the view of the feed.

She's having to readjust the layers and finds it difficult whilst simultaneously delivering fresh bagita along with piping hot coffee to the table.

I only wish Waleed would extend her the same courtesy as the Lieutenant.

He is nursing his cup of coffee at the kitchen table, angling for a top-up, whilst simultaneously trying to humour Margot who is drumming the table leg with a wooden spoon. He is preoccupied with Baby Claude's feeding routine and more specifically by the tantalising thought of glimpsing Mother's naked breast.

Louis is intent on gathering his books for the day and Mother is coaxing him to the table by slathering his favourite mushed tomatoes onto a heel of the sliced bagita.

Waleed has his greedy eye on that too but is distracted by the unruly din Margot is creating. He takes the spoon off her with a manic wide-eyed glare and she thinks about crying but resists. Her lower lip wobbles instead. "So, we will be taking the children to Madame Hachemi today, Basira?" he enquires, smiling broadly at Margot to placate her, then giving me the evil eye. "And it looks like you will be going with Lieutenant Mauritz."

Mother is clearly not happy with the arrangement. She doesn't want the soldiers driving me away in their vehicles yet again as they did last Monday morning.

She hasn't yet recovered from the shock of that. I'm not sure she will ever erase it from her memory.

"Why can't Shimeun come in the bus with us? We'll drop him at the school gates on the way."

"This is the express wish of Captain LeBoeuf, Madame…I'm sorry, but I have my orders."

Lieutenant Mauritz is still trying his utmost to avert his gaze from Claude's tiny puckering mouth locked onto Mother's teat. His eyes are directed out towards the yard through the open door where a chicken is fossicking around one of LeBoeuf's staff car tyres, trying to dislodge some seeds from its tread.

"Let him go, Basira," pipes up Waleed, "He'll be fine. He'll be safe with the Lieutenant here. The Lieutenant is a good man. Would you like some of this bagita, Lieutenant?"

"Thank you, no. I've already eaten…"

I am indignant that Waleed is offering our breakfast to Lieutenant Mauritz without asking for Mother's say-so. Just as I'm disappointed that I haven't been consulted about going to school.

The adults want to resolve the issue without me. They are rattling on as if I wasn't there, putting about as much value on me as a farmer does on a lame nag.

I make sure they're in no doubt about it.

"I'm not going…"

Waleed tuts again. As if I hadn't heard him the first time "…and you think you have a say in it do you?"

I appeal to Mother, but she has neither the energy nor the capacity to take issue with the Lieutenant. She thinks it's a good idea that I go anyway.

Lieutenant Mauritz takes her silence as assent and an end to the matter. "Come! Or we'll be late…"

"No!" I protest.

Lieutenant Mauritz takes a step into the kitchen.

"Oh, Simeon. This is all very tiresome." sighs Waleed, moving to grab half of Louis's breakfast off his plate.

Mother slaps Waleed's hand away and glares at him, knowing his ill-timed intervention just makes matters worse.

She knows exactly how to play Waleed.

It's a presumed intimacy on his part. He is starting to behave like her husband and our stepfather, as if he owns the place—which of course he says he does. And Mother sees the need to remind him every now and again that his sense of entitlement is totally baseless.

Lieutenant Mauritz is starting to stiffen and bristle at my open display of petulance.

"Spare your Mother any more grief," he says quietly. "You will go back to school. And you will come with me now."

The delivery of this simple command stops everyone in their tracks. Even little Margot. There is something incontestable in this statement. Something implacable that makes me shudder.

Lieutenant Laurent has learned a great deal from his master, LeBoeuf. I realise that I have little choice in the matter.

As we drive past the para guard in the car, Mauritz tells me how lucky I am that Captain LeBoeuf is in good spirits today.

He explains that it's a red-letter day for the Captain because the General Strike has been smashed. Another line to add to his glowing résumé. Consequently, he will excuse my rebelliousness in the classroom as nothing more than an aberration. A blip. And so will Madame Alaric.

"But don't think that is an end to it, Simeon. As our American cousins say, three strikes and you're out! By my estimation, you are on strike three.

Patience is wearing thin. Blot your copybook une fois de plus and your directrice will certainly never let you back in her school."

I ask myself again why LeBoeuf is taking such a close interest in my progress. Then I put the question openly to Lieutenant Mauritz.

"I would have thought the Captain has better things to do with his time than check up on my school timetable," I assert.

"He is involved. Let's leave it at that."

Lieutenant Mauritz is doing Captain LeBoeuf proud. He is giving nothing away and that is exactly what the Captain wants.

Lycée René Coty, Medea Wilaya, 8 February 1957

The week has passed without incident. My mood has even started to lighten. I've joked about with Christophe and Verna at break time and taken lessons in my stride. I've sat quietly in class, studiously working through my course notes and staying out of Madame's way.

Mademoiselle Richemont has retained her irrepressible cheerfulness, of course. I find that the longer I am in her class, the easier it is to accept—even to return—her bonhomie. Indeed, against all expectations, I am starting to find it offers me some relief from a heavy heart.

Despite this, all is not perfect with the Mademoiselle. Something is keeping me on my mettle around her. It's not just her implied criticism of Monsieur Gazides. There's something else.

I stare at her in lessons, study her, keep trying to understand what it is about the blithe Mademoiselle Richemont that is out of keeping. The answer eludes me until one day half-way through the afternoon, I finally work it out.

The Mademoiselle is explaining the periodic table to a stupefied class and playfully suggesting some amusing acronyms for chemical symbols.

When I study her closely, I find that whenever her mouth forms a smile—which it often does—her eyes remain lustreless and sad. Which is to say that, despite her natural gaiety, she never leaves me with a smile in my mind.

I'm sure my feeling is shared by the class as a whole. I've no doubt she always intends a smile, but I don't believe that she actually means it.

I find this extraordinary given she is, as Madame Alaric puts it, "one of life's radiators."

Or maybe it's just me…

You see, I am gripped by that infernal procession of images.

The hanging Lieutenant Laurent comes back to haunt my dreams regularly most nights. 'Invasion of the Body Snatchers' is a recurring nightmare. I continue to dream of Mother and Father and our walk on the salt flats, although recently the human eagles have appeared in that dream too. Scavengers high up in the sky waiting for me to drop.

Night after night, I wake in a muck sweat with Louis and Margot slumbering beside me, blissfully unaware of my returning night terrors.

As for Monsieur Gazides, I long to hear word. But I also fear it. I'm not quite sure which feeling tugs at me more. All I know is that with each day that passes, receiving any news of my erstwhile form teacher seems an increasingly remote possibility.

I mention it to Christophe in the yard.

"Have you heard anything?"

"No," he replies, and then adds "Why? Are you expecting to?"

"S'pose not. Not really. Well, kind of…Hope so."

That is the genius of Major Paul Aussaresses and his acolytes—how the torturers can make the disappeared and the dead taunt the living.

The Road to Medea, Medea Wilaya, 21 February 1957

I am growing used to the morning routine again.

The grinding of the gears on Waleed's bus, the wheeze and chug of the engine as it labours up the hill towards Medea with a full complement of passengers on board, the casual jostling and barging at the bus stops along the way.

My para escort is sitting on the back seat surrounded by Pied-Noir office workers and Arab women on their way to the souk carrying empty shopping baskets.

He is making a vain attempt to edge their baggage out of his personal space, trying to secure a zone interdite around himself.

As more people pack into the bus, however, he finds that he can no longer hold out.

He resigns himself to sitting atop the incoming tide of bags, crates and cases-perching as comfortably as a French soldier can among a bus load of Pieds-Noirs and Francophile Muslims, trying not to lose face.

Lieutenant Mauritz hasn't been to our farmhouse for several days now. He has been assigned to the Zone Autonome d'Alger in the Casbah where, far from winding down, Colonel Massu's operation is gaining momentum.

Needs must.

Captain LeBoeuf's men may have seen off the strikers, but the ringleaders and agitators have only temporarily gone to ground. They will be back.

The threat to the Fourth Republic is undiminished. Indeed, the strike has made it more real.

General Massu has set Captain LeBoeuf the task of not just breaking the strike but demolishing it. And then clearing away the collateral damage.

In the aftermath of this demolition, a pall of dust has risen up from the ruins of a febrile city. As the people of Algiers wait for these clouds to settle, they wonder what they are in for next.

It doesn't take an oracle to know the answer. Nor even an educated guess. It is transparent to most. The citizens of Algiers are waiting for the bombs to go off again all over their Wilaya. They have no idea where or when. They just know that it is coming.

The thought is etched into the lost and frightened faces on Waleed's bus. I encounter them every morning and most afternoons.

The Pied-Noir commuters are bug-eyed with fear and sleeplessness. They have transformed into nocturnal pacing animals, insomniacs, weary of the struggle, the killings, the perpetual tripwire vigilance.

Their faces have turned liverish beneath their olive complexions. Each one of them knows of a friend, relative or colleague who has been cut down by an assassin's bullet or blown to kingdom come. And each one knows there but for the grace of God or Allah...

Likewise, the Algerian Arabs who catch Waleed's bus every morning to reach their places of work in the fields and factories along the way. Made third class citizens in the country of their forefathers. Their faces are pale and raddled too. They could speak at first hand of inhuman acts—from Sétif to Philippeville and now Algiers. But they choose to remain silent. They have lost loved ones, sacred ones, innocents. That is why they all appear to have aged five years in as many months.

Both of these tribes are under no illusion that the end of the strike is just a temporary reprieve from the hostilities.

The 'collection service' has stopped. The calls of the FLN organisers and activists have been muted, and Captain LeBoeuf must surely be due a promotion. But celebrations are not exactly the first thing on their mind.

There is another entirely contrary mood circulating in the narrow alleys and passages of the Casbah, the boulevards and avenues of the European quarter.

Those colons and Pieds-Noirs foolhardy enough to raise a glass to the end of the strike may live to regret it. If indeed they live at all.

Today, they may feel that they are on the right side of history. They may feel entitled to make a home here for good within this old Phoenician port, this jewel of the Ottoman empire set beside an azure sea. They may assume that a comfortable rhythm will return to their daily lives here in this Département of France on the North African Riviera.

But if they do, they deceive themselves. Because there is something they haven't bargained for.

The quashing of the General Strike in such a brutal, boorish way has let loose an unstoppable moral force. A clamour for independence that will not be quelled until the flag of Abdelkader is raised above the ancient medina.

It won't be long before the bomb carriers once again come knocking on the doors of the bomb-making factories. Soon the detonators will be connected to the explosives, the bombs planted, and plans executed. And these deadly devices will keep coming like the waves that smash at the harbour wall of Algiers. They will keep coming if it takes the next year, the next decade, the next millennium to see French resolve crumble into the Mediterranean Sea.

The tide may have gone out for now. But those connected with the French are under no illusions. Not really. They may keep on enjoying their privileges day to day, but deep down they know that they are living on borrowed time.

Somewhere right now in the Casbah, a boy even younger than myself is carrying five-gallon jugs of acetone and ammonium nitrate from safe-house to safe-house right under the noses of French paratroopers.

Somewhere a man baking kalb elouz at the back of his shop is offering blessings to black and white photographs of ALN fellaghas as they prepare to shoot down paratroopers in the Boulevard Verdun.

And somewhere one of Yacef Saadi's bomb-runners is touching the stones of the mausoleum of the Marabout Sidi Abderrahmane before handing his bombs over to the mujahidats so they can sow death in the El-Biar Municipal stadium.

This is just another day in the Casbah, strike or no strike. And the suburbs are not exempt from its shockwaves. Algiers is on high alert and Medea Wilaya is in its ambit.

Here outside the Lycée René Coty, the Harki presence has been scaled down, though they have strict instructions to shoot on sight anyone they suspect of being maquis or ALN.

For now, however, all is well-meaning pandemonium. Harki troop transporters doubling as school buses and the armoured vehicles of the tenth para have been replaced by the usual jam of civilian vehicles in the narrow road up to the Lycée.

Normal service has been resumed. Parents are dropping their offspring, the bus drivers are upbraiding them for dawdling and holding up the traffic. Their strident voices are raised in protest at the delays. Harki hands are held up not to obstruct but to pacify, direct, and negotiate.

Cars are manoeuvred, paths through the traffic cleared. The school is in business for the day.

I am at the school gates now, having just jumped off Waleed's bus, which is slowly pulling away with Mother and the family on board.

I feel a wave of tenderness towards our tight-knit little family unit.

Louis is pulling a silly face through the window, licking at the glass and writing his name in the sticky saliva with his finger.

Mother is trying to contain Baby Claude who is kicking and punching at her breastbone with his pudgy limbs, wanting to be released from her arms.

Margot is standing on her seat yawning and peering over the headrest at the back of the elderly man's head in front of her. She is enchanted by his protruding ears and slowly reaches out to touch a giant earlobe.

Waleed pulls the bus out into the steadily moving stream of traffic and I finally lose sight of them.

Distracted, I find myself caught up in a crowd of parents at the gate.

I am searching for a way through the hubbub to the school yard when I become aware of a woman in a jilbab right beside me.

She is steering me discreetly by the elbow out of the group and away from the gates. At first, I think she is being helpful, a good citizen. But as she retains her grip, that thought quickly evaporates.

I instinctively move to edge her off me, but she resists. She has my arm firmly in her grasp.

She is strong. Under her loose jilbab, there is a woman with an athletic gait and an irresistible forward momentum. She strolls with urgency at getaway velocity, neither too fast to set off alarms, nor too slow to risk being caught.

I have an idea she must be concealing a revolver within the folds of her garb. The thought makes me bend to her silent force.

I squirm at the thought of an assassin at my side.

Zohra Drif, Djamila Bouhired, Samia Lakhdari, the mujahidat. Have these women come for me now?

The woman is nudging me towards an improvised car park strewn with rubbish, a convenient dumping ground used by the residents in this part of town.

She has one eye on the Harki guard still attempting to hold back the tide of parents and pupils outside the school gates.

She opens the passenger door of a decrepit deux chevaux-vapeur, its paintwork encrusted with guano and pitted with rust. As I plant myself inside, I am hit by a strong whiff of roadkill and puke. Quite a funeral casket, I think. I can almost hear the marabout offering prayers as I am entombed in it.

At this point, the thought of running away or putting up a struggle hasn't even crossed my mind. The woman moves with such agility and stealth I can't imagine being able to escape from her. She gives me little choice but to go along with this quietly efficient abduction. And I watch her going about her operation with mounting fascination as if I am on the margins, an observer to it, not at the centre of it, the target.

There she is darting around to the driver's door. Here she is already beside me in the driver's seat. And there is her hand turning the key in the ignition and wrestling with the gearstick.

I sit very still as she slips the car into gear and starts driving. I am in shock, but twice removed and floating above myself as I did at Au Bon Marché department store last Monday morning.

I see the Lycée slip away in the wing mirror as my kidnapper moves up through the gears and we accelerate off up the road.

We are quite a distance from the Lycée now.

And it is then, whilst the car is picking up velocity that I come to my senses.

I am seized by the overwhelming compulsion to save myself.

I dive for the door handle and snatch at it. The passenger door swings open, the car veers wildly to the left and I move to throw myself out into the road.

The woman in the jilbab has other plans.

She is determined to keep me in the car at all costs and forms a tight brace against my chest with her outstretched arm.

She has phenomenal strength.

Pulling on the passenger-side seatbelt, she smartly wraps it around my neck like a garrotte and ties me in. I am trying to release myself, but the more I fight it, the tighter it becomes and the more entangled I am.

The car lurches from left to right as she grapples me with one hand and the steering wheel with the other.

She flings the car back to the right with a squeal of tyres and straightens the vehicle just in time to prevent it from skidding into an oncoming truck, its horn blaring in our ears.

There is now a restraining hand around my throat. She has me in a chokehold. I clear my airwaves violently as if that will somehow make her ease off.

But she is having none of it.

She pins me to my seat, pulls at the wheel and turns the car into a side street—a short strip of concrete that peters out into scrubland. She pulls the car to a halt and reaches across me to slam the door shut. The car takes a final lurch before the engine putters and stalls.

She slaps me around the face repeatedly. Hard.

"What the fuck…!" I scream in shock.

She is simmering. Her jaw is clenched. Sweat trickles down the furrow of her brow from her hairline. She wipes it away with the back of her hand and her mascara smudges. She takes a few moments and then turns to me.

"Calm down, my little wingman…"

She is a crazy woman. A psychopath. This time I am going to bolt for it. I flail around, pushing the seatbelt off me with thrashing hands as if a boa constrictor has wrapped itself around me and I must release myself from it by any means possible before it squeezes the life out of me.

I throw open the door, fling myself out of the seat and charge across the waste ground away from her grasp. She instantly pursues me. It's a desperate foot race now. A mortal chase. But she is too fast. I can't compete. She is behind me in a flash, tackling me from behind and pulling me down. I lash out at her with my legs.

"Simeon! Stop it!" yells Father, straddling me and trying to pin my arms to the ground.

I kick some more, then freeze and take in the face beneath the hood of the jilbab. Rouge, lipstick, eyeliner. Enough foundation to coat the closely shaven stubble of his chin with flesh-tinted powder.

A clown.

I want to laugh—and my laughter becomes a deep roar of pain.

I lash out at him with everything I have. Arms. Legs. Forehead. Punching. Kicking. Head-butting. Sending a cloud of dust up into the humid air.

I catch him in the groin with my foot and he falls off me, groaning. I roll over and start pummelling him with my fists as though I am in a playground scrap.

I am incoherent. I scream at him between heaving sobs. Starbursts of pain and loss are flashing before my eyes.

"You left me…you left me for dead…you blew me up…then you killed him like you wanted to kill me…you left Mother, Louis, Margot, Claude…you left us…you left us…and Laurent…you hung him from that tree…you hung him…you left him for the crows…you fucking traitor…you fucking coward…"

Father is jerking his head from left to right trying to avoid my punches most of which land in the dirt, grazing my knuckles.

"Not my face, Simeon," he cries, "Please! Anywhere but my face!"

But I keep going at his mouth, his nose, his cheeks. He continues to shield himself and my blows land on his forearms, his wrists, his hands.

"I came to you and you weren't there, like you weren't there in the Casbah before and you haven't been there for me since…and you left me to that man LeBoeuf…you left me to him…you let him torture me…you didn't come for me…you fucking coward…how can you?…how the fuck can you? How can you choose to blow me up? Your son."

"Not the face, Simeon. Do you hear? Not the face."

It is raw. It is wild. And it continues to pour out of me.

"How can you kill a man like that? He was our friend. Our last chance. He could have got us out of here. You have done this…you! I hope they catch you…I hope they catch you…the Army…the fellaghas…whoever the fuck it is you work for…I hope they catch you and string you up like you did him. And leave you for dead like you did to me…you fucking cowardly traitor…"

My fists are still flying at him, beating out my words on his hard body.

Father is trying to hold my wrists to restrain me. He is wincing with each blow. He will continue to take them until the fire burns itself out.

"Shh…" he tries to calm me. 'Simeon. Simeon. My little wingman…" But his pacifying tone just makes me want to thump him more.

"Stop calling me that! I'm not little. And I'm not watching your back any more…"

The muscles in my leg are aching and my breath is short. I am starting to flag. My fists are slowing. My arms are shot. I am devoid of energy, but my blows are still coming. I drag up every ounce of strength. From where, I have no idea.

I punch the dry earth beside him with gasps and sobs.

"Why?" I bellow from the depths of my gut. "Why have you done this to me? What have I ever done to you?"

I am on all fours like a dog that's been whipped and burned. I am bawling into the ground now. I throw up bile and I spit mucus which sinks into the giving, loamy earth.

Father has a hand on my shoulder. He is now sitting on his haunches beside me as he did in the ravine when we hunted the deer. Keeping low. Staying out of sight. His eyes glisten and he is trembling. He is trying to soothe me as I heave and shake.

"Shh…breathe, my boy…breathe."

I take a deep breath just like he says.

"Tell me…please…tell me…what have I done, Father?"

"Come!" He stands unsteadily, offering me his hand. I take it and he raises me up from the dirt. I can see he is sore.

He puts his arm around me and leads me back to the car. We sit and stew in silence. My heart is racing at a thousand kilometres an hour. Tears run down his cheeks.

After a short while, he reaches for the glove box. He takes out a lady's compact mirror, a tissue and a lipstick, checks in the rear-view mirror, dabs concealer and powder on his face and lightly colours his lips.

"What the fuck are you doing?" I ask incredulously.

"It's survival, Simeon. You and I are survivors. That's the way it has to stay."

He drives in silence towards Algiers, looking over at me every so often, reaching out to touch my arm and check that I am alright.

Approaching Algiers, he passes me a taqiyah.

"Put it on! We are going to the souk. We will be grandmother and son."

Mother was right. He is quite demented.

He drives towards the Marine Quarter. A party of gendarmes and soldiers at a roadblock are checking cars. I squirm in my seat, but they don't seem that interested in us. I look to Father again for clues. He offers none.

I take in the sight of the port and the sparkling Mediterranean. A sweep of French colonial houses faces out to sea where blockading French frigates ply the horizon. A pleasure boat heads out to Djerba with no passengers on board.

Arabic fishermen slouch, smoke and brag on the quayside. A Pied-Noir family is playing on the beach.

Father turns off the Boulevard de Marine and into a ruelle leading away from the quay. A sign on the side wall of a ship's chandler proclaims the Rue Quincie. This quiet street is lined with garages and the odd makeshift lean-to. At the top of the street, a fishing boat on a trailer has been hauled out of the water and is now stranded in the dry dock of an abandoned lot, its mast flat to its centreboard. Its barnacle-encrusted hull and cracking paintwork point to its neglect.

Further along, an old man lazily weaves a wooden bar through the mesh of a fishing net laid out on trestles on the pavement.

Father drives to the end of the street and pulls the car up outside a garage whose hinges are black with rust. There are fissures in the wood and the bottom edge of one of the doors has warped and splintered so badly that it's possible to see underneath to the inside.

He shakes the dust from his jilbab and takes an empty shopping basket from the back seat.

I hear a pop of gunfire from further up in the medina. I look up to the sight of the Casbah rising beyond the old colonial edifices of the Marine Quarter.

I wait for Father to lock the car.

"You can never be too safe…" he says, pocketing the keys.

"Where's the truck?" I ask.

"I traded it for this. With a farmer in El-Achour."

I can see who came away with the better deal.

"Come! Let's go shopping!" Father says.

He walks carefully with small steps. His head is fixed on the ground. He takes my hand and holds it tightly in his grasp.

"Remember, we are mother and son on our way to market…"

A convoy of Army trucks lumbers up the road behind us. The soldiers watch us absently as they pass, but they don't stop. Traders whizz past us on their scooters and in cars but are too focused on the business of the day to spare us their time or attention. An old boy flays his yoked oxen with a bull whip as he hauls a cart heavily laden with stone bolders up the incline from the port.

We proceed largely unnoticed. Nobody gives a second look to a Muslim matriarch with clown make-up and her morose grandson, teetering up the hill towards the central boulevard of the Casbah and the souk.

After a few minutes, I take a look to see how far we have climbed. Quite a way in such a short period of time.

The steep streets and stairways cascade down to the Mediterranean stretching out behind us. Way beyond the harbour wall, I can just make out the natural breakwater of islands—El Djazair—standing sentinel out to sea.

We strike off the main road and enter a world of shadows.

We scale stone staircases, pass under cantilevered overhangs of mud and brick, propped up with beams like a cohort of invalided war veterans on rotting crutches.

We pass under a vaulted first floor chamber arching over our heads and teasing gravity.

We scurry along alleyways off which impasses lead to dead ends of cracked plaster and pockmarked masonry. We head down narrow ruelles pitted with cracks and potholes, flanked by stucco facades.

Within this ramshackle tangle of buildings and winding streets, there is one constant. Hardly a wall or facade is untouched by the scars of bullet-holes and blast radius.

Father knows exactly where he is going. I accidentally collide with him as he makes sudden turns and unexpected breaks into the mouths of ever-climbing passages and alleyways. He urges me to keep up with him and stay beside him so that we behave to all intents and purposes like grandmother and son out shopping for the daily staples.

As we walk side by side, hand in hand up through the Casbah, Father quietly confides that in our scenario the grandmother will rely on her young charge to do her fetching and carrying in the souk. To help make light work of the grocery errands. And the son will respect the wishes of the mother.

I tell him I cannot help him with this play-acting as I have no idea why we are here or what he is up to. He scowls back at me from under his jilbab, putting me further on edge.

The role of dutiful grandson? Fuck you!

I am angry as hell with him.

"Perfect," he jibes, "you are in character already."

As he pulls me along, I peek in through the bombed-out portal of an Ottoman loggia. Above the shaded courtyard rise three storeys of arched gallery. I notice a couple of little girls with smudged faces clinging to the cracked balustrades of the first floor whilst their mother in niqab pegs out the washing.

I think of Mother and Margot and Louis and what they would make of Father now.

The cupola and tower of mosque and minaret reveal themselves to us, rising above the medina at every corner and through every aperture, vying for airspace with the dome of the Cathedral of Saint Philippe in a monumental stand-off.

An ascending flight of red-tiled roofs with tightly abutting terraces reminds me of our dash from the fellaghas. How Father leapt like a cat across the rooftops.

I hope and pray there will be no such frantic chase through the Casbah today. Though I can't say—I really haven't a clue what trap Father is leading me into now.

We hear the souk even before we see it. An inchoate burble of sound that comes at us full blast as we draw closer—a wall of chat and gossip punctuated by the cries of delivery men and traders.

We head down passages which now seen more familiar to me. The narrow course between shops and stalls is strewn with waste, abandoned baskets, rubble, splintered crates, empty bottles, cast-off boxes. Stray cats and dogs mark their territory.

The shopkeepers' wares and goods spill out into the gullies between the shops—pallets, display stands and shelves. Vendors choose to sit outside their stalls directly in the path of passing trade so they can greet old customers and waylay new ones.

Some keep an ear out for Radio Algiers which blares out from transistors in shop doorways, others read 'El-Moudjahid' in open defiance of Army patrols.

The paratroopers will no sooner spot the masthead of this banned newspaper than pluck its reader out of the souk, pin him up against a wall and 'disappear him' to a centre d'hébergement for further questioning.

Father hands me ten dinars from a purse.

"Shimeun. Go buy five juicy oranges, harissa, chermoula, honey, a quart of couscous—and an artichoke from that vendor over there. I will let you do my buying."

"You choose to call me by my Arab name now!? What's going on?"

"I will tell you in due course."

"Now!" I insist. "Tell me now!"

"See that café over there? I will be there at the far table in the corner. When you've done your shopping, join me. Then you can put to me any questions you want to ask. But do this first. Now go!"

Father hands me the basket and makes a beeline for the café.

It takes longer to shop than I thought. I can't find my bearings as I spin from one stall to the next to fetch the goods on Father's...or should I say grandmother's...list.

I am finding even basic tasks are becoming harder to accomplish. My head is frothing with pure fear—panic, confusion and dread. I can barely put one foot in front of the other, let alone make a transaction over an artichoke.

Having completed my errands, I am relieved to be seated, even if only within a lightless, airless café in the dimmest and dingiest section of the souk.

"Did you get them?" he asks.

"Yes," I reply, presenting him with the shopping and a few dinars in change.

"Good boy. Now that we have a full basket you can start to play the part. You will have to get into your role. Give it a bit more belief. That way you will get to stay alive."

"What?"

"Coffee?"

"Coffee...!" I exclaim, exasperated, "You owe it to me...what do you mean by 'stay alive'...what is going on here?"

"First things first, my little wingman. This place serves the best coffee in the whole of Algeria. This is Jameel's café. You remember Jameel? My best customer?"

I do remember. I remember approaching the café from the other end of the souk the night Father killed the deer. I was tremulous then. I am scared witless now.

I recall him delivering the fresh venison carcass to Jameel's kitchen and Jameel giving him forty dinar and a bottle of Pernod for his troubles.

Indeed, Jameel is settling with a customer right now. Father waits patiently for the patron to pay.

"Father, you said I could ask you anything..."

Father leans over to me and whispers discreetly in my ear.

"Call me 'Father' once more and I will rip your head off and give it to a Mexican to use as a skull on the Day of the Dead."

I recoil. Is he joking? No, his eyes flare and he is in earnest. He is quite insane.

"Surely no one can hear us," I say, innocently enough.

Father is angry, but vigilant. He is careful to modulate his voice under his breath.

"Do you know where you are? Do you even understand how dangerous this is? Do you know how FLN cells operate? How they communicate with each other?

By virtue of couriers and informants on street-corners and in cafés such as this one. You cannot see them. But you can smell them.

Sniff the air now! They are all around us. The treacherous stink. Spies, messengers, snitches. That is why we're here…"

I have had enough of this. I deserve answers and he is the one bombarding me with questions.

"Yes, I think I can smell it. It's coming off you right now."

Father delays his reaction long enough to let my insult rebound off him and back at me.

"One day you will realise. One day you will know your father. But right now, right this minute, I don't have time for your pathetic backchat…"

We both check to see whether Jameel has yet managed to disentangle himself from the irate customer who thinks he is being overcharged.

I turn to Father.

The powder, the mascara, the lipstick. I could swear he has even teased a black curl out of his hairline and down over his forehead to try to make himself appear winsome.

I want to kill him. Right now, I want to plant a fork in his eye and winkle it out. "Won't Jameel see through your disguise?" I ask.

"I sincerely hope so," Father replies. "He is in on it. We have business. Today I am his customer. But I am buying more than a coffee and oublis for breakfast."

"You are buying lunch too?"

Father pinches my cheek and lightly slaps my face the way a proud matriarch would. I resent him for this role-play.

"Very funny. You are regaining your sense of humour, see. And getting into the part. There, I told you it would be fun…

His sarcasm is mean-spirited and cheap. No, he didn't tell me. And I am a long way from having fun...

"Today, I am buying information off Jameel. Important information," he continues. "He says at the right price, he will fetch it for me. We shall see whether or not he sells me a pup...or whether his dog can hunt."

I have no idea what he means.

"What are you doing here?" I ask earnestly, trying my hardest not to provoke him.

"I told you. Keeping us alive."

He has hooked me again. My temper rears up and snaps back at him. "Keeping us alive! From the man who blew me up, that's quite something."

"Keep it down, my dear grandson. I did it to save you..."

"Save me? You brought the Casbah down on top of me."

"If I had allowed those fellaghas to take you out of that square, it would have been the end of you...they would have butchered you alive..."

"So you decided to kill me first..."

"Can't you see, I saved you..."

"Mon Dieu, you have some gall."

"You're here, aren't you!"

"And Lieutenant Laurent?"

"What about Lieutenant Laurent?"

"Why did you kill him?"

"I didn't..."

"You are lying!" I say, raising my voice a notch.

"Keep it down..."

"You are lying," I repeat in a hushed voice. "You strung him up from the branch of a tree and you left him to rot. You are a liar and a murderer. I know you were there at Koudiat el-Markluf. I went there to find you. I found him swinging from a tree instead."

"I swear to you, my little wing man...I had nothing to do with Lieutenant Laurent's death. You have to believe me."

I am thinking that the onus is on him, not me. He has to win back my trust. Isn't that how this works? Or am I missing something here?

"Are you telling me you never met with him at the ravine?" I say.

"Oh, I met with him alright...or rather he met with me...but it wasn't me who killed him."

"Who, then…?"

"Lieutenant Laurent had come very prepared to kill me."

"So, you killed him in self-defence? Then decided you should string him up like a game bird for good measure…?"

"Enough!"

Jameel has finally extricated himself from the complaining customer and is approaching us. For a man of such considerable girth, he moves swiftly between tables.

"Ah, Fatiha…Mahmoud, so good to see you! It's been a while. My, haven't you grown, Mahmoud…"

Jameel has not just been expecting me, but to weave me in to this charade. Between him and Father, they have their story all mapped out.

"…Your usual, Fatiha?"

Father nods.

"Absolutely," he says scribbling the order on a pad of receipts, tearing one off, slapping it down on the table and pushing it under a sugar bowl.

"And oublis for you, Mahmoud? Your favourite, I seem to recall."

He has never served me oublis in my life.

"Thank you." I hesitate to go along with it, but Father has left me little choice.

"The oublis is on the house…I'll be right back!"

Our host retreats. Father glances at the receipt. A sharp intake of breath.

"A little steep for coffee…" He replaces the slip of paper back underneath the bowl. "But at least Jameel has what I want on his menu. He is in play."

I don't hear him. I crave answers, not riddles.

"I don't believe you…about the Lieutenant. I don't believe you."

"As you wish," says Father noticing a sudden commotion further up the alleyway.

A patrol of paratroopers is barrelling its way through the throng, scattering goods and kicking over chairs.

Four soldiers in the vanguard dart away from the group and storm an electrical shop. The remainder of the patrol mobilise around the shopfront, rifles trained on the interior.

A man charges out into the alley and is brought down amid a clatter of lampshades and electrical parts. There are scuffles, a cry of "sur le terrain! Maintenant!"

Two other men, one younger than the other—young enough to be the other man's son—are thrown face down on the ground and their hands cuffed behind their backs.

The soldiers form a human cordon around the three captives, backing away from a hostile crowd, weapons at the ready.

The crowd presses in, hurling jibes. The paras push them back. A few soldiers wield batons.

I watch the battery of French muscle retreat with its human catch as quickly as it has arrived.

I notice that during the course of the fracas, a sheen of sweat has surfaced on Father's forehead. He is scared, but he will not let that deflect him. This is our game of un, deux, trois, soleil—but this time the souk is our hunting ground.

He speaks sotto voce behind his jilbab.

"The French are conducting ratonnades all over the Casbah. And they are fucking it up. Going for the hammer-blow rather than the squeeze…

As a result, the once unwary are now wary. The ZAA is on high alert—the Casbah is a coiled spring. Can't you feel it? It is like the seconds before an electrical storm.

No one can manoeuvre in such an atmosphere. That's why I am playing the part of a woman—your grandmother. Because I am well known here. If I didn't, I would attract suspicions. They would take me, kill me, dig a hole and pour quicklime over me like the rest of the 'disappeared'."

"Is that what they'll do to me now I am with you here?" I ask.

You are not known. Neither am I—as a woman at least. This role-play gives us the space to operate…"

"Operate? You mean spy? Is that why we're here?"

"Before, we listened in at cafés for the voices of dissenters. The maquisards gave up their secrets all too easily. By listening, we knew who would be breaking the curfew. We knew who would be making the next move.

This is the same, except that the stakes are far higher since the strike ended. And now everybody is listening in to everyone else…

The FLN see their defeat in the strike as a public relations victory because the world is watching what happens. They are now desperate to force home the advantage in the worldwide court of public opinion…

The Army want to finish the job they started. They are equally desperate to find the men who organised the strike and extinguish the nationalists once and for all. They can only do this by killing the snake at its head…"

"Ben M'hidi," I say, recalling LeBoeuf's plan to stage a suicide in the farmhouse.

"Ben M'hidi. Or if not the biggest fish, others in the shoal…

This is the endgame either way."

I have the terrible presentiment that events are repeating for Father and myself. And I cannot go through it again. I cannot face it.

"So, you are still working for LeBoeuf?"

He thinks about it.

"Ultimately no. I am working for myself. Myself, you, your mother, sister and brothers."

"Ultimately, maybe, but right now?"

Father is still at it, twisting the truth. His lies and evasions offer no real answers. No real hope. He is deceiving me as he has done time after time. And cheating himself.

"Right now, I work for the highest bidder."

He leans into me. "You see, the only way to survive is to play both sides. The clever part is to let neither know I am working for the other."

"Clever or suicidal? Is that why you have been seen in the company of Ali La Pointe and Saadi? Around his bomb-making factory. In the passages de grenade?"

"The Army found the factory. Saadi escaped. To where is anyone's guess. He is about to wreak havoc."

"Did you give away his location?"

"I am trusted by both sides…"

"Answer the question, damn you! Did you give away the location of Saadi's bomb factory?"

"I am building a nest-egg for us."

"You are crazy, Father. Mad. Mother was right. You are demented. They will kill you. You will get us killed. If you work for both sides and you are here in this get-up, then I take it you are being hunted by both sides."

"I am a free agent. The hunter, not the hunted. I tread my own path."

"I get it. You are not selective in your treachery. You are a traitor to everyone."

"You can only betray what you truly believe in."

"Is that why I am here? So that you can betray me again?"

"You are all that I believe in. You, maman, your sister and brothers. You are my life, my faith, my world…"

"Then why am I here?"

"For the same reason I have always chosen to take you with me. Watching my flank. Watching my back. My little wingman. My second set of eyes…"

"Yes, I served your purpose well last time didn't I. You offered me to the fighters as your sacrificial lamb."

"I understand why you are angry. But you are so very wide of the mark. I saved you that day. One day you shall see that and know it. That is the nature of the truth. It will reveal itself over time."

He disgusts me.

"Who killed the Lieutenant?" I ask once again.

He thinks about it.

"LeBoeuf…"

It's a stunning answer. A body-blow. I reel with it.

"LeBoeuf?"

"It is his calling card—to make murder look like suicide."

"But why?"

"Army Intelligence does not just keep watch on the enemy.

The Army also likes to keep an eye on itself. Lieutenant Laurent worked within the GRE to build a secret dossier on Army missteps.

He was occupied with counter insurgency directed at the FLN but was also busy investigating his own.

He was a covert division of Army Intelligence that is keen to root out certain unacceptable practices within the Army's ranks. These sordid practices have LeBoeuf's grubby fingerprints all over them…"

"What practices?"

Father deliberates on whether to tell me. He knows that once he has done so there will no turning back for me. He feels the weight of that responsibility.

He toys with a used coffee spoon, turning it over in his fingers.

"I am talking torture…Massu and Aussaresses are torturers-in-chief and LeBoeuf brings them fresh meat. That's the way it works…"

Just as in my dream. I am reminded of the ravening eagles.

"The General Assembly in Paris is not a big supporter of these methods," Father says. "They are certainly not a vote-winner in France.

Lieutenant Laurent had been investigating LeBoeuf and his associates from a long way back. Reporting into his paymasters back home. You and I, my little wing man—I'm afraid we fall into the category of LeBoeuf's associates."

"So that's why Laurent wanted to catch up with you so badly…"

"Of course. He knows I know a great deal about the Captain and his illegal operations—way back to Philippeville. I would be a principal witness in any trial on the torturing practices of the French. Laurent wanted to take me back to Paris to give evidence against LeBoeuf, and LeBoeuf wasn't prepared to let that happen."

"But Waleed is tighter to LeBoeuf than you are…why didn't Laurent target him?"

"Waleed is a stool pigeon. Waleed is also slave to his own appetites and easily manipulated. He is an idiot, an amateur bomb-maker with no knowledge of the ZAA. Which is limiting. He drives a bus to the European Quarter. He does not know the Casbah. He rarely goes there himself."

"But he planted the bomb you detonated in the Casbah…"

"And caused a lot more damage than LeBoeuf bargained for. The bomb may have spared you, but it killed fifteen Muslim citizens. These are not the kind of people LeBoeuf wants dead. Their killings turn public opinion. And that only makes Lieutenant Laurent's brief a more pressing one.

There is never a good place to plant a bomb, but Waleed really couldn't have chosen a worse one if he'd tried.

Had he known where he was and the extent of collateral damage a bomb of that size was likely to create—with women and children living above…a learned man of faith too who taught in the madrasah…he would not have put his explosives in that passage.

I was horrified when LeBoeuf revealed its location…he made a big mistake sending Waleed in there to wire it up. The only thought going through his mind was to avoid risking his own men—and so he didn't give a second thought to where Waleed put it…

He should have done."

"Waleed is a spy then…?"

"Waleed cannot spy for LeBoeuf in the Casbah. He is a dullard and a liability. As such he is of no great use to the Captain and has therefore been of no great importance to Laurent in his investigations.

No, Waleed is only useful to LeBoeuf in that he can snitch on me from next door. When LeBoeuf agreed to us taking the farmhouse as our home, he made sure he recruited our good neighbour to his cause first.

LeBoeuf is afraid of me. I know too much of what he has done. That is why he sent me into that trap in Place Jean-Paul Sartre. He didn't expect me to come out alive. And he didn't bargain on you being there with me."

"So, you think you are different to Waleed. Better than him?" I suggest.

Father senses the precocity in my question and ignores it. "I know this place just as well as I know the European Quarter. The upper Casbah. The lower Casbah. The souk. The whole Arab Quarter. I supply customers with my wild meat. Why shouldn't I do the same when it comes to supplying information?

I keep the French Army informed of FLN movements. I keep the FLN informed of what the Army is thinking…

Eating is universal! I have found a good clientele here in Algiers. Ali La Pointe and Yacef Saadi have to eat in the same way as the men of the tenth para or the counter-clerks in the Credit Lyonnais Bank. And they too enjoy their venison and rabbit as much as the Captain loves his boar. Why shouldn't they? They are all men of taste and appetite and do not wish to scrimp on their food."

"So, you have met with Yacef Saadi and Ali La Pointe…"

"Of course. The rumours are true. But this is not news to LeBoeuf. He is not stupid. He relies on me to get him information he couldn't come by otherwise. He knows to do that I must get closer to my sources here in the souk.

Without my knowledge of this place and my various alliances to people here, the Army would not have learned the location of Saadi's bomb factory."

It is starting to make sense to me. Why LeBoeuf was itching to see me in hospital. Why Laurent was so insistent on tracking Father.

"So, Laurent would have got you out of the country."

"From Oran, yes, on a boat to Marseilles. That was his plan. He was getting uncomfortably close to shutting LeBoeuf down. He wanted me to give evidence against the Captain, to expose Aussaresses and his butchers and bring them to book.

There are voices in the UN urging these men be brought to trial for crimes against humanity. To set up a Nuremberg style courtroom for the French. To expunge their own demons."

"But why aren't the FLN after you themselves?"

"Because those ALN fellaghas were not exactly loved by the FLN. When the ALN went into the optician that night, they assassinated two of the FLN's most priceless assets. Monsieur et Madame Courvois were double agents, working for the nationalists…"

"But they were Pieds-Noirs."

"Alain Courvois was a staunch Arab nationalist…it was a double bluff, a cover, a backstory. And we were drawn into the reprisal killings every bit as much as LeBoeuf…

The ALN murdering two of their sharpest operatives does not sit well with the FLN leadership…

Make no mistake, they were most grateful we took the fellaghas out…

As for the collateral damage, yes, the FLN vow to avenge every Muslim death…

But it also helps the nationalist cause when a single bombing can provoke such a huge volume of sentiment in the international courts and in the eyes of the world. Strategically, it is all to the greater good of independence…

That's not to say I am immune from reprisals. Following the bombing, I thought it best to lie low…

LeBoeuf knew I had information on the whereabouts of FLN bomb-makers and the FLN would want to make an example of me…"

"So how did LeBoeuf find you at the ravine?"

"He was planning to force the information out of you, my little wing man. But he'd learned that Laurent had been admitted to the Trinitarian hospital with an undiagnosed condition.

He is not stupid, LeBoeuf, despite being an oaf. He knew Laurent would be drilling you for any news of my whereabouts and he knew the Lieutenant wouldn't leave your side without it. So, he let Laurent do all the hard work. When the Lieutenant released himself from the Trinitarian, LeBoeuf was waiting to follow him to Koudiat el-Markluf so he could get to me first and kill me.

I wasn't exactly surprised. I was expecting to be tracked there. Part of me wanted LeBoeuf to find me. But I didn't bargain on Lieutenant Laurent."

"I don't understand…you said Lieutenant Laurent wanted you out of France to give evidence…and yet he wanted you dead?"

"He is a man of principle. But also, a man of passion. I told him I was not prepared to leave Algeria without my wife and my children. It was a pre-condition. And I know your mother is not willing to go.

Laurent had all eventualities covered. He came armed not just with pen and paper for me to sign a written confession. But with a revolver…

I told him if I signed his piece of paper, I would be signing my own death warrant—not just for me, but my family. Can you imagine what LeBoeuf would do to us all if I testified against him?

…Laurent sat me down in the boar hide. Held a gun to my head. Threatened me, you, maman, my flesh and blood. Said he would have no hesitation in blowing my brains out and feeding me to the boar if I didn't sign the confession. So I agreed. He told me he was going to 'lash LeBoeuf to the mast of public opinion'. LeBoeuf would 'go down with the ship of the Fourth Republic'. He certainly had a way with words, that man."

"And LeBoeuf stopped him?"

"The two of them fought. But LeBoeuf got the better of him. He took the rope I used to tie the legs of the boar. He strangled Lieutenant Laurent, marched him up the hill to a tree and, well, that was that…"

Lieutenant Laurent forcing a statement out of Father at gunpoint to incriminate LeBoeuf for crimes against humanity? My head is a muddle. I struggle to understand what is real and what is not. Where the good stops and the bad starts.

Jameel approaches the table with two more kahve finjani.

"You like my coffee, Fatiha?"

Father nods.

"The Turks were good for something, eh?" he says, slapping my back. "Well, they had more than a few hundred years to get it right…your oublis are on their way. And I will give you my speciality creppone to go with them. You are a growing boy, you must be famished! He is getting tall, Fatiha!"

"So, Fatiha!" he pulls up a chair and sits down next to Father. "I hardly get to the upper Casbah these days. How goes life in Bab-EL-Oued?"

Jameel's voice lowers as Father sips at his coffee. He reaches for his purse, grabs a handful of notes and slips several of them under the saucer.

I can't help myself. I reach out to touch a note. I've never set eyes on individual pieces of currency with such a value attached, let alone come to hold one.

Jameel, however, is less impressed. He is disappointed at the amount tendered.

"Ah, Fatiha! And here I am offering you a complimentary breakfast..." Both men talk in whispers.

"You are a bandit, Jameel."

Father discreetly augments the pile of notes with two crisp additions. Jameel flicks each one at its corner with the brisk efficiency of a bank teller, rolls them up tightly together and slides the roll into his waistcoat pocket.

"We are good..."

He leans forward, planting his elbows on the table and rubbing the palms of his hands as if gently washing a stain from them.

"As you know, my wife is a good listener. People like to gossip, and she is often detained in the street by friends who love to chitter chatter..."

"...one of them is utterly convinced that her husband is cheating on her...

He is a mechanic in a repair shop on Rue Marengo...where he works all hours. Hence the suspicion...

Unlike most days of the week, every Tuesday and Thursday he returns home in his stinking overalls, yet apparently only on those two days is he free of grease on his face and his hands...and he smells of patchouli.

As you can imagine from a wife who suspects her husband of infidelity, there is little loyalty left in their marriage. She is not exactly backward in coming forward about his peccadilloes."

"Come to the point, Jameel," whispers Father, "You have your money. I want my goods."

"Ah, be patient won't you...I can assure you, this information is roasted, ground and filtered. It is quality."

"Get on with it, Jameel."

Jameel will take as long as it takes.

"The husband is occasionally called on to service cars that have broken down or are generally misbehaving.

Last week he was called out to Rue Claude DeBussy—to the apartment of the owner of a car that wouldn't start. A Siata 308S. Do you know of that make and model?"

216

Father shakes his head.

"They have very weak engines…You see, this woman's husband is the sole importer of small-block V8 engines and is regularly replacing the misfiring Italian duds with the Yankee real deal.

…These Italians, eh!" he blows his cheeks out in exasperation "They are all swagger and style, no substance. That is how the Yankees have conquered the world.

But I digress…Siata's loss is his gain…"

Father's leg is jiggling under the table. The table is gently shaking with the vibration of his knee.

"Anyway, he went to the address as instructed, knocked on the door and was met by a young lady who handed him a set of car keys. He happened to glance over this lady's shoulder into the hallway of the apartment and who do you think was there?"

He pauses for dramatic effect.

"Yes, yes," says Father, "This prick tease routine may work for you, Jameel, but it doesn't do it for me. Who did he see in this corridor?"

"Benyoucef Benkhedda"

The table stops shaking. Father stares at his interlocutor in disbelief.

"So was the coffee worth the wait after all?" teases Jameel.

Father has been broadsided. He is speechless. Jameel is content to watch him swill the information around in his skull.

"Do you have the precise block and apartment number on Rue Claude Debussy?"

"It's right there on your receipt…Do not leave it behind. And that's not all, Farouk. There is more," he whispers.

But Jameel won't give it away all at once.

"I will fetch your oublis, Mahmoud. My chef is being somewhat tardy today. Apologies—another coffee?"

Father is lost in thought next to me and doesn't hear him.

"Fatiha!" Jameel barks.

Father looks up.

"Another coffee?" he asks again…

Father nods.

Jameel disappears with the empty cups, leaving Father to his thoughts.

"Benkhedda?" I ask.

217

Father slips the receipt into his purse.

"He is the man…Along with Ben M'hidi, he is in control of the Zone Autonome d'Alger."

"The money you handed to Jameel just then…where did you get it?" I ask. Father is starting to tire of questions.

"Where do you think?"

"You robbed a bank?"

"Don't be snarky, my boy…it's not funny and it doesn't become you."

"LeBoeuf, then…"

"As I say, I sell information to the highest bidder. I am merely the middle-man in the deal."

Father catches me frowning.

"Don't worry, my little wingman. I will be applying a handsome mark-up for this information."

"What are you planning to do with it?"

"What do you think! Sell it on to the man you just mentioned…LeBoeuf! It will be worth a lot more to him than Jameel. It may even be enough to pay for a new life for us. If I can set the right price…"

He leaves the thought hanging tantalisingly.

"What is the right price…?"

"Stop with your infernal questions for now, please! You have had a good run. My head is spinning with your damned questions. You are worse than the Prefect of Police."

LeBoeuf has made many promises to Father and failed to deliver on every one of them. I wonder what makes him think this time will be any different.

I fall silent by his side and wait for Jameel to return.

He reappears carrying a small platter of thin grey pancakes smothered in melting lemon sorbet. He props another two cups of kahve finjani on his forearm, balancing them as if on a narrow tray.

"My apologies for the somewhat anaemic dessert. It's been thrown together at the last minute by a chef who is present in body only. Sadly, his head is elsewhere and has not yet returned to work from the General Strike."

I dip my spoon in the smear of sorbet and lick the back of it. It is chilled, tangy and soothes the back of my throat, still raw with the heat and dust of my fight with Father.

Jameel is once again at the table, now in the role of fulsome host. He is spouting small talk to allay any suspicion among his regular patrons.

"There is news in 'Le Monde' of a flu pandemic coming out of China…they think it's from geese…

Here I am thinking the empire will be the undoing of France and it may all come down to their love of fois gras."

Jameel laughs although Father remains stony-faced.

"There's the joke of it. We are busy cooking up bombs, and the foie gras producers may end up killing us all. Is the second coffee as good as the first?" Jameel leers at Father.

This time it is Father's turn to lean in.

"I don't know. I haven't tasted it yet."

"I think you will find it better. These beans are the first press canephora…the flavour improves with every taste."

Father takes two hundred dinar notes and slides them under the saucer. Jameel takes the money and pockets it. He cannot resist licking his lips.

"How is the garage in the Rue Quincie…"

"Basic," says Father, thinking Jameel is now pressing him for the rent.

"The camp bed is to your liking?"

"No. Neither is the smell of creosote."

"It's nothing to do with me. It comes from the garage next door. The man paints and repairs old boats. It's where he keeps his materials."

"Is your neighbour also responsible for the stinking drains?"

"As I say, the garage was not meant to be lived in. Not by humans at least. By boats and cars."

"Well, for a garage that's not meant to be lived in, you are certainly charging me a live-in rent."

"You will find the garage a competitive price for the Marine Quarter, but only if you keep up the payments and avoid penalties."

"Your lodgings might be competitive compared with a palace, but not much else. You are changing the subject, Jameel. This is a ruse. I'd guess you have nothing more up your sleeve by way of information. The cupboard is bare."

Jameel is thrilled to prove Father wrong. He grins knowingly and whispers. His lips are closer to Father's ear than it has been throughout the entire course of the conversation. It's an uncomfortable proximity.

"You do realise don't you, Farouk, wherever you find Lou Costello, Bud Abbot is never far away…"

I am perplexed. Father is too.

"What the fuck are you on about…?" Father mutters testily.

"You know…Abbot and Costello, Hope and Crosby…Daher and Retief. What a forward pairing those guys make for MC Alger, eh? Long ball to Daher. Takes it on his chest. Holds up the defender. Creates space for Retief to score…"

"Get to the point. Please, Jameel. I do not want to wear this jilbab any longer than I have to…and the make-up is wearing thin—like your conversation."

We watch two young men pass by carrying Kalashnikovs. They are in drab, creased suits, frayed Oxford shirts and sandals. They stop to peer into the same electrical shop the Army raided not ten minutes before.

"Laurel and Hardy, Astaire and Rogers, sackcloth and ashes…

…I guess what I am saying is that wherever Benkhedda goes, Ben M'hidi is not far away."

We are off the streets and back in the garage at the Rue Quincie a half hour before curfew.

Up on the hill away from the port, the lower Casbah flickers with small arms fire well into the night as troops of the tenth para skirmish with FLN activists.

They will be going house-to-house this evening as they have every evening of the strike, pulling out activists on the flimsiest of charges and stuffing their centres d'hébergements, jails and containment centres with frightened bodies. Some of those bodies will quake all the way to the guillotine.

I watch the sporadic light show in the Casbah from Jameel's 'live-in rental apartment' as the Marine Quarter falls quiet and the Mediterranean pounds the harbour wall.

It is rough out there tonight.

We are both famished and exhausted.

We have the contents of the shopping basket from the souk. Father fires up a small gas stove that Jameel takes with him on the occasional outings across to the islands.

He boils some water, cooks the couscous, steams the artichoke over the watery chorba and waits for the fleshy leaves to soften. We eat the artichoke with the spiced couscous and flavour it with the harissa. It is succulent but stringy.

I have already asked Father to take me back to the farmhouse. I have no way of contacting Mother—no way of letting her know I am alive and well and residing with Father.

I fear she will think that I have been executed by ALN fellaghas as a reprisal for sending their three Muslim brothers to Paradise. And in all likelihood it will send Mother that way too.

Father tells me he cannot afford to go back to Medea. He has unfinished business here with LeBoeuf in Algiers.

The Captain has him in his pocket.

If he were to break cover and bail on LeBoeuf, the Captain would have him arrested and imprisoned for the bombing and murder of civilians in Place Jean-Paul Sartre.

And anyway, before he allows me to return, there is one thing he would like me to do for him.

He pulls a photograph from Jameel's old nautical map drawer.

The print is badly cracked and feathered.

It shows two men and a boy. One of the men is in his mid-twenties, the other older man resembles Jean Gabin. The boy looks no more than twelve years of age, though all of them proudly display their guns on a street in the Casbah—similar to the trio of resistance fighters we observed in the souk earlier today.

Father paws over it.

"This is gold-dust. It was taken by a fighter for 'El-Moudjahid' as a propaganda photo to stir the hearts of the nationalists.

Benkhedda was the editor and withdrew the photograph for publication when the strike was announced. For obvious reasons. The FLN bombers need to keep their faces hidden to avoid being targeted…

But Jameel has managed to get his grubby hands on a print of the photograph from an informer…at a price, of course.

That man has been put on this Earth to trade…"

Father puts his arm around me and points to the individuals beaming their broad grins down the camera shutter.

"Apparently, the one on the left is Ibrahim Najjar. He is one of Yacef Saadi's bomb transporters.

Since the discovery of his bomb factory, Saadi has gone to ground, but Jameel informs me Najjar is out there actively fetching and carrying.

I want you to remember this face. Commit it to memory. He will eventually lead us to Ali Ammar, aka La Pointe."

"And who are the others?"

"That's Saadi on the right and the anchovy in the middle is Little Omar, Yacef Saadi's nephew, the liaison officer for the FLN."

I stare at the photograph. So, this is the great man Saadi himself. The swashbuckling warrior with the Hollywood looks who the fighters lionise.

The three generations stare back at me out of the shot, frozen in time. They are goading me. The boy in particular. 'I dare you', he is saying. 'I just dare you…'

"Little Omar is their Chief Liaison Officer?"

"I know…Big title for a boy whose balls still haven't dropped. But there are advantages to being small and part of the family. As Yacef Saadi's nephew, he is personally connected to the FLN leadership, Abane Ramdane, Krim Belkacem, Rabah Bitat…Ali La Pointe.

He is the ideal size and stature for liaison too. A skinny one. But he sure can crawl through tight holes.

They say he skips around French roadblocks and confounds LeBoeuf's paratroopers at every twist and turn. He is a valuable asset to Saadi."

Is that what Father thinks of me—no more than 'a valuable asset'?

It sounds expendable however you say it.

"You should get some sleep, my little wing-man. Tomorrow is a big day. We are meeting with the Captain himself…

Today was an unexpected bonus. We have some good news for him…

You are my good-luck charm. I knew that having you along with me would give me hope. It will certainly make the Captain's year.

Here. Have the camp bed. You have earned it. I will take the floor."

At this he fashions a nest out of pillows and blankets thrown down on the hard, cold concrete. He curls up and falls asleep instantly.

A creamy light from the half-moon floods the floor of the garage. I lie awake studying the photograph, but it is the face of the boy that fascinates me, not the bomb transporter.

Father's snoring is peaceful tonight—more the purr of a contented cat or an idling Bugatti.

I lie watching him. I could so easily cave his head in with a boat hook. It is not long before the purr of his engine sends me off to sleep.

The Marine Quarter, Algiers, 22 February 1957

There is a light tapping sound coming from the floor-space around the camper stove, not far from my bed. My eyelids are opening, though I am resisting the shock of morning and my pupils are adjusting to the day.

I am trying to find the source of the sound.

I see something bounce across the concrete into a shaft of watery daylight. Dust motes dance across my vision.

I hear the faintest hint of what sounds like a shuffled deck, and for a split second I think I am back in bed at the farmhouse with Louis and Margot, listening out to Father touting a new game of cards with Waleed.

But I now realise I am hearing the flutter of tiny wings.

A hop, the merest flash of red and more tapping. Tap tap. Hop. Tap tap. Hop.

I am waking to the sight of a small bird pecking at spilled couscous grains by the stove. A robin. I lie there and follow its foraging.

It has a delicate strength.

The bird tips its head to one side as it watches me, black pin heads for eyes, tripwires for legs. We are both fragile survival machines. We are both still. We are both beady-eyed living things in the pale dawn with a mutual yearning to hold on to existence for as long as possible.

I am momentarily at one with my little friend.

That is, until Father decides to shoo the bird away with a kick of his loafers and a grunt.

He lifts a steaming coffee-pot off the burner ring and pours one for himself. I look up to see his jaw covered in creamy shaving lather. I think about protesting, but I am too tired.

The robin has darted away towards the partly open window. It dwells a while on the sill, takes a fleeting look back at the two humans it has left behind and, without the slightest regret, flits off.

"Ah, shit…" I moan, disappointed that the bird has departed.

"Morning!" comes Father's gruff voice, cracked and croaking with the first cigarette of the day.

He goes back to the business in hand. He is now at the old rusting faucet, dragging a much-used razor down the side his face, trying to rid his chin of that tenacious stubble.

"You like robins, eh?" he says, stopping to take a sip of coffee from an enamel mug.

"Don't let the cute little buggers fool you. They are real scrappers. There are plenty up in the Bled Atlas at wintertime. Like the French colonists, they flock to Algeria in the European winter and fly back to Northern France in their spring…opportunists, the lot of them…"

He wipes away the remaining dabs of shaving foam from his ear lobes with an old rag, gives his face another splash of ice-cold water, dries his chin, wipes his eyes, pours me a coffee and hands it to me. All in the short time it takes between sleepy blinks.

"Do you know why the young don't have red chests like the adults?"

The mug of steaming liquid warms my hands. I press it to my chest. I shake my head. It's too early to speak. I crave this injection of coffee.

"Because robins hate red…" he says, answering his own question. "Seriously! The bird with the red breast, its least favourite colour is red."

He can see I'm surprised.

"Yep, it's true…they'll attack anything that's red. Literally anything. Ketchup. MC's home kit. The Tunisian flag. So, if the young have red chests, they're doomed. There's nothing the parents would like to do more to a youngster than peck it to death.

For a robin growing up that's a hell of a place to be isn't it…caught between a rock and a hard place…"

He gulps a mouthful of caffeine and goes back to examine his remaining stubble-shadow in the mirror above the faucet.

Satisfied, he picks up a lady's compact from the side of the sink and starts in with the concealer.

"So, given the young robins can't defend themselves, they go without red chests until they're fully grown. Which is why you never see a baby robin redbreast. What a beautiful quirk of nature that is!"

"Is it beautiful?" I ask.

"Don't!" Father shouts, emphatically.

"What?"

"Don't do that."

"Do what?"

"That thing where you ask a question that isn't a question. Where you don't need an answer. It's so fucking high and mighty. You get it from your mother…"

I choose the line of least resistance, pulling on my clothes in silence and wetting my head under the running faucet to wake myself up fully.

Father goes about applying his face paint with an unexpected precision. He pulls the jilbab over his head and slides it down over his shirt and trousers. He smooths down the whole ensemble.

"How do I look?"

"Like a mother…"

"Good. Put on your taqiya. You are still your grandmother's grandson. Be respectful to the dear old bird."

We are ready to go.

Father tells me we are due to meet with Captain LeBoeuf along the coast. He says it's a safe house, somewhere we can talk freely.

The very mention of the name LeBoeuf sets me on edge. The murderer of Captain Laurent, the tormentor of Monsieur Gazides, the man who put us in harm's way, the instigator of this whole destructive series of events.

Father eases the deux-chevaux through a French Army roadblock just west of the Marine Quarter. He flashes a note at the officer who waves us through.

We head out on the road to Mostagem, beyond Tipaza. The road clings to the coastline and my spirits soar at the sight of the Mediterranean breakers and golden beaches.

I trail an arm out of the passenger side window to catch the offshore gusts of air. Life can be good, I think.

A few kilometres further on, Father turns the car onto a switchback road that snakes up through a forest of Mediterranean pines for a good few kilometres.

The feelgood melts away as quickly as it arrived.

We turn a bend to find LeBoeuf's barnstorming circus—a handful of troops manning a line of armoured vehicles and staff cars parked outside a neat colonial mansion.

It is the most unlikely sight, out of place and out of time, a whitewashed plantation house seemingly transplanted from antebellum South Carolina to twentieth century North Africa.

I stare in wonder at this big wedding cake slab of otherworldliness.

A solidly proportioned stucco fascia holds up a steep pitched roof over high narrow windows. A colonnade-lined portico runs along the front of the house at the centre of which, right in front of the main doors, as if on sentry duty, stands Captain LeBoeuf.

He is flanked by two paratroopers and is in the middle of a terse exchange with Lieutenant Mauritz. He breaks off once he's spotted us.

Somehow LeBoeuf looks more imposing, more puffed up than when I saw him last in the Casbah.

He is no doubt basking in his victory over the General Strike. I am sure a triumphal cigar has never left his mouth since the FLN's capitulation in the face of his ingenious strike-breaking interventions.

As a direct result of his actions, the FLN leadership committee has sloped off back to their rat-nest hideouts as wanted men. And now Father is about to deliver one of them—Benkhedda—on a plate.

What an immensely satisfying moment this will be for the St Cyrien blowhard—the coup de grace that will seal LeBoeuf's reputation as the poster-boy of the tenth para, a sure-fire promotion prospect and a legend in his own camo jacket.

More importantly to LeBoeuf, it will give him something he needs far more than validation. It will give him vindication. His torture methods will now become the standard playbook of truth-extraction.

He is pleased to see us. It's another chance for him to tease and toy with us. Another chance to turn the menace on and off at will. To make us his friend, then his nemesis.

"Ah, Farouk, Bellissima! Your disguise is most fetching. And convincing. If didn't know better, I would eat you up!

And powder monkey!

My two super-spies…Come!"

The tamed, symmetrical exterior of the building does not prepare us for the grandeur or style of its interior.

We stand together in the atrium over which hangs a copper lantern the size of an oil drum.

As I look up, I have a sense of the imposing scale of this mansion.

A single central staircase splits into two flights that lead up to a first-floor gallery, wrapping around three sides of the mansion's vaulting heart.

Balustraded and panelled, it is a riot of ivory and teak.

A stained-glass skylight in the roof admits a shaft of pastel colours that set off the sparkling tesserae beneath our feet.

There on the floor is a peacock in full strut—an explosion of iridescent glass fragments. Eyes of ochre, orange and purple on aquamarine tail feathers fan out behind its proud head. Its exaggerated crown extends across the floor towards the oak doors of the main salon.

LeBoeuf is matter of fact. He doesn't feel at home with this level of ostentation.

"The President has his Brégançon, the Pope his Castel Gandolfo. This is Mont-Les-Pins—the summer residence of The Governor-General of Algeria…"

He steps forward to run a finger along the plinth of the ball-cap finial at the foot of the stairs. He examines the dust on his fingertip and flicks it off.

"…Except nobody knows about this place. And Governor-General Lacoste is now skittish about coming here—as was Jacques Soustelle before him…for fear of what the people might think…"

The opulence of this house sends the wrong kind of signals to the citizens of France. Best left or turned into a museum…

"Shame to let it go to waste," says Father, overawed.

"Indeed, it is! So General Massu uses it as a base for the tenth para whenever we are planning operations and need to locate ourselves outside the medina. This is where we can regroup safely. Did you stop to look outside? Commanding views of the Med, don't you think…Come!"

He leads us through the oak doors off the atrium to the main salon, offering up a tour of the house as if he is a homeowner grown weary of his mansion and we the hopeful buyers ready to breathe fresh life into it.

LeBoeuf isn't exactly cut out to be a curator or tour-guide. For one, he is a man of little patience. He's not on home ground explaining at length the provenance of the many artworks and artefacts that adorn the place. To him, art and fashion are a mystery akin to ancient religions and cosmology. But his memory is pin-sharp. He has the script memorised.

He tells us as much as he knows of the house by rote. He has clearly been through this routine before. I suspect it's the part of his job he least enjoys, guiding visiting generals and dignitaries around the premises in lieu of the Governor-General.

The house has its very own catalogue of antiquities and ornaments which LeBoeuf pulls from the drawer of a bureau that stands under the salon window. He uses the copy as his guide. I am taken aback by the incongruous sight of the bull-necked Captain playing museum curator.

We learn that the walls of the salon are hung with champagne velvet and play host to portraits by Boucher, Fragonard and Delapierre, with landscapes by Vernet and Delacroix. The statue of a seventh century Hindu deity stands in pride of place on the mantel above a large Adam fireplace, flanked by Roman amphorae, salvaged off the coast of Marseilles, and gurning Tahitian tribal masks, stolen by an unscrupulous French explorer and never returned. A Napoleonic era granite maquette of an Egyptian sphinx, a marble obelisk and an ornate mantel clock in the shape of a lyre complete the mantelpiece.

Above the fireplace is a distressed Empire mirror. To one side stands a fin-de-siecle tapestry screen featuring a scene of negro slaves working the fields surrounding a plantation house that looks uncannily like this one. The fire-irons are tipped with the brass heads of Afghani hunting dogs.

The room is furnished with Persian carpets and silk brocaded curtains behind which louvred shutters reduce the damaging effects of the sun's rays on the precious artworks and artefacts.

A mahogany drinks cabinet stands against the far wall, a peace offering from Castlereagh to the House of Bourbon following the Congress of Vienna.

Next to them stands a brace of Tsarist silver samovars, their imperial curved surfaces buffed so mercilessly that we can see our faces reflected back at us as caricatures.

LeBoeuf insists that Father sits on a formidable marble-inlaid Syrian throne-chair, designed more for an Emir than a chasseur.

"Fit for a queen!" says LeBoeuf having a laugh at Father's expense.

The chair dwarfs Father's wiry body. He looks fidgety, although he does his best to remain still. It is not a chair designed for relaxation, despite the single decorative silk cushion, its only concession to comfort.

I perch on a nearby chaise longue which has been newly upholstered in crushed purple velvet. It makes my skin crawl. I cannot settle.

This maison de maître has borrowed so indiscriminately from every corner of empire that the interior has become something of an incoherent mishmash.

It is a ghoulish Frankenstein of a house.

His hosting duties done, LeBoeuf soon draws us back to the business in hand. That of information pending.

"So, this had better be worth it, Farouk… General Massu is waiting to sign off my expenses. The Army has handed you quite a tidy chunk of sou for your intelligence. Paying for information is not a practice we generally endorse in the Army. We prefer to use more interrogative techniques. However, I have reassured him this is an experiment that's going to pay off. I have told the General to 'trust to my sources'.

He doesn't, of course. And he won't until he sees the results.

Just to say, he holds me personally accountable for the quality of your information. And if I am, then you certainly are.

Do not fuck it up for me. I am riding high like Napoleon at the Saint Bernard pass. Do not give Massu any cause to swap the white charger for a manky mule now. I would certainly take a dim view of that. So, what do you have? Go on! Surprise me!"

Father shifts in his seat.

"I am rededicating myself to finding Ali La Pointe and Yacef Saadi."

"Rededicating! Rededicating? That is not new information," blusters LeBoeuf "That is the same old manure!"

Father interjects.

"I think I have a new lead. The identity of a puppet-master in the FLN ranks. I think he will lead us to Saadi."

LeBoeuf raises a sardonic eyebrow.

"This sounds more like stasis to me. Like nothing is happening, but very slowly.

I have been extremely generous to you, Farouk, but Major Aussaresses and General Massu are going to need more than that to go on…

You have had enough time since that shit-show in Place Jean-Paul Sartre to reconnect with your Muslim brothers in the Casbah."

Father is shrinking back into the seat.

"With respect, we are looking for a needle in a haystack, Captain—two men among four hundred thousand."

"I'm not interested in your excuses. I'm only interested in taking Ali Ammar and his chief bomb-maker out of circulation for good."

"It takes time…"

"Don't talk to me about time.

How much time do we have before the people of France vote De Gaulle back in, before we are forced out of Algeria—and you, Harki, are left to rot here in Algiers…

You need us to protect you. Or you and powder monkey will be strung up from a lamppost by your fellow countrymen…"

The idea makes me shudder.

Lieutenant Laurent's face looms large in my mind. I imagine this man before me looping the rope around Laurent's neck, leading him up the hill like a beaten cur, pistol whipping him to his knees and hauling him up into the bough of the cork oak as his feet pedal the air and he gasps for breath.

I imagine watching the life drain from Laurent's body as he hangs inert like one of the portraits in this house of horrors.

This is LeBoeuf's way. As Father says, it is his calling card.

"It is a ticking time bomb," LeBoeuf goes on. "The longer it takes you to defuse it, the more likely it is to go off in your face! So, don't talk to me about time.

Time is not on your side…I am."

Father knows the conversation is going badly. But he is aware he can salvage this. He has his ace in the hole.

"Well, I have Simeon by my side now. We are good cover for each other. We will find the targets…"

LeBoeuf chuckles away to himself.

"So, is that your news? Young powder monkey here!"

"No, I'm just saying…"

"Get out of here! You have nothing for me but pipe dreams and your circus-barker act. Get your wizened-faced, bitch-arsed carcass out of here before I throw you out. Go on!"

Father leans forward.

"There's something else, though…" he adds.

LeBoeuf is about to grab Father by the sleeves of his jilbab and clobber him. Father rises to his feet before the Captain has the chance to land a blow.

The two of them are face-to-face, no further than the distance of a rabbit punch. There is a glimmer in Father's eyes that stays LeBoeuf's fist.

"Hear me out!" urges Father.

"I heard word only last night of the possible location of the lodgings for a certain member of the FLN committee of coordination and execution."

"Oh?" LeBoeuf is clearly unsure whether this is a stalling ploy. Father can tell that the Captain's interest has been piqued by this tantalising snippet of intelligence. "Well, go on…Which of the buggers is it?"

"Benyoucef Benkhedda."

LeBoeuf is silenced by the news. Father is quick to elucidate.

"By chance, Benkhedda called up a connection of my source to fix his car. I think he must have gone through the Algiers phone book searching for a specialist in his make and model."

LeBoeuf is mute. He is thinking. Calculating.

"Apparently, he is staying at an apartment on the Rue Claude DeBussy in the European Quarter."

LeBoeuf is smiling.

"Block five. Apartment eight."

LeBoeuf is grinning.

"And he is there now…"

LeBoeuf is sniggering.

He moves to bear-hug Father. Father does not stand or reciprocate in any way. It is a strange and sudden rapprochement that fails utterly.

Father pulls me up from my seat and makes to leave. He doesn't want to spend a second longer in LeBoeuf's company than is necessary.

"Where are you going now?" asks LeBoeuf.

"We are going back to my digs," says Father.

"Oh, no. No, no, no…You are staying put."

This is not turning out the way Father anticipated.

"But I have given you all I know," he pleads.

"You have…and it is good news…" says LeBoeuf.

"So, we can go…"

"But what if it isn't?"

"What?"

"What if it isn't good? What if your source isn't good? What if this information is pure fiction and we have blown five thousand francs—that's twenty thousand dinars to you, Harki—on hot air?"

"My source is reliable…"

"As you say. And your source had better be reliable. As I say, I have staked a lot on your word. But if I find it all to be a pack of lies, you are a dead man…"

"Go and find out," says Father. "Go to Rue Claude DeBussy and see for yourself!"

"Oh, I fully intend to. And you will come with me. Because if this information turns out to be a canard, General Massu will want you shot on site as a counter insurgent. You and powder monkey here. Our friend Aussaresses may have something to say about it too."

I know that Father is having visions of Aussaresses' escadrons de la mort. He maintains he never shows fear, but there is terror in his eyes now.

"Massu will not suffer fools and nor will I. Do you understand me?"

I notice a single bead of sweat running down Father's jawline and drop onto the neck of his jilbab.

LeBoeuf sees it too.

"I am telling you, Farouk, if you are wrong about this, then the Rue Claude DeBussy will be the last stop you make on your way to the Villa Tourelle."

Mont-Les-Pins, Algiers Wilaya, 22 February 1957

We have been here all day in this salon. LeBoeuf has no sooner left the room than we hear the sound of a key turning in the lock. This is to be our gilded cage for the rest of the day.

LeBoeuf has food brought into us from the kitchens, although our forced confinement just makes us more attuned to the movements beyond the door. We register the continuous tramp of boots on the floor of the atrium and the gravel paths outside.

We watch the sun set over the Mediterranean through the gap in the shutters and night invades with stars like spotter flares in the night-sky.

Father urges me to nap. I try to curl up on the chaise longue, but the mantel clock regularly chimes the quarter hour. I would even prefer the creaking camp bed in Jameel's garage to this.

I am unable to stop thinking about the night ahead.

Father paces a lot. We talk a little. I tell him I am desperate for Mother to know that I am alive.

"Let's get through the night first," says Father, ominously.

Just after nine, the key is turned in the lock, the door swings open and LeBoeuf appears with Lieutenant Mauritz by his side.

"It has been decided. General Massu and General Salan have agreed this will be a joint operation between the tenth para and the third para of Colonel Bigeard. You will come with us now."

We are back on the coast road east as LeBoeuf's convoy sweeps down to Algiers.

Father and I are squeezed inside the belly of an armoured car along with Lieutenant Mauritz and two of his men. They are combat ready.

LeBoeuf travels up ahead with a signals officer. He is in continual contact with General Massu.

Lieutenant Mauritz is silent. But I cannot hold my tongue.

"What happened to Monsieur Gazides?" I ask.

"That is classified information."

"Did you hand him over to Aussaresses?"

"That's Lieutenant Aussaresses to you, son."

He turns to look me straight in the eyes. A penetrating gaze tinged with regret.

It is enough for me to know that Monsieur Gazides is dead.

The European Quarter, Algiers, 23 February 1957

Father is not short of questions for Lieutenant Mauritz. He appreciates that we have arrived at our target destination. But with such a limited view of our precise location from inside the car, he wants to understand what is happening.

Lieutenant Mauritz is reluctant to share the knowledge with him. There is an embargo on news for civilians like us.

"We are waiting," is all he says.

Father presses him some more.

"We are waiting for further command."

And again.

"We are waiting for further command on the next action."

Father explodes.

"Tell us! Our lives depend on it!"

"Control yourself!" urges the Lieutenant, then relents.

We learn that we are two hundred metres from Rue Claude DeBussy in Avenue Jean Moulin—a street that runs directly behind the apartment block.

Troops of the third para are positioned on the corner of the Rue Anise and Rue Claude DeBussy with a direct line of sight to the front of the building.

The tenth are waiting for the 'Go' command to surround the exterior of the apartments while the men of the third go in, led by the indomitable Bigeard.

For now, we are positioned in side streets. We will be here until the lights go off in the apartment so as not to raise any alarm.

LeBoeuf has been liaising with Massu and Bigeard for over three hours now. The night is sticky and humid, and the stale, heated air is suffocating in this enclosed space.

The door of our vehicle opens. It is LeBoeuf.

"Get out and stretch your legs," he orders, curtly.

We jump down.

LeBoeuf has forgone his signature cigar tonight and is lighting a cigarette. He props himself against the vehicle and passes the cigarette to Father who takes a long lingering smoke.

"We are ready."

"What are you waiting for then?" asks Father.

"It is too early. The lights are still burning inside. If Benkhedda is in there as you say he is, then he will still be up. We need him sleeping, not scheming."

Father offers to return the cigarette to the Captain. LeBoeuf lets him keep it and lights up another for himself.

"If you don't mind me asking," Father says tentatively, "why is your boss sending another soldier in to make the arrest? I've given this information to you."

LeBoeuf merely harrumphs.

Father is wily. He is trying to win back LeBoeuf's confidence with flattery. He will keep working this scratch until it becomes an open sore.

"I mean your men broke the strike didn't they…Bigeard wouldn't be here without you. You extracted the information, not him."

It doesn't take much to rile LeBoeuf.

"Bigeard is a soldier through and through. Tough as old boots. But a soldier's soldier if you know what I mean. He is much respected for his soldiering."

LeBoeuf hits the 's' of 'soldier' hard as in the sense of 'smug', 'swindling' and 'scoundrel'.

"He is fit as a butcher's dog, much decorated and loved by his men. Professional to the core. Though he is old school. A battlefield soldier. The finer points of urban street-fighting are lost on him. He does not understand asymmetrical warfare."

LeBoeuf takes another puff of his Gitanes.

"Ah…" murmurs Father.

"General Massu thinks the high-profile arrest of a figurehead such as Benkhedda merits the more soldierly approach.

He is inclined to play by the rule book. It is more apt that Bigeard takes the lead. I can't argue with that."

But Father senses the opposite is true—that LeBoeuf is desperate to take issue with the General's decision.

Another hour elapses. My bladder is fit to burst. I ask Lieutenant Mauritz if I can be let out again to relieve myself and he accedes to my request.

I step down from the vehicle into the night air and see LeBoeuf standing by his signals vehicle two up in the line. He is still waiting for the 'Go' from Bigeard who watches for the lights to go off in the apartment from a few streets away.

"Where do you think you're going?" he shouts.

"I'm bursting…"

LeBoeuf strides towards me, telling Lieutenant Mauritz—now following me out of the vehicle—to stand down.

"Don't you dare piss anywhere near my vehicles, you little rat. It is bad luck to urinate on Army property. I will go with you."

He leads me up the road to the intersection with Rue Brèves where a telegraph pole offers a more suitable urinal.

It seems that half the dogs in the neighbourhood have had the same idea.

I urinate whilst LeBoeuf stands by.

The curfew has tamped down all sound in the city. Amid the quiet, my stream of piss sounds like a waterfall and I can hear LeBoeuf's breath behind me loud as a snorting bull.

I am just buttoning up as we hear something else. It is abrasive and sonorous—the sound of dragging metal across concrete.

LeBoeuf is startled. He looks around sharply and I follow his gaze out to the middle of the street some twenty yards away—where the Avenue Jean Moulin meets Rue Claude DeBussy.

Through the darkness, we catch the fleeting sight of a silhouetted figure disappearing quickly below ground.

LeBoeuf grabs hold of me and pulls me along with him towards the spot.

As we approach, we can make out a manhole cover that has been pulled back to reveal a dark space beneath the road surface.

"Vites!" shouts LeBoeuf. He charges the remaining distance to the hole, half-dragging me with him. "Go!"

"What?" I say.

"Go! Now!" He pushes me down into the gap. My legs and hips are grazed by the edges of the manhole and I yelp "Go, damn you! Go! Go!"

I release my grip from the hole's rim and drop down into the darkness—I have no idea how far I will fall, though my feet immediately splash down through water to hard concrete.

My legs hold and I find myself standing in a rivulet of sewage some five feet below the road surface. A sticky sludge rises to my calves and soaks into my shoes, congealing around my legs.

I feel if I don't start moving, it will suck me down.

Sulphurous fumes hit me immediately. A miasma of expelled lunches, dinners and snacks. The putrid fug makes me heave and wretch. I have nothing to throw up but acid that burns my throat and mouth. I gag repeatedly.

The only light that penetrates down here is the thin stream of moonlight through the uncovered hole. LeBoeuf jumps down after me and waits in the darkness, listening.

"Shhh…" LeBoeuf is still. I try to suppress my gag reflex, but I wretch instantly.

We hear echoes created by someone moving further down the tunnel, breathing heavily and splashing through the effluvia. The person is panting hard—sobbing and moaning mournfully like a snared animal whose life has just started to ebb away.

LeBoeuf swiftly reaches into the breast pocket of his camo jacket and produces a torch which he flicks on, shining its thin beam down the tunnel.

I see the walls start to move and contract—and I think for one fleeting moment that I am inside the belly of a monster organism—moving through its muscular intestinal tract. The belly of Algiers.

I am then struck by the curious notion that these sewers must resemble the gut of that spy Terrare. Then I see it—a wall of crawling rats. Hundreds of them, scattering and scuttling over one another in the torchlight. Beneath this shifting sea of vermin, white maggots glow against the dark fat that coats the walls.

Drips fall down from above—the sweat of condensed gases.

LeBoeuf squints into the beam. We see the blur of an escaping figure some twenty yards away. Or could it be just a smudge on my eyeball?

"Benkhedda!" LeBoeuf shouts. He wades relentlessly through the liquid shit and I follow. Sewer gas is making my head whirr and my sinuses scream.

LeBoeuf ploughs on through the muck. He moves with swiftness and sewage splashes up into his open mouth. He doesn't seem to care about the consequences.

I am convinced he is not even aware he is ingesting raw sewage, or even tasting the effluvia, so driven is he by one thing and one alone. To hunt, to kill.

He wades to the end of the tunnel where it joins with another channel through a slim aperture. The hole is too narrow for his bulky frame to pass through. All the while, we listen out for the splash and the wash made by the paddling limbs of a desperate man further up the tunnel.

"Benkhedda is a much smaller man than me. You go!" urges LeBoeuf, pushing me towards the opening. "Take this!" He hands me the torch.

"What do you expect me to do?"

"You are younger and fitter than Benkhedda. He has asthma. Keep going and he will tire. He sounds done for already. Catch him! Then subdue him! You can bring down an exhausted man. Drown him in shit if you must. But do it!

Don't cheat me, powder monkey! Or I will have my sappers blast this sewer wide open and I will find you. Do this and you, your father and your family will be free of me…Fail and you can forget about seeing them ever again. Your choice…"

"But Father's information was good," I complain, "You know he was telling the truth. You have your man as promised!"

"Do I? Where? I do not have him yet. You must deliver him to me!"

I climb through the gap and jump down into the scummy soup of the main channel. Crumbling ridges run along the side, highways for the rats encrusted with excrement. These disintegrating bricks are held together by the grease and fat that clog them. I cling to them nevertheless, using them as handrails whilst managing to stay upright.

My footholds are uncertain. I am kicking unseen objects under the surface of the slick that disintegrate with contact and set my heart thumping—and I am trying my hardest to avoid tripping and going under. I am straining to move forward against the downward pull of this hellish river.

A bloated dog drifts by, ready to pop. Islands of human hair and soapy gunk brush past me, a shoe drifts like a boat on this tide of decay.

The torchlight is picking out the shape of the escaping man more clearly now. He is ahead of me, labouring through the channel which has become a river of human waste. He is coughing repeatedly and gasping for air. He can hear me pushing through his bow-wave and he is panicking and gasping. It is a desperate sound.

He keeps going. I keep following. There is nothing to indicate a route out, just a seemingly endless, viscous torrent.

I can feel the wash that has rebounded off the side walls. Benkhedda slows to a crawl. He is almost within spitting distance now, out of puff and wheezing heavily.

He wades two more steps. And he stops.

Suddenly, he lets out a roar—the last exhausted cry of resignation from a man who knows he can fight no more. LeBoeuf's hunch was right. And Benkhedda knows it. There is no strength left in this man.

He turns to face me. I shine the torchlight directly into his eyes. He squints back.

I am surprised by his appearance. I expect to encounter a fearsome warrior, a superhero, a man of steel.

Instead, a bookkeeper stands before me dripping in sweat and sewage.

There is something dignified about Benkhedda, though—something that reveals itself through all the shit.

I can see the neat, proud man beneath.

I see the head of thick cropped hair, the clean-shaven face, the well-tailored suit jacket now smeared, spotted and stained. And the most remarkable thing of all—throughout this chase, he has managed to keep his spectacles straight on the bridge of his nose.

I decide what to do next.

I am back at the ravine in Koudiat el-Markluf looking directly into the big black eye of the wounded fallow deer.

Do I try to drown him? Do we tussle and pull each other down into these eddies of piss and crap? Do I reason with him?

What can I, a fifteen-year-old boy, say to persuade a grown man of more than three times my age and experience to return with me so that he can be despatched directly to Aussaresses' torture chamber?

He is Algerian like me. He is covered in sewage like me. He is terrified like me. He could easily be me thirty years older.

We are both trying to find the energy to stand, let alone wrestle with one another.

I don't know what to say. And clearly neither does he. We dither and circle each other in a ridiculous danse macabre.

From far off, I hear LeBoeuf's voice booming down the tunnel. "Powder monkey!"

I have been shining the torch into Benkhedda's face for several seconds now and realise I must be nothing more than a shadow to him.

I lower the torch and angle it upwards between the two of us so that the beam illuminates both our faces at once.

I can see he is just as surprised to find a fifteen-year old Algerian boy standing in front of him.

An instant look of mutual recognition passes between us. I nod and point the torch beyond him, illuminating the passage ahead.

"Shukraan jazilaan," he says, his palms pressed together in thanks.

Then he turns and slowly wades away.

I return to LeBoeuf weary, cowed by my failure to bring Benkhedda back with me. I scramble up towards the aperture, LeBoeuf pulling at the back of my shirt to yank me through. He seizes me by the scruff of my neck and pushes me along the narrow conduit towards the column of moonlight that arrows down from the street. The rats swarm about us.

He has grabbed the torch back off me. And notices something large lying on the ridge of the tunnel.

He takes a closer look, shining his beam full on.

In its beam lies an eyeless human corpse. The rats have gnawed at the grey flesh and the internal organs. Tattered clothes hang of the cadaver.

LeBoeuf shines the light up onto the walls. The brickwork is newly punctured with bullet holes. There has been a recent skirmish here.

LeBoeuf processes the scene perfunctorily like a gendarme noting a traffic violation and moves on, dragging me towards the descending shaft of light from the street.

Lieutenant Mauritz is peering down from above, his arm extended. He grabs me by the hand and pulls me up onto the road above. LeBoeuf jumps from below, grabbing the rim of the manhole and pulling his weight up through it, swinging his legs and using his elbows to lever his body back up and out into the warm night air.

We are both breathless, coughing and spitting.

LeBoeuf is furious with me.

"You let him go, didn't you, powder monkey." He turns to Mauritz. "Powder monkey here has let Benkhedda escape."

"He got away from me…" I protest.

"You are a liar," retorts LeBoeuf, giving me a short, sharp clout around the back of my head with his palm.

"He outran me!" My ears are ringing.

"Out-ran you, indeed! Benkhedda couldn't outrun a geriatric snail. He is asthmatic…"

"I came back didn't I, like you wanted me to," I say, keeping my tears in check.

"And you think that's going to save you and your old man? What a fucking aborted excuse for a human being you are."

"But you promised…"

"Sir…" Lieutenant Mauritz interrupts. "There is good news from Lieutenant Bigeard and his men…outstanding, in fact."

"Oh…?" enquires LeBoeuf distractedly.

"The third para have been into the apartment. They found a man there in his pyjamas…"

"And what's so amazing about that?"

"It's Larbi Ben M'hidi…"

Mont-Les-Pins, Algiers Wilaya, 23 February 1957

"Fuck you!" shouts LeBoeuf. "How can you demand a French visa when you have put France in danger?"

I have washed. My clothes have been burnt by Lieutenant Mauritz in the garden fire pit. I am wearing the thobe, serwal and sandals of a Mont-Les-Pins house-boy, specially sequestered by the Captain.

He has just told us his news. It comes with mixed blessings.

The FLN's kingpin and principal architect of the General Strike, Larbi Ben M'hidi has been captured and detained for questioning by the French Army.

However, General Salan has decided that Colonel 'Bruno' Bigeard will be the man for the job, not Captain Gregory LeBoeuf.

Ben M'hidi has been taken in an Army jeep to Colonel Bigeard's Headquarters in Medea.

He was last seen two hours ago entering the building smiling and joking with French paratroopers. He even stopped to pose for the cameras on the way in. Apparently, it all looked very pleasant, like a Sunday morning stroll in the park. Word has reached LeBoeuf that he and the Colonel have even sat down to lunch together and are busy breaking bread, one commanding officer with another. It sounds cosy.

LeBoeuf is sick to his stomach.

It may be from ingesting raw sewage during the night-time's escapades. Though given his sturdy constitution, that is unlikely.

The gripes in the Captain's gut are more likely to be caused the Generals' preference for Bigeard as M'hidi's interrogator over him.

He is blaming Father and I for this outcome regardless.

"You have done exactly what I asked you not to. You have made me ride a mule. I am ridiculed and scorned by the Generals for allowing Benkhedda's escape. My men see me as a laughing-stock and I have now been punished by General Salan who has handed Ben M'hidi over to 'Bruno' Bigeard for questioning…"

Father is determined not to be browbeaten by the Captain this time.

"We delivered top-grade information. We have been as good as our word. Benkhedda's escape was an operational failing, not a failure on our part."

LeBoeuf is less than impressed.

"Don't play the smart-arse with me, Farouk. I know what you're up to with your double bluffing…

This morning, I had a notion you may even have found a way to tip Benkhedda off."

"That isn't true."

"You didn't alert him to our operation in advance, then?"

"Of course not. How could I? I was with you. That was the point!"

"You can do many things I thought were beyond the realms of possibility. Shall I give you the full report or an executive summary…?"

Father is unresponsive. LeBoeuf has taken all the air out of him like a flat tyre.

LeBoeuf starts counting on the fingers of one hand.

"You move through the souk as you are, disguised as an old woman—and no one bats an eyelid…

You blow up fifteen Muslims and the FLN can't track you down. Either that or don't want to…

You attract the attention of an unofficial internal enquiry into Army interrogation techniques…

You string Lieutenant Laurent along when you have no intention of giving him what he wants…and I have to save your bony arse…

You move with impunity through the Casbah…"

Exhausting the fingers and thumb of his right hand, he now moves onto his left.

"Then you pinpoint a key terrorist suspect…with information that happens to fall into your lap…

And he gets away just at the point we are about to take him down. I mean, who the fuck are you, Farouk?

Who are you really? What is this really all about?"

I am studying Father's face for the merest flicker of a response.

I'm not sure that I know who he is either.

Far from stamping a visa on his passport and approving his safe passage to France, LeBoeuf has run out of patience.

"What is stopping me from booking you in on Aussaresses' death flight. Today, I mean. Over the sea. Right opposite this house. Powder monkey here can spectate from the balcony. It's a clear day. He'll get a good view of you free-falling all the way down to the brine. You will make quite a splash! What do you say? Shall I call the Major right now? He will be delighted. I can almost hear his rotor engine starting up.

He is as frustrated as I am seeing Bigeard play host to Ben M'hidi. He is itching to have a go at the man himself."

Again, I recall LeBoeuf's revelation back at our farmhouse that it is to be the setting for Ben M'hidi's murder and staged suicide.

Father tries to recover his dignity, though he knows LeBoeuf has reached the end of his rope and is one call away from making this execution happen.

Father knows he has delivered on his side of the bargain. Equally, he knows it is pointless to reason with the Captain. A waste of breath.

Frustrating as it may be, Father has settled for the fact that paranoia and suspicion guide this man, not logic.

"Let me show you. Let me deliver Ali La Pointe and Yacef Saadi. Then we are all square…"

"We have been over this. You want time. And that is not something we possess. We must stamp out the FLN now. We must press home the advantage while their leaders are scattered—either abroad, on the run or in custody. We are stepping up our raids in the Casbah. We are removing a whole level of support. I know that La Pointe and Saadi are pimpernels, but it can't be that difficult to track them down."

"So, let me find them. I can do it. Give me one shot at it and I'll do it. I promise you."

"What, after last night's farrago?"

"I promise I will find them."

"On your knees?"

"What?"

"Promise me on your knees."

Father is dumbstruck.

"Promise me on your knees and kiss my shitty boots. Do it in front of your son so he can see you have made the pledge in all seriousness."

Father does what he's told. He sinks to his knees and touches the sewage steeped leather of LeBoeuf's boot with his lips.

He stays down.

"I promise I will bring you Ali La Pointe, and Yacef Saadi."

"Now swear…"

"What?"

"Swear on your life!" Le Boeuf puts it to him.

"On my life," Father concedes.

"And the life of your boy…"

Father hesitates.

I feel that my heart has stopped beating in my chest.

Father has sorrowful eyes, full of loss, regret, fear and self-loathing.

It is the same expression he wore when he crouched in that passageway off Place Jean-Paul Sartre, his finger hovering over the switch of the detonator.

The Arabic Quarter, Algiers, 4 March 1957

Father and I are moving around the Casbah now. We have spent endless days trudging the staircases, passages and impasses, stopping at cafés and browsing in the souk. We are two sets of eyes and ears and make sure we are always seen together—grandmother and son going about their daily business.

We have stopped by a few times at Jameel's café, though Father does not want us to stay in any one place for too long.

Jameel has no more titbits of information to speak of. Nor does Father expect that much from him. After all he has already fulfilled his brief by delivering the intelligence of Benyoucef Benkhedda's whereabouts—and for the time being, Jameel is all out of miracles.

Jameel's network of informants tells him that the FLN leader, having escaped through the sewer system, has now crossed the border into Tunisia and is directing operations from Tunis.

Father is not proud of the part he has played in the capture of Ben M'hidi. But he is still extremely proud of his family. He hopes that we are strong enough to survive the scrutiny of the French Army.

I'm not sure that any of us would feel the same way about him.

As a consequence of his intelligence, Larbi Ben 'M'hidi has been apprehended. And—something Father has yet to find out—our family home will soon be turned over to French military intelligence for his execution.

With every day that passes this feels less like a partnership and more like a hostage situation. My abduction from outside the Lycée René Coty is for real after all. Father's latest act of betrayal leaves me in no doubt. He is holding me against my will.

It appears that Father is incapable of standing up to LeBoeuf and will do and say anything to survive one more day.

He cuts a sorry figure in his face paint and jilbab.

I stay with him for the very simple reason that I fear for the life of Mother, my sister and brothers at the hands of LeBoeuf.

Like it or not, I am part of the hunt for Ali La Pointe and Saadi. The Captain is using my family as collateral. And there is no way I can abandon that mission without risking them.

Father has sworn he will lead LeBoeuf to the hideouts of the FLN's bomb-maker-in-chief and the leader of its military wing…and he has sworn on my life.

As we left Mont-Les-Pins that day to return to Algiers and resume our spying mission, I asked Lieutenant Mauritz if he could make sure Mother knows that I am alive. I don't know whether he has or not. I think there is some good in the man. I hope so.

LeBoeuf has set us a strict timeline. He has given us a week to make progress on our search through the alleyways and ruelles of the Casbah. And our time is up. We are due back at the headquarters of the tenth para for a de-brief and progress.

We have precious little of substance with which to update him.

In the meantime, we have been extra vigilant in the Casbah, not just for our own protection, but to make sure that if we are in the same place at the same time as little Omar or Ibrahim Najjar, we can spot them in the crowd and start tracking them to Saadi and La Pointe.

There have been several false alarms. On one occasion, I thought I glimpsed little Omar running down the Boulevard. On another, I was convinced I spotted Najjar delivering a pallet of tomatoes to a grocer. Then I was sure I spied him in a café.

Of course, it turned out that, whilst the faces of these people strongly resembled those that have stared out at me from the photograph in Jameel's map drawer, they are not one and the same.

Like so much in this city of falsehoods, they are nothing more than a chimera.

It's something Verna once told me about myself. That I'm a dreamer and there are times I want things so badly that I'll imagine them into existence.

Today we trudge disconsolately back to the Rue Quincie and Father starts up the deux chevaux. The journey along the coast road to Mont-Les-Pins is not as carefree as the first time. The sea has lost its lustre. Everything is held in a flat monochrome light. Even the beaches seem more grit than powder today.

We are about to arrive empty-handed and we have never felt more naked.

The Mediterranean has taken on an altogether different aspect since LeBoeuf issued his ultimatum to us.

Today I am more aware than ever that within its depths are hundreds of the 'disappeared'. The bodies of lost souls who have dropped out of the sky. Major Aussaresses' quarry. And the Captain will soon be sending Father to join them.

He spends the journey quietly calculating how he can pull off another act of escapology and what kind of humiliation he will have to endure to do so.

I fear the worst.

To me, our process through the forest of pines over crunching gravel is more tumbrel to the guillotine.

We turn the bend to find LeBoeuf in his usual position by the grand front doors of Mont-Les-Pins, legs astride, smoking his regulation robusto cigar.

To our astonishment and relief, he appears to be in good spirits as he opens the driver's door of the deux chevaux with the flourish of a hotel valet.

"A votre service!"

Father doesn't quite know what to make of the reception. He waits for the scorpion tail to curl as we follow Captain LeBoeuf into the house.

LeBoeuf has coffee waiting in the salon.

"Shall I be mother—or should I say 'grandmother'?" he quips as he eyes up Father's jilbab and make-up.

Pleased with his joke, he chuckles to himself before pouring thick black coffee from a dallah into two bone china cups on a silver tray.

"I asked the house-boy to rustle this up. Special qahwa for a special occasion." LeBoeuf hands Father his coffee with a steady hand.

Father is nervous. Steeling himself for another lacerating onslaught. The abused flinching from the whip. He can't conceal it, much as he wants to. His hand tremors slightly. It is accentuated by the rattle of the cup in the saucer.

"Don't worry, Farouk. I don't expect you have any news for me…" he chirps as he passes me a cup too.

"Erm…well…possibly…"

"As I thought. Don't try to fudge it with me, Farouk. You make yourself look even more foolish than you do already in that get-up and lipstick…

No matter. This time I have news for you…"

LeBoeuf puffs out his chest.

"We finally have him," he crows.

"Who?" asks Father.

"Ben M'hidi. He was transferred into Major Aussaresses' control yesterday afternoon. They should be through with him at Villa Tourelles…" He glances at his watch, "…within the hour!"

LeBoeuf pours himself a coffee and plants his feet by the fireplace. He checks his timepiece against the mantel clock.

"Over the last seven days, Colonel Bigeard and Ben M'hidi have been running some kind of mutual appreciation society.

Bigeard has declared his admiration for his adversary's courage and resilience…and, can you believe it, his dignity. He has forbidden anyone to use torture on his prisoner!

Ha! This has emboldened Ben M'hidi. He sings the 'Chant des partisans' behind the walls of El-Biar.

Word has got out that 'Bruno' Bigeard is in awe of Ben M'hidi. A crush even! Ben M'hidi can do no wrong. He is the Tristan to Bigeard's Isolde. A lion, no less! An Algerian patriot, holding firm in his conviction that the people of Algeria will be liberated. He treats his adversary like a matinée idol and smothers him with praise for his warrior spirit. They say he refuses to use coercive interrogation techniques on the man…

I tell you it is neither big nor clever of Colonel Marcel 'Bruno' Bigeard…as Ben M'hidi now laughs at the tricolour. And that is a capital offence.

Well, he has it coming…General Massu has stepped in. He has had enough of this pussyfooting. He has removed the man from Bigeard's charge and handed him over to the 'escadrons de la mort' of Major Aussaresses".

Father is wary. He still doesn't know whether LeBoeuf is suckering him in by bringing him into his confidence. He keeps his counsel lest he provoke the Captain, inadvertently or otherwise.

"Major Aussaresses has put me on alert. We are his 'special unit' and we will soon be setting off for Medea via Villa Tourelle.

"Medea?" asks Father.

"Ask powder monkey here. Basira has very kindly agreed to give us your farmhouse to host Ben M'hidi."

"What?"

"This is of course confidential information."

"Our home?"

"There speaks an absentee father. I think it stopped being your home the day you killed eighteen people in the Casbah.

To be frank, Farouk, it has never really been yours anyway. We are your landlord, remember? Us and Waleed. We can do with your tenancy whatsoever we wish..."

"What is the meaning of this?"

"Do not push your luck, Farouk. You are not in a good position to do so.

Had you come to see me yesterday morning you would be at the bottom of the Mediterranean by now...I have been nursing some very deep grievances since our botched operation on Rue Claude DeBussy.

However," he says, more cheerily, "since yesterday afternoon these misgivings have been assuaged...

I am back in favour with General Massu and Major Aussaresses. I have climbed back on my mount, that white charger, so to speak. I have crossed my Alps!

It is only this news that has spared you. I am in quite a forgiving frame of mind. Keep on the right side of me and it will stay that way."

LeBoeuf replaces his coffee cup and picks up the cigar he has nested in an ashtray whilst performing his duties as 'mother'.

He checks his watch again before continuing.

"I feel I have to give you some credit. I have underestimated you, after all. You have worked hard to cultivate your informants. And you have brought Ben M'hidi to me. You should at least be rewarded by tasting the fruits of your labours. I would like you to grasp the prize. Hold the trophy. Shake the hand of Larbi Ben M'hidi, the man you have helped ensnare. And anyway, it is about time you visited your family. They will be eager to see you again, as I'm sure you are them."

Father is turning the proposal over in his head. He doesn't know what to make of it.

"I'm n-not sure...I..." he hesitates.

"Oh, come, come, Farouk. You deserve it. And anyway, I am reluctant to let you out of my sight knowing what you know...and who you know. These are sensitive times."

"You are about to witness history in the making...I wouldn't want you to miss it."

Waleed's Bayt Rifi,
Medea Wilaya, Algiers,
4 March 1957

To our surprise, the armoured vehicle has turned off the road and up towards Waleed's house before reaching the turning for the track leading to our farmhouse.

We are greeted by Waleed himself. LeBoeuf shakes his hand. He hails Father, though Father does not reciprocate.

Father stands back as Waleed ushers us into his sparse kitchen. Margot and Louis immediately rush into our arms, delirious with reunion.

Father picks them up and twirls them around. I hug them tightly and hold on to them like I will never let them go.

He asks Waleed where Mother is, and Waleed leads us to his bedroom.

She is facing away from us, curled up under a thick blanket fast asleep. Her hair is tousled, and she has her arms around Baby Claude who is stretched out next to her, his tiny mouth blowing clusters of minuscule bubbles as he dreams.

LeBoeuf is watching Father whose eyes are welling up. Frustration, hurt and fury are mixed in with his tears. The sight of Mother lying in Waleed's bed is too much for him to bear. He turns and heads out of the door to recover his composure. LeBoeuf follows him leaving me with Waleed and the children.

"Don't worry, Simeon. Lieutenant Mauritz told your maman where you have been hiding out. She knows you are still with us," he says.

"When did he tell her?" I ask.

"Last week."

"And what's she doing here? In your bedroom…"

"She is resting. The tenth para have taken over your farmhouse. Temporarily. You probably know why, don't you…?"

I nod.

"I have been looking after your maman and the family. Keeping an eye on them while you have been away."

Is he serious? Does he honestly expect my thanks?

"She took your disappearance very badly. Worse than last time. I think she is quite ill with it. Sick at heart. And in here…"

He taps his cranium with his forefinger.

"Your papa's arrant behaviour has tipped her over the edge…"

The door opens and LeBoeuf enters with Lieutenant Mauritz.

"Your Father is coming with me," informs LeBoeuf. "You will stay put. Lieutenant Mauritz will be here to look after you."

He turns on his heels and marches briskly out of the door. Lieutenant Mauritz grabs a chair and sits down. He kicks another chair away from the table and invites me to sit with him.

After a few seconds, Louis and Margot come in from the bedroom followed by Waleed. The children drape themselves over me. Margot sits on my knee.

Waleed grabs two tumblers and a bottle of brandy. He pours a glass for himself and Lieutenant Mauritz.

Mauritz declines. He is not in the mood. Waleed takes his glass and the bottle and wanders into his living room.

"Thank you for letting my mother know," I say to Lieutenant Mauritz.

He is deadpan.

"Do you know what's going on up at the farmhouse?"

He looks up at me.

"Do not concern yourself with it. It's best that you don't."

"Why has the Captain taken Father there?"

"He wants a photograph."

"A photograph?"

"Of your Father and Ben M'hidi. Together. Just in case…"

"In case of what?"

"Just in case…"

A little while passes. I am tucking Margot and Louis into Waleed's big bed alongside Mother and Baby Claude when I hear the latch to the front door lift.

Father is back, but this time without LeBoeuf. He is pale. He doesn't talk. I don't think he can.

We sit in silence. I stare at Waleed's toile wallpaper. Rustic scenes of courting couples and voyeuristic shepherd boys in a drab Provençale blue.

The formica wall-clock above his sideboard tells us that we have to sit and wait.

My head on Waleed's table, I start to drift again. A hot-headed feverish dreamscape in the gap between wakefulness and sleep. Eagles circling. Wolverines baying. Mother and Father strolling on salt flats. Distant cries and screams in the dark.

I wake with a start and look up.

It is two-thirteen. I hear the scrunch of tires on aggregate and the sound of LeBoeuf's heavy boots outside.

The door-handle turns, the door swings open and he stands on the threshold.

He looks different. The swagger has gone. The energy has faded—face harrowed, brow puckered.

He calls wearily to Lieutenant Mauritz who stands, comports himself, fixes his beret and strides past the Captain out of the door without a further word.

LeBoeuf addresses Waleed slowly. His voice has lost its bellow. It is flat and monotone.

"Waleed—you have your instructions. You will call this into the gendarmerie in Medea. They will alert the Prefect of Police in Algiers.

You will report what you have seen at the farmhouse as you find it. I need the gendarmes to log it tonight.

We have not been anywhere near here. You have no knowledge of our being here tonight or at any other time—myself, Lieutenant Mauritz, any member of the tenth para, any French Army presence whatsoever, be it regular, Harki, auxiliary or motorcycle fucking display team. Not a trace, not even a boot-mark...

You will stay put here tonight and we will return in the morning to clear it up.

Only Waleed goes to the farmhouse tonight. You two..."

He waves his hand at Father and I.

"...You are not here. You continue to work for me as my intelligence gophers in the city. Got it? Farouk, you know I have some compromising photographic evidence of you with the false martyr Ben M'hidi. I can spin it either way. That you conspired with him against us or collaborated with us to betray him. I can make you a pariah to either side, or both. I will not hesitate to use this evidence against you if you violate my orders...

Do I need to repeat myself?"

Father shakes his head solemnly.

"Good. And you, powder monkey. I need you to acknowledge these orders too."

I follow Father's lead. I nod.

"Thank you…"

Having gained our assurances, LeBoeuf now switches his focus to Waleed.

"I will see you in the morning. Waleed. Remember, I am relying on you to call this tragic incident in within the next hour. Keep the family here. If you need to drive to the gendarmerie to do it, so be it…"

At this he leaves.

We are all looking to each other.

"You knew this was planned?" Father says to Waleed. He stands up, takes two steps across the room, pulls his neighbour up by the collar and pushes him into the wall.

Waleed is choking.

"So did Simeon. He did too." Our neighbour is quick to excuse himself. Father releases Waleed. He turns to look at me and slumps down in a chair. We sit for several minutes not knowing what to say or do.

Waleed breaks the silence. He puts on his coat.

"Where are you going?" says Father, dazed.

"You heard the Captain. I need to visit the farmhouse," replies Waleed.

Waleed heads to the door and leaves. I hear his laboured footsteps trudge away into the night.

Father is done. He takes one look at me, turns and shuffles away into the bedroom.

I sit.

A few minutes pass. I look in on Father.

He is curled up on the bed alongside Mother and the children—a cluster of sleeping bodies locked in a deadly family embrace.

I follow Waleed out into the night and traipse uphill across the fields that separate our two houses. I reach the brow and see the familiar silhouette of our farmhouse against the night sky.

The lights of our farmhouse are off, though there is a glow coming from the barn. I can see the silhouette of Waleed entering some two hundred metres ahead.

I plod silently across the dry earth until I am on the lane that leads up to the house. I don't want Waleed to see me or know I've been here. I don't need him reporting my disobedience to the Captain. I circle the barn by the far field and close in. I crouch down by the loose boarding along the back wall and carefully part the boards.

I silently slip through the gap into the musty barn.

A brightly burning hurricane lamp swings from a hook on a low beam above the tool chest. It throws dancing shadows across the dirt floor. That's when I see the upturned seed-barrel, then the stockinged feet floating in space. I see Waleed standing staring up at a figure hanging by white strips of cloth from a cross beam.

The trousers of the hanged man are soiled. They sag below his waistline. His upper half is bare except for a bloodied vest. His head lolls. His lips are blue and his mouth is black with dried blood. There is a small chunk of flesh in the straw directly beneath him.

I think he must have bitten off his tongue.

I look more intently at him. He has a compact frame, gentle features, a head of lush short-cropped hair—a man I would like to have known.

This is Aussaresses' signature. This is LeBoeuf's calling card.

I see Lieutenant Laurent in the face of the hanged man. It flickers back to the features of Ben M'hidi, then away again to Laurent dangling from the cork oak in Koudiat el-Markluf. Barn. Cork oak. Barn. Cork oak. I am spinning with it and reach out to steady myself.

Waleed hears me and turns to catch me lurking in the shadows.

Despite LeBoeuf's strict orders, he doesn't appear to care that I am there.

"You heard the Captain. I have to call the gendarmerie…" he says, "Larbi Ben M'hidi has killed himself."

Part Three
Jameel

Mont-Les-Pins, Algiers Wilaya, 18 March 1957

"It has changed the game," crows LeBoeuf as he greets us in the atrium of the grand mansion. "The demise of Larbi Ben M'hidi has done something I never thought possible. It has silenced the FLN.

They are on their knees or on the run.

Half the committee has fled to Tunis and Tangier and the other half, well, they dare not show their faces anywhere around Algiers...

Come! I want you to meet someone."

We enter the salon where a soldier sits on the marble-inlaid Syrian throne-chair, clutching a document case, looking intimidated by the gewgaws all around.

He is relieved to have some company to distract him from the gilded ornaments and portraits—and stands to attention immediately.

LeBoeuf waves him back to his seat and introduces us.

"This is Lieutenant David Rousseau of the third para. Colonel Bigeard's man."

Rousseau extends a hand. His grip is limp and clammy. He is willowy, bordering on gangling. He is not as tall as he looks, though his patrician bearing somehow lends him more height and maturity. He is twenty-three going on fifty.

I fancy that his bloodline must be noble and that he is some Second World War General's fast-tracked son or the nephew of a Minister for War in the National Assembly.

He is so much the foundering foal that he couldn't have possibly arrived at this lofty point in his career entirely without a leg-up.

LeBoeuf continues.

"Lieutenant Rousseau is too modest to admit he is something of a high-flyer in the corps...

I hope you don't mind me saying that, Lieutenant."

Lieutenant Rousseau offers a polite gesture of acknowledgement. LeBoeuf takes this as his green light to launch into a tribute to the younger officer.

"Lieutenant Rousseau here sailed through the Academy with distinction and is the youngest of his rank of any division under General Massu's command. He has risen so high so fast that his doctor has prescribed him nose-bleed pills.

He is a man of considerable intelligence and extraordinary ability. Do not think that he will suffer fools...

Lieutenant...meet Farouk Abu, aka Fatiha Mokrani...and his, or should I say 'her'...grandson, Mahmoud...aka 'Powder Monkey', Simeon, Farouk's boy."

Confused by these noms de guerre, Rousseau clears his throat.

"I have heard a lot about your work undercover. It is to say the least...unorthodox." His eyes flicker nervously between Father's jilbab and his overly reddish lips.

"Lieutenant Rousseau will handle matters with you from here on..." says LeBoeuf casually glossing over this surprise announcement.

He could just as well have been speaking of tomorrow's weather forecast or the latest price on the Bourse.

I am stunned by the news. LeBoeuf registers Father's palpable sense of relief.

"I know how sad you must be to see me go, but General Massu has reassigned myself and the tenth to Kabylia and I cannot refuse a challenge.

Now that we have pushed the FLN leadership out of Algiers, we are pressing home our advantage and following them back to the highlands—their spiritual homeland.

The General wants boots on the ground there, not ballet pumps...

...If only we were there last September, eh?" he sighs, "We could have nipped this whole thing in the bud at Soummam.

Never mind—we now have to make sure they don't rally around a sense of birth right, let alone a green and white rag with a fuzzy felt crescent and star inside it.

Over to you, Lieutenant..."

Father is finding it difficult to switch his gaze from LeBoeuf. He is trying to get used to the idea that he may never have to lay his eyes on his tormentor ever again.

Lieutenant Rousseau of the third picks up the baton from the Captain of the tenth. LeBoeuf steps back to allow him his own introduction.

"Though we are united, we have our own informants in the third parachute division—our own credible sources.

However, it may not surprise you to learn that we are finding it as difficult as you to locate the murderous FLN terrorists.

Their political representatives may be subdued, but their chief bomb makers and mischief makers are still at large. Disappointingly so…"

Rousseau's voice is timorous and soft. He talks from the gullet, unlike LeBoeuf whose diaphragm heaves like a pair of forge-bellows whenever he opens his mouth.

Rousseau seems uncharacteristically callow for a soldier of his rank. Perhaps this tenderfoot is to 'Bruno' Bigeard's taste—a neophyte of the officer class who has not yet fought in a major theatre and who he can mould in his image.

It's just as well LeBoeuf is about to pack his kit bag and head off to Kabylia. The Captain would be bored out of his skull if he were forced to stay any longer in the company of this young pretender.

LeBoeuf feels the need to shake things up, to add a little spice to our meeting. He can't resist it. He is full of himself today.

"The FLN cells are tight as a gnat's arse…" he chips in, "They are so tight they don't know even who their own comrades are. Most of them have never even met each other. They communicate through dead drops, numbers stations, one-way voice links. It makes for great spy craft but a lousy orgy."

"Quite!" says Rousseau. "Having said that, it looks as if Yacef Saadi is becoming more careless. His female operatives are sighted in the Casbah on a relatively frequent basis…

I fear he may be planning a repeat of last September—the bombs at Place Bugeaud and on Rue Michelet.

The mujahidat managed to walk into the Milk Bar and the Cafeteria and trigger their bombs with remarkable ease. The femmes fatales melted into the bars of the European Quarter."

Rousseau is pleased with the pun. He feels 'femmes fatales' may be a slick way to describe female killers without glamorising them. They kill, after all.

"I guess it's not just down to their gender, but their youth, fashion, cosmopolitan behaviour…all ideal camouflage for terrorists."

He speaks like a man who has lived a conformist, catholic life yet is prone to the occasional lapse—and therefore weighs his words carefully, policing them for any faux-pas.

"We have seen nothing of Zohra Drif since, but our informants have sighted Hamia Toari on several occasions. Unusually, she takes the same route every day from her place on Rue Constantine. She meets with a man in a café and returns home. Regular as clockwork…"

I am wondering whether the café is Jameel's. I can tell Father is having the same worrying thought.

"We believe she is planning an imminent attack and we would like you to be our eyes and ears in the Casbah.

We are aware the FLN may be resorting to the same tactics as last year. They're desperate to notch up a few PR victories having suffered such catastrophic losses…"

Again, LeBoeuf must have his say. Like the bells of Notre-Dame de Paris, he must be heard loud and often.

"Bigeard's men have been trying to come at Saadi from another direction, but it would be a far more effective use of resources to pool our efforts now," the Captain says. "It will take more than one rat-catcher to subdue the king sewer-rat of Algiers!" he adds.

Lieutenant Rousseau reaches for the document case and passes us a black and white photograph.

"This is her. This is the Toari woman."

We see a studio portrait of a young woman dressed in a white chemise with nipped in, high-waisted slacks, her long, crimped hair flowing out behind her.

For some reason, the photographer has chosen to give her the dramatic pose of an artist, with her easel just forward and out of frame.

Such is the intensity of her expression that it looks as if she is about to lunge at the canvas with a rapier, not a brush. She observes her subject with the unerring gaze of a fencing master or sharpshooter.

She resembles Hedy Lamar in a Hollywood publicity shot. And I am instantly captivated by this revolutionary firebrand.

"Keep it. You may need it."

Father takes the photograph from Lieutenant Rousseau who continues with his briefing.

"We would like you to follow her. Just follow her. We think she is planning an attack on the European Quarter. We believe that is Yacef Saadi's next move...

Naturally, the moment she leaves the Casbah, we will arrest her.

But, in the meantime, we—or rather you—will track her every move and report back.

She may, just may, contact Saadi in person. And if she does, we will have him."

He snatches a sprite from the air and clenches it tightly in his closed fist.

"As soon as you have an inkling of Saadi's whereabouts, send young Simeon here on a foot race to alert us. And we will be there in force."

As we go to leave, LeBoeuf hands Father an envelope stuffed full of dinars. Father tries to take it from him, but LeBoeuf keeps a firm grip on it. A polite tug-of-war the Captain is destined to win. He won't let Father have the blood money before hearing him out. It is a polite tug-of-war.

"This is the last set of expenses I will give you. Lieutenant Rousseau will be your cashier from now on.

Remember, Farouk—If you're going to sell your soul, make sure you get a good price."

Father and I return to the Casbah that afternoon. We spend a few hours walking Hamia Toari's daily route as described by Lieutenant Rousseau.

Obligingly, the young Lieutenant has provided us with a marked map.

We familiarise ourselves with the various shops, recesses, natural resting places and stop-off points along the way from Rue Constantine to the Mosque. These will make it easier for us to follow Toari without being seen ourselves.

Father says that having failed to locate Ibrahim Najjar thus far, it is good to know that we will finally have one of Saadi's associates in our sights.

I run errands in the souk for my pretend matriarch. Father sits in the smoke-wreathed corner of Jameel's café while I go scouting for provisions.

Jameel's rent is due and Father places it for him under his saucer.

We quietly watch the swell of humanity in the surrounding streets. The tide rises and falls with the hour. At around three o'clock the stalls open for business. At four, there is a trading frenzy, a dash to transact in the hours before the curfew falls. At five-thirty, the young fighters come out for their show of strength...

They promenade and sing the 'Le Chant des Partisans' in solidarity with Ben M'hidi and in defiance of Aussaresses' death squads...

They brandish their weapons as a sign to all Muslims that they will not stand for French encroachment into the Zone Autonome d'Alger. Not tonight or any night. For this is Arab Algerian territory and these are Arab Algerian lives.

They know only too well that the French enforcers will be around after dark to collect the dues of empire in the form of secret abductions and detainment without trial.

Captain LeBoeuf may have left the scene, but the work continues unabated.

Jameel is eager to talk. He joins us at the table.

"Fatiha! It's been a while…Have you been keeping well? And you, Mahmoud. Are you taking good care of your grandmama? You are without coffee, I see. This won't do. My waiter is getting as lax as my cook. Would you like some?"

I am late to the punch today. Weary. And, whilst Father never speaks in the persona of Fatiha Mokrani, Jameel still requires an answer.

Father jabs a discreet elbow into my ribs to prompt me.

"Speak, you sloth. Or I'll give you something to talk about later…" he whispers under his breath.

"Yes, please," I say lustily back to Jameel. "Two cups…I have had a good day in the market thank you—we will run our shopping up to our cousins in Bab-el-Oued later…"

"Ah, good, good…taking care of family as well as your grandmama. You are a good boy…"

Jameel drags his seat in closer to the table, lowering his voice.

"Ben M'hidi's demise has repulsed the people of Algeria and enraged the nationalists. Nobody is listening to this suicide riff from the Army and the Governor-General. It's self-serving gibberish.

There is now talk of all-out North African war with France, enlisting the help of the Arab League…this lull will not last…it will explode soon enough…

It is getting unseasonably hot around here, my friend. The temperature rises with every day that passes. I would advise you not to come here again for a while…

If people knew what had been going on between us, they would string us up from the nearest lamppost and disembowel us…"

"I didn't expect Ben M'hidi to be murdered."

"Then you are a fool. Everything is possible. Once information is out, the law of unintended consequences applies. And nobody is above that law…"

Father has been itching to say something. The longer he keeps it inside, the more intensely it burns in his chest.

"I want to put things right. Balance things out, try to make my peace," he asserts.

Jameel looks shell-shocked by this. I didn't see it coming either.

"Who do you think you are? Captain America? The time for justice has long passed, my friend..."

"Can you pass messages to the FLN?"

Jameel frowns.

"For the right price, I can do anything. I'm like you. Enough dinar can take the fear out of any situation. It's a question of the break point, that's all...and it's just good to know if I go down you go down with me...

Why do you ask?"

"Let Saadi know that the French are on to him. Let him know that Massu's spies are following Hamia Toari."

"Saadi? You believe I can bring you the organ-grinder when I only deal with the monkeys?"

"You do yourself a disservice, Jameel. Benyoucef Benkhedda was no monkey..."

"I told you, Benkhedda was a glorious golden meteor that fell into my lap as a gift from the stars...and Ben M'hidi was the unexpected consequence...

But Saadi! Saadi is a mythic warrior, another matter entirely..."

Father is not to be deterred. He glares back at Jameel. It is a most effective weapon. I know he will keep it up until he receives the answer he wants to hear. Sure enough, Jameel finds it hard to ignore despite his continuing protests.

"Are you joking with me? Why do you think I am trading photographs of his bomb-makers and gophers with you?

Do you not stop to think that if I knew of Saadi's whereabouts, I would have sold that information to General Massu in person, then scooted off to Monte Carlo for an easy life, to play at the gaming tables?"

Father continues to fix Jameel with his impatient stare, forcing the big man to throw him a few crumbs of comfort.

"I know people who may know people. That is how it works. Benkhedda and Ben M'hidi were a lucky strike. A freakish, accident. A one in a million."

Father bucks up.

"Will you let the people who may know people who know Saadi…know of this then? Please."

"And how much do you want them to pay for this information?"

"I want nothing."

Jameel is non-plussed. To the seasoned black marketeer and horse-trader, this makes no sense.

"Nothing? What kind of a businessman are you?"

"I'm not a businessman."

"Clearly…!"

"I don't know what I am…"

"An idiot? A suicidal idiot?"

"I want you to talk to somebody who can get word to Saadi that the Army is on to Hamia Toari," he repeats. "You can set the price for this information. Have this one on me. Pocket the lot. I don't want a sou. That's it. No strings."

Jameel shakes his head in disbelief.

"Just those strings that are intertwined into a rope, looped into a noose and attached to a lamppost…" he comments, "This is a very reckless game you're playing, Farouk. If you send out a message like that to Saadi and his men, you will get backwash from Ali La Pointe himself.

"And that backwash may pull you under. He will show you no mercy if this ill-advised show of contrition inadvertently alerts the Army to his whereabouts."

He reflects some more.

"This sounds more like the indulgence of conscience to me. It is certainly not the action of a rational man."

"It is just a way of levelling the score." Father concludes.

Jameel doubts that. Father is keen to win over his number one snitch, but he's a tough nut to crack.

"What's so unusual? I have given you information on French Army movements before now. I did Ben M'hidi wrong. I want to make up for that and I want to wound LeBoeuf in the process."

Jameel extends his arms, appealing to a greater god.

"All the tea in China. All the tears in Algeria. Nothing in a million years will make up for Ben M'hidi's death. You are the chaser of lost causes. And you put us all in jeopardy with this triple agent act of yours."

But Father won't back down.

He will sit here until hell freezes over if that's what it takes to bend Jameel to his will.

After a short while, Jameel breaks the silence.

"Alright, alright, I will seed your information with my network, then see whether Saadi bites…

But there is something I don't understand, Farouk…"

"What's that?"

"If you already know of Hamia Toari's whereabouts, why don't you just tell her that the Army has tumbled her?"

"Toari is a foot-soldier. She is unreliable," replies Father. "If she knows the Army is on to her, she may just fly the coop without telling Saadi and then we will never reach him.

No, we must make sure this intelligence reaches Saadi himself. At least then he can judge whether the information is useful to his operations and take the appropriate actions…I feel thus in my gut. And my gut is rarely wrong…"

We are back at the garage in the Rue Quincie with some hot food in our bellies, using the camp bed as a bench, an upturned lemon crate as a table.

Father is gnawing on a heel of bagita, dipping it in the dregs of a thin cholaba, textured with sweet potato and cilantro.

It is not tasty. We eat without joy. Father is a hopeless cook. And he has put neither spices nor heart into this meal.

Indeed, he has lost his appetite altogether. He is shedding weight. He has a gaunt and hunted look.

He entered Waleed's home the other night as a revenant, returning to a family he hadn't seen in months. But unable to feel, touch, or connect with anything he held dear in his life before the bombing at Place Jean-Paul Sartre.

He couldn't bring himself to revisit our own farmhouse that night, to behold the handiwork of Aussaresses' torture squad.

He daren't. It would have destroyed him.

He is too unstable to take much more punishment. I know this for the simple reason that the sight of Mother asleep in Waleed's bed hardly raised a flicker of recognition.

He may have been reunited with his family for one night, not as the fully sentient head of it, but as a ghost, already dead.

We left early in the morning before Mother even had a chance to open her eyes. LeBoeuf saw to it that we were spirited away without any shedding of tears.

Mother would have realised he'd been there, of course—even before an excitable Louis and Margot jumped on her to wake her up, as they do on the morning of Eid al-Fitr when we all look forward to helping her bake the bread and the boureks for the table.

I can see their bright little faces now. I can even hear their voices, "Father is here, maman! Dressed like you! Father and Shimeun-frère!"

The children would no doubt have bubbled over with excitement at the thought of breaking the good news. They would have searched Waleed's house for us—only to have their hopes dashed yet again.

In the kitchen, they would have found Waleed asleep in a chair by himself. No sign of 'papa' or me.

We would have been long gone by the time they roused themselves from sleep. Headed back to Algiers with LeBoeuf and the tenth. Tramping the streets of the Casbah, paving the way for 'la mission civilisatrice'.

But the scent of Father's sweat would have remained on the pillow beside Mother, and she would have woken sensing he had been there.

By that time, following Waleed's detailed statement to the gendarmerie in Medea, the clean-up would have taken place at our farmhouse. The body would have been cut down from the beam in our outbuilding and despatched to the mortuary at the Maillot hospital.

And Major Paul Aussaresses would have left the farmhouse with his little box of tricks and his 'special unit', having turned the scene of a war crime into that of a 'misadventure.'

Jacques Massu would be claiming that Ben M'hidi was still alive on his way there in the ambulance and that he had hanged himself with an electrical cord during the night.

The next day Governor-General Lacoste's press officer would draft an announcement to the effect that Ben M'hidi had committed suicide by hanging himself with strips of material torn from his shirt.

And the following day the world would be greeted with the breaking news that Algeria's most wanted had taken his own life.

Of course, I knew differently. I knew all of this to be a pack of lies.

No wonder that Lieutenant Laurent was seeking to build these soldiers their very own Nuremberg courtroom.

And no wonder, since my night-time visit to our farmhouse out-building, I have been abstracted, distanced from everyone and everything.

I have become a stranger, even to myself.

I am struggling to keep a purchase on my world.

The two hanging men who plague my dreams are those of Lieutenant Laurent and Larbi Ben M'hidi, but they may just as well be Father and myself.

LeBoeuf may be on his way to Kabylia, but it feels as though, in us, he has two more live bodies dangling in the wind.

Rue Constantine, The Casbah, Algiers, 2 April 1957

We arrive in the street just as Toari emerges from a doorway. She wears a hijab and striped green and brown jellaba under which she moves with the nonchalant grace of a ballet dancer. She is entrancing.

We start tailing her along the crumbling stone gullies, the back-doubles, the narrowing chutes of rubble and refuse.

As we drop down through the Casbah, Father notices Toari's black canvas basketball shoes.

He tells me that she can make good headway in those rubber soles. They grip the foot-worn stones, the grooves, the uneven surfaces of the rapidly descending staircases and alleyways.

What's more, once she has disposed of jellaba and hijab, this footwear will not look out of place in the fashionable European bars around the Rue Michelet.

He speculates as to what she is wearing under her jellaba.

"What do you think, Simeon? What would go with basketball shoes? My money's on white pedal pushers and a bowling shirt to pay off the Yankee look. 'Rock Around the Clock' style…"

Toari is already fifty yards ahead of us and we are losing touch.

"She moves with great speed. We must hurry without hurrying," he says, "She is looking to see if anyone is shadowing her. She has seen us, but not registered us. Not yet. We must be very careful."

I have no idea how Father can tell these things. I cannot see what he sees.

We follow along the route so precisely marked out by Lieutenant Rousseau. She is true to her calling, never wavering from her course. We pass the imposing facade of the Dar Hassan Pacha with its serried balcony balustrades and grand entrance.

She stops as expected at a café close to the southern perimeter of the Casbah on the esplanade outside the Ketchoaua Mosque.

Here she orders mint tea and meets with a young man in a dark suit, open neck shirt and sandals.

After twenty minutes, the man pays and she retraces her steps. All the while we are trailing her, we are also looking out for Ibrahim Najjar—in shops, cafés and doorways, through side streets, conduits and alleyways—in the hope that either of these targets will lead us back to Saadi.

We report back to Lieutenant Rousseau every third day. He prefers the more modest surroundings of an empty parking lot some way off Chenoua Plage back along the coast road from Mont-Les-Pins towards chichi Tipaza.

The beach is a popular destination for colonials seeking a day at the seaside, although the parking lot is located so far from the beach that few day-trippers bother to use it.

"Good afternoon, gentlemen. What a perfect day!" Rousseau breathes in the ozone and stretches his gangling legs like a loose-limbed foal.

"I bet you can see all the way to Majorca from the top of that ridge," he declares, peering up into the low sun towards a steady ascent of pines and shielding his eyes in a kind of limp salute.

"How is our Casbah commuter…?"

"Keeping good time," Father replies.

"From the Rue Constantine to the Ketchoaua Mosque in eleven minutes. Ten minutes spent in conversation with the man in the black suit. Fourteen minutes back again…uphill."

Lieutenant Rousseau nods sagely as if these latest timings give him some deep insight he doesn't really possess.

"If you don't mind me asking," says Father, "who is the man in the black suit?"

"I was about to ask you," replies Lieutenant Rousseau. "I have no further intelligence on him."

The days repeat themselves. The same routine. Toari emerges at exactly the same time. She makes her rapid descent from the medina to the lower Casbah where the streets level out and widen, past the front of Dar Hassan Pacha, then along towards the Mosque. A mint tea at the café with the man in the black suit, and back again. A thirty-five-minute round trip—almost to the second.

"Perhaps he is her boyfriend," I speculate one evening at the garage in the Rue Quincie. "Perhaps it is nothing more than a lover's tryst. Her parents disapprove of him. She is well-to-do. He is from the wrong side of the tracks…And hey presto! They meet to gaze into each other's eyes at the same time every day."

Father senses how much I am enjoying my made-up scenario.

"Ha! She is certainly worth gazing at. She is very beautiful…Are you in love with her, Simeon, that headstrong young woman…?"

"I feel I know her."

"In your dreams, maybe…"

I do not tell Father, but at night, far from putting the photograph of Toari to one side, I slip it under my pillow.

If I wake up before him, I gaze some more at the woman of my dreams and once, just once, I even snatched a kiss off the photo…I was immediately ashamed of myself.

We are growing used to the routine. It repeats day after day for ten days. All that changes is the movement of the clouds and the sweet song of the goldfinches that flit around the Casbah and never stay in one place for long.

Otherwise the sights and sounds are a constant. Even the smell of mimosa, pine, spice and coffee are wafted at us from the same doorways, the same courtyards, the same places along the route.

Father says this is the everyday banality of war. The kind of reality they didn't show in the movies. The interminable wait for the opening salvo, the endlessly repetitive drill-square preparation, the rhythm of extreme nothingness. Then the sudden outbreak of something psychotic, summary, cruel that we could never conceive of if we hadn't lived through it.

He urges me to guard against complacency. Routines are there to be broken and once they are, it can be difficult to reorientate around new events.

It is a human point of weakness, a blind spot. In the wake of the unexpected, in those split-second moments of readjustment and indecision, people can lose their lives.

He has seen it many times whilst serving in the Harki Army. A lapse of concentration caused by something as sudden as a songbird flying up from a ground nest or a mosquito landing on a soldier's neck.

It breaks the routine, the concentration gone and wham! A tripwire is triggered, a grenade explodes, someone forgets to keep their head down and takes a bullet in the brain. One fatal moment and the lights go out on their world.

"Do not let it go out on yours, Simeon!"

On the eleventh day, something unusual occurs. Toari passes a note to the man in the black suit over the café table as they touch. There is a lingering stroke of her hand in his and the man then slips a piece of paper into the inside pocket of his suit jacket. I long for the beautiful assassin to stroke my hand too.

On the twelfth day, the skies darken, and we hear the drumbeat of rain on the masonry and the ancient stones across the Casbah. We stop in at Jameel's café first thing. Father wants to check something with him.

We are soaked as we sit down and Jameel brings us an umbrella—one of the many unclaimed pieces of lost property that patrons have left down by the side of chairs or hanging from coat hooks in their haste to plunder the souk for bargains.

"Here, Mahmoud, you will need this. Keep the rain off your grandmama. You know how she suffers with pneumonia."

I think Jameel is starting to believe the role play.

"I do. I will, thank you," I reply loudly and courteously, taking the umbrella with a small respectful bow of my head.

"Did you pass on my message to your contacts, Jameel?" whispers Father. "I did," Jameel confirms. "I can do no more. However, there is one thing."

Jameel is either reluctant to tell Father or doesn't quite know how to put it.

"Well, what is it…?"

"A message has come to me via the dead drop. It rarely happens that word comes back along the pipe. It asks for the name of my Army informant. In truth, it demands the name of my Army informant."

Father sits back on his chair.

"There is no suggested price attached. Just a threat…"

"A threat?"

"If I don't reveal the name of my source, I will take an assassin's bullet…" He sees doubt cast its shadow across Father's face.

"Don't worry…I'm not giving you up…

That's why I use dead drops. I am anonymous and therefore so are you. You are safe for the time being…

But I have to tell you, Farouk, this is highly irregular.

273

I am very uncomfortable with it. The jackals are circling…and don't say I didn't tell you this would happen! It was foolish of you to insist on reaching out to Saadi.

We must be very careful. I have told you already not to come here…this time I must insist…"

Despite Jameel's efforts to reassure Father, fear is etched into the expressions of both men. Between them they are catching the terror like a virus—and infecting me.

"As of today, I am shutting up shop…you will have to leave the Rue Quincie as of tonight."

"What?"

"I am in fear for my life. You should be too…we cannot be seen together…we cannot afford to be connected."

"Where will you go?"

"Believe me, not far…I would advise you to do the same. For the sake of Simeon here if nothing else.

The Casbah is no place for games. You are playing both sides. And that cannot last…

Ben M'hidi was their totem, Ali La Pointe is their talisman. Yacef Saadi knows they cannot afford to lose both standard-bearers in the space of a single month. He is their sword of retribution."

We leave Jameel for Rue Constantine. It will be the last time we say our goodbyes.

By the time Toari leaves her recessed doorway, dark clouds have massed over the medina and a thin mist shrouds the Casbah.

Descending the stone staircases, heavy raindrops bounce off the steps which become slippery. Toari glides her way down towards her assignation, with the sure-footed agility of a mountain goat.

I try to hold the umbrella up for Father, who is struggling to keep sight of the mujahidat. In the narrow alleyways, it is virtually impossible to keep the weather off his head without scraping the walls to both sides with the ends of the umbrella spokes.

The rain arrows down into the slits of passages. The wind whistles off the Mediterranean and through the ancient ravines and blows the umbrella inside out.

I ditch the wreckage in an ancient water trough and Father surrenders to the driving rain.

His eyeliner is streaking his face and he is forgetting himself, losing his matriarchal disguise and forgoing his short steps in an attempt to keep up.

He is taking paces and skipping over the puddling hollows in the stone that have been eroded by civilisations of footsteps.

I am reminded of his words earlier: 'In a lapse of concentration caused by something unexpected…in one forgetful, fatal moment, the lights go out on your world.'

I realise that in haste and fear, he is flouting his own rubric. Forgetting his disguise. Panicking all the way down the hill. And leaving himself exposed and vulnerable.

As we cross the street by the Dar Hassan Pacha, a thunderclap booms overhead. Flashes of lightning strobe the hurrying form of Hamia Toari, illuminating El Djazair and electrifying the grey-green Mediterranean with a sparkling phosphorescent glow.

As we enter the esplanade, we are passed by people rushing to escape the torrential rain.

An old man in a fedora and high-collared raincoat crosses our path, holding the hand of a small child, possibly his grandson. I deduce they are on their way to school and long to be back there myself. Hurrying into view is a middle-aged woman wearing a heavy light blue coat and a flower pattern hajib. She collides with a young man in a smart waiter's uniform who is drenched and harried—I can only guess he must be late for work in the European Quarter.

We slow when we reach the Mosque and look in under the bright red awning of the café.

No Toari. No man in the black suit.

Father glances up and down the esplanade.

He catches sight of the man in the black suit walking in one direction, Toari hurrying in the other towards the European Quarter.

She is carrying something under her jellaba, now heading for the perimeter of the Casbah and turning a corner into Boulevard Abdelkader.

We follow in her footsteps to find her walking straight into an Army checkpoint.

Soldiers turn to look. It is too late for her to pivot around or back up along the street without arousing suspicion.

We realise this misstep may cost Toari her life. As does she.

She is just metres from the barrier where a Zouave soldier stands in a newly installed sentry box checking the passing drivers' tickets of sojourn. A group of troops and gendarmes are stopping passers-by at random and searching every other car.

Toari slows. We slow. She is agitated. It is the first time we have seen her lose her poise.

"This is it…This is her hour of reckoning," confides Father quietly, watching his target as if back in the ravine.

It becomes clear from her faltering steps that Toari is trying to estimate the frequency of the spot checks.

Every third person is searched. Males are prioritised.

I feel the heat radiating from her.

Can she blather her way through, flirt her way around, or challenge this all-male group of guards to frisk a Muslim woman by kicking up such an unholy stink that she passes unmolested—sending them away with the Koranic text ringing in their ears and their tails between their legs? Which is it to be?

She is edging ever closer to the paratrooper at the barrier, sizing him up, calculating the odds of going undetected, unscathed.

We are holding our breath.

A step. Closer. Another step. She is third in line now.

The citizens are keen to hurry things along and escape the rain. The gendarme has asked a man on a bicycle to dismount. The Zouave soldier has waved down a car. The paratrooper is waving through the man directly in front of Toari. It is the man in the fedora who passed us earlier with the child by his side.

It looks as though they will go through unchecked.

This is Toari's chance.

She tucks herself in behind the man. Perhaps the soldier will mistake her for the child's mother.

One more step.

She thinks she's through.

There's a tap on her shoulder.

Another soldier is telling her to step to one side.

He points to her midriff.

She objects.

She shouts at him.

He shouts back and reaches to liberate the sidearm from the holster on his belt.

He is now grabbing at the handle of his service revolver...

There is a sudden blur of light blue. A figure rushes in from nowhere with pistol raised. There is a flash. A crack. Toari drops to the floor. A woman takes flight. Light blue coat. Flower pattern hijab. Pelting up the street.

Weapons are drawn. Gunshot. Two pops. Then a third. Four, five, six.

We crouch and watch as a hail of bullets flies past. The escaping woman turns the corner and is gone.

Only seconds have elapsed.

The gendarmes and soldiers can't even give chase. They have been caught flat-footed and now they have a dying young woman on their hands with a bomb under her jellaba that she could still activate.

They push each other back to a safe distance, guns raised and pointed. The soldier takes charge.

He steps forward, raises his rifle and pumps two more bullets into Toari's body in quick succession. We see her stiffen and strain, then go limp and still.

We back away slowly. Father places a hand on my shoulder and urges me to walk, not run.

I take one last look at Toari. I can see her black canvas baseball boots under her rucked jellaba. I can see the wires and the explosive device underneath. Her ankles are bare, but I glimpse the thickly stitched hem of a pair of blue denim pedal-pushers.

We go briskly in the direction of the Marine Quarter without speaking.

At Rue Quincie, we silently pick up our belongings from Jameel's garage and leave.

Father drives without thinking, without talking.

He takes the road west through thrashing rain as if he is going to Mont-Les-Pins. Visions of the incident are dancing in front of his eyes, repeating again and again. He is walking himself through what has just happened. Over and over. He cannot stop. His eyes are growing dark, sombre.

He pulls the car into our rendezvous location. No Lieutenant Rousseau today. This is not a scheduled stop. The parking lot behind Chenoua Plage is deserted. More desolate than ever in this squall.

We sit in the vehicle staring out at the dense fog through a sheet of a water. The horizontal downpour pummels the windscreen and raindrops strafe the car. Bam, bam, bam.

The rising pines at our backs aren't even visible from where we sit. They are saturated in a thick mist. If it weren't for the salt tang of the sea, we could easily be floating in the clouds thousands of feet up.

We sit in silence, insulated except for the drumming splatters of heavy raindrops on the roof of the car, which are starting to slow. We listen in silence to the softening rainfall.

"Saadi got my message," says Father after a while.

"How do you know?"

Father is gently knocking his head against the steering wheel, gripping tightly with both hands.

"It was right under my nose and I missed it."

"Missed what?"

"Look at me, Simeon. Look at my disguise! I have been in this jilbab now for seventy-three days. Seventy-three days plastering powder on my face and dragging lipstick across my mouth.

Seventy-three days and no let up!

I have looked at the world through mascara eyelashes. I have worn this jilbab and hijab like my birth-suit. And I have held my tongue through all of that. Farouk Abu alias Fatiha Mokrani, the widow from Bab-el-Oued with her goitre and her pneumonic condition…"

I need to remind him that it has been a trial for me too.

"And I have been the dutiful grandson for over half of that time…taken against my wishes and forced to be a part of this charade. You have led me into the jaws of hell…" I add querulously.

"Indeed, Simeon…I am sorry."

He stands corrected.

"…We have put ourselves through all this together. And guess what—there he is right in front of us taking a leaf out of my book…and I don't even notice.

Fool…fool!" he goes on, "I am such a fucking idiot…"

"What are you talking about?"

"It's as if he is mocking me…"

"Who?"

"If only I had seen it, Simeon!"

"Seen what?"

That woman…The shooter…it's only just dawned on me…did you see her face…that was our chance."

I haven't a clue what he is saying.

"We should have followed her…I wasn't thinking straight…" he goes on.

He is disturbed, distracted, rambling.

"She was too fast for us…it all happened so quickly," I say in a vain attempt to join in.

But he can tell I am a long way from understanding.

He is looking at me just as he did the Syrian throne-chair at Mont-Les-Pins. As something out of time, out of place, out of touch.

"What?" I ask, trying to read his expression.

"You don't know who that woman was back there, do you? The one who murdered Toari?"

"No."

"That woman was him—Yacef Saadi…The bomb-maker just shot his bomber."

Mont-Les-Pins, Algiers Wilaya, 4 April 1957

"The paratrooper who shot Toari has been disciplined," Lieutenant Rousseau informs us.

"It was Saadi who delivered the kill shot," Father tells him.

"Yes. He would rather kill Toari than see her arrested," Rousseau confirms.

"He would do anything to stop her giving away his location under interrogation. Even risk being caught himself.

That is how desperate he is becoming.

It's just unfortunate that we fell for his disguise. But then you have gone undetected for months with yours.

The fact is we let him get away and lost our lead for good in the process. I would call that a bad day at the office."

"Just to be clear, I don't believe Toari would ever have led us to Saadi. He is far too wily to allow it." Father is certain on that point.

"And yet that was quite a daring stunt he pulled off in the Lower Casbah," says Lieutenant Rousseau.

"A calculated risk…" Father corrects him.

Rousseau is becoming quite peevish. The head of housekeeping at Mont-Les-Pins calls him "un homme doux'. But I'm not so sure.

It's true that this 'sweet man' doesn't have LeBoeuf's quick temper, but there is still something astringent in his sugar-coated personality.

"You look very tired, Farouk. As does your son."

"We are working all hours."

"On high alert. Always on call, eh? That's the spirit. Although…"

His nose twitches.

"…you must not sacrifice personal hygiene in pursuit of the cause…"

"My cause is my family, Lieutenant…"

"Very noble…"

"To which point, we would like to visit them soon…"

There is a sharp intake of breath from Lieutenant Rousseau.

"I'm afraid that is impossible…"

"Impossible…" echoes Father.

"You see, unpalatable as this whole thing is, the farmhouse is the scene of a death by misadventure…the family currently resides with your neighbour, Waleed. I believe that is his name.

Your farmhouse has been made a zone interdite for the time being…the Prefect of Police is investigating. You can see how your being there would attract the wrong kind of attention."

"How about me? Can I go home now?" I ask.

Father appears angered by my suggestion. To his relief, Rousseau dismisses it out of hand.

"I'm afraid you have become an essential part of your father's cover story here. And a messenger. If you find Saadi you, Simeon, will be our Pheidippides…and deliver the news directly to us."

His reference is lost on me. I have some way to go at the Lycée René Coty before I start studying the classics.

"So, no. Whilst Ali La Pointe and Yacef Saadi remain at large, then so do you…"

My heart sinks.

"Will you please make sure our family are safe, Lieutenant. Protected, I mean…" I urge him.

"I can tell you for free they are in a far safer place at your neighbour's house than at your farmhouse.

We are keeping the whole area under close watch. The FLN have their reasons for sniffing around the scene. They have a different take on Ben M'hidi's suicide…

But you have nothing to fear.

The third para have now replaced the tenth as your family's cordon de sécurité—both at your neighbour's house and the farmhouse…it is as if no one has lived there.

I believe not many know you live there anyway. According to Captain LeBoeuf…"

I wonder what LeBoeuf is doing now. Whether he is busy erasing our nation's history with the same nonchalance he uses to despatch his enemies.

Father and I have speculated long into the night.

Whilst I cannot forgive him for all he has put me through, our time spent together has given me the opportunity to talk freely with him about matters I already know but don't fully understand.

Such as why, when we arrived at our farmhouse from the east and settled there courtesy of the French, we stood by as the Army cleared a Berber farmer out of what is now our home.

In justification, Father tells me that was the same for most Arabs in northern Algeria where the French Army were instructed to move the Pied-Noir settlers in and the Berbers out.

We were a notable exception among indigenous Arabs. In our case, Captain LeBoeuf allowed for Father's excellent service record with the blue caps, the French auxiliary Arab forces.

I tell him Mother says we are generally mistrusted for that in Medea and that, by pitching the Arabs out of their homes, the French have created a Francophile enclave around the capital. Father thinks the sooner they get the job done, the sooner we can settle in mainland France. But whenever he drinks, his tongue loosens, and he becomes more bitter towards his masters.

He tells me the French are keen to repeat that trick in the rural west—in Kabylia, the spiritual homeland of the nationalist struggle and in Aurès, the mountain stronghold of the maquis.

At this very moment, he says, LeBoeuf and his men are razing the villages, laying to waste the crops, rounding up the Berber Arabs and creating ghettoes for the misplaced. He says the historical record will be written by the victors who will exculpate themselves from their crimes.

The truth, however, is that in some communities, girls as young as fourteen will be gang-raped by French soldiers and every third Muslim man will be lynched.

In others, pregnant women will be violated so badly that their offspring will suffer birth defects and Muslim males will be taken and summarily shot, their bodies buried under quicklime in mass graves. The evidence eradicated. Thousands and thousands of lives expunged.

LeBoeuf, of course, will punish this wrongdoing. He will come down hard on the violators. General Massu may describe their actions as 'maladroit'. He may say it is required to root out the terrorists hiding within the Berber population. Or he may choose to say nothing.

But in reality, these are the officially sanctioned methods of the tenth para. Major Aussaresses has practised them behind the walls of El-Biar and he will do so again whatever the backdrop, provided his methods bear fruit.

It worked in Sétif, where the French stoked the fire of nationalism by giving Arab homes to the Pieds-Noirs, seizing the land by decree, enforcing zones interdites where nomads once roamed, and handing all French settlers privileges over the indigenous tribes.

Enfranchised and newly entitled, the Pieds-Noirs became France's proxy population in North Africa. And hostility grew. It reached its nadir at Philippeville.

But, as I said, Philippeville is Father's very own no-go zone and he will not talk about it.

What is common to all of these conflicts across Algeria according to Father is that LeBoeuf has led the tenth from the front into every one of them, with Aussaresses' torture squads never far behind.

He and Aussaresses have been there at every swing of the scythe.

As I understand it—and this is Father quoting Mother—'the last battered stump of Algerian nationhood stands at Kabylia and Aurès'. And that is precisely where LeBoeuf is now.

He is completing the last leg of his sweep from East to West—the direction in which the Romans, Phoenicians and Ottomans travelled in their own pursuit of Algeria's annexation.

For the French empire-builders, however, this was never a natural direction of travel.

The French Fourth Republic prefers the direction of heel on throat to the sweep of a cloak—that is to say, they favour north to south over east to west.

Perhaps that is why they have stayed in Algeria for such a long time.

Perhaps that is why their foray into Indochina has been, to use LeBoeuf's words, 'such an unmitigated cluster-fuck.'

For the French, it was simply the wrong direction of travel.

No, LeBoeuf is a downward pressure boot-on-skull kind of soldier. North to south. Up and down.

And his boots are always the first on the ground wherever the Frenchman reaches with his mission civilisatrice.

Father tells me all this in the time we have spent together at Rue Quincie and in the Casbah.

He is definitely not shy of giving history lessons, though I have to say he is hardly self-taught. Much of it is gleaned from Mother.

Infuriated by his outrageous backsliding at Philippeville, she has given him several stern lectures on the Algerian struggle, berating him for his serial flip-flopping and fence-sitting.

To Mother, he is a man with an arse full of grazes and splinters.

"Do you know how many times the French invaded Algeria, Farouk?"

"No, but I've a feeling you're going to tell me, my love."

"Fifteen! Do you know the first time they came here in eighteen thirty, it was a blood sport for them?"

I remember Father raising his eyes to the heavens, knowing this was her pet subject and she would treat him like a dunce.

But then, just as Mother dismissed his grasp on events, Father consistently underestimated the fire inside her.

"No, I mean it quite literally, Farouk. Literally, a blood sport."

"Literally, my love? Surely not," was his riposte.

Mother was not one to pussyfoot around the facts with a man who had no interest in in the birth of nationhood.

She rammed them home.

"The French invaders laid out hundreds of dead Arabs along the coast so that French sightseers could watch the body-count through their telescopes and binoculars from their pleasure-boats out in the bay.

The aristos arrived from Marseilles for the day. They even drank champagne and stuffed their faces with amuse-bouches as the fighting continued in Algiers and the disembowelled corpses of Algerians were assembled like so many eviscerated wild boar on the harbour side…

All trophy kills! Yes, trophy kills! And these European butchers have been killing us ever since…And you ask me now why I am not desperate for a visa to live in France?

Shame on you, Farouk Abu!"

I am back in the room.

"Where do you bivouac?" asks the genial Lieutenant Rousseau.

"We have accommodation," replies Father, evasively.

"You live in that car of yours, don't you..." says the astute Lieutenant with a touch of pity.

"We like to stay mobile. It is the best way in the Casbah. We are not safe..."

"Night after night in a tiny jalopy. Surely, it's no place for a boy, Farouk..." advises Rousseau.

"I am not a boy," I protest, "and in case you hadn't noticed, I am here."

I am ignored again.

"Bear with us, Farouk. It won't be much longer. Once we have the bomb-master we shall be free of the terrorists..."

"And then what?" I ask.

"Then we will all be in clover. Talking of which, do avail yourself of the facilities here at Mont-Les-Pins should you so wish...

Now that Captain LeBoeuf has gone away on tour of duty, General Massu has given Colonel Bigeard and the third para free rein of the house—his way of compensating us for our humiliating loss of M'hidi to the tenth...

I share Colonel Bigeard's view. Personally, I loathe the place. It is the most vulgar white elephant. To be frank, I would rather bed down in a flophouse in Saint Denis. It reminds me of the chateau in The Ardèche that my father owned when I was a boy..."

A shiver comes over him.

"I much prefer barracks closer to Algiers. This feels so wantonly ostentatious."

Father agrees with the Lieutenant. He is reluctant to receive French Army hospitality in such a lavish setting, if at all.

Despite knowing that we would give our eye teeth to lie flat on a soft mattress, we resolve to take our chances in the car.

Before we do, however, Father makes sure he has a wash and brush up in one of the many en-suite bathrooms on the first floor.

Here he reapplies his make-up and refreshes his disguise. His jilbab is starting to stink and the head of housekeeping insists on giving it a wash before we go anywhere. It delays our departure for a good few hours.

In the meantime, Lieutenant Rousseau insists we eat a hearty meal before we return to the city. And encourages us to continue using the mansion as our 'arrêt confort' if only to ablute and freshen up.

Fully refreshed and restored, we return to central Algiers, though by the end of the day, we will have wished we'd stayed away.

The Arabic Quarter, Algiers,
10 May 1957

Father and I are outside Jameel's café.

The streets are almost empty, the shops boarded up. One merchant is open for business a little further up the alleyway—a man and his daughter selling lemons from a barrel. We hardly notice them.

What is in front of our eyes holds our gaze.

Jameel's café is a scene of utter devastation.

Shattered crockery and copper dishes are strewn everywhere. Cutlery drawers have been emptied. The legs of tables have been torn from their brackets and used as cudgels. Seats have been ripped from chairs only to be repurposed as projectiles which are now scattered across the streets.

In the kitchen it is worse. The place is infested with flies. The stove Jameel so lovingly installed from his mother's house on her death has been desecrated. People have pissed here. Someone has defecated on the hob. They have turned on the gas burners and singed the ceilings. Wooden counter tops are charred. The wall-tiles are scorched. Jameel's larder and cold store have been raided, leaving puddles of milk and cream souring on the floor. His beloved coffee machine has been vandalised, its parts torn from their fixings and the once gleaming body he polished every morning battered out of shape. It is annihilation.

A storm of brick-dust has settled everywhere from the enormous holes that have been punched in the walls. Great cave-like openings revealing tangles of wires, powdery render, dry rot and a single rat waiting for our departure so that it can feed safely off the scraps of mouldering produce on the kitchen floor.

Pipes have been smashed in the latrine and the sulphurous stink of sewage is seeping up through the walls.

Father pushes open the door to Jameel's small back office and we enter Hades. Our mouths fall open.

There is the big man, naked down to his underpants, tied to a chair, trussed and bound.

He wears a tall, round white plastic hat.

His face is unrecognisable. His head is a bloodied lump of gristle and bone. His eyes have been scratched out of their sockets. The skin looks as if it has been whitened with a powder giving him the look of a Pierrot. The powder has since hardened into a thick crust.

But that is not all.

A knife has been taken to his body. His torso has been gouged with crimson crescents like the patterning on a clown costume. Jameel has been cut many times.

I have to avert my eyes.

We stand there for what must be minutes.

The shock has a numbing effect. We are only gradually beginning to process all this.

In our silence, we know too that we are paying our solemn respects to the café owner.

Father cannot bring himself to speak. Nor me to look.

I need air. This air inside Jameel's office is fetid and rotting. I walk outside through the carnage, leaving Father with his friend.

Out in the alley, I double up. I feel a cramping seize my gut. My eyes are prickling with the sight of Jameel. I am losing balance, seeing stars. I throw up.

I feel a steadying hand on my back and hear a consoling voice.

"Get it out. Get that poison out of you. You'll feel better for it."

I straighten up. The lemon-seller is by my side. He has left his daughter to mind the stall.

I look over at her and wonder whether she too has witnessed this. I pray to my personal god that she hasn't.

"Did you know him?" asks the lemon-seller.

"Jameel? He was an acquaintance—a friend of the family."

"Is it wise to leave your mother in there? It is a brutal sight."

"She is my grandmother, and she is paying her respects…"

"No one has dared go near this place since it happened. The people around here fear they may come back."

"What happened here?" I ask.

The lemon-seller shakes his head.

"I still don't quite understand, and I have spent many years on this planet. I cannot explain why human beings do this to one another."

"Please try to tell me what has been going on. Jameel was a friend to our family. He did many kind things for us."

The lemon-seller takes a deep breath. He feels he owes me an explanation even though he is at a loss to find one.

"Two days ago, midway through the afternoon…

I was down there doing good business…

I heard cries of 'Traitor' and 'French poodle' coming from up here.

That's when I saw the five ALN fellaghas with Kalashnikovs come for Jameel.

I hadn't seen him for days. He'd shut up shop, so I was relieved for him. I assumed he wasn't there…

The fellaghas couldn't find him so they started tearing the place apart. Ripping the shutters off. Throwing around the furniture Jameel had stacked inside the café. Threatening us.

They tried to rouse us, all the shopkeepers, to join them in ransacking the place. 'A traitor's lair,' they called it.

But we were scared of them and held back.

We have no issue with Jameel. He was making a living like us. We all mind our own business around here. We have to. Including Jameel.

The fellaghas were happy to carry on without us. Tearing at the furniture, raiding the empty till, smashing the bottles, the glasses, hurling everything around.

It was a whirlwind of destruction.

Then they disappeared inside, and we heard more smashing and banging. We smelled burning. We thought the whole place was about to come down…

They were trying to smoke him out.

They must have heard him coughing. They found him hiding in the walls.

He'd been there for days apparently…crushing that big body into the wall cavity behind the kitchen…can you imagine?

They stripped him and tied him to the chair as you saw…

And then they came back out on the street.

They turned the guns on us, on all the shopkeepers. They threw furniture at us. They were crazed.

They said they would kill us if we didn't each take a slice of yellow-belly pig from the café.

They lined us all up in Jameel's kitchen, made us wait outside his office door.

One of the fellaghas—a kind of master of ceremonies—had a carving knife in his hand.

He handed each of us the knife in turn and we went in one by one at gunpoint to carve our slice out of Jameel.

He was alive and begging us to stop.

We tried to make small nicks in his skin at first to spare him as much pain as we could, but the fellaghas had their guns pointed at us and they demanded we take bigger, meatier cuts away with us.

We each returned the knife when we were done…

I couldn't believe a man could make such a squeal. It was like nothing I have heard before.

The last of us that went in, the old tailor, he has a shop further up this street, they told him they would 'cure' the meat of the pig to preserve it so that others could see what happens to a traitor.

That's when they fetched an enormous tub of cooking salt from the larder. They made the tailor tip the salt all over Jameel's raw wounds.

The whole of the Casbah must have heard those screams.

I believe they were planning to cut Jameel's throat and finish him off, but his heart must have given way first. Bismillah."

I see it now. The hat. An inverted tub with the words 'du sel/milh' scrawled on the side. The powder-encrusted body discoloured with sweat and blood. The whiteface salty clown.

"They left telling us that's what happens when you inform on your brothers.

Most of us have stayed away since. We are all in shock. I have only just returned. I am ashamed that Jameel's body is still in there.

Normally, the FLN would help us clean up. But they are at sixes and sevens. And anyway, this is the ALN's doing.

We will need to bring the gendarmes in. But how can we when the streets are a tinderbox?

My daughter is expecting a child. Though few customers will venture into this corner of the souk now. We do what we can…"

Father is staggering out of the café, gulping air. He turns to walk up the street. He has not forgotten his disguise.

"You had better look after your grandmother," says the lemon-seller. "Take care as you go. I have heard that two paratroopers have been shot and killed this morning on the street…"

We are sleepwalking our way through the Casbah now—neither Father nor I are thinking about direction or destination. Our feet are carrying us forward despite ourselves. They are leading us along Toari's route, which ends at the esplanade café outside the Mosque.

.Neither of us can explain how or why we have arrived here.

Father moves towards the interior of the café. Apart from the counter, there is a small table with two chairs covered in garish red leatherette.

Both chair seats have worn patches that go through to the padding—rubbed by the arses of two thousand customers in as many days.

A woman is washing cups in a back room. A man I take for her husband is flicking through 'El-Moudjahid' and grunting at the column inches dedicated to Larbi Ben M'hidi, the martyr of Algiers.

There is much speculation as to his death which the newspaper reports as 'state-sponsored murder'.

Father directs himself to the corner seat while I ask the man behind the counter for coffee.

I sit opposite Father.

We do not talk.

We cannot. There is nothing to say. I cannot even bring myself to look at him.

We hear gunfire. It is muffled, a smudge of sound, but prolonged. It could be the distant click clack of a train going over points. But it is too irregular for a train.

It falls on our ears in sporadic bursts, going on for so long that we are waiting for it to cease, thinking every rattle is the end of it.

It goes on like a drunk man pissing…a splurge, then a dribble, a torrent followed by a trickle…until the last shakes of sound are wrung out.

We see movement outside in the street. Muslim men are shouting at paras. The paraphernalia of Army moves into the streets of the Casbah. Armoured cars. Heavily armed troops.

The people think this is it. This is their end of days. The Casbah will be wiped off the face of the map for good.

From where we are and what we can see through the café and out into the street, the soldiers are asking more questions of themselves—and of their Zouave and blue cap auxiliaries—than they are of the Arab citizens.

Nobody seems to know what is happening. There is much confusion.

The café owner tells us to stay put. It is the safest place to be. There is pandemonium out on the streets.

We hear sirens going off in all parts of the Casbah. Paramedics are trying to find their way through. Some elderly Arab men are shouting at the troops, the Zouaves and Harkis. They are sheepish. They don't know precisely what is going on either.

We are waiting.

A man rushes in. He is breathless. The café owner's wife stops work in the kitchen when she hears his voice. The café owner knows him and is trying to calm him. The man's eyes are bulging and his speech is more a wail of pain.

"qutil aljunud alfaransiuwn muslimin fi alhamamati. hunak thamanun qatilanaan."

The café owner is incredulous. He cannot believe what he is hearing.

There is a frenetic exchange of words between the two men. The wife joins in the fray.

"My friends," says the café owner once the tempo of these quick-fire utterances has slowed, "I was wrong. I am afraid we will have to ask you to leave. It is not safe to be here or anywhere outside. If you have a home to go to, then go to it. And may Allah go with you and look over you and keep you safe."

The café owner is pushing us out onto the street so that he can bring his shutters down behind us with a final shuck.

"We must find Lieutenant Rousseau," says Father.

We are racing to the car now. We fear that all cover is blown in Algiers. That up is down, right is wrong, black is white and the line between life and death, real and unreal, is about to be completely erased.

Father has heard the words of the Arab in the café, but he cannot figure out what that means for us. He needs to verify with the Lieutenant.

He thinks the Lieutenant may have his hands full at the moment. He thinks the third para may be tied up in it somehow. Whatever 'it' is.

He suspects 'it' is a heinous crime.

He is like a drunken man, stumbling and slurring his words.

I am at the point where I would welcome total extinction over this.

I would choose to be vaporised by an atom bomb.

I pray to my private god that the Yankees will launch a fleet of B52's and drop its load right on top of my head. That a shadow silhouette of me on the café wall in the pose of a frightened rabbit will be all that remains in the atomic flash.

We are wraiths.

I am convinced we are on the verge of a massacre of souls the likes of which has never been seen in the history of Empire, that pure evil has been unleashed on the city and no one is safe.

The skies glower. The humidity is smothering. I miss Mother like crazy. I have no home. No family. I fear Father has taken leave of his senses.

And yet remarkably, despite the horror show, the turmoil all around him in the seething streets, he still seems to know what he is doing.

Call him what you will. A survivor. A prophet. A charlatan. An idiot. Through all of this, he has the presence of mind to find the car, find the car keys and drive away from Algiers just at the time the combined forces of the French Army are driving towards it.

The troops flood in on high alert from their blockhouses in Hussein-Dey and El-Biar.

And yet Father appears to know exactly where he is going and what he needs to do…

The car careens towards Mont-Les-Pins and Father steers it towards our rendezvous with Lieutenant Rousseau and into the obsolescent parking lot behind the beach.

Father has the notion that it is time for our status report.

"Why are we here?" I ask after a little while.

"To meet with the Lieutenant."

"He won't come today. He has the whole of Algiers in lockdown."

"He will come. And we will wait for him as long as it takes…"

Father stares towards the beach defiantly. It is a clear day. We can see the breakers in the far distance.

Within the half hour, an Army staff car approaches slowly down the sandy track towards us. It pulls up beside us.

A man who we recognise from the grand mansion as Lieutenant Rousseau's aide-de-camp steps out. He signals to us to join him outside the car.

A small man with horn-rimmed glasses, he introduces himself simply as Bertaux. He knows who we are. No need for introductions.

"Lieutenant Rousseau sends his apologies. He is detained in Algiers. He wonders if you would wait for him to return at Mont-Les-Pins."

"What is going on?" Father says lamely.

"Why don't you follow me there…" Bertaux can see Father is distrait. He feels that under the circumstances, it is wise to escort him to the grand mansion.

We follow the staff car along the coast road and up through the drive of pines to the big white house. There is a pair of sentry guards but no Army vehicles or units present at the grand mansion today.

Bertaux conducts us into the salon and brings tea. He closes the door behind him without turning the lock.

We are free to leave at any time.

Father sits on the floor.

"I sent Jameel to his death didn't I. Just as I did Ben M'hidi. Me and my levelling the scores."

There is no modulation in Father's voice. It is flat.

'The law of unintended consequences,' Jameel said. 'Once the information is out, nobody is above that law. Not even you, Farouk.'

I find talk impossible. I cannot disagree with Father. He has been a fool. A distinguished blue cap has made a dismal spy.

He has allowed the demons into his work.

His momentary distractions have put our lives at risk. The circumstances that have led to Jameel's killing are down to Father's call of conscience. His own bird flying up from the ground nest, his mosquito on the neck. It has all been so futile, so unnecessary.

He has lost focus.

He is coming to terms with a reality that is apparent to me now. Me! Fifteen years old, him a fully-grown man of thirty-eight who has fought in the Army.

He cannot be a soldier of fortune in this war. He cannot simply fight for family. A family that is now scarred, divided and separated.

This war forces people to take sides.

He is curled up on the floor now. In the foetal position. I use the chaise longue as a day bed. We are both drifting with the gruesome image of Jameel the Pierrot caked in salt just behind our eyelids.

By the time the door opens, darkness is descending. The room is gloomy. A shaft of light now falls on the mantelpiece reflecting off the empire mirror onto the wall.

The upright form of Lieutenant Rousseau stands in the doorway to the salon, silhouetted by the light of the giant lantern burning in the atrium.

He is drunk, using the frame of the door to prop himself up.

"Gentlemen…what can you tell me?"

He slurs his words. We are silent.

"Alright, let me tell you something then. This afternoon, we sent the mutilated body of a man in the Casbah to the hospital mortuary. They will have a hard time cleaning him up.

Perhaps you can throw some light on that?"

Still nothing from us.

The Lieutenant expels a loud, raking burp.

"The men are blaming me for the lack of movement on Ali La Pointe. They say his butchers are free to roam the streets and shoot our paratroopers at will.

They took down two of my men today in broad daylight.

Well, I'm afraid my men have taken things into their own hands…catastrophically so…"

He heads to the drinks cabinet and pours himself a brandy which he downs like water.

"You are not doing your job.

We have lost our lead, lost an opportunity to get Yacef Saadi, and now this."

I am tempted to ask what 'this' is. But I don't think I need to. This is turning into a drunken confessional anyway.

"An eye for an eye. Isn't that what the ancients believed…

Well, this is more like a heart, lungs and spleen for an eye…

Jesus said it was a bad idea. Turn the other cheek, he said. I think my men have long given up on Jesus."

He pours another tumbler of brandy. He is holding the full glass of spirits, gesticulating and splashing much of it on the carpet.

He cuts a sorry figure, this mischievous child raiding his Father's drinks cabinet while the old man is out doing a proper job.

"Did you have anything to do with that café owner? Poor sod. I'm told he was an informant working for the French. But he's not known to us…"

We are mute.

"Silence is not a good look right now, gentlemen. I wonder why Captain LeBoeuf spoke so highly of you. Your double act has turned up nothing of interest for Colonel Bigeard or my men. That is why they have gone to town…"

We are blank.

The acid is starting to surface through the sugar-coating.

"Oh, you don't know? You haven't heard? My, my, what have you been doing with yourselves?

'Monsieur Tout-Le-monde' might think you have been squandering his tax francs by wasting your time idling in doorways."

This is an absurd statement to Father, who feels he has worked his balls off for the people of France. I think Lieutenant may have a point, albeit one fuelled by the Governor-General's private stock of three-star Pinet Castillon cognac.

"We have run amok at the hammam. It is a massacre. My men have brought their own brand of justice to town."

We are still looking blankly at him, two incredulous numskulls. Is this true? Lieutenant Rousseau elucidates.

"The comrades of my two murdered paras have taken semi-automatics into the bath-house…and let loose.

Bodies everywhere. Changing room. Hot room. Cold room. Latrines. Up in the galleries…all over the baths…so many bodies I lost count…I have never seen anything like it."

He staggers and rights himself.

The Lieutenant is starting to take on the unblinking wide-eyed stare of a man driven to madness. He is reliving the scene.

"There were blue ceramic tiles on those floors in the hammam…

I couldn't see the blue for the crimson. Maybe they were crimson after all…"

He has laid down his glass.

"Eighty Arabs for the lives of two French soldiers. Muslims with towels against commandos with sub-machine guns…

Would you call that a fair trade in the souk?

One Arab…he was so perforated with bullets they nearly split his torso in two. Another…his head was gone completely. Right off his block.

Is this war, Farouk?

Or is it a duck shoot?"

Father cannot answer. But then, no answer is required.

"The Colonel, of course…Colonel Bruno…he has fought far and wide. He fought off the Germans in Alsace, he led the resistance in Ariège, he commanded the tirailleurs in Senegal…he led Thai units in Dien Bien Phu.

The President has pinned the Legion d'Honneur to his chest for Christ's sake…he has seen many things, and he is no saint, believe me…but he has never seen anything like this…"

Lieutenant Rousseau is trying to think straight.

"My soldiers blame you. Well, they blame me. The Colonel is beyond reproach.

He is a decorated war hero with an unimpeachable reputation…

No, it is me whose obituary will be asterisked and footnoted with this slaughter. And, by implication, you will carry it too, as you have failed me and them…"

In his intoxication, he is quite capable of ordering his men to take us outside and shoot us.

And not for the first time, I am thinking what a blessed relief it would be to put an end to all this. If it were quick and painless, I would take that way out.

Instead, he goes the other way. Maybe he can see in us something of himself now—the union of the eternally damned, a worldwide brotherhood bonded by bloody witness.

"It is best that you lie low here for a little while. You are still a prized asset, so treat this as your safe house.

We can do with your knowledge on the streets.

But reprisals are in the air.

Use this room as your quarters. There is a basement bathroom you can access via the back staircase. Keep the shutters closed and the door locked. Bertaux will attend to you.

And whatever you do, don't let my men see you here. They are inflamed and out for revenge.

But then, not being seen is what you do best…"

He is debating with himself.

"The Casbah is not the place for spies right now…" he repeats, "I don't know whether you're a help or a hindrance to us in Algiers at this moment in time…

But I do know this—you are not to suffer the same fate as the man in the café…Ghastly, just ghastly."

I recall Jameel's words to Father—'We are attached to each other—if we go down we go down together…'

"Jameel was the name of the café owner, I gather. Jameel Rahal. Do you know him?"

We both shake our heads.

I think it strange. Gruesome as his killing is, Jameel is just one man to the young Lieutenant. Eighty more have been slaughtered in the hammam. His men have turned the bath house into an abattoir.

But maybe the Lieutenant cannot dwell too long on the crimes and misdemeanours of his fellows. It is the French way.

"I still have faith you will lead us to the bomb-maker. It will now take us more time, but we will prevail…

Besides, I would have Captain LeBoeuf to answer to if I decommissioned you…or worse."

The 'or worse' lingers in the air as a veiled threat.

Lieutenant Rousseau of the third para slinks off to his temporary bed clutching the brandy bottle to his chest like a teddy bear.

Mont-Les-Pins, Algiers Wilaya, 14 June 1957

Father and I have become more distant with each other.

We have hardly spoken at all—rather we co-operate on the functional stuff of living day-to-day, working out between us how to go unseen by the staff and the troops stationed in and around the house. We decide who uses the bathroom first, when it is safe to communicate with one another, that kind of thing. For the time being, this house is both our prison and our fortress. We are aware that what separates us from a fate like Jameel is that the well-meaning Lieutenant Rousseau keeps us hidden from those who seek retribution.

We may have swapped the streets for the salon, but it involves the same subterfuge. Making ourselves smaller, insignificant, invisible.

Bertaux brings us food, water, and fresh clothes in our gilded confinement. The housekeeper is aware that we are to be treated as house guests but that this information is to be kept to herself on pain of instant dismissal.

It has been a truce of sorts, although the longer I dwell on the horror of Jameel's end, the less I trust Father and the more resentful I am towards him.

By all rights it should have been Father stewing in that salt crust at the back of Jameel's café.

The ALN targeted the lesser traitor.

We are thankful to the gauche Lieutenant, for he has undoubtedly saved our skins. And we are careful not to push our luck.

Since arriving here with Bertaux, we've been quiet as the dead. Compliant in every way.

At night, Father has slept on the Persian rug with me on the chaise longue.

I've woken a few nights to find Father just staring at me in his sleep. I think he is using night time to work things out. And I am a touchstone of sorts.

Father has also picked up a book to keep the demons at bay—a leather bound tome from the bookcase, 'The History of the Decline and Fall of the Roman Empire, Part One', by an Englishman named Gibbon.

The contents of the bookcase in the salon at the grand mansion are antique though virtually untouched by human hand.

The pages of this one have never been thumbed.

To call this a collection of classics is to overstate its value. It is really a form of three-dimensional wallpaper.

I think Father brave for tackling this virgin, weighty volume. There are no pictures to alleviate the eye, just dense type, unreadable fly-shit. I begin to suspect he's taking very little in. Anything to kill time.

We have started to lose a sense of how long we've been here at Mont-Les-Pins, despite that infernal mantel-clock marking every quarter hour.

Unfortunately, the housekeeper has insisted on coming in regularly to wind up the time-piece—and has succeeded in doing the same to us.

Father wanted to kill the sound by sabotaging the clock. I told him that would be an abuse of hospitality, not to mention the Governor-General's property.

It was the only time he'd become irate throughout our whole stay here.

"Hospitality? Don't let them deceive you. They are fattening us up for the slaughter. That day will come soon enough."

Up until the point of this outburst, we'd managed successfully to ward off the furies. But for some reason, Father felt he had to let them back in. Perhaps to remind me the uneasy ceasefire between us was only temporary.

I had bad dreams after that. And I could see that look of self-loathing return in Father's dark, deep-set eyes and the surly set of his mouth.

One early morning on the way down the back stairs I thought I saw Lieutenant Laurent smoking on the lawn just above the basement window.

After watching him a while, I realised it was a moustachioed paratrooper with the same uneven tapering hairline at the nape of his neck and a similar aquiline profile.

The man in question didn't appear to radiate the same aura as the Lieutenant.

Strangely enough, it was only then that I realised it couldn't possibly be Lieutenant Laurent. Because the Lieutenant was dead.

All of this has happened in a vacuum—Father and I bumping along together in our confinement.

Today, however, is different.

The uneasy peace has been shattered by external voices.

An argument has broken out in the atrium and it sounds very much—at least from the fragments of conversation we hear through the closed door to the salon—that Lieutenant Rousseau is coming in for a drubbing.

"…time after time…tit for tat…escalation…get a grip…no meaningful intelligence…"

We press our ears to the door and the voices take shape.

A gruff-voiced man is haranguing the hapless Lieutenant Rousseau.

"Why has this come as any surprise to me…your Father wasn't even a soldier…he was a bureaucrat, a marquis…General Massu persuaded me to take you on against my better judgement because he thought it would play well with our political pay-masters in the National Assembly. God knows why I agreed to it…"

I allow myself a moment of pride.

I was right.

This confirms my theory that Lieutenant Rousseau is an officer of noble stock with his commission and rank a result of who he knows, not what he has accomplished. Regardless of his social status, he is giving a good account of himself.

"With respect, Colonel, I think that is unfair…my father owns a chateau in the Ardèche. It is hardly the Loire. It is certainly not Cheverny. He was a farmer and a mayor of the local town. We are by no means privileged…"

Bigeard explodes.

"It is a privilege to serve in this regiment, Lieutenant. That is the only privilege that means anything to me, and don't you forget it."

"Of course not, sir…"

"This is the second time General Massu has let me know he has had enough of the shilly-shallying in my unit.

It is a point of dishonour, so how in God's name can you tell me you're surprised at his decision?"

"I will get you Saadi, sir. You can count on it."

"Well, now we will have competition…

The casino was the last straw…"

Gruff-voice's boots are pacing around the floor, circling for the kill.

"After that shit-show at the hammam, how in the name of sweet Jesus do we allow Saadi's bombers to breeze through the casino doors and stroll right up to the roulette tables?"

"They were determined to kill Pieds-Noirs at play, sir. The casino is a place of leisure for Europeans as are the hammams for men of Islamic faith…mirror violence…tit-for-tat in every respect, not just the numbers of dead."

"Ah, yes. Numbers. Nine Europeans dead, Lieutenant, more than eighty wounded. That is quite some 'tit-for-tat'."

"It is the way of Algiers…"

"Well, it's not my way, soldier. We do not allow the Muslims to just walk in to our casinos like croupiers and start calling the odds on people's lives…

Nor do we allow Pieds-Noirs the space to launch reprisals within hours. To go on ratonnades at Muslim funerals on the same day? Whoever heard of such a thing!"

Gruff-voice sounds like he's reading off a ledger.

"Nine Muslims killed, Lieutenant. Fifty injured. What kind of a funeral party is that?"

"I'm very aware of the numbers, sir."

"Oh, are you? Are you really? Well, get your head around this one then…

We have more than three hundred and fifty thousand French troops in Algeria. Three hundred and fifty thousand men…

And yet we still cannot find one man…one man! That is all we need. Just the one…

This Yacef Saadi…this one-man bomb-making machine. Nor can we subdue any of the operatives delivering his bombs…

So, I ask you again, Lieutenant Rousseau of the third para, why are you surprised at the General's decision? If I were Massu, I'd do exactly the same…"

At this, a pair of boots storms out of the atrium. They crunch on the gravel outside our window. A car door slams, an engine starts and a car rolls away down the drive.

We hear another set of footsteps approach from the atrium and we back further into the room.

There is a loud rap on the door.

Father turns the key from the inside and opens it a little way. He peeps out and gives way.

"It's only me, Farouk," says the Lieutenant, sidling into the room.

"We have an issue…and I need your advice."

This truly is a turn-up for the books.

"General Massu is…how shall I say…disappointed at our progress. The maquisards are wreaking havoc all over Algiers. Every day brings something new by way of escalation."

"Have you been fired from your post?" Father interrupts.

"Not exactly. But I need you to throw me some fresh meat. Something I can…"

Ever the diplomat, he is reaching for his onboard lexicon and repeatedly clicking his fingers to summon up the right word.

I find it for him.

"Something you can leverage?" I suggest.

Lieutenant Rousseau clicks his fingers once more.

"Yes, that's it. Precisely…But it must be soon. Colonel Bigeard is getting very…anxious."

Father nods. Lieutenant Rousseau continues.

"…It's hardly surprising given that General Massu has ordered the tenth para to return from Kabylia."

The news hits me straight in the solar plexus.

LeBoeuf is back.

The Ketchoaua Café,
The Casbah, Algiers,
25 August 1957

We sit at a table to one side of the patio.

Father is back on his game.

His eyes dart around the esplanade. Men are entering the Ketchoaua Mosque for midday prayers. A man hails another in the street with an "Asalam alaykum" and places a hand over his heart.

Two men shake hands and smile as they swap stories.

A few other elders in stiffly laundered thobes are talking family business or politics. But even they cannot resist the odd aside to a friend or acquaintance and one of them manages to crack a smile through the starch.

I spot an old man being helped up the steps to the main doors by his two adult sons. They are greeted with open arms by fellow worshippers. The senior has only two rotting stumps for teeth in his head, but his pride in his family brings a grin to his face and a glint to his eye that lights up the esplanade.

A group of Muslim women congregate on the far side of the Mosque waiting to go in through another door. Some laugh and chat, others take a quiet moment of reflection before prayer. They are natural and easy in each other's company.

The communal scene fills me up. It is heartfelt and genuine. The sunlight on the front elevation of the Mosque is watery and bathes the wide esplanade in the light of renewal.

Father, dressed again in jilbab and hijab, takes a sip from his cup. The coffee is lustrous and viscous, hot, sweet and strong, as he likes it. He leaves a faint rosy lipstick mark on the rim.

He is watching the gathering of Muslim women to the side of the Mosque, examining their mannerisms.

He is always seeking to improve his disguise by discreetly studying the opposite sex. He has become fascinated by their comportment, the way they behave with family, with each other, with men. He notices the subtle changes in their facial expressions and practices them to himself when I'm not looking. Occasionally, I will catch him tilting his head forward in a modest bow or averting his gaze to the ground in a gesture of humility.

This is a good morning. My personal god is in his heaven. And this is going to be a day to remember for the right reasons.

We partly have LeBoeuf to thank.

He swept in to 'Mont-Les-Pins' yesterday with his cortège like a returning Odysseus to Ithaca. Lieutenant Rousseau was there to greet him.

LeBoeuf was surprised to find us lodging in the salon and immediately challenged the Lieutenant.

"You don't lock your weapons in the armoury when the streets are running with blood. Farouk and powder monkey are our prospectors. They need to be out there on the streets of Algiers panning for gold again."

Before LeBoeuf sent us out to the Casbah, he once again dangled the incentive of a visa to France in front of Father. And decided to season it with something extra tasty.

"If you find Saadi, I will find you a modest apartment on the outskirts of Paris—you and Basira and the family."

I have become weary of hearing LeBoeuf's empty promises. He is full of hot air. But there is a gleam in Father's eye every time he makes them.

Father feeds on impossible dreams. He feels he can persuade Mother to go with him. And the prospect of that is even less likely.

LeBoeuf knows he has Father on a leash. That he can call Father to account for the deaths of fifteen Muslims in Place Jean-Paul Sartre. That he can throw us to the wolves on both sides.

However, I still cannot fully understand his determination to stick with us— why he keeps on turning us out into the streets of the Casbah as his eyes and ears.

Why rely on the ineptitude of a gumshoe blue cap with his powder monkey sidekick?

We have been out here in the Casbah for weeks, searching for Saadi's bomb transporter.

The café owner remembered us from the day of the hammam massacre. He and his wife welcomed us back and apologised for pushing us out that day.

"My wife was scared. I was too. Those soldiers could have gone anywhere with their weapons. I have been told they went to the bath house because they thought the FLN were there...

I have since learned that they weren't.

The coffee is on the house."

Father was insistent I pursue the chat with the café owner further.

"People who know where the FLN aren't may also know where they are."

But my attempts resulted in nothing more than the café owner speculating about my virginity and sharing some salacious gossip about the sinful khans of Rahbat al-Jammal.

He urged me to travel to Constantine just as he himself had done as a fifteen-year-old boy. He said the whores were so much more attentive than those in Algiers, because in Constantine they serviced French soldiers in mobile bordellos, like the refreshment vans around the MC Alger stadium.

The whores of the Army's mobile bordellos were less likely to have contracted venereal diseases given the Army's exclusive use of them.

He said he has paid the French pimping money to gain access to the women—and they have turned a blind eye to having an Arab in their midst."

"I was a fox in their hen-house..." he boasted.

He said the French were more demanding in their preferences and it sharpened the girls' talents.

He asked me not to share any of this with his wife. He was just helping me out with a few timely recommendations, as he guessed my adolescent angst needed relieving.

He went on to say he was sick of the pimps of Algiers—common criminals like Bud Abbot running operations in the lower Casbah.

These hucksters and fraudsters used the FLN to legitimise their scams.

He preferred good honest pimping and thought the legitimate claims of the nationalists were being undermined by their association with these manyaks.

I know Mother has accused Father of going with the daughters of the Ouled Nail, but I never really understood what that meant until now.

This was as close as I came to information on the FLN which an ungrateful Father immediately dismissed as 'fool's gold'.

"LeBoeuf will have me pistol-whipped if the only intelligence I take back for him is that the FLN run all the bordellos in Algiers.

It's not relevant nor is it true. It is tittle tattle."

However, Father felt the café-owner's confidences could prove useful to us in time—and the Ketchoaua café became our new base while we reconnoitred the Casbah daily.

There was, of course, another reason for us to regroup at the Ketchoaua café during our long days plying the streets of the city.

The question of the man in the black suit.

We knew this café as Toari's meeting-place with that man, though his identity remained a mystery to us.

Father of course prompted me to raise the subject with the café owner. I said I didn't know how I could do that without arousing his suspicions. But Father has an answer for everything.

"Tell the café owner you like the cut of his customer's cloth.

Tell him you'd like to wear an Armani-style suit that looks just like the one his customer wears, but you can't afford the price tag.

Tell him you've been wondering how you can obtain the name of his customer's tailor.

Then ask him for the name of the man in the black suit."

I tried it. Of course, the café-owner was clueless on the subject. He couldn't even recall seeing a man in a black suit.

And yet that very man is here in the café today.

He is sitting not ten yards from us on the patio of the Ketchoaua café ordering a mint tea from the café owner's wife.

A slim young man in sunglasses, open neck shirt with button-down collar, sandals and, yes, dressed immaculately in a black linen suit.

Father and I simply cannot believe our eyes.

"He is right there!" I say to the café owner at the counter out of earshot, pointing through the open café doorway at the small, wiry man sitting alone at a table outside.

"You mean him!" replies the café owner, somewhat surprised, "Why didn't you say? He is no man. He is a boy. And that suit is not black. It is midnight blue."

The café owner peers out at the young man, scrutinising his face.

"I suppose he does look quite grown up. He started coming here with his old man just last year. But his father died. Now he comes here by himself to meet with people. Men. Women. He's not choosy.

He must have grown six inches in as many months...They grow fast at that age—well, here's me telling you that. I can't remember it myself. I think I must have come out of my mother's birth canal wearing a beard and a kufi..."

I take the news to Father who has been watching the man in the black suit for the past fifteen minutes while having the same thought.

As we centred on Toari, we never really studied the features and bearing of the man she was meeting.

Father now sees him in a different light. He murmurs into the menu as he scans it.

"I can hardly believe our good fortune, my little wingman. He is one and the same. The FLN's very own Liaison Officer. We have been searching far and wide for Ibrahim Najjar to the exclusion of 'Little' Omar."

I look again.

"When was that photograph taken of the boy with his uncle Yacef and Najjar?" he asks.

I am unsure. Father speculates.

"My guess is last year after Soummam. Round about October time, when the FLN set their sights on attacking Algiers.

He appeared in the publicity shot alongside his uncle.

Benkhedda was the editor of El-Moudjahid and he advised against publishing."

"That's a full ten months ago," I say.

"And ten months in the life of an adolescent boy can be the difference between a child and a man."

I can see it now. There is less of the 'Little' about 'Little' Omar. He retains the retroussé nose of that photograph, the dark arched eyebrows, the thick lashes. But looking at the boy now in the flesh, he has lost the baby face.

His face is leaner. His mouth has matured and when he removes his sunglasses, I notice that the big round eyes of the photo are now more ovoid in shape, more creased around the rims.

His handsome features are already starting to resemble those of his Uncle Yacef, with his film star looks. And he has grown some six inches.

'Little Omar' is developing into a fine-looking young man.

"We missed it again..." says Father. "We are hopeless spies, always looking in the wrong place..." Omar finishes his meeting, settles the bill and departs.

We follow him at some distance. It is easy to do so in the wider streets of the lower Casbah, but when we cross Rue Mohamed Bencheneb, the chase stutters amid a muddle of tapering staircases, impasses and alleys. We are struggling to keep Omar in our sights. He is fleet of foot. Yet his stride is not as lengthy as ours. Father is able to keep pace, concealing much of his movement under his jilbab so that he appears to glide rather than rush.

If Father feels we are too close to Omar, he will stop to take a breath and stoop to rub his calf muscle. Over the months, he has learned to dissemble the ailments of goitre and pneumonia convincingly.

The upper Casbah is more of a challenge.

Omar takes the staircases two steps at a time and I think the trail has gone cold before I see his head bob up again on another flight of steps ahead of us.

I am intent on holding on to Father. I fear that if I lose touch with him now I'd never find a way out of this tangle of streets.

The dense latticework of alleyways becomes tighter and gloomier the higher we climb. The further we penetrate into these musty passages, the more the walls close in on us.

Daylight is a thin streak of white above us now and, when we pass under bridges connecting both sides of the street, it feels like we have entered a dark tunnel.

This far up towards the medina, the number of passers-by thins out. The gradient steepens. There are steps on steps, twists on turns. North, south, east, west, are lost amid this confounding maze. We are in the middle of an Escher riddle. Only by turning to glimpse the landmarks of the city below and the Mediterranean beyond in the gaps between buildings can I determine our direction or height of travel.

Omar sashays along the snaking pathways, the colour of his suit starting to blend in with the shadows. We strain muscle and eye to keep up.

When I first set foot in these streets, it was all about the broad brush for me. The blue shutters, neat squares and wide arcades of the French city, the mosaic of rooftops over the Casbah from the old fort and medina to the Marine Quarter and the sea, the Great Mosque with its towering minaret.

Now, senses alerted, I am noticing the small details that stand out in the half-light. A Star of David etched above a doorway; a glazed tile inlaid into a wall depicting the patron of Algiers, Sidi M'hamed Bou Qobrine, teaching in the madrasah; an MC Alger pennant taped to the inside of a porthole window just above street level—alongside the torn-out page from a fanzine showing a sun-bleached first team photograph.

Behind the walls of these dimly lit passages are thousands of huddled lives packed into a hive of rooms, galleries and corridors.

Yet there is no way of knowing. There are few windows giving out onto the alleys and those that do are defended by iron grilles.

By the time we turn into Impasse St Vincent, we are exhausted. Up ahead, we see 'Little' Omar step off the street and disappear. Father releases my hand and hurries up the remaining flight of steps to check the number on the doorway.

He looks further up the alley and leads me towards a nook with a ledge set into the white wall of a house. This recess is intended for people to rest as they toil up the hill. The house itself looks on the point of collapse, leaning precariously into the passage. It is only kept from falling into the property opposite by the thick timber struts that push against the fascia of the neighbouring building.

We sit. We listen.

We hear children at play in a courtyard somewhere close by; the clank of a copper pan placed on a hob; the raised voices of a couple in an upstairs room; the growl of an angry mastiff pulling on a chain; a goldfinch singing its tiny heart out.

We wait.

Squeezed onto that bench together, I notice that Father's hand is trembling as his fingers clasp mine. I can feel his bare wrist pressing on my forearm. His pulse is frantic. He knows we are close now…

Close as the thickness of a Casbah wall.

We are there in Impasse St Vincent for an hour or so. Father keeps his eyes on the doorway. He could sit here for all eternity. I try to keep my breathing shallow all the better to listen. The alley is deserted and, during the time we are there, not a soul goes up or down.

There is a sudden movement in the street and the FLN Liaison Officer emerges from the doorway carrying a honey-coloured valise that is larger than the man himself.

Omar Saadi pauses outside the door and glances up and down the alleyway, checking his bearings, configuring his route.

He is extra careful not to give the suitcase any sudden jolts.

His arm works as a gimbal for the valise as he mounts the steps. A capable bomb transporter, he makes sure the luggage makes its smooth passage up the staircase unimpeded.

But we are anxious.

He is coming our way. Too late to make an exit off Impasse St Vincent, Father gives me some rapid direction on our grandmother-grandson play acting.

"I am exhausted with the climb. You want me to feel better."

Father starts panting, gently rocking himself back and forth on the bench. I place a caring arm around his shoulder.

"How are you feeling, grandmother?" I enquire affectionately, though a little more loudly than is natural, "we should get you to a water fountain. These steps are deceptively steep, and you are no use to anyone with heat-stroke. Rest here while you get your breath back…"

Omar is coming up to pass us, taking it steady. He treats every step with extreme caution. The valise dwarfs him. He looks like a mountebank, a travelling carpet salesman or a ventriloquist on his way to a cabaret. I think the luggage is going to catch on the edge of a flagstone and send the whole of Impasse St Vincent sky-high.

And yet as he passes, he does the most extraordinary thing.

He gently places the valise down and stops beside us.

"Your poor grandmother," he says, "Is there anything I can do? A glass of water perhaps?"

"Thank you," I respond, "That's very kind of you but she'll be fine. She just needs to recover her breath."

'Little' Omar gives me a sympathetic smile and, in a gesture that I will never forget, he touches Father's shoulder lightly with one hand.

"Hafidaka Allah," he says and goes on his way.

We wait for him to turn the corner at the top of the steps. And then follow on behind.

Rue Caton is further up towards the Medina. More cramped houses straddle the strangulated passage. Even more families vying for space beneath the Moorish citadel, stuffed between walls into spaces barely large enough to house rats.

We trail Omar with every expectation the valise will go boom and the higgledy-piggledy houses will collapse in on one another like so many dominoes.

He arrives at his destination unscathed and we are not far behind. He raps the brass knocker on a recessed door and is admitted off the alley. From our side-on perspective, it looks as if he has somehow magicked himself through a wall.

Father makes a note of the house number.

Number three…

then turns to me.

"We have seen enough for one day."

Chenoua Plage, Algiers Wilaya, 26 August 1957

"You wanted us to throw you something. Here it is."

Lieutenant Rousseau is a like a boy on Christmas morning. Father delays the moment, giving the Lieutenant a few more seconds of exquisite anticipation.

We are standing by the deux chevaux in the beach parking lot. Bertaux has gone for a stroll in the pines, finding a suitable place to relieve himself. He is now back at the edge of the trees but stretching his arms up towards their upper branches, greeting the elements like some latter-day Zoroastrian.

The day is crisp and clear. There is a whipped-up chill in the air, keeping us alert. The distant breakers on Chenoua plage roar their approval.

Father gives it a few more beats.

"You can't keep me in suspense for ever. Tell me you have found Saadi."

"Not quite…"

Lieutenant Rousseau's face drops.

"Najjar?" he asks hopefully.

Father shakes his head.

"Who then?"

"'Little' Omar."

"Who?"

The Lieutenant is hard work today.

"Saadi's nephew…"

A flicker of recognition from the Lieutenant but nothing too excitable. "…and Chief Liaison Officer," Father adds.

"Not Najjar, then…" confirms Lieutenant Rousseau by way of clarification. "No, not Najjar. 'Little' Omar Saadi."

"Ah…yes…well, great!"

Father has left a tricycle under Lieutenant Rousseau's Christmas tree when he really wanted a scooter.

Mont-Les-Pins, Algiers Wilaya,
27 August 1957

"Christ on a bike! You must have a death wish, Farouk!" exclaims LeBoeuf, as he paces the salon. "What the fuck were you thinking giving vital information to that sorry excuse for a foetus…"

Lieutenant Rousseau has fallen a long way in LeBoeuf's estimation over the past six months—from high-flying star of the Academy to this. And Father is equally as low in his eyes now.

"I thought you might be pleased…"

"Pleased?" LeBoeuf rants, "Pleased that Saadi's chief bomb-maker and deputy have been killed maybe. Pleased that Bigeard's men didn't take them alive? You're having a laugh…"

He steps closer to Father who is stood to attention. They are face to face. "Is that the point of this, Farouk? That you can laugh at my expense…"

"It's a victory for the Army…" says Father. "I thought you'd be pleased."

"You don't work for the Army, Harki. You work for me…"

"…and Lieutenant Rousseau and Colonel Bigeard," Father corrects him.

"Me!" LeBoeuf bellows so that the whole house can hear. "Me! Me! You work for me! Tu m'emmerdes!"

"No one said…" mutters Father, meekly.

"Do you see what you have done, you connard?"

I can tell Father knows exactly what he has done. LeBoeuf cannot appreciate the complex calculus going on behind those dark eyes of his.

"You have let Saadi off the hook by sending in the third para when you could have turned Saadi's deputy and chief bomb-maker over to the tenth and Aussaresses…"

Instead, the jejeune Rousseau went in all guns blazing. Raided the place like a cat among pigeons.

How could they fail to take those bastards alive when I would have made it mission-critical?

Major Aussaresses would have squeezed them 'til their gonads squeaked, but all Bigeard got was a couple of casualties on our side and a couple of dead on theirs. Ibrahim Najjar included.

What use is dead deputy to us when he could have led us to the chief?

Recognise the pattern, Farouk? Do the names Benyoucef Benkhedda and Larbi Ben M'hidi spring to mind?

Your actions are completely reprehensible…no, worse, they are incomprehensible…

We are in stasis.

Again…

When we need to bring an end to this once and for all."

Father offers no further resistance. He knows LeBoeuf cannot subject him to any more than this verbal lashing. General Massu will be delighted at the outcome of our sortie into the Casbah yesterday. So will the other Army chiefs. It is a timely propaganda victory and General Massu will be lapping it up on behalf of all RP units.

For Colonel Bigeard and the men of the third para it has thrown them the kind of morale-booster they were demanding. And Lieutenant Rousseau will have gone up in the estimation of his gruff-voiced commanding officer.

But for LeBoeuf it is undigested meat, giving him heartburn. Fresh back from Kabylia, he feels he deserves more than this. He smarts.

"As for victory, Saadi is still out there, his chief bomb transporter, his network is intact. And Ali La Pointe is still whipping up dissent.

I ask you, Farouk. What kind of victory is it that leaves the opposing generals in the field, heavily armed and still commanding their troops?"

But Father knows otherwise.

He is just a heartbeat from Saadi and Ali La Pointe.

Far more importantly, he has advanced his own cause.

Father knows that LeBoeuf and he are tied at the hip. He knows he is one step closer to that visa and apartment in Paris that LeBoeuf promised…and he knows that LeBoeuf cannot collar him for the bombing of Place Jean-Paul Sartre as long as he holds one new vital piece of information back.

That information is reserved exclusively for LeBoeuf. It is Father's vital piece of collateral. And he will serve it up at the right time when he knows for sure.

It is the other location in the Casbah—an address he holds close to his chest. The door behind which he suspects Saadi may be hiding…

Just four words will be his final piece of leverage over LeBoeuf in Algiers. 'Number Three, Rue Caton.'

Rue Caton, Algiers,
7 September 1957

There is no easy method of surveillance here. It would be like having to cling to a high, smooth, sheer rock face unobserved by other climbers.

The street is far too narrow and offers no natural vantage point or place of concealment.

We recce the adjoining streets and find wider tributaries feeding into the steps of Rue Caton—streets that cross the staircase both above and below the doorway of number three.

We decide to do something we have never done before. We split up so that we can cover off Rue Caton in both directions.

I take up position below on the steps of a disused stone fountain fifty yards along Rue Honore Balzac with a clear view of the intersection.

Father perches above on a bench next to the doorway of a small Byzantine church on the corner of Rue Caton and Passage de Thagaste.

We take it in ten-minute spells before swapping over with each other, making slow sweeps up and down Rue Caton before repairing to the Lower Casbah.

The Café Ketchoaua is always the first and last stop of our day.

It is a balancing act. Father does not want to outstay his welcome in the upper Casbah, so we spend little time around Rue Caton but frequent it every day. We stay in position until a passer-by notices either of us for the second time, at which point we will switch stations with each other. That way we remain unobtrusive.

We stick to our rule and don't dwell in one place for longer than an hour at a stretch. Father's final memory of Jameel is enough to keep us moving on.

He has instructed me to look out not just for 'Little' Omar, but for any of his possible associates. We have no means of visual identification for anyone other than Omar, his uncle and Ali Ammar, who Captain LeBoeuf prefers to call by his alias La Pointe. We choose to follow anyone who emerges from number three Rue Caton in the hope it may unearth another location.

Most of the time, these journeys are of little consequence—menial trips to the souk for provisions or a kiosk for cigarettes and a newspaper—but today is different.

Today I glimpse 'Little' Omar skipping down the staircase past the intersection with Rue Honore Balzac.

I move swiftly along the street, expecting to encounter Father crossing my path. But there is no sign of him descending Rue Caton and I am already in pursuit, so cannot wait for him to appear.

For the very first time since being chased by the ALN fellaghas towards Place Jean-Paul Sartre—that time I lost sight of Father in the jumble of roof terraces some forty feet above me—I find myself on my own in these streets.

Without Father, the going is more rapid if less certain. This time, the rat run traverses the hill.

Even though the route is mainly on the level, only occasionally taking us down passages and up rises, it's still a challenge.

Omar bounces along, eager to reach his destination. Even though I can follow at a clip, free of the faux matriarch at my side, the going is tougher for its unfamiliar terrain. And I now realise how much Father's knowledge of the Casbah's street layout has helped to propel us along together at speed.

At one point I am waylaid by a party of children being led by their teacher from the madrasah to the Mosque. At another, a cart loaded with bricks, beams and buckets straddles the alley in front of a crumbling stucco facade that is being repaired. I dance around a mule, its head buried in a nosebag, straight into the path of an Imam on a bicycle. Collision swerved, I catch sight of Omar's trailing leg just disappearing around the corner of a prayer hall.

The further north we go, the less dense the buildings, but the more crowded the streets. Those citizens of the Casbah who are on the move weave intricate paths around the many in the community who choose to dawdle and chat.

The further I go, the more I dodge and sidestep to avoid them, and the more strangers I encounter the more out of my depth I feel.

Omar turns sharply to his left and enters an alley between two towering tenements.

Here, there are buildings on top of buildings. Some are stacked in steps crowned by roof terraces. Others appear as sheer walls comprising the various strata of building materials spanning different chapters in the city's occupation. Phoenician, Ottoman, Moorish, French. White render surmounts mottled brown above red stucco. A filled-in colonnade holds up an adobe terracotta roof. A brickwork buttress supports a stone partition. Nothing makes sense.

Down below, a passage flanked by walls made from concrete blocks leads into the bowels of the building.

I follow Omar into one of these passages. The path quickly dips down into the darkness—a blackened corridor broadening into a space like a crypt.

His quick footsteps start to bounce off the walls.

This subterranean chute is fed by wide concrete pipes—with a radius large enough to take a person standing up—which lead into the walls of the building.

We soon emerge into the light of another street flanked on both sides by similar stratified buildings.

Omar stops in front of an arched oak door, its stone lintel engraved with an iris and the number 'five'.

He knocks twice, steps back into the street and looks up to the floors above. A face appears fleetingly behind the balustrade of an upstairs balcony.

A few seconds later, the door opens, Omar enters the building and the door shuts behind him.

I walk to the end of street with no idea where I am.

A blue street sign reads 'Rue des Abderames'.

I've no hope of retracing my steps to Father. The only way I know is down. Down through the tightly woven streets of the upper Casbah.

I reach Rue Mohamed Bencheneb just as the sun breaks through the clouds. From here I see clearly down and outwards—out beyond the lower Casbah to the Marine Quarter and the wide Mediterranean.

A solitary shaft of late afternoon sunshine breaks through, sending evanescent striations of amber, orange and gold across the sea.

It momentarily lifts the jewel-like islands of El Djazair out of their cerulean setting.

It illuminates the emerald green garden terrace of the Jardin d'Horloge and spritzes the cobbles of the harbour, lighting up the creamy facade of the post office like alabaster and flaring out eastwards towards Philippeville.

Then it fades as quickly as it has appeared.

I shiver and pull my collar tight around my neck.

I head down through the ancient town. I am being watched. Followed. No, chased down…hunted by the spirits of Lieutenant Laurent, Ben M'hidi and Jameel—the spirits of the murdered in pursuit of the condemned.

My step quickens as I catch sight of the cupola atop the Ketchoaua Mosque and pass the Dar Hassan Pacha.

Whatever has been shadowing me is closing in. It is a powerful palpable sensation, not far behind, just out of sight.

The landmarks I have come to know so well over the course of several months feel unfamiliar to me now.

The esplanade is deserted, and the café is shuttered.

I sense this malign force trailing me is catching me. It is at my back, pushing me on in a state of mounting panic.

I know where I am, but without Father here, I have entirely lost my coordinates.

The sensation grips me. I feel it is right behind me now. Over my shoulder. I turn.

"Ha!"

It is Father.

Relief floods my body. And without thinking, without speaking, I hug him.

"You had no idea, did you…" he grins, knowing he has succeeded in his subterfuge.

"I followed you all the way from Rue Caton. Just to see if you had it in you…

Well, I'm pleased to see you do. It's sink or swim up there…"

"I have to be on my wits…"

"On your wits? You were magnificent! Masterful! A true hunter. I see you navigated the maze of passages without any trouble. That mason La Pointe makes some impressive rat-runs. My little wingman has earned his wings. You are now fully fledged…"

"Five, Rue des Abderames."

Father nods.

"You have unearthed one of Omar's contact-points. A bolthole. Another piece of the puzzle. And such perfect timing. Tomorrow is our rendezvous with Captain LeBoeuf…Tonight, we drink at the Bar Chenoua Plage!"

"There is a bar at the beach?" I ask.

"There soon will be…" Father replies.

"The car…" I conclude, "Classy…"

"We can make it so. I will introduce you to the mysteries of the green fairy and we can dance with the devil…I have two bottles of Pernod in the car.

We can even take some Daughters of Nailya to liven things up…"

I fall silent as we walk towards the car. He regrets these last remarks. I am not his drinking buddy nor his friend. I am his son. He would do well to remember that.

We both feel Mother's absence as he drives the car away from the centre of Algiers to connect with the coast road west.

"I'm joking about the whores, Simeon…We need to talk, you and I…"

We sit in silence for the rest of the journey. There is much he is not telling me today.

It is dark outside.

On the bends, the car headlights catch the needles of the roadside pines whose shadows dance deep into the forest.

Father is thinking about his options following our day's work.

Arriving at the Chenoua Plage car park, he fetches a box from the trunk of the car.

He removes a bottle of Pernod and unscrews the cap. The sickly alcoholic aroma of liquorice and bonbons floods my nostrils and throat and I gag.

"Have it neat," he says. "No sugar cubes. Not tonight. Go on…straight from the bottle. It won't kill you…cats and rats, maybe, but not you…"

There's the Pierrot in him coming out.

"Why does it smell like death?"

He takes the bottle from me and sniffs at the neck.

"That's wormwood. It smells of dreams, that's what it smells of…the best Parisian bars, the Left Bank, the first rain of springtime in the Tuileries Gardens. All that jazz. And maybe tomorrow some of those dreams will start to come true."

And there's the poet coming to the fore.

I should explain.

Mother told me there are three types of drunk. The Pierrot, the poet and the pugilist. And Father combines all three. They sometimes appear in that order. At other times they turn up separately to the exclusion of one another. She let me know she could never tell which would appear in Father after a night playing baccarat with Waleed.

Tonight, I'm waiting to see. I have spotted two at the party already.

The evening on the beach, however, has not turned out as Father has anticipated. He has become morose.

He is reflecting on his time, kicking over the traces of everything Captain LeBoeuf has said and done. Looking for dying embers to rekindle, then fan into a flame of hate.

This is Father all over.

We have taken the bottles to the beach and have perched on the promontory of rocks which form a natural breakwater.

We are idly skimming stones into the sea. Father is downing the Pernod— four slugs to my half-hearted one—when the pugilist arrives at the party.

"I'm going to kill LeBoeuf," he says, "I'm going to take his visa thank you very much, and before I board the boat at Oran, I'm going to take him around the back of the customs hall and put a fucking bullet right there."

He tries to plant a fingertip in the middle of my forehead, but his aim is off, and he pokes me in the eye.

"Ow!" I yelp.

He doesn't say sorry. He just slurs his words as he goes off on another detour.

"When I was a squib, younger than you, my grandparents sent me off to the madrasah in Constantine. They wanted me to stand on my own two feet. Be a proud Berber.

You know, your grandad grew date palms in the Maghreb…Hard-working grower that he was, he was more like a plodding pack-horse than a thoroughbred racehorse…"

In spite of the fact that Mother has taken the time to explain all this to me, it's clear that Father wants to tell me himself.

"He struggled. He was always struggling…it was the way he was made. Middling. He could never shed the dullard label. But your grandma always wanted exceptional, never so-so…

She wanted him to be much more than a fruit-grower and picker, you see…she wanted him to be an exporter so that she could go and pray alongside all the other well-heeled merchants' wives in the mosque.

The French offered to take his plantation off his hands for a notional sum. He asked them for more. Of course, why wouldn't you. How do you put a price on your birth right?

So, they took all his cash crops anyway, put Mum and Dad in a bidonville in Constantine and moved colons on to their farm.

I watched Mum and Dad visibly shrink with it. Dad went mad with despair…and it broke Mum's heart. They passed away within six months of each other.

I vowed to myself I'd never be like them. I'd look after my own. I'd play the Frenchman at his own game…"

Father is drowsy. He repeats again that he will kill LeBoeuf, this time with a stiletto to the heart. He rather fancies himself as a duellist.

He starts orchestrating the constellations, humming a Malouf tune using his finger as a baton, repeatedly jabbing it at the night sky. Then he falls asleep against a slab of rock, snoring into the cosmos.

I walk along the beach, leaving Father to his slumbers. I don't disturb him. After all, tomorrow is a big day.

Tomorrow is the day Father will show Captain Gregory LeBoeuf of the renowned tenth para what he's made of.

Never again will LeBoeuf underestimate the blue cap spy and his 'little wing man'. For the Harki is about to claim his visa along with a modest little apartment on the outskirts of Paris. And his 'little wing man' has now well and truly earned his wings.

I watch the starlight glint off the water, feeling an aching homesickness—a longing to be reunited with Mother, Louis, Margot and Baby Claude for good—and I send out my prayers for my personal god to bring them sweet dreams across the blue-black night.

Mont-Les-Pins, Algiers Wilaya, 8 September 1957

"Not before I have the visa…"

"What!" booms LeBoeuf, "Can you understand nothing of what I've told you…"

"Not before I have the visa…" Father repeats. He is emphatic about it. "I can't do that."

"Then the information stays with us…"

LeBoeuf's body goes rigid. His face starts to flush.

"You are playing with fire, Farouk…"

"I am used to it, Captain…I have asbestos fingers…"

"You do know that I can pick up the phone to Major Aussaresses right now and have him get the information out of you…"

"I have no doubt about it…but it would be easier to obtain a visa I can assure you. And far less messy…"

I am impressed with Father's composure. Although under his jilbab his heart is pounding like a field gun.

On the coast road back into Algiers, Father asks me to check for other cars. He suspects we may be followed.

He parks the car in the disused lot at the Marine Quarter and we make our way up through the Casbah. This time, we continually change directions and double back on ourselves to avoid detection by Army spies and informants. We are all too mindful of Jameel's fate and the dangers we face just being here.

Reaching the top of the town we find our way to the streets around Rue Caton where we resume our positions and dig in for the waiting game.

It will be the familiar pattern of staking and switching.

We have seen enough of 'Little' Omar and are now after a sighting of Yacef Saadi himself.

For over two weeks, we eat off scraps from the Ketchoaua café, provided for us like stray dogs at the beginning and end of every day. I spin stories with the café owner about our journeys across the city—how we spend our days looking for work in the Casbah but that 'my dear grandmama' is a little 'touched in the head' and therefore appropriate work is hard to find.

He takes pity on us. And my pretend grandmother's supposed diagnosed melancholic condition keeps him from trying to converse with 'her' any more. It also conveniently accounts for the rather taciturn, introspective manner of Father's adopted persona.

We are due back with Captain LeBoeuf within the week. And four days have elapsed since we tracked 'Little' Omar to Rue des Abderames.

I am sitting on the step by the fountain in Rue Honore Balzac, glancing at a comic-book and peeling an orange, when an old white-bearded man emerges from a doorway nearby carrying a glass of water. He stops to chat and hands me the glass. I thank him.

"I see you sitting at this fountain," he says, "and I feel sad for you. You always look so desperately thirsty…"

"Thank you," I reply, "I am fine…but this is most welcome," I add, sipping the water.

He stands with hands on hips waiting for me to drink it all and pass him back the empty glass.

"They say this fountain has had no water for over seventy years—it dried up the day Abdul Kader died…"

I haven't studied the stone fountain that much. But now I see it is engraved with the figures of an emir and an emperor side by side—the inscription reads 'Abdelkader—Friend of France and Napoleon III.'

"I think the water will come back the day the French leave Algiers."

I drain the glass, wiping my mouth with my sleeve, hand it back to him and he disappears through the door.

It is my cue to switch places with Father.

I make my way along to the intersection and start climbing the staircase of Rue Caton.

As I approach number three, the door opens, and a woman emerges with a shopping basket.

A man standing inside the doorway places a hand on her arm and they exchange words. He is partially obscured by the door frame, but as I pass close by, I see clearly the high forehead, flashing eyes and matinée idol features.

I proceed up the steps towards Father outside the church on the corner of Passage de Thagaste.

"Simeon, who was it? Who was she talking to? I couldn't see."

"It was Yacef Saadi…"

Father is ecstatic. This is turning into another very good day indeed.

Mont-Les-Pins, Algiers Wilaya, 22 September 1957

"You have it?"

We are all standing in the salon. No one feels that comfortable sitting any more.

LeBoeuf strides over to the bureau under the window and slides open a drawer. He holds a piece of paper in his hand. Marching swiftly back towards Father, LeBoeuf raises it up to Father's face so that he can read every word.

"Take your time, Farouk."

It is a decree in the form of a letter:

délivré le 22 septembre 1957

avec l'autorité investie en moi par l'Assemblée nationale de France, je confirme, par la présente le statut de Farouk Abu en tant que citoyen français.

A l'activation de cette commande, le susdit et sa famille légale—Basira Abu, Simeon Abu, Louis Abu, Margot Abu et Claude Abu—ils auront droit à toutes les protections légales, civiles et éthiques accordées par la constitution de la France.

liberté, égalité, fraternité

signé Governor-General Robert Lacoste.

Father reaches to take the letter, but LeBoeuf snatches it away and takes a step back.

"No, no. I will keep this. You have your visa, Farouk, but you must give us Saadi before it becomes active."

Father feels as if he's been tricked.

"I cannot have my cake and eat it?"

"Of course. But a visa is only as good as the person who issues it, not the paper it's written on. You have your visa, but as far as this person is concerned you still need to earn the right to use it."

Father is thinking.

"Come on, Farouk, we've played this cat and mouse game for far too long…"

Father is resolved.

"You will find Yacef Saadi at Rue Caton. Number Three."

LeBoeuf steps back in. I think he is going to take a swing at Father. He thinks Father is blagging and searches his eyes for signs of deceit. He cannot find them.

Now I think he might kiss Father on both his cheeks like a diplomat.

He turns on his heels and strides out, calling for Lieutenant Mauritz. Then he shouts back at us. "I want you here tomorrow morning."

We are left in his wake, stunned.

Father realises LeBoeuf has taken Governor-General Lacoste's letter with him.

He paces and thinks. We hear excited conversations, summary commands, telephone conversations, troops loading ammunition boxes and weapons into vehicles on the gravel outside.

We cautiously step out of the room, through the atrium and onto the portico just in time to see LeBoeuf's circus roll off down the drive.

"Come on," he says quickly, "we're going back to Algiers."

"But the Captain wants us here tonight."

"No, he said he wants to meet us here tomorrow morning. It's a while between now and then."

"Are we going to follow them?"

"No. There's no point. We can't do anything."

"So, we're not going to Rue Caton?"

"No, Rue des Abderames."

It is a long time after dark when we arrive. The curfew is in force. It has been for several hours. We climb the Casbah, keeping close to the walls, veiled in shadow. The streets are deserted.

We arrive at Rue des Abderames as a faint purple glow starts to gather in the eastern sky.

We pick a spot just thirty yards from the front entrance of number five, shielded by a rainwater tank set into the patio of a derelict house whose walls have buckled and caved. We sit with our backs to two spiral columns either side of a bricked-up doorway.

We wait.

The early morning is still. A cat slinks past, caressing the wall with its bony flank. We hear an Army helicopter whirring above the old town. A gust of wind seizes a paper bag, making it jig and waltz along the street. It is joined by a dirty sheet of newsprint and the two enter into a gavotte.

A goldfinch is singing. Maybe it's the same bird as before, the only goldfinch in Algiers, following us.

From another part of the hill, we hear bursts of gunfire.

"It has started," says Father, "Now let's see."

I don't know what Father has been expecting, but no faces show at the upstairs windows of number Five, Rue des Abderames. No lights go on inside. No maquisards run from the building to help their fallen comrades across the old town in Rue Caton. There is no sign of FLN or ALN, no sign of life here whatsoever.

Father is disconsolate. His calculations have failed him.

He is about to drag himself up from the ground when two figures hurtle across the dimly lit street, skimming over rubble and refuse, then tripping up to the main door of the building.

In the low light of dawn, I recognise one of the men from his movement and outline. It is 'Little' Omar.

The other is taller, of slim, athletic build. He carries a semi-automatic rifle in one hand and as he turns to look out to the street, I see the unmistakably high cheekbones, strong jaw line and handsome face of Ali La Pointe.

Mont-Les-Pins, Algiers Wilaya, 23 September 1957

LeBoeuf is celebrating with his men. We stand on the patio of the grand mansion—uninvited guests at the wedding breakfast.

The Captain is back-slapping and shaking hands amid cries of "Great night's work!" and "Well done, men. That'll show 'em!"

Once his back is turned, his mood shifts.

"Eels!" he exclaims. "Slippery eels! La Pointe, Benkhedda, they are like octopi. They escape down holes they have no right to get through. They run from the teeth of battle by shapeshifting."

LeBoeuf is not a man to dwell on his victories. The ones that slip away are the itch he can't scratch.

We are in the atrium with expectant faces when he rounds on us.

"Well, what do you want? A gold star? An apple from teacher?"

"Did you get him? Did you get Saadi?"

"Of course, we got him. It's the other fuckers who got away from us…Ali La Pointe, 'Little' Omar and most of Saadi's crew."

"So, the information is good…" Farouk confirms.

"Half good, Farouk…which means it's half bad."

"Half good?"

"You gave us Yacef Saadi at Number Three Rue Caton. You just failed to mention Ali La Pointe right across the street at Number Four…that pimp and murderer got away.

Mind you he has plenty of form in that regard.

The man uses his masonry skills to good effect. He's able to put up walls faster than we can blow them up…and he's broken out of prison. Not once, but twice. If he can escape from Barberousse and Damiette, I'm sure Rue Caton presents no particular challenge for him…"

Father is astounded we have missed that vital detail. For LeBoeuf it has taken the gloss off the night's successes.

"But you got Saadi…" Father is keen to check with LeBoeuf that he has fulfilled his side of the bargain and met the conditions for obtaining his visa.

"Oh, we got Saadi alright. He did his best to hide away from us, but he put up a good fight once we'd found him hiding in the walls with Zohra Drif.

What a man that Saadi is. Who'd have thought an illiterate baker could be such an asset in battle.

You'd think he'd come out fighting with bread rolls rather than grenades.

One of my sappers blew a hole in the wall and out the two of them came kicking and screaming like children who'd been found out playing sardines at a birthday party. Hardly the vaunted mythic warriors we expected to see.

We were so busy dealing with the grenade Saadi lobbed at us, we didn't notice his little nephew and Ali La Pointe bailing out across the street…

By the time we found the tunnel between the two houses, 'Little' Omar and La Pointe had escaped."

LeBoeuf is in need of a drink. He marches through the open door of the salon and attacks the drinks cabinet, reaching in for the bottle of the Governor-General's best cognac.

He pours more than a swill into a balloon glass and raises it to us.

"General Massu owes me this…here's to the General…santé."

He bolts down the burnt-umber liquid.

We have followed him into the salon assuming he wants to carry on our conversation.

It turns out to be more diatribe than dialogue.

He pours himself another, having downed the first.

"A toast! To you, Farouk. To your powder monkey. And your dear, sweet family.

Here's to loyalty…to belief…to honour…"

The toast goes unreturned.

"Oh, I'm sorry you don't have a glass. Maybe that's because you possess none of those things…

You are a traitor, a heretic, a man of no integrity…you betray your family, your friends and your own country…and then you tell me want to go and live in mine—a country that enshrines all the values you lack. That's a bit rich, don't you think, Harki?"

"Where's my visa?" Father asks.

LeBoeuf brushes the question to one side.

"I mean, who are you, Farouk? Really. Who the fuck are you?"

Father does not deign to respond. He knows LeBoeuf does not intend it as a question, nor would the answer make any sense to him. Or me.

"General Massu wants us to go easy on Saadi," LeBoeuf continues. "After all that!

The man has become a cause célèbre in France, no less. Untouchable! This bringer of death, destroyer of worlds!

We take the man alive having tried to blow us up and then we are expected to treat him like a film star! In France, Yacef Saadi is a hero! A hero! This terrorist is a freedom fighter. This murderer is a nationalist icon. Apparently, students swoon after him. The people think he is Gerard Philipe in 'The Red and the Black'.

General Massu is just keen that Saadi does not end up like his character—his head rolling at the base of a guillotine.

He says the last thing we need in Algiers now is another martyr who plays well with public opinion in Paris…not after Ben M'hidi, that salaud, fils de pute of the first order!"

Father stands patiently, waiting for LeBoeuf's invective to burn itself out. I am fidgeting, feeling the hot sparks fly off the Captain, but Father has not moved a muscle throughout.

"Major Aussaresses and I may be under orders not to touch a hair of Saadi's neatly groomed head, but France doesn't give a flying fuck what happens to you.

I could crucify you and stick your body on the ramparts of the medina for all those bourgeois Parisians care—and they'd be none the wiser in the morning. You'd be lucky to make it into 'Le monde' as a by-line on the sports pages.

How about that? Your own personal calvary up there above the Casbah? To show all your Muslim friends what a treacherous bastard you've been…They'd love to know how you've sold them down the river to the wicked invaders who have brought them their liberté, their égalité, their fraternité."

"You have my visa, Captain…?" Father holds his nerve.

"Have you listened to a word I've said…?"

"Of course. Where is my letter from Governor-General Lacoste?"

"I told you, your visa is not active. I could have Robert Lacoste's order rescinded at any time…"

Father is not going to be denied. He storms towards the bureau and jerks open the drawer. LeBoeuf seizes him and throws him to the floor. I go to help him, but he pushes me away, picking himself up to face his aggressor.

LeBoeuf spots Father's clenching fists.

"Oh, you want a piece of me, do you? The treacherous coward wants to take on the Captain who has kept him alive…well, go ahead. Let's have it out. Here! Now! Fair fight…"

"Where is my visa?"

"I have it," says LeBoeuf, "Don't you worry."

"What are you waiting for? Why don't you give it to him?" I shout. LeBoeuf grins back at me.

"He speaks! Powder monkey, the protégé, a chip off the old block. You can speak up for your père, eh? Well, while you're speaking up for him, why don't you tell me what you really think of him."

"Leave the boy alone!" urges Father.

LeBoeuf ignores him and continues to grill me.

"Can you vouch for your Father? Would he make a fine upstanding citizen of France? Has he proved his chops? Are you impressed with his work here in Algiers?"

I am silent again.

"Erm…not exactly a ringing endorsement is it, Farouk. It may have something to do with the fact you left powder monkey here for dead in the Casbah…your own son. That is stooping low even by your shoddy standards…"

I can see Father's head drop.

"…or maybe he is pissed off that you have ripped him away from his family…from his schooling…from his friends…and that you have dragged him around Algiers with you to protect your own sorry hide…putting him in peril…exposing him to God knows what…

Do you wonder what Basira thinks of you using your son as your shield in this way—violating everything she holds dear?

Well, Basira has well and truly forsaken you now. She is living with the bus-driver full-time now that we have requisitioned your farmhouse for the Army…

It appears you have lost everything, Farouk…your home…your wife…your family…it's a wonder you still hold on to your sanity…"

Father looks beaten in both senses of the word.

"Except you still have me…"

It is a marked and instant change of tone by the Captain.

Father's head goes up.

"I am still looking out for you. I may not like you, but I still believe in you…"

I am astonished.

"If you are in any doubt about that, then bear in mind the lengths I have gone to obtain that order from Robert Lacoste. I have even asked General Massu to intervene on my behalf. On your behalf, Farouk. Do you have any idea how difficult it is to gain French citizenship for a non-French Arab? How far I have stuck this neck of mine out? And as you can see, there's not much of it…

I wouldn't have done it if I didn't believe in you, Farouk…you'd do well to remember that."

What is it that Father knows? What is it between them that so hooks Captain LeBoeuf and keeps Father jiggling on a string?

"What do you need from me now?" asks Father submissively.

"Ali La Pointe…

I want to finish this thing in Algiers once and for all."

Rue Des Abderames,
The Casbah, Algiers,
6 October 1957

I cannot think why we are still here, why we don't give LeBoeuf the location of Ali La Pointe's hideout right now and be done with it. What is Father waiting for?

Why does he prefer LeBoeuf to believe we are still searching for the chief assassin of the FLN in the Zone Autonome d'Alger when we know the man is there right now across the street behind the door of number five?

La Pointe has a considerable reputation as a killer, the de facto head of the FLN/ALN compound. It is rumoured that part of his recruitment test the day Saadi interviewed him was to kill an informant on that very same evening.

La Pointe's thuggery looms large in the Zone Autonome d'Alger. He sows fear around the Casbah as much through the reputation that precedes him as the trail of murder that follows him.

Father believes it was La Pointe's men who brutalised and then despatched Jameel.

It is hardly a surprise, therefore, that Father has demanded he now carries a gun as protection. He can no longer live on his wits alone when he feels he is a wanted man. He senses Saadi's operatives may have identified him as an Army informant. But he cannot be absolutely sure.

LeBoeuf has reluctantly obliged, supplying Father with a Manhurin Walther PP semi-automatic pistol which he conceals under his jilbab.

Father checks and cleans the weapon every morning, making sure it is always fully loaded even though he knows he has not discharged any bullets from the barrel.

These checks are a part his French-instilled Harki discipline. It seems you can take the man out of the Army but not the Army out of the man.

I carry the spare ammunition—as is my role—in the shopping basket, an accessory that helps with our guise as grandmother and her dutiful young charge on the way to and from the souk. I have three boxes of bullets, twenty rounds in each.

Our surveillance has changed in its nature since Rue Caton.

We are now hidden out of sight rather than just disguised.

The derelict building that we used as cover before now provides us with an elevated, concealed space to observe the comings and goings in the Rue Des Abderames.

Every morning, we pick our way through the crumbling ruin as if we are scavenging for scraps and cast-offs. We enter through a side door that swings off its hinges and we make our way up to a casement-room on the first floor—at the top of a stairwell that is missing both balustrade and the occasional step.

No doubt the room was once used by the maître de maison to store linens and air bedclothes.

A small casement window, long since voided of its glass and open to the elements, affords an unobstructed view down the street to the doorway of Number Five.

We are also wary that LeBoeuf's spotters may be following us. We move through the medieval streets with great stealth, careful to make ourselves slippery by using the same double-back evasions we have come to practice recently.

Father carefully plans our route through the Casbah to Rue des Abderames with the specific intention of shaking off any potential shadows.

We spend many long hours in that crumbling room, taking turns to watch and snooze.

It gives me time to dwell on Captain LeBoeuf's tirade and think about where this is all going.

It is not a pleasant prospect.

LeBoeuf is right about Father in practically every respect.

Father is a spineless, hollow man, a man without principle or precept, without common sense or rational judgment. A quixotic dreamer. A dangerous fantasist. A farceur. An idiot.

And it has rubbed off on me. I am a worm for having gone along with his plan. For he has had none. Not really.

He has had a horizon line in his sights, that is all. He has nursed the idea that a promised land lies just beyond it, an illusory land entirely fabricated in his head.

It is an agreeable place where he can take his family and be received with open arms by everyone.

This shining city of his dreams closely resembles the European Quarter of Algiers, with colonnaded and cobbled squares, tram-lined boulevards flanked by pollarded lime trees and Gothic fascia with their high blue-shuttered windows and finely filigreed iron balconies. This city will be bathed in a perpetual spring light. Temperate in the winter months, and enough cool shade in the summer for everyone to enjoy.

And who would that 'everyone' be?

Father dreams of a city populated by friendly tribes of North Africans, Gulf Arabs, Eastern Europeans, Chinese, Mexicans and Russians, who freely mix and merge in the open markets. They are at peace with one another and their metro-European surroundings. Families rally and dance to the sound of musicians playing in the parks and squares. Teachers lead crocodile lines of dutiful children across the broad avenues and squares to the museum, the gallery, the observatory. Nannies with prams sit gossiping by cool marble fountains as their juvenile charges splash in the shallows. Everyone prospers here.

That is the divine place just over Father's far horizon.

No plane lands there, no ship docks there, no road or rail links cross its borders.

He has no idea how it can be reached.

Because it simply doesn't exist.

Yet he has to believe in it. He has to believe he can attain it for himself and his family.

Because that is his only vindication, the only way he can justify why we have spent six months traipsing around this beautiful, decaying, corrupt, volatile, magnificent, bloody stinking hole of Algiers.

Believing in his illusory destination is the only way he can square away the fact he put my life at risk and fed me to the hyenas that day in Place Jean-Paul Sartre and has been doing so ever since.

Believing in it is the only way he can tolerate the abiding image of his friend Jameel the Pierrot mummified in salt crust, the only way he can live with the memory of Larbi Ben M'hidi hanging by the torn-off strips of his shirt from a beam in our farmhouse outbuilding, and it is the only way he can excuse himself for abandoning Lieutenant Laurent to his fate at the hands of an Army Captain hell-bent on spiking the big guns of international opinion—so that the French Army can persevere with the mission civilisatrice of the Fourth Republic unmolested.

He has a name for this place of his dreams. He calls it 'France'.

One afternoon nearing the end of our day, Father decides we should stay on through the night at the derelict house in Rue des Abderames—if only to observe what happens during the hours of curfew.

I feel compelled to ask him.

"Father, what are we waiting for?"

"Eh?"

"Why are we here? Why the wait?"

Father sinks into himself. He doesn't answer.

The next morning, I ask him again.

"Why don't you tell Captain LeBoeuf? You want your visa. He will finally give it to you if you tell him Ali La Pointe is here."

Father is weary after a night-time's watch. Something is troubling him. "I can't stop thinking about the young man in Rue Caton..."

"Who?"

"Yacef's nephew, Omar..."

"What about him?"

"He was genuinely concerned..."

"What about?"

"About us. You. Me. Mother and son. He wanted to give us some water..."

"Well, yes, it was very good of him..."

"He's younger than you..."

"Yes..."

"He put his hand on my arm..."

"He did."

"And he is across the street right now. There at Number Five..."

I wonder where he is going with this.

"Tell me, Simeon. Do you think I am completely without compassion?"

"No," I answer, perhaps a little too quickly and defensively, as if Father is accusing me with this question.

"That's a shame. I think I am. I think I must be..."

338

Is Father playing mind games with me?

"You ask me why I wait to tell Captain LeBoeuf. I wait because I am weary of this. I think I am doing a good thing. And yet so many people, Simeon, so many dead."

He is jaded. Depleted. Dog-tired.

"You know, the papers report Yacef Saadi has been sentenced to death in El-Biar. General Massu has rowed back on public opinion in France and no doubt that Rottweiler Aussaresses has been unleashed on the bomb-maker.

Saadi is not strong—he will bend under pressure.

It's only a matter of time before LeBoeuf finds out this address for himself and comes here looking for blood…"

He looks me straight in the eyes.

"So, what do I do, my Little Wing Man? Do I bring this to a conclusion myself here, this carnage—or leave it to LeBoeuf so the blood is on his hands?

I feel I have plenty enough on mine."

"The longer you leave it, the more destruction there is…" I argue.

Father shakes his head.

"I disagree. The longer I leave it the more information we glean. And the more information we glean, the more death is avoided in the long run.

We have seen so many people come and go over the last forty-eight hours. We can identify the bomb transporters by sight."

"When did you start caring?" I ask.

"What?"

"When did you start caring about people dying? Was it over a coffee, in the street, while you were watching me about to die in the Casbah, when you watched LeBoeuf string up Lieutenant Laurent, seeing Jameel shredded? When did you start caring about people dying?

Because LeBoeuf was right. All of those people have died as a result of what you've done.

Except for me, of course. I'm not dead, despite your best efforts, only I think that I might like to be.

So, I ask you again. When did you start caring about people dying?" I feel I must have broadsided him with the question. But I am mistaken.

"That was my original question to you. Am I entirely without compassion, in your opinion?"

This is ridiculous. We are going around in circles. He is not hearing me. "They are planting bombs, Father.

The maquisards go all over the city, not just the Casbah, but a long way out. LeBoeuf says the whole of Algiers is now a playground of terror, from Pointe Pescade to Hussein-Dey and Maison-Carrée.

And every day they leave from that door right over there and we just sit here like mannequins and watch. Are we going to just watch them go off to sow death and not put a stop to this?"

"Simeon, hear me out…"

"Hear you out? You haven't heard a word I've said…"

Father goes on.

"Little Omar, Yacef Saadi, Zohra Drif, Benyoucef Benkhedda…all those voices have a right to be heard too. And I am about to betray all that. The FLN cannot take this shock. La Pointe is the last man standing. We need to keep him alive, not give him up to be slaughtered. Because with him the voice of Algeria will be extinguished. LeBoeuf is right. This is my country too."

I can't believe what I'm hearing.

"Father, this is all too little too late. You cannot do this just because it makes you feel better. You have no right…"

This riles him.

"Right? You think I have rights? I have been shorn of my rights! The rights of conscience are the only rights I have left…"

I can't take any more of his nonsense.

"No! You can't speak of this. It's grotesque that you talk about your conscience now. After all you have done in the name of the French."

Father is trying to keep up this absurdity, but he simply doesn't have the energy for it.

"I am a free man. I can talk about whatsoever I choose." His words merge into each other now as one continuous lazy drawl. He is tiring. He is maddening.

I am incensed.

"Where was your conscience in Place Jean-Paul Sartre, in the hills of Koudiat el-Markluf, in Rue Claude Debussy, at Jameel's café? Where was your conscience when you walked out on Mother?

And yet you tell me a boy puts a hand on your arm in Rue Caton and you feel the pangs of conscience?

Grow up, Father!"

But Father is asleep.

"Fuck you!" I say softly peering through the tiny window down into a deserted Rue des Abderames.

Mont-Les-Pins, Algiers Wilaya, 7 October 1957

"Be ready…"

"What are you talking about, Farouk?"

"Have your men ready tonight in the medina."

"What, and you cannot tell me why…I might suspect you were leading the tenth para into a trap if I didn't know any better."

"That is your gamble. Be there, Captain."

Last night, we watched the bomb transporters head out from Five Rue des Abderames to all points north, south, east and west, fanning out across the city.

The mujahidat in their jellabas, young men carrying shoulder bags and backpacks. And then 'Little' Omar slipping out of sight with a heavier tread and a thicker waistline than was natural for his slim form.

Once they'd departed, Father rose to his feet.

"It's time," he said, before leading the way down the steps to the ground floor and slinking out into the shadows of the street.

We scuttled down the hill in silence, keeping close to the walls and gullies by the side of the alleys. We encountered no passers-by and no paras making their night-time door-to-door incursions to snatch FLN sympathisers and informants.

We breathed easily once outside the range of French snipers. This far up towards the medina, pot-shots were commonplace during curfew. Snipers of the tenth para used night-sights to pick out their targets and it was common to find a man lying dead in the street the following morning as if he had just fallen out of the sky overnight.

In the car, Father spat onto his shirt sleeve, wiping away the face paint and lipstick which he said was starting to itch like sunburn.

We arrived at Mont-Les-Pins at first light, just as LeBoeuf was being served a coffee and brioche on the patio by the attentive Bertaux.

As Father stands here bedside me with LeBoeuf seated in front of him, I fear it is too late to stop a wave of bombings from inundating the city's hospitals and mortuaries.

LeBoeuf has agreed to our request. He wanted Father to give La Pointe's precise whereabouts to him there and then.

But Father declined, still prey to the vicissitudes of his new-found conscience.

LeBoeuf vowed to speak to General Massu later that morning and assured us the tenth para would be on standby at the top of the hill once curfew had started.

Between now and then, there is time for Father to go through one further pointless crisis of conscience. One more futile round of self-examination.

But as we depart Mont-Les-Pins, I can tell he is done with this.

From here, Father drives to the beach car park and we fall asleep in the car.

I dream again of the eagles under De Gaulle's protective wing feeding on the carcasses of Algeria's citizens. Of Mother and Father abandoning me on the salt flats. Of 'Invasion of the Body Snatchers' and the elongated form of a hanging Lieutenant Laurent.

Father snores heavily, muttering and shouting in his sleep, and he farts loudly. The gases are seeping out of him at both ends and the sulphurous fug fills the car. It is as if Father, like Terrare, is rotting from within.

I wind down the window, unable to sleep and then go for a stroll in the pines.

We return to Rue des Abderames later that afternoon to hear the bombs going off across Algiers. The potent thunder of acetone and fertiliser chemicals rolls across the Wilaya.

Father plugs his ears with his fingers every time he hears a boom.

He is shutting the stable door after the horse has bolted.

We sit and wait in the derelict house for the last time. We watch 'Little' Omar scamper across the street and the bomb transporters return empty-handed.

The lights of the bomb factory blaze into the night. At two o'clock, the light goes off in the window above the doorway. All is still and silent within number five Rue des Abderames.

"Go!" shouts Father. "Up to the medina with you and give LeBoeuf this address. I'll stay here just in case Ali La Pointe leaves. I'll follow him so I know where he goes."

"You promise me," I say.

"Promise you what?"

"You don't do anything stupid."

"Stupid. Like what?"

"Like warning La Pointe that the Army are coming for him. Answering a last-minute call of conscience."

Father deliberates.

"Would that be stupid?" he asks.

He offers no assurances, no certainties. I realise I have to take my chances just as I have done every day since the bombing of Place Jean-Paul Sartre.

I set out for the medina.

I can see the landmark of the Grand Mosque and minaret above the terracotta tiles and roof terraces. I use it as my guiding star.

I creep along the passages riddled with night terrors. The sound of every movement bounces off the walls and trails me up staircases. I climb higher and the minaret vanishes. The steps zigzag and make my head spin.

I need to stop. I have no idea whether I am going east or west, just up.

At that point, I hear a fizz nearby. A pop. A cry.

I am looking down on myself again from on high. The altitude at which my own personal god looks over me.

I see a man coming in on me at speed with an attack rifle from further up the staircase.

He is bounding down with the force of a rockslide, skipping, bouncing and jumping three steps at a time.

He is firing with one hand as he steadies himself against the wall with another. Another fighter emerges into a ruelle to my left, screaming blue murder.

I take off. My legs are pumping like locomotive connecting rods, driving me through the narrow alleys. I head down a passage and up into a courtyard, scrambling through a gate and out onto another staircase.

I keep racing upwards. There is gunfire in front of me now which makes me slide and whirl on the steps as if dancing on embers. The bullets ping off the stones around my feet and the walls behind me.

I am certain the fellaghas are still behind me so start to panic at what is happening up ahead.

It suddenly dawns on me that I am being targeted by the snipers of the tenth para from the ramparts of the medina.

I dart to my right down an impasse that blocks their line of fire and dive behind a dweb.

I am praying to my personal god that the fellaghas haven't seen me. Please, please, let them walk on by. My prayers are answered. The fellagha passes without so much as a glance down towards my position.

There are further volleys from above and I turn to see the same fellagha tumble back down the steps across my line of sight.

He is hit several times in the chest and the heavy fire propels his body into a doorway. He jerks like a marionette until he slumps down to rest sitting upright against a door.

I make my way back along the ruelle and see the fellagha in the pose of a mendicant, legs astride into the street and arms out.

Somewhere down there is the second fellagha. He hasn't braved the staircase. I'm sure he is hiding in some shadowy corner.

I stay where I am and take a few seconds to recover my breath. I listen out for noises, commotion of any sort.

There is none.

I wait for a few minutes, then quietly steal back out onto the stone staircase.

I take stock.

The fellagha is lying dead. A dribble of blood issues from his mouth and his eyes stare at the opposite doorway. His rifle has slid down a few steps.

I pick it up.

I register no movement down the passage. Up the other way, I am relieved to see the large shapes of Mosque and minaret standing out against the purple of night, and beyond them the geometric outline of the ramparts.

I crawl up the staircase, trying to make myself small and soundless.

I am in some hellish crossfire. No, worse than that even. I am the intended target of two opposing sides from two opposite directions.

The whole world is firing at me.

I cannot see straight. My eyes are swimming, my vision blurred, but even so, I am sure the figure of a man is looming up the steps towards me.

Within a split second, I see him clearly—the second fellagha. I don't think he has seen me.

Instinct keeps my body tucked into the dark shadow of the angle between the steps and the wall, frozen like a statue. 'Un, deux, trois, soleil'.

I hope against hope that the snipers of the tenth are picking up the second fellagha in their night sights right now.

All gunfire has ceased from the direction of the medina ramparts.

The fellagha is now just ten yards off and closing in—making cautious progress up the staircase, clinging to the opposite wall, with his rifle pointing up the steps straight at me.

The dead fellagha's rifle that I took from the steps is by my side.

Any movement on my part will alert the second fellagha. Any further movement up the steps on his part will reveal me lying there.

He is too close not to see me.

I am left with no choice.

I take a deep silent breath while I silently count down.

Three.

Two.

One.

Go!

I roll into the middle of the alley and sit up, bringing the semi-automatic to my side and pulling the trigger. I think it has jammed.

Bullets strafe the steps around me as the fellagha fires into the space I've left. They ricochet wildly of the stonework.

I pull back on the trigger again. My rifle spits fire. The weapon jolts, pushing me onto my back and I shoot at random into the night sky. I sit up again and keep spraying the staircase with bullets until the cartridge is empty and I drop the rifle.

I cannot see through the clouds of brick and smoke. But the angry exchange of fire has set off further rounds of sniper fire from the ramparts.

I scramble further up the steps into a hail of bullets from above. I sprint for another ruelle, clear of the fusillade, behind buildings and away from the line of sight of the medina.

I am expecting a rush of angry fellagha footsteps behind me as I career along the path. I vault over a low wall and onto the patio of a house. A searing pain shoots up my leg, pounding at the walls of my heart and stabbing at the inside of my skull. I hobble back up to the street, feeling my nerves hurl daggers at my brain.

I stagger up another staircase past the outer wall of the Grand Mosque and crouch down beside a pillar.

Now I can see clearly the tenth para manning the ramparts. Hundreds of troops.

I see LeBoeuf directing his snipers, marching up and down the line. Is the Captain trying to kill me or was that friendly fire? I am trying to calculate, but my head is a haze. I cannot think.

That's when I hear the familiar voice of Lieutenant Mauritz.

"Simeon! At last...we were beginning to think you weren't coming!" Lieutenant Mauritz leads me to LeBoeuf. I am breathing heavily.

"Steady on, powder monkey. You're panting louder than a bitch on heat in the Maghreb."

I regain my breath.

"Where is Farouk? This had better not be another chasse aux oies sauvages!"

"My Father is in Rue des Abderames. Ali La Pointe is in the house at Number Five."

LeBoeuf mobilises his men. He doesn't need me any longer. I am left with Lieutenant Mauritz.

I am seething.

"You fired on me, you bastard. Your snipers. As I was coming up the hill."

"You're not a boy, Simeon. This is war. You know the risks..."

"But you fired on me! I had the ALN firing from one side, you bastards from the other. What were you doing?"

"We couldn't be sure it was you. And there was gunfire. We thought you may be one of them and our positions were being attacked...

As I say, war is messy. It happens. Get over it..."

Lieutenant Mauritz leaves to join the briefing. I see LeBoeuf surrounded by senior troops plotting points on a street-map of the city which is spread out across the hood of a jeep. I perch on the rampart wall, my heart ready to leap from my chest, looking down towards the Bay of Algiers.

The sight momentarily soothes me. My heart rate slows.

The scene is like a romantic painting. It reminds me of the landscape by one of those French artists whose works grace the walls of the salon at Mont-Les-

Pins. Vernet. Fragonard. Delacroix. I hear the unlikely tones of LeBoeuf the curator reading out the list from the catalogue at Mont-Les-Pins.

Lieutenant Mauritz soon returns to explain that Captain LeBoeuf will move ahead with an advanced unit of paratroopers. They will take up their positions in Rue des Abderames before sun-up. A back-up unit will go in to secure the site and provide cover, whilst a rear-guard column of troops supported by Zouave auxiliaries will contain any backlash among the general populace and repel the actions of any other ALN cells in the vicinity.

The French don't want to turn The Zone Autonome d'Alger into a killing ground this morning, but everyone inside its perimeter will know this is the last throw of the dice by a beleaguered group. Once cornered, they will fight like wounded animals.

It only leaves the paras a few hours for the raid.

I ask to go with the tenth.

"Request denied," says LeBoeuf as he crashes in on our exchange.

"Denied? But Father is there. He needs me with him. He will expect me back."

"This is no place for a boy…"

"A boy? I've just fought my way up here to bring you the message." I'm pleading with the Captain, holding back tears.

"I've lived in a fucking cloud of death," I continue. "I've seen things you wouldn't believe. I've—"

"Okay, okay…enough…come!"

LeBoeuf leads an advance line of paratroopers down into the snaking streets. I am tucked in behind Lieutenant Mauritz and a signals officer. I hear a background of white noise, the receive and transmit of a high frequency radio.

At one point he stops to let Mauritz talk on the radio transmitter. Mauritz heads up the line, exchanges words with LeBoeuf. Mauritz peels off to the left taking a few of the paras with him. I see them heading down towards Rue Mohamed Bencheneb and disappearing out of sight.

The line continues silently towards Rue des Abderames where the paratroopers take up position in the surrounding streets.

"Take me to your Father," LeBoeuf demands.

I lead him, his signals officer and two of his men behind the tenements and along the subterranean passage through which I followed 'Little' Omar.

We pick our way across rubble and waste to the rear of the derelict building in Rue des Abderames and ascend the disintegrating stairway to the first floor.

As I peer around the door frame to the casement room, I see Father with his revolver drawn. He looks terrified. Paralysed by fear. The blood has drained from his face and he is a ghost.

LeBoeuf pushes ahead of me.

"Put it away, Farouk."

He edges towards the window and glances down the street.

"That's number five?"

Father confirms with a nod of the head. I see him swallow hard.

LeBoeuf backs out of the room. I can hear him mumble to his signals officer, followed by frenetic radio chatter. He sidles back into the room.

"We have half an hour before sunrise. We must go in now. You two. Stay here. Do not move. I know where to find you."

LeBoeuf leaves the room. We hear cautious footsteps recede down the stairs and crunch lightly across the debris.

I am left with the shell of Father.

"What have I done, Simeon?"

I can't answer. I can only look at him and wonder.

He pulls himself up from his perch by the window. He is looking at me strangely.

"I can see him in you…"

"Who, Father? Who can you see?"

"I must go to him."

I start to panic.

"Who?"

"Omar. He's in there. I must go to him. I must tell him to get out of there…"

"Are you mad?"

But Father isn't listening. He is pushing past me, heading for the stairs, "Stop this!" I shout, but he pushes on.

"Father, stop!" I lunge at him, pushing him over onto floorboards that creak and crack under his weight.

He tries to stand up. I launch myself at him again. We tussle on the stairs. He has me by the throat. I punch him on the jaw and he releases his grip.

349

I am grappling him now at the top of the stairs. We roll together and tumble down the stairway. The damp wood splinters, bends and snaps and we crash through the steps to the ground below.

My head cracks on a sharp brick.

I am out for what seems like minutes but can only be seconds. I see Father already crossing Rue des Abderames. I hear gunfire and shouting. A cacophony of sound. All is confusion.

And then…Boom!

Father is thrown backwards across the street. The buildings opposite turn into a fireball. A massive blue and yellow flame licks at the sky. A wave of red-hot stone and bricks flies towards us. Fragments pummel my body. A cloud of dust and smoke billow out from the hole that was number Five Rue des Abderames.

A barrage of black ash and soot blast across the street and smother us. I am choking now. Coughing up gritty phlegm and yellow bile.

I hear muddled voices. I see a paratrooper kneeling by Father.

I black out.

I am propped up against a wall. A soldier is pouring water on my face, asking if I can breathe. I nod.

Father is beside me, holding my hand. He is pleased to see me open my eyes.

I see the familiar, stocky figure of LeBoeuf emerge from what is left of number Five Rue des Abderames. He saunters towards us, stopping to swap a few words with a party of his men. Soldiers are tearing away at the rubble of collapsed houses along the street while others have sealed off the entrance to Rue des Abderames, weapons at the ready. I see that the conflagration has taken out several houses in the street. Their charred wooden and brick frames are smoking and spitting fire.

He speaks briefly to the medic who has been attending to us.

He stands legs astride, fists on hips, looking down at us. Despite the carnage, I can tell he is all poised to break out another cigar.

"Destroyed," he says, "Ali, Omar, one of his bomb-transporters…all in bits. I don't know how many Muslims we'll find in the wreckage."

"What have you done?" I shout.

"Done? La Pointe has done, not me. He went hiding in his fucking wall behind one of his false partitions.

I had one of my sappers blow a hole in it. How was I supposed to know he had a whole bomb factory in there with him? I thought we'd recovered all that at Rue Caton."

He lights up a torpedo cigar.

I am silent. Father is drinking water from a canteen. He drenches his head with it and wipes away the last remnants of make-up from his cheeks. I have left him with a bruise around the orbit of his right eye.

I have smashed my head and my hair is matted with blood.

A medic is finishing up wrapping a bandage around my head when I see Lieutenant Mauritz having a quiet word with LeBoeuf.

Mauritz takes a step to one side as LeBoeuf hangs his head.

I stare back at him.

I have never known LeBoeuf to let a cigar just slip from his fingers.

I have never known him have to lean on a fellow soldier so that he can keep standing.

Yet that is what he is doing now. And all the while is looking over at us, at Father and me.

I stand and walk towards him. I see his eyes are wet.

Lieutenant Mauritz is glancing nervously from LeBoeuf to me and back again.

I am looking for clues in their faces. Mauritz averts his eyes and LeBoeuf gently clears his throat.

"Yesterday, the bomb transporters planted bombs in streetlamps at bus stops in the centre of Algiers…eight Muslims killed, over ninety wounded, Muslims and French.

Your maman, brothers and sister had just boarded Waleed's bus on their way back from the souk when one of the bombs went off…

They are dead, Simeon. Your mother, Louis, Waleed. By some miracle, your sister and baby brother are safe.

Lieutenant Mauritz has instructed paras to take Margot and Baby Claude back to the farmhouse.

We need to go there now. Do you want to tell Farouk?"

I turn to look at Father. He is still manically rubbing at the face paint, trying to erase the stain.

I am numb. I tell Father by rote exactly what LeBoeuf has just told me.

It doesn't sink in. Nothing is sinking in about this day.

I cannot even remember stumbling down the staircases of the old town to the waiting Army vehicle on Rue Mohamed Bencheneb or the drive south to Medea. I still struggle to recall anything about that journey other than Father, LeBoeuf and I sitting in a stew of incomprehension, loss and self-loathing.

Apparently, Lieutenant Mauritz explained that Mother, Louis and Waleed had been taken to the Maillot hospital, but Waleed and Louis had passed away at the scene and Mother had died on the way there.

I cannot recall arriving at the farmhouse. Just picking up the trembling bundle that was Margot and holding her tight, then taking a wriggling Baby Claude from the arms of a soldier and handing him to Father.

What happened next, however remains pin-sharp in my memory to this day.

Lieutenant Mauritz is handing Father a velvet pouch.

"This was in one of the pockets of your wife's coat."

"Here, Farouk, let me take Claude from you," says LeBoeuf.

LeBoeuf lifts Baby Claude out of Father's arms so that his hands are free. I see the Captain trying to sniff the fontanelle on the top of Claude's head, but Claude is an infant now and LeBoeuf finds the smell hard to locate. It makes me feel queasy to see the man flaring his hairy nostrils and dragging his nose through the child's wispy hair.

Father takes the pouch and looks at it blankly without a flicker of recognition.

"It was your gift to Mother for your wedding anniversary," I say to Father, "You gave it to Waleed for safe-keeping. Don't you remember?"

I am going through the motions. Everything I say, everything I do is as if someone else is saying and doing it, not me.

I am floating up there with my personal god watching Father open the soft blue envelope and pull out a silver object.

I see it is an apostle spoon on a chain. The handle is embellished with a Christian saint.

"This is not mine," says Father.

Lieutenant Mauritz thinks Father is in shock and confused. He tries to clarify.

"No, I think what Simeon is saying is this is your gift to your wife…"

Father erupts.

"I don't need you to tell me! I bloody well know what my son is saying. And this is not my gift to my wife."

Captain LeBoeuf requests his Lieutenant leaves and takes Margot with him out of harm's way. Lieutenant Mauritz dutifully obliges.

"This is not mine," repeats Father. "This is not mine. It's not even the kind of thing a Muslim man gives his wife on the anniversary of their wedding. Or Christians for that matter. It's a christening gift. A Christian gift."

Waleed…that snake. Waleed always admiring Mother. Always wanting to supplant Father in the affections of my family. Ingratiating himself to Mother with a christening present for Baby Claude. And him a Muslim.

It still doesn't make sense.

Captain LeBoeuf leans over to examine the silver curio in Father's hand. "Who is the saint, Farouk?" asks LeBoeuf, coolly.

Father is confused.

"Who is the saint on the apostle spoon?"

"How the fuck am I supposed to know who these followers of Christ are? I was born into Islam…"

"I rather think it's Saint Philip."

Now I am bewildered.

"A very influential apostle. The Greeks couldn't get to Jesus without going through Philip first. Like you couldn't talk to Governor Lacoste without going through me."

I hold Margot tightly. LeBoeuf is gently bouncing Claude in the air with two outstretched hands.

"You don't know your Last Supper, Farouk?

I believe it was Saint Philip who asked Christ, 'Lord, show us the Father,' and Christ replied, "I am in the Father, and the Father in me. Got that? I am in the Father and the Father in me," he repeats, his eyes flitting between Father and myself and then down at Baby Claude.

LeBoeuf is gently jiggling the child, now making baby-talk and gurning a smile at him. My stomach is churning.

"The apostle spoon is my gift…my gift to Basira and through Basira to this little chap."

Remember Philippeville, Farouk? You remember Philippeville, surely."

Philippeville, Skikda Wilaya, 20 August 1955

The words flow trippingly off Gamal Abdel Nasser's tongue on the sawt al-Arab radio station. There isn't a consonant out of place, not a single hesitation or misspeak. He is a smooth orator.

We listen attentively, Father, Mother and I, while Margot crawls around our feet and under Mother's jellaba. Even Louis, sitting still on Father's lap, is tuned in to Nasser, thinking he is listening to a storyteller reciting a nursery rhyme.

"Imperialism is the historic enemy of the Arabs and Arab nationalism. Its sole aim is the liquidation of Arab nationalism…"

Father can't resist carping in his Harki uniform—the outfit of a French policeman, the blue cap of a French soldier. I find it strange, this mimicry of French forces. But he thinks it gives him the authority to take pot-shots at the radio and challenge the leader of the United Arab Nations.

"That jumped up young Army officer. What right does he have to set himself up as the modern-day Saladin, the voice of every Arab. He is a fraud…"

"Shh, Farouk, listen!"

Nasser's honeyed tones are sending Louis off to sleep.

"Just as we say 'What has imperialism to do with the Arabs'…Just as we say 'What has imperialism to do with Egyptians'…so we stand shoulder to shoulder with our Arab brothers throughout North Africa and say to the Frenchman 'what has imperialism to do with the Arab Algerian—the only true Algerian?"

Father is at the radio again, spitting his dissent at the Egyptian President's inflamed anthem to the FLN.

"He has never set foot in Algeria, this Gamel Abdel Nasser. What does he know?"

"He knows that French hands are dipped in our Algerian blood," says Mother, "He knows that our workers and farmers, women and children deserve better than this…supplanted by duplicitous colons and obsequious Pieds-Noirs…"

"Bah! You're as lunatic as he is…"

Mother is aggravated.

"Perhaps you should show a little more respect for your wife in front of your children…"

Nasser goes on. He is milking Radio Cairo for every last drop of airtime.

"The world is watching. And I say to the aggressors, we will not hesitate to support our Algerian brothers with the bonds of nationhood—Cairo and Algiers united as one!"

Nasser's voice gives way to the plangent tones of Umm Kakthum. The diva 'pearl of the orient' is singing a dirge to the Aswan Dam.

Father has heard enough. He huffs, switches off the radio and rises from the table.

"I am due in Philippeville," he says, making for the door with his French Army issue duffel bag.

Mother won't let the topic go.

"At least Nasser has the best interests of your fellow countrymen at heart—the workers and farmers. You have only the needs of the colons in your sights."

The words stop Father in his tracks. It is an argument that Mother uses often enough. But he rises to it every time.

"How many times, Basira! I have a skill for soldiering as I have for hunting in the forest. The French are prepared to pay me for that. It puts bread on the table and a roof over our heads. I don't have a quarrel with my fellow countrymen. It is nothing more than a financial transaction with the French."

And on that, he takes his leave.

A little later that morning there is a hammering on the window grille. Someone is rattling a metallic stick across the iron bars outside. We are startled by the sound.

Mother goes to the door and opens it to the sight of three men, two in shirtsleeves, khaki trousers and ragged jumpers, one wearing a leather bomber jacket. They all carry rifles. She has never seen these men before.

"You heard the radio?" says the man in the leather jacket.

"I'm sorry, I didn't catch your name."

"Rafiq El Zawi, coordinator of the FLN Constantine branch. And I asked you if you have been listening to the radio."

"Do you mean the Voice of the Arabs?"

"I mean Gamel Abdel Nasser…"

"Yes, I heard him…"

"Where is that Harki husband of yours?" asks another of the young men. I recognise him from school. He is the older brother of a classmate.

"You mean Farouk…He went to town some forty minutes ago…"

"I bet he did, the traitor…" says the third man under his breath.

Mother is uneasy. Since Father was enrolled into the blue caps, we have encountered some hostility in the neighbourhood. It has come mainly from the Algerian Muslims in the bidonvilles but also the colons and Pieds-Noirs in town.

Our saving grace has been that the women in the town know Mother to be community-spirited and obedient servant of Islam. The men therefore have largely let us be. Not that we have avoided their abuse altogether.

We have been spat at in the streets a few times and called names on several occasions, but that has been the full extent of our neighbours' show of disapproval for the Harki head of our household. Mother thanks Allah we have escaped their condemnation so lightly.

This, however, marks an escalation.

We have not been confronted by gunmen before.

She hopes these ones are about to go hunting in the hills.

The man in the leather jacket, the more senior of the three, is certainly in a hurry to be somewhere, but I'm sure it's not the hunting grounds.

"Nasser's speech is the prelude to revolution. It starts here in Philippeville. Right now! An Egyptian force has landed on the coast to support the Arab cause…Come! Bring the family. We will have a day out in town—a picnic to celebrate our victory over the French."

Mother quickly realises there is no room for negotiation.

"Shimeun," she says, "We must go with these men. We will be safe. Take Louis, I'll bring Margot."

The men scrutinise me as I step out of the door with Louis in my arms. Once outside, I put my little brother down on the ground before hoisting him up on to my shoulders. He giggles.

I am frightened of these men, but Louis thinks it is all quite fun. A new adventure. And he is riding tall on my shoulders. He can now look at the world from a higher position than me. He is an emir in his own lofty palace.

Mother takes Margot in her arms and follows me. The FLN trio knock on other doors from behind which men, women and children emerge—and we join up with other families in the main street. Here I notice that large numbers of Muslim citizens in the throng are bearing knives, cudgels and pitchforks. And the march starts to take on a different complexion.

My fears are confirmed when I overhear a farmer talking with a mechanic.

The farmer wears a leather belt and sheath around his waist from which protrudes the bone handle of a large hunting knife. The man in overalls is carrying a wheel wrench.

"That thug Superintendent Filiberti went out to Karim's place to arrest his brother for a domestic breach of the peace. A whole column of fellaghas were waiting for him when he got there…he and his gendarmes managed to get away unscathed by all accounts."

"How did they manage to escape?"

"No idea. Fellaghas chased them back into town. Now we have FLN commandos and fellaghas backing us up. We will take Philippeville."

I had assumed that the two men with Rafiq El Zawi were FLN commandos, but soon realise they must be FLN agitators. They have unfurled party banners and hold them aloft, waving flags of Abelkader and punching the air. They appear to be choreographing the march, leading the crowd in an unruly chorus of 'Le chant de partisans'.

We are soon joined by the fighting men—commandos in combat uniform, armed for a frontal assault. And the fellaghas bristling with Kalashnikovs. We are several hundred strong. There is a high-voltage buzz of excitement in the ether.

"We march on the garrison!" shouts one of our number.

The FLN officials put us to the front of the march along with other unarmed men, women and children. I take Louis down from off my shoulders and hold his tiny hand as he trots alongside me, but the crowd is surging forward behind me with such speed that his little legs can't keep up and I have to carry him.

"They are using us as a shield," says Mother softly as she walks in lock step by my side, clutching Margot for dear life.

As we near the centre of Philippeville, I notice ALN fellaghas and FLN commandos split off in raiding parties. I see them smashing windows, turning over cars and ramming in the doors of houses with rifle butts.

I see them forcing Pieds-Noirs and those I assume to be Muslim collaborators out onto the streets. I see men being beaten to their knees, with words of condemnation thrown at them. I see women and girls being taken away by FLN commandos. I see Pieds-Noirs and Muslims brawling. We are aware of hand-to-hand fighting taking place behind us as we push forward.

The route of the march has been planned to take us into the centre of town past the homes of the great and good. Philippeville politicians, Pied-Noir businessmen and well-heeled colonists. The FLN are determined to make an example of them right up at the front of the march and within sight of the garrison troops.

The commandos haul many people out of their homes and set about them with fists and clubs.

It is a very public summary court.

Accusations come thick and fast.

"You passed a law that took away our rights. You gave away everything that was ours," shouts an FLN commando at his genuflecting colon captive—a local councillor.

"You have sucked the cocks of the imperialist aggressors!" shouts another at a known Muslim collaborator so terrified that he is soiling himself.

A little further on in the centre, a Pied-Noir is extracted from his office and set upon.

"We have been patient with you, but no longer—you have been only too happy to take our homes and livelihoods. Now take our revenge like a man!"

"Look away, Shimeun! Look away! Cover Louis's eyes."

I do as she says. I hold Louis tight. I hear gunshots and livid screams.

We are still marching. The banners and flags are still flying. Now there is gunshot from all over the centre of town. Murderous shrieks like the cry of fennecs in the forest, skirmishes, chaos.

And then a barrage of bullets from behind us. We are caught in a crossfire. An ambush.

The marchers scatter. Commandos scuttle for the cover of buildings, Mother and I run clasping the children. We run and run and don't stop until we find ourselves entering a small park on the western fringes of the town. We cower behind a plinth on which stands the bronze statue of Marshal Oudinot.

"We must find your Father," says Mother, "and you must try and banish from your mind all you have seen today and all you may see. You must be strong, Shimeun. Strong, do you hear? This has been coming for a very long time and the French will not let this lie."

We wait for the gunfire to die down before venturing out into the surrounding streets of the town.

We wander back towards the centre of town on our wits, through lines of French soldiers and police, not quite knowing or understanding how we fit in to all this, who is our friend, who our enemy, who the authority, who the aggressor.

I am not even sure they know.

A huddle of Harki auxiliaries are standing nearby.

We hope to find Father among his comrades, but he isn't here. We continue looking.

The carnage is plain to see all around.

We see mutilated bodies everywhere, in blood-soaked doorways, hurled through shop windows, bayoneted against wooden doorways.

Mother tells me to look away again. She tells me there is a sight over my right shoulder that she cannot describe or even explain. I see her shock and horror reflected back at me and I cannot bring myself to look back.

Sirens bray. Ambulances race around town ferrying the dying and wounded to hospital. All is in flux. All is chaos.

We are crossing the main square in the centre of town when I spot Father.

He is among an attachment of blue caps helping to clear bodies from the street. Citizens have appeared from every quarter of Philippeville and are catcalling and yelling. The police are trying to shepherd them away from the centre. They are in a state of abject distress. French colons, Muslims and Pieds-Noirs all around us are in shock—some dumbstruck, many weeping, others wailing.

There is no sign of the marchers.

The FLN commandos have dispersed, the fellaghas have melted into the surrounding streets. The tempest has blown over Philippeville for now.

And yet Father goes about his business with an unflappable efficiency. It is a side to him I haven't seen before. And it makes me wonder at what point in his life he became so hardened to the sight of the dead.

He is working with a fellow Harki, metronomically slinging bodies onto the back of an Army troop transporter like so many bagged boars.

Once he sees us, he quickly breaks off from his grim work, leading us away from this mobile mortuary and asking another blue cap to step in for him.

He guides us towards a stone bench in the square. Mother and I sit.

"I had no idea," he says, "If I'd known, I would have stayed at home. It was all a big trap."

Mother is having none of it.

"Oh, come on, Farouk. Don't be so naive! The Army must have known what the FLN were planning here today. You must have known the French have strength in numbers and we were walking into an ambush…"

Father pleads with her.

"I swear, Basira, I had no idea Army intelligence saw the FLN coming.

They knew the fellaghas were gathering up in the hills. They've known for the last week that FLN commandos have been hiding out in the cellars of the houses here in town…

That's why they brought in the tenth paratroopers. To add to the four hundred troops already here.

But you know they don't share that kind of intelligence with us Harkis. We are just grunts…

Nasser's speech was the trigger for them…They lured in the FLN. And the FLN lured you in ahead of them…"

"Your French Army buddies are waiting for you," says Mother, distracted by a group of senior officers who are staring over in our direction. A bull of a man with a cigar clenched between his teeth can't take his eyes off her.

Father continues.

"The FLN have conned their own people, you know, Basira.

They put innocents at the front of the march. They used you and the children to protect them…"

"I'm not stupid, Farouk. I know what the FLN are capable of…"

I catch a low rumbling sound over the sea. From the north appears a squadron of ten Dassault Mystère fighter bombers in diamond formation, the size of midges. In no time, they grow large in my sight like condors and roar overhead towards the mountains.

The officer with the cigar looks up. About time. Time to rain fire.

What I do not know but am about to find out, is that nearby in Constantine Wilaya, in the village of El-Halia, Pied-Noir workers have met with a similar fate.

Just before midday today, as the FLN were knocking on our door in Philippeville, FLN commandos were moving from house to house in El Halia.

While the men of the village were away in the sulphur mines, they were plucking Pied-Noir women and children from their homes and slaughtering them with their bare hands in the streets. Knifing, strangling, pistol whipping amid cries of 'Imperialist scum!' and 'French cock-suckers!"

The men returned home from their shift in the sulphur mines to be dragged from their cars and shot. Thirty-seven Pieds-Noirs were killed. Many of them women and children.

The bovine paratrooper with the cigar is now being handed the latest news of deaths and casualties and I catch faint fragments of sombre conversation across the square.

"Scores of French killed…women and children…"

"How many?"

"Thirty at the last count…the final toll will be higher."

I can see the fury rise in the officer's barrel chest. His face turns crimson. The air around him crackles with a ferocious static.

His rage radiates out to his men. They sense a seething contempt for his surroundings. He is now commanding without the need to communicate—they are attuned to his fury and ready to wreak vengeance on his behalf.

Passionate, undying loyalty to their commanding officer flows through their veins. They are quite capable of carrying out his orders as a muscular reflex whilst the blood is still ringing in their ears.

At this moment Father just happens to be in the officer's eye-line—the first Arab face the officer has seen as news breaks of the scale of French deaths and casualties in El Halia.

An innocent Muslim auxiliary with his family on a stone bench has now been transformed into a destroyer of worlds in the fevered mind of a French Army officer.

The officer now has it in his head that Father is singlehandedly responsible for the deaths of French citizens in this latest killing spree. A kind of cypher for this massacre. A mythic nemesis.

The officer looks set to string Father up from a lamppost, to have us, his family, watch and then do the same to us one by one—to gather his rage into one massive electrifying thunderbolt and hurl it down on all five of us.

But he can't.

The officer can't kill a Harki in cold blood. That would be against the Army code. He would be subjected to a court-martial for such an action.

He has to take his vengeance elsewhere.

The officer will not let this figure of hate off the hook. In his mind, the Harki must be punished.

If he cannot be made to experience the wrath of the tenth para, then he must bear witness to it.

This Arab must see the full extent of the officer's ire—he must be made to feel its destructive power rain down on his Muslim countrymen.

The officer approaches.

"You! Come with me," he commands Father. "Bring your eldest boy! You!" he says, pointing at Mother, 'You stay here with your kids! We'll be back!"

Father and I trudge off behind him. He is followed by a column of wild-eyed paratroopers. He has whipped them up into a lather. They bubble with menace. Fifty or sixty soldiers of the tenth para prowling the streets of Philippeville, ready to rampage among the town's Muslims.

Mother has been eager to protect me from the sights that this man is now so adamant that I see.

He leads us into a side street where six soldiers are tormenting a young Muslim woman. A soldier has tuned a radio to the sound of 'Papa loves Mambo' and is controlling the volume and laughing. They have ripped at her jellaba, torn at her hijab. They are spinning her around from man to man in a game of pass the parcel. And when Perry Como stops crooning, the soldier who has received her last puts another tear in her clothes. The music is turned up and the game resumes while the officer claps out the rhythm.

The game goes on to the point the young woman is grazed and bloodied and semi-naked. Her clothes are in tatters and the soldiers' hands are all over her. She is screaming at them to stay away, but they have pulled off her undergarments and now all taking it in turns to paw at her.

I can't watch and turn around, but the officer makes me stand and demands that I keep my eyes open. I try to roll my eyes up into my head.

The young woman is pushed to the floor and has her eyes firmly shut throughout her ordeal. The men take in turns to violate her. One takes off his heavy belt and whips her with brute force through gritted teeth. They all goad each other. They have lost all sense. They have forgotten about us and the other troops forming a circle around them like a playground fight. We do nothing.

The young woman stops struggling.

Her eyes are shut tight.

She opens them once to stare at Father. She can see he is Arab like her and, in her mind, an Arab is her only salvation.

"You do something," she says, "you stop this, you do something. Please." But Father does nothing.

When it is over, the officer dismisses his troops and tells them to report to his Lieutenant. As each one of them slopes off, I notice how young the six of them are. Raw recruits, not long out of the academy.

"You go home now," says the officer to the young woman, letting her pick herself up in front of us. "These streets are not the place for you."

The young woman opens her eyes and stares at Father. She can see he is Arab like her. He cannot return her look and casts his eyes to the floor.

She gathers up the strips of clothing from the ground and covers as much of herself as she can with them. She stumbles away silently.

"Let's go!" says the officer, leading us out of the side street into a main thoroughfare.

"Why didn't you do anything?" I ask Father, distraught.

"What?" he replies, "What do I do? Tell them to stop? Shoot at them? Tell the officer I shut my eyes? Everyone shut their eyes…These are my buddies…I have to work with them."

Further up the town, the officer is joined by other men from his unit. A jeep pulls up with a signals officer on board. He patches the officer through to another field radio. There is a prolonged and intense conversation during which a grin starts to spread across the officer's face.

"We have the Muslim murderers. Come with me!"

He insists we ride with him in the jeep south of the town.

We arrive at a municipal recreation ground—a patch of scrub bookended by rusting goalposts and some broken swings. I can see a crowd of Arab men being herded by soldiers of the tenth para into a tight group within the centre circle of

363

the football pitch. They are being jostled and corralled by twenty paratroopers at rifle point.

The officer climbs down from the jeep and strides over to the group. Legs astride, hands on hips, he scans the group from left to right. He then calls us over.

"Recognise anyone here?" he asks Father.

Father looks.

"No," he says.

"You!" he says to me," You tell me. I don't know your name. I don't need to. I shall call you powder monkey…"

My hackles rise but I am helpless to object.

"Recognise anyone from this lot?"

I look.

I can see clearly among the crowd Rafiq, the FLN party man in his leather jacket and the two FLN fighters who stood at our door. I also spot one of the men who pistol-whipped the Philippeville counsellor and, I assume, subsequently put a bullet in his head."

"No," I say curtly.

The officer smiles.

"I know you're fucking lying, powder monkey. If I can recognise them a hundred yards away from the roof of the Hotel de Ville, you can recognise them standing right next to you at the front of that march."

He strides off to consult his Lieutenant. Father and I exchange glances.

We both know what we've done. Or rather what we haven't done. We are both bonded by the guilt of having done nothing. Not speaking up for the young woman. And now we are trying to allay that guilt somehow. Just so that we can carry on living with it.

She won't be able to shake off that violation, so why should we? I know we share the same thought, Father and I. This is not what I understood by 'war'.

We both let the young woman suffer. We know it. She knows it. The officer knows it. The rapists know it. We are damned.

"Stand away," shouts the officer, quickly followed by "This is for our Pieds-Noirs dead…Fire!"

The troops controlling the group stand back as ordered.

They suddenly raise the stocks of their automatic weapons to their shoulders and fire, raking the group with repeated rounds. The Muslim men jig, jerk and fall. Further rounds. A wall of fire hits them again. More flail and drop. Fifty, sixty. Toppling into one another, spinning, smoking, writhing.

I am sobbing to the rhythm of the rounds, willing them to stop. But the soldiers keep firing until the bodies are still. Even then my sobs are lost in the repeated crack and smack of the bullets, which eventually cease.

The soldiers pick over the bodies, kicking them over in heavy boots to check for signs of life, firing sporadically into the dense heap to cancel out any residual twitches or spasms.

They fire off shots until they are sure the last pulse in the final living soul has ceased. Eighty or more of them. Gone.

We return home that evening wondering why we have survived this day as a family. More so, whether we can live through another one.

There is no return from this. Father vows he will protect us and not let us out of his sight until we have reached a place of safety.

"Like you protected that girl today…"

"What girl?" asks Mother.

Neither of us wants to speak about it.

"There was a girl who needed our help and we failed her…"

We leave it at that. Mother doesn't pursue it. She won't let him spill his guts around her.

She is brooding on Father's deceit at joining the Harki ranks and betraying everything she stands for.

We are all numb.

The two of them sleep separately as they have done for months now. She sleeps with Margot. I am in with Louis. Father is camped out in the kitchen on a makeshift bed he has laid on a floor by the stove—no better than a dog. More a bedroll that he stows away every morning, the fastidious soldier and hunter that he is.

I am not about to sleep. I can't stop thinking about the young woman and the dancing bodies on the recreation ground. It makes me wonder what the officer has seen in us that has made him think we deserved to bear witness today.

Father has resolved in his head to take us away from Philippeville. Somewhere closer to Algiers, perhaps. Closer to the French.

He sees it as a contract.

He has thrown in his lot with the French Army. He has taken great personal risks to do so. Now he needs their protection in return—for the sake of us all.

Perhaps he will seek the help of the officer of the tenth para first thing in the morning. He knows it will not be easy.

Philippeville, Skikda Wilaya, 21 August 1955

"You what?" says the officer.

"I would like to request a move to Algiers…"

The officer chuckles.

"We haven't finished our work here yet and the Harki is already requesting a new posting. Who do you think you are? General Massu?"

We are standing in the central square of Philippeville to one side. Father will not let us out of our sight. But he has promised himself and us this conversation.

"No more talk of postings, Harki. We have work to do here. The Pieds-Noirs are retrieving the bodies of their loved ones and burying their dead. You must marshal the mourners."

We are not through with the bloodshed. Not by a long way.

Seventy-one wooden boxes in a field behind the church beside an open grave. As usual, Father's blue-cap comrades have done the grunt work, working hard overnight to cover some of their tracks.

They have been out to the municipal recreation ground with a mechanical digger requisitioned from the yard of a builder's merchant outside Philippeville.

They have prepared a trench for the Muslim slaughtered, throwing in the Army's murdered Muslim informants after them. The bodies of the Muslim men have been covered with quicklime and the Harkis have ploughed back in the freshly excavated earth. The burial attachment has returned to hallowed ground behind the church for the interment of the Pieds-Noirs and colons. A priest officiates.

Many mourners attend. The mood is dark and menacing. It is too soon for the mourners to allay their anger. Their blood is running red-hot and raw with it.

The families of the dead are allowed a minute for their eulogy. Each can have their say, though many are too stricken to even stand.

Few decide to speak.

The husband of one of the slaughtered stands beside his wife's coffin and addresses the sea of faces. The whole population of the town have turned up to pay their respects—colons, Pieds-Noirs and Francophile Muslims alike, though they eye each other with a clear and deep mutual mistrust.

"They did not spare her," says the husband. "They know no mercy. These men of stone. No, not men. Monsters with their cold, cold hearts. They violated my lovely wife. They took bottles and forced them inside her. The bottles broke and cut her inside…they just stood by like they were watching a football match, cheering on every fresh laceration."

There are gasps of horror from the mourners. Scuffles break out. Father steps forward to intervene. The officer puts a restraining hand on his shoulder.

The service over, the tide of mourners washes back towards the town while the Harki soldiers lower the boxes into the pit. Paras look on.

The officer asks us to stay close behind him as he follows the throng, his para unit not far behind.

We see a sudden rush forward. Parties of mourners are breaking from the crowd, chasing Muslim men and women. They fall upon the first Muslims they see, kicking and mauling them, wrapping loops of rope around their necks. Young Pied-Noir men go shinning up the stanchions of lampposts to loop the ends around the crossbars and haul up their victims. Five, six, seven Muslim men and one woman dragged down the street and raised into the air in formation. One by one from alternate lampposts.

Mother watches them kick and struggle. She pleads with Father to cut them down. Father tells her to be quiet or she will get us all killed. He reminds her that we too are Muslim Arabs and the protection of our French escort will only last as long as we keep our mouths shut.

The tide surges further out of the town and towards the football stadium. The paras follow. Father stays close to us. He has long since given up on his Harki duties. He is now a bystander. We tag along behind the guard of the tenth para under the protective watch of our tormenting officer. He wants to keep this one Muslim family alive. He wants us to see what transpires today. He will keep us in his thrall.

The raucous crowd passes through the bidonvilles. Muslims are being rounded up and herded like cattle as the riptide of hate sucks them in towards the stadium.

Mother is still trying to process all this. She is desperately appealing to the officer, tugging on the sleeve of his camouflage jacket, trying to make him hear her.

"Please officer, stop this. Your men have weapons. Yet you do nothing. I beg you."

The officer brushes her off. She now clings to Father and shouts at him as he moves alongside the officer.

"Farouk. Please. Tell your comrades to control the crowd. Use your rifles if you must. I don't understand. Why are you letting this happen?"

But Father is unmoved. He can do nothing but caution her, just as he did nothing to help the young woman yesterday, just as he watched his Muslim brothers fall and die.

The crowd is stampeding now, desperate to enter through the gates of the stadium.

The officer brings the para escort to a standstill. They form a cordon blocking the main street to the stadium.

The stadium gates close behind the Muslims and their Pied-Noir tormentors.

I know these to be the gates to hell. And these are the screams of the damned. A roar goes up from inside. Not the kind that usually fills the stadium, more a baying clamour. Gunfire fills the air. The screams and cries intensify. I block my ears and look to the skies. I pray to my own personal god that this will not go on for much longer.

Margot and Louis are wailing hysterically now. Father is holding them, kissing them, trying to make them stop blubbing. But they are inconsolable.

Mother is begging the officer to stop the bloodshed.

"You cannot let this happen. I will not have it!"

It is too much for her to bear. She breaks through the line of soldiers and darts towards the stadium.

"Basira, no!" shouts Father, but she is sprinting now, flying towards one of the side entrances.

The officer raises his semi-automatic rifle. I push it away to stop him from shooting. He scowls at me.

"Basira!" cries Father as the children shriek in his arms.

Suddenly, the officer charges beyond the line of paras and sprints after Mother. I see her disappear through the gate, leaping the turnstiles and I watch the officer go in after her.

My prayers have not been met.

The tumult is never-ending. The detonations of gunfire continue to echo around the stadium, its high-walled precincts swallowing the repeating sound, deadening it and muffling the cries inside, which evaporate into the thick concrete—as if the stadium itself is determined to keep its secret to the bitter end.

Half an hour later, all noise subsides. All is quiet but for the shuffling shoe leather of Pieds-Noirs who emerge from the stadium in dribs and drabs, insensate, drained of life. They saunter past us in silence.

I see the officer stride out from the stadium side entrance and march back towards his cordon of troops, a fastidious soldier straightening his beret, checking that his belt is correctly looped and his sidearm is locked in its holster.

"Where is she?" asks Father, "Where is my wife?"

The officer turns to regard the Harki.

"She is fine. She is safe. Making herself look presentable for you again. She will be out in a minute."

And at that very moment, Father knows.

The Farmhouse, Medea Wilaya,
8 October 1957

"He is mine, Farouk. You know it. I know it. Basira knows it.

Claude is the only one of your family entitled to French citizenship. And I will make sure he gets it."

Father draws his revolver. LeBoeuf reels back.

"Whoa, Farouk! Careful, now…you wouldn't want Claude here to be one more stain on that conscience of yours now, would you…"

"Give Claude to me, Captain…" says Father.

"My men are right outside that door. You do know that, don't you. Lieutenant Mauritz will not hesitate to shoot you down like a dog if you make any move on me."

"I said give Claude to me…" repeats Father.

"I suppose you can take one moment to say your goodbyes to him…"

LeBoeuf carefully passes Baby Claude across to Father in his outstretched hands.

"You'd better change his nappy while you're about it. God knows he needs it. I will have a nanny attend to him once he's back in Paris with me.

At least one of your family will be going back with me when I leave your god forsaken country…well, you never really expected me to give you citizenship did you, Farouk. That letter from Lacoste was a fake. I mean, I know you're a dreamer but so gullible with it…"

Father cannot take Baby Claude and hold the revolver at the same time. "Here, Simeon, take this, keep it pointed at the Captain…"

He hands me the gun. I take it and hold it steady while Father holds the grizzling, gurgling infant.

LeBoeuf switches his attention.

"Powder monkey performing the role your Father always intended for you."

371

"Stop calling me that!" I protest.

"Have you heard of onomastic determinism?"

He is playing his mind games again. I don't know what he's talking about.

"It is the strangest phenomenon where people are likely to take occupations according to their last names.

It's funny how many goat-farmers are named Chevrolet and shepherds Berger.

You would expect a man named LeBoeuf to have a barrel chest and no neck…and here I am!

That's why you will always be powder monkey to me, Simeon…"

"I said stop with that. I can't abide that name. Mother hates it…"

"Hated it, Simeon…" LeBoeuf corrects me, "I'm so sorry for your loss…of your maman and Louis, powder monkey."

"I said stop it!" I scream into his face, my finger gently compressing the trigger.

"Simeon…" says Father, trying to calm me down.

"Yes, Simeon," says LeBoeuf, "uncannily like 'simian' isn't it. You are named after an ape, I fear, African Arab boy…monkeys are less than human…"

I pull the trigger at point blank range and put a smoking hole through the middle of LeBoeuf's forehead.

He drops to the floor.

Father stares disbelievingly at LeBoeuf's collapsed body, then at me.

We hear a commotion outside. We hear Lieutenant Mauritz shout "Captain LeBoeuf. Are you there? Show yourself, please…Captain LeBoeuf."

I turn the revolver towards Father. I am bursting with rage. It is burning a hole in my heart like the still smouldering bullet in LeBoeuf's head.

"You have destroyed us. Mother is dead because of you. You allowed the bombers to go out from Rue Des Abderames. They planted that bomb at the bus-stop, and you could have stopped them. Just as you did nothing to stop the murder of Laurent, Ben M'hidi, Jameel. You're so fucking weak, weak…"

"Simeon! Put the gun down…Claude is not safe. Put the gun down…"

I sink to my knees and sob uncontrollably. A river of grief and pain, of loss and longing. I keep pointing the revolver at Father. I am going to kill him. I am finally going to kill him.

"Take Claude. Give me the gun…"

I hold onto the weapon. It is all I have left. My eyes go from Father to Baby Claude and back.

"Give me the gun, Simeon..."

I don't trust him. I see his face as it was when he crouched in the doorway of Place Jean-Paul Sartre. As he abandoned me, packed me off to a certain death. But this time he is the one doing the pleading.

"Please don't, Simeon. Please don't. There is a better way."

I am gently squeezing the trigger. I look at Baby Claude, LeBoeuf's Claude.

"You knew he wasn't yours, didn't you...so did Mother. You kept it a secret all this time..."

"I did everything to help us survive..."

"Survive? What kind of a life is this?"

Outside, Lieutenant Mauritz is becoming more agitated.

"Captain LeBoeuf," he is shouting, "show your face, sir. I will give you a countdown...

Ten..."

"I did my duty, Simeon..." pleads Father.

"Nine..."

"I always put family first..."

"Liar!" I shout.

"Eight!"

"Everything I did, I did for you..."

"Seven!"

"Give me the gun!"

"Six!"

"Give it me, Simeon!"

"Five!"

"There is a better way," he pleads.

I feel myself sagging, my body sinking through the floorboards and down past the earth's crust to its molten core.

"Four"

I am tired. I am weak.

"Three"

I hand Father the revolver. He gently puts down Baby Claude who starts to crawl towards me.

"Two"

Father holds the gun up. I think he is going to shoot me.

"One!"

"I am coming out!" Father shouts. Mauritz is silenced.

Father steps towards the door, briefly placing his hand on my shoulder and squeezing it as he goes. I hear the latch lift and feel a blast of air on my face as Father stands in the open doorway.

"I have just shot dead Captain LeBoeuf!" he exclaims.

There is an instant volley of gunfire.

I hear Father's dead weight drop to the gravel outside.

Baby Claude reaches out towards me with his tiny fingers.

Epilogue

I discovered Eloise's business card in the lining of my hunting jacket some two months after the enquiry opened into the killing of Captain Gregory LeBoeuf and the subsequent shooting of Farouk Abu by soldiers of the tenth para.

The inquest concluded LeBoeuf was murdered by Farouk, an-ex soldier in an auxiliary Harki unit, who'd previously served under the Captain out in Philippeville. According to the commission, Farouk had been settling an old score, the nature of which was never fully determined. In the eyes of the military, however, the matter was closed.

The death of Lieutenant Laurent was determined as suicide, though the Army never managed to close the book on the staged suicide of Larbi Ben M'hidi. His murder and the subsequent attempt at a cover-up, wiped away any moral authority left around 'la mission civilisatrice' in Algeria.

My view is that the attenuation of the French Fourth Republic started with Ben M'hidi's killing. I believe the event accelerated De Gaulle's election in December of 1958 at the head of a Government committed to a policy of national independence and state centralisation. France's colonial ambitions were effectively deemed a dilution of its grandeur, unsustainable and corrosive.

Lieutenant Laurent's work was not quite as influential. The United Nations failed in its efforts to bring to book the torturers of Algiers, the International Court of Justice deeming such a trial illegitimate outside a conventional theatre of war.

As for me, on the death of our parents, Governor-General Robert Lacoste's office ordered that Margot, Claude and I were to be made temporary wards of court.

For the time being we would live with a foster parent in a bidonville outside Oran until further arrangements were made for our care.

The found business card bore the name 'Eloise Marchand', the title of 'Directeur' and the address of the head office for the centre socieaux in Oran.

Our foster mother lived close by the centre socieaux and I therefore decided one day in April of 1958 that Margot, Baby Claude and myself should pay Eloise a visit.

It wasn't easy to evade the watchful eye of our foster parent, although Claude's hacking cough presented me with the perfect opportunity.

I asked that we go into town to pick up some cough mixture from the pharmacy. She agreed on the proviso we hurry back afterwards and the three of us set off in the morning before the opening of business so that we could be there in good time—me carrying Baby Claude in my arms whilst Margot toddled along beside me the few kilometres to our destination.

The centre socieaux turned out to be a prefabricated concrete block on a busy access road to the main port of Oran. Whilst we were there, the offices shook to the thunderous rumble of container lorries and Army transporters that seemed to continue without any let-up.

I was informed that Eloise was on business in the south but that she'd be back later that day. And so, I decided we'd wait for her return.

We spent much of the day watching the French warships taking on supplies in the port, the vast oil tankers edging out to sea and the leviathans of shipping heading off to foreign lands carrying their cargo of heaven knows what to God knows where—I think it was sodium chloride, dates and wheat. That's if my memory of Monsieur Gazides' geography classes serve me correctly.

When we arrived back at the centre, Eloise was there waiting for us with open arms and a welcome hug. She was delighted to see me again and to meet my siblings, expressing her sorrow for our loss and eager to hear my story. My first thought was to tell her that, on the day we first met, I left her flamiche on the back of a truck full of farm workers. She laughed and told me that, as long as they enjoyed it, it was all to the good.

She too had a story to tell regarding her life partner, Alice Reyes—a teacher at the Ecole Normale of Bouzarea.

It transpired that when she returned home to her Oran apartment on the first day of the General Strike, Eloise's worst fears were realised. The apartment had been ransacked, the contents of drawers spilled, files emptied from her filing cabinet and papers scattered all over the floor.

Alice was nowhere to be found.

The neighbours informed Eloise that the police had come for Alice during the late morning on that Monday. A file of photographic prints was missing from a bureau in the study.

The headmistress at the school said that Alice hadn't reported to work that Monday morning either. And Eloise's mood had started to turn from worry to fear.

Eloise has since gleaned that Alice had refused to break the strike that Monday morning and, as a result, had been driven east to Algiers to be questioned by Major Paul Aussaresses of Army Intelligence counter insurgency.

Eloise's subsequent requests for information proved fruitless. She understood that Alice had been removed from the Villa Tourelle and taken to the women's section of the Barberousse prison.

Eloise received no further word of Alice's whereabouts after that. The police and Army claimed never to have seen an Alice Reyes or processed any such detainee. The prison archives contained no records of a prisoner ever having gone by that name. There was no evidence that Alice Reyes had entered the gates of Barberousse in the first place. She simply disappeared off the face of the earth.

Eloise would never stop in her search for the truth about Alice right up until her death a few years back. And even after Eloise's death, Margot and I kept a vigil for her lifelong partner and campaigned hard to make sure the book never closed on her life and death.

Once Eloise had taken us under her wing, I enquired into the subject of Alice's photographic collection and why Army Intelligence had been impelled to take it away.

She told me Alice had been making a series of photographic portraits of the victims of torture in Algeria since the struggle for independence first started in 1954. It wasn't so much a record, more an artistic study of the human spirit under extreme duress.

She added that I was not to worry as Alice had handed Eloise the negatives which she had kept safely under lock and key ever since. She entrusted them to me just as I had entrusted the lives of my sister and brother to her.

Eloise and Margot are the only two people alive who know who Claude's birth father really is.

We never told Claude right up to his death from pancreatic cancer in 2005. But Eloise maintained until her dying day that it didn't really matter. That parents are only parents in the heart. And love is always earned, never anyone's by right.

I learned a lot from Eloise.

Eloise passed away in a nursing home outside Deauville just before her ninety-third birthday in 2010.

It feels in my heart that she's a true parent to me. I believe Margot feels the same way, though she has never declared it.

We've kept a flame alive to the big love of her life, Alice, by honouring her memory on this, the fiftieth anniversary of Algeria's independence from France. And by sponsoring an exhibition of her portraits to commemorate the occasion this 4 July 2012. The reason I am here in Paris today.

We commemorate her just as we have kept a flame burning for Mother, Louis, Claude and, yes, even Father.

We are all survivors in our own way.